Divas [▪] KT-466-429

Belinda Jones's first paid job was on cult kiddy comic *Postman Pat*. Since then she has written for a multitude of magazines and newspapers including, *New Woman*, *Empire*, *FHM*, *heat*, *Elle* and the *Daily Express*. Belinda's widely acclaimed first novel *Divas Las Vegas* was voted No.2 in the *New Woman* Bloody Good Reads Awards in 2001 and *On the Road to Mr Right* - a non-fiction travelogue love quest was a *Sunday Times* top ten bestseller. Her new novel *The Paradise Room* is available now in Arrow Books.

Acclaim for *Divas Las Vegas*

'A glitterball romp' *Company*

'Great characters ... hilariously written ... buy it!'
New Woman

Acclaim for *I Love Capri*

'A deliciously entertaining beach read' *heat*

'With more twists than a bowl of fusilli and more laughs than a night out with the girls, *I Love Capri* is as essential as your SPF 15' *New Woman*

Acclaim for *The California Club*

'A perfect, sunny read' *B*

'A riotous page-turner, full of witty observations on life and love' *She*

Acclaim for *On the Road to Mr Right*

'Essential for that girls-only summer trip' *Company*

'This is definitely worth cramming in your suitcase'
Cosmopolitan

Also by Belinda Jones

I Love Capri
The California Club
On the Road to Mr Right
The Paradise Room

To embark on more fabulous journeys with Belinda Jones, visit
her website: www.belindajones.com

BELINDA JONES

Divas Las Vegas

arrow books

Reissued by Arrow Books in 2003

9 10 8

First published in the United Kingdom in 2001 by Arrow Books

Arrow Books Limited
Random House UK Ltd
20 Vauxhall Bridge Road, London, SW1V 2SA

Random House Australia (Pty) Limited
20 Alfred Street, Milsons Point, Sydney, New South Wales 2061, Australia

Random House New Zealand Limited
18 Poland Road, Glenfield
Auckland 10, New Zealand

Random House South Africa (Pty) Limited
Isle of Houghton, Corner Boundary Road & Carse O'Gowrie,
Houghton, 2198, South Africa

The Random House Group Limited Reg. No. 954009
www.randomhouse.co.uk

A CIP catalogue record for this book is available from the British Library

Papers used by Random House UK Limited are natural, recyclable
products made from wood grown in sustainable forests. The
manufacturing processes conform to the environmental regulations of the
country of origin

Type by SX Composing DTP, Rayleigh, Essex
Printed and bound in Great Britain by
Bookmarque Ltd, Croydon, Surrey

ISBN 0 09 94 1492 9

For James
(and everyone who dreams in neon)

Acknowledgements

Unlimited thank-yous to: Emily O'Neill – the ultimate Vegas Vixen – for inspiring this book, Lizzy Kremer at Ed Victor Ltd for having the x-ray vision to see I had a novel inside me (you deserve a dozen beaded cardis!) and Kate Elton at Arrow for her much appreciated encouragement and enhancing editing. Also fellow Arrow Angels, Anna Dalton-Knott, Grainne Ashton and Sarah Harrison for their enthusiasm.

Sandy Battaglia, without your help and patience this book wouldn't exist (nice storage unit, GB!), and as for the hugtastic showboys – Danny, Frank, Graham, Pete, Les, Darren, Brian, Kenny A, Kenny D, Ed, Eric, Phalps, Doris-crooning Don and the main man Tom Jones, y'all rock my world.

Cheers to my fabulous champagne showgirls: Amanda, Sarah, San, Nige, Chee, Maddie, Christie and Line – Vegas vacations with you send my spirits soaring as high as the Bellagio fountains.

Gratitude a go-go to Richard Bartlett-May for speed-of-light research (I'm sure those Apache wedding vows will come in useful one day), Shane Ford for being my Sag soulmate, James Breeds for obscene generosity, patronage and Cabbage, Gilly for bacon-saving, Chip for acting as banker, brother Gareth for test-reading *Divas* when your preferred books are carpentry bibles and, finally, my beautiful mother Pamela for being the ultimate believer and my lucky charm.

1

We're on our way to Las Vegas to get married. Admittedly we're a little light on grooms – only Izzy has a fiancé and she has no intention of marrying *him* – but still, we're optimistic: with statistically one wedding taking place every six minutes, the air in Vegas is practically 70 per cent oxygen, 30 per cent confetti.

Add to that the fact that drinking hard liquor 24 hours a day is (near enough) compulsory, and we reckon the odds of us finding I do-able men in under a month are stacked in our favour. What do we have to lose, anyway? Lacklustre jobs and men with a gift for making us feel more alone than when we were single.

We've been led – rather brutally – to the uneasy realisation that we're tolerating rather than embracing life. Wishing for a miracle isn't netting us the results we need so we've decided on a more hands-on approach to our fate.

Izzy has packed 72 condoms instead of her usual 36 and I've got a family-size jar of Marmite wrapped in my pyjamas – proof indeed we have no intention of returning to England until our lives are well and truly 'altared'. Well, there comes a time when you have to take a stand. As Izzy says, 'There's only so many crap boyfriends a girl can take.'

At twenty-seven we're plenty old enough for crap husbands.

'There it is!' screeches Izzy, spying her first Vegas light bulb from 12,000 feet up. The solo glow suddenly erupts into a shimmering mirage of chameleon neon. We gasp in unison, severing the circulation in each other's arms with a white-knuckle grip of excitement. I place my other hand over my heart to stop it leaping from my body. It's as if a huge, leaden treasure chest had been prised open to reveal its glittering booty: the Kryptonite green glow of the MGM Grand, the fizzing pinks and oranges of the Flamingo Hilton, the gleaming gold of Mandalay Bay, the polished jet of the Luxor pyramid. . .

It's all so beautiful. My eyes blur with tears, creating swirling kaleidoscope patterns.

'I can't believe we're here . . .' I breathe.

'I can't believe how far the lights spread out,' says Izzy, craning to take in the million golden spangles scattering into the desert. 'I thought there was just going to be one main street.'

Of course we'd heard rumours that there is life beyond the glitz – that people raise families here, and go to school and college. There's even talk of people mowing the lawn. But we're not interested in hidden suburbia. We need to believe there is a place where

9–5 rules don't apply, a place where ovens clean themselves and ironing is a felony – hell, you'd only melt the sequins.

Marriage may be our mission but we're also craving Sin City's extremes and the excess. We need to escape reality, to be where men walk around dressed as Egyptian pharaohs and no one tries to look up their skirts; where its not unusual to find Tom Jones impersonators performing on the same night as the Sexbomb himself. We want to shop in places that sell plastic Elvis sunglasses with built-in fun fur sideburns, and stroke one of Siegfried and Roy's white tigers. We want to stand on escalators with newlywed women wearing frilly lace garters with cut-off denim shorts. On a more personal note, I'm looking forward to being around people with bigger debts than me.

'Furnace alert!' Izzy reels as we emerge on to the street outside baggage claim. 'We must be under a faulty air duct, move along a bit, Jamie.'

We drag our straining suitcases further down the pavement but it still feels like the entire staff of Vidal Sassoon are blasting us with their hairdryers. We fall into the taxi with relief.

'Where IS that heat coming from?'

The driver gives us a weary look and sighs, 'The sun.'

'I didn't realise we were actually ON it,' scoffs Izzy.

It's 8 o'clock at night and easily 90 degrees. The news on the radio tells of a two-year-old boy who got second-degree burns from falling on the pavement

3

and not being able to scramble up quick enough.

'I think we'll keep our heavy drinking sessions to carpeted areas,' Izzy squirms.

The airport is but a dice-throw from the Strip and within minutes we're entering the dazzling rainbow kingdom, squeaking rapture at a level only dogs can hear. It's curious how multiple wattage can fill you with such emotion. Imagine the heart-warming sight of fairy lights on a Christmas tree combined with the thrill and wonder of a firework display. Liberace must have felt this way every time he opened his wardrobe door.

'There's the Statue of Liberty,' yawns the cab driver pointing at New York, New York casino with its red rollercoaster wrapped like an undulating ribbon around the replica Manhattan buildings.

'Caesar's Palace,' the driver nods to out left. 'A classic.'

'Wow!' We contort to take in the cloud-nudging Roman columns, gold emblemming and mighty statues. Tourists crowd the pavements to gawp, kitted out with foot-long margaritas, livid sunburn and perms that should have been outlawed in the seventies.

'Neil Sedaka!' yelps Izzy.

'Where?' I gasp.

'No, you fool! On that billboard . . .'

'Crystal Gayle!'

'Earth, Wind and Fire!'

'Taylor Dane!'

We call out the names as we flash by.

4

'Old rockers don't die, they just play Vegas,' opines the driver as we pass the oriental blue neon of the Imperial Palace.

'Where's *our* hotel?' says Izzy, sounding about four years old.

'Just a bit further down, we should see a pink metallic roof . . .'

'Circus Circus sounds so cheesy,' Izzy pulls a face. 'And I thought clowns gave you the creeps.'

'They do,' I reply, 'and I'm not thrilled about the cat they've got riding a unicycle across a high wire, but a free room is a free room.'

'Yeah, you're right,' Izzy concedes. 'Anyway, I don't care where we stay, just as long as I get to meet my millionaire.'

The cab driver snuffles into his stubble.

'Pardon?' I enquire.

'You won't find any millionaires at Circus Circus! It's full of obese families and LA gang bangers!' he snorts.

Fantastic. No, I mean it. The naffer the better as far as I'm concerned. If I can mentally picture my sister Nadine recoiling and reaching for her facial mist I know I'm on course.

'If you're looking for the big spenders, you wanna get yourselves over to the Las Vegas Hilton or the Desert Inn.' He eyes us for a second, then adds, 'Nah, too classy.'

Charming. We're about to take offence but he realises his tip is at stake and starts talking moolah again.

'Here's a tip for you girls: the casinos wanna ensure the flow of money is not disturbed by some dumbass tourist risking his mortgage on number 15 just because his pet mutt died on the 15th of the month, so you know what they do?'

'What?' we chorus.

'They give the high rollers their own private gaming zones – a lot of these areas are just cordoned off so you can see them in action.'

Izzy lets out a gurgle of anticipation. I take it she finds the idea of clusters of hyper-rich men – ready sorted and sifted – hugely appealing.

'I wish you luck though, most of those guys only have eyes for the croupiers,' he notes, turning into a driveway marked by a monstrous ginger Afro-d gatekeeper.

'That's Lucky the Clown – he's made up of three-quarters of a mile of neon tubing!'

We force out an 'Ooooh'.

'Like you give a shit!'

He's right. We prefer his hints about meeting millionaires.

As we roll under an entrance canopy emblazoned with infinite winking and red and gold lights, Izzy whispers in awe: 'I feel as if we're about to be sucked up for a close encounter by a UFO.'

A man dressed in ringmaster livery opens the cab door and the heat oven-bakes us again. But not for long. The air conditioning in the hotel is positively Arctic – if we were cartoon characters, we'd have gone from molten, steaming heaps to freeze-framed ice sculptures in seconds. We'd heard stories that they pump extra oxygen into the casinos to keep people awake so they can gamble longer, but it seems they're also experimenting with cryogenics to keep gamblers immortal.

'Reception this way!' Izzy shivers. We give each other a nervous look – the driver has made Circus Circus sound so bargain basement we're expecting walls papered with discarded popcorn boxes and a sawdust-strewn floor – but instead we find a foyer lavish with regal purples and golds, hand-painted murals and velvet tasselled chaise longues. Okay, so we're the only people not in jeans formerly worn by hippos but remove all the guests and this place would be *plush*.

A Hispanic man on reception beckons us to the check-in desk and then taps our names into the computer.

'Ah, Miss Miller. It looks like our publicity department have left a press pack for you. Are you with the media?' His eyes light up.

'I . . . er . . . well . . .'

'You're looking at the *Express & Echo*'s finest pet and wildlife contributor!' Izzy answers for me.

The receptionist looks bemused and I don't bother explaining that up until recently I actually worked in a poxy call centre and my forays into journalism can only be classed as a hobby. Still, with any luck this trip will change all that. With any luck it will change everything.

The receptionist switches to autopilot as he runs

7

through a booklet describing Circus Circus' various restaurants, facilities and attractions. He then pushes forward a map detailing the wings, towers and extensions of the hotel. There are 3,743 rooms that aren't ours. The odds of us being reunited with our suitcases don't seem great.

Izzy hands over her credit card to be imprinted (mine has been cut up and returned to First Direct) and we sign our names on the registration form: Izzy Ingham and Jamie Miller.

'Just think, this might be the last time we register under our maiden names!' I muse.

Izzy narrows her eyes muttering, 'So long as I don't end up Mrs Copperfield!' and I smile, remembering her leaving card – her temping agency had doctored an old paparazzi shot of David Copperfield and Claudia Schiffer, superimposing Izzy's face over the supermodel's.

'If my hair ever looked that good, I would believe in magic . . .' Izzy had sighed, eyeing Ms Schiffer's glossy vanilla river.

Izzy's hair is the bane of her life. By her own admission it's the texture of straw, fractured with split ends and so choked with hairspray she lives in fear of brushing up against lit cigarettes. She's the only person I know who can actually relate to the women on *The Jerry Springer Show*.

She is unquestionably blonde but it's hard to describe the exact hue – sometimes she's pale honey, sometimes Pammy peroxide, sometimes she comes out of the bathroom shrieking, 'It's *peach*! Peach, for God's sake!'

The Timotei ads she saw as a teenager torment her still and she is constantly on a quest for the ultimate Nordic-blonde hair dye. Not to mention the styling product that will change her life. She takes what men say with a pinch of salt, unless they happen to be Daniel Galvin, Nicky Clarke or Charles Worthington, in which case she'll fall mousse, gel and serum for their line of products promising tresses like spun gold and follicles that no longer cry out for mercy.

For someone so despairing of her hair she wears it big and proud. And men care not that a caressing hand may never return from a forage in her killer tangles – she fulfils the fantasy cliché of Long Blonde Hair and that's good enough for them. It also explains why no matter how many times she wails, 'I'd look better bald!' she will never consider having it cut or returning to her natural colour, whatever that might be.

Despite these horrors, she's undoubtedly a babe. What she lacks in grooming she makes up for in raw sex appeal. The inside of her leaving card was peppered with quips like, 'She puts the "bed" in bedraggled! The "ass" in sassy! The umbrella in the cocktail!' and the majority of bon voyage messages included references to her most infamous feature: 'Las Vegas or Bust!' 'The Grand Canyon's got nothing on your cleavage!' etc. It's not exactly that her boobs enter the room a good ten seconds before her, it's the way she wears them. She has a gift for arranging them like some people have a gift for flower-arranging. A strategic slash, zip or scoop can do so much and she swears by buying bras a size too small to give a 'spilling forth' illusion.

I secretly admire the way Izzy embraces slutdom. I've always said she's more of 'a slag with a gag' than 'a tart with a heart'. She makes no apologies and she can get away with it (even with a fiancé in tow) because she's got such a smart mouth. Men are initially lured by her bod and then wowed by her wit. With that combination – and the fact that she's so good at flattering them – they naturally think they are in love ten minutes after meeting her. I suppose she's not an obvious choice as Best Friend because she's such a man's woman – some people say any man's woman – and I certainly know more reliable, sweeter people than Izzy, but none more fun. She leads me astray and I like it that way. We've shared a flat for the past five years and been friends since we were seven. (It amuses me greatly to think I knew Izzy when she was a virgin.)

We met at a Christmas panto in Plymouth – when Buttons asked if there were any birthday girls in the audience our hands shot up simultaneously, just two seats apart. Egged on by near-hysterical parents we went up on stage where Izzy threw Roy Hudd off his stride with her pre-Lolita flirtations. Naturally we slaughtered the 'Birthday Boy' team. Afterwards, we polished off the sack of prize sweeties leaving only a candy bracelet each – a memento of our triumph.

We've hooked them over a succession of dressing-table mirrors, unnibbled, for the last twenty years, but today they are stashed in our hand luggage.

Izzy jingles another bracelet as she takes the room keys and flusters the chap on reception by winking 'You know where to find me . . .' It's a silver charm bracelet – our mums conspired to buy us matching ones for our fifteenth birthday and each year we have a ritual exchange of charms. We were eighteen when the Vegas obssession kicked in – I bought her a mini Elvis head, she bought me lucky dice studded with eensy-weensy diamanté. And now here we are, finally putting Project Presley into action. I would never have guessed it would take us this long to get here, or predicted what prompted us to make the leap. But right now that doesn't matter. The night is young and we're overdue for some fun.

'Look, I know we said we wouldn't,' Izzy whispers, ' but shall we?'

So much for our pact to steer well clear of gambling – we haven't even got as far as the lifts and Izzy's Devil horns have sprouted. Obviously we have nothing against a big win but we don't want to end up down at the pawn shop trying to convince the broker of the value of our make-up bags. Still, a little flutter couldn't hurt . . .

'Okay, but no more than $10,' I insist. 'We can't ruin ourselves on our first night. At least not financially . . .'

2

The jangling-clanging-bleeping-ringing of the infinite fruit machines assaults our ears like anarchic percussion as we step into the casino. To our right a cascade of coins clatters noisily.

'Now that's what I call music!' Izzy cheers.

The room is the size of a big top with rows of old ladies in garish appliquéd blouses sitting mindlessly feeding quarters into the machines, sometimes playing two simultaneously, eyes flicking between them entirely expressionless, even when they win. People always harp on about how depressing and disturbing this phenomenon is. We're delighted.

'It's all real!' we whoop, with no sense of irony.

We change up a $20 bill – well, there are two of us – and prowl around attempting to sense which machine is ready to give birth.

'Use the force!' I mutter, passing on Fast Buck but feeling drawn to the Zodiac grouping. Unfortunately the Sagittarius seat is already taken so I settle for a *Wizard of Oz*-themed machine called Ruby Slippers. I feed in a dollar bill and after a few spins it rewards me with a $10 payout. I'm shaking from the thrill. Looking around I see people helping themselves to the plastic pots stacked on the top of the machines so I grab one and shovel in my coins, feeling wise to the scene. It occurs to me that if I collected a logo-d pot from every casino they'd make great kitsch plant pots. I'm already having far too much fun and I've lost Izzy.

After twenty minutes trying to track her down aisles where all the machines and the people look the same, I take a wrong turning and find myself waist-deep in children in the amusement arcade. It seems that the universe intends to test my insistence that I'm through with younger men for there, across the room, stands the ultimate temptation: an angelic manchild with a halo of gleaming blond hair peering in my direction from beneath feathery lashes. I look behind me, expecting to see some fifteen-year-old Britney Spears babe with a bare midriff and combats. Nothing but a bank of video games. I watch a kid shoot a mini basketball hoop and then look back at the teen angel. He is still looking at me. I watch another kid slam a mole on the head with a mallet and look back again. The yearning in his eyes is unmistakable.

'I'm an on-the-shelf, jet-lagged hag and I'm getting attention from an American Adam Rickett? How fantastic is this?' I think gleefully.

Being the older woman, he is clearly waiting for me to make the move so I sidle over to where he's standing at the top of the escalators and give him a 'Go ahead – I'm all yours' look.

Falteringly he inches closer, looking enticingly embarrassed.

'Errmm,' he begins.

'Yes . . .?' I encourage gently.

'I was wondering . . .'

'Yes? . .' I smile indulgently, tingling with expectation.

'The security man won't let me in the games area unless I'm accompanied by an adult . . .' he mumbles.

I'm gobsmacked. 'Oh, right, I—'

'Would you mind saying you are my mum?'

My jaw dents the floor. I look at him in absolute wonderment. The cheek! Just how old does he think I am? Oblivious to my mortification he continues to look imploringly at me.

'You just have to walk in with me . . .'

Perhaps it isn't entirely necessary to drag him in by the ear but I feel it adds authenticity.

As I attempt to retrace my steps to the main casino, I wonder if the teen angel humiliation is a sign that I should choose an adult male for my future husband. That concept could take some getting use to as I'm almost exclusively attracted to younger men. I've heard all the cradle-snatching comments like, ' Should he be out on a school night?' and 'How nice, he's only seventeen – you'll get to spend all his important birthdays together: eighteen, twenty-one . . .' Very droll.

Normally I just laugh it off but I have to say I did cringe when people asked Brent how he broke his arm and he replied, 'I fell off my skateboard!'

He was a full-grown nineteen-year-old but this immediately made him sound twelve. People would give me rueful looks as if to say, 'Give him back his Curly Wurly and send him on his way.'

The outside world may not take these relationships seriously but in a way that removes a lot of the pressure, so the focus is simply on having a rip-roaring time. And that's not the only bonus. Here's what I consider to be the the top 10 advantages to dating a boybabe:

1. All his ex-girlfriends are schoolgirls with Saturday jobs in Budgens so you won't feel intimidated by them.

2. He has a lovely lean body – the puppy fat has fallen away and the beer belly isn't due for another five years.

3. His heart has experienced ten to twenty years less relationship hell than the average older man so it's still squidgy and available, not cowering beneath his ribcage.

4. Dating an older woman is every young man's fantasy – suddenly you are Isabella Rossellini and you didn't even need surgery.

5. He brings out the frisky, live-for-today, kiddy-playful side in you. (Just as well because being mature around him would make you feel like his mum.)

6. He thinks that by your age you've tried every sexual position (twice if you like it) so he tries extra hard to impress you in bed.

7. He's so easy to buy presents for – a little bit of Tommy Hilfiger goes a long way.
8. Young guys totally dig equality with women – they're not as confused as thirtysomethings about the role of men and women today. As far as they are concern, *there are no rules*.
9. He'll stay up all night eating Häagen-Dazs, watching videos and snuggling you because he doesn't have to get up for work the next day. (And even if he does, he can survive on two hours' sleep.)
10. It does your ego good – why do you think older men have been dating teen bimbettes for so long?

Of course it won't last. But what relationship does?

Only one boy has ever really got to me. His name was CJ. It's amazing how some people penetrate your heart and take root, but I'm tired of feeling in pain every time I think of him, and one of the main aims of this trip is to get over him once and for all. People think I was upset when Travis (the last in a string of loser boyfriends) dumped me three months ago, but that was nothing. He told me: 'The fact you don't take drugs means you must be harbouring latent disapproval for my, er, recreational pursuits and I cannot be with someone who does not accept me for how I am.'

I would have debated the point but he passed out. I'm feeling pretty unsteady myself right now – small wonder – its 5 a.m. back in Britain and we've been up for 21 hours. I have to find Izzy and get to our room.

I'm looking around for her, absently humming to the piped casino music when I feel my heart lurch and I'm swamped with emotion. It's as if CJ had just kissed me. It takes me a few seconds to realise it's because 'our' song has come on.

Tonight I need your sweet caress, hold me in the darkness, croon Breathe.

I say 'our' song, CJ never even liked it but for some reason whenever I hear it, I'm consumed with love for him. I feel churned up, as though my internal organs are swapping places, and this shifting summons up other memories of love and disappointment – the CJ domino knocks into the Travis domino which in turn topples the teen angel domino. Half an hour ago I was on a major high, now – woozy and wilting from jet lag – I seem intent on grabbing at anything to OD on self-pity and there is only one conclusion. Here we go . . .

I tilt my head back to stop my eyes over flowing but a trickle of Maybelline Great Lash mascara escapes . . . I try to smear it back in place but the Shu Uemera peach shimmer shadow is also in motion. The designer brands get no special treatment – Dior Touche Éclat concealer mingles with Rimmel eyeliner and streaks down my face as one. These are not tears that can be dismissed with a sniff and a 'silly me' laugh. I sense the tidal wave gathering momentum and hurtle towards a nearby ladies'. The cubicle offers little sanctuary with its voyeur-friendly gaps around the door but I don't care.

I'm just glad to be surrounded by reams of toilet paper.

3

Over the last ten years I've replayed the memories of CJ countless times, struggling to preserve every detail and conjure up the exact sensation of lying in his arms. Falling in love with him shaped my life and yet Izzy has only just found out how much he meant to me.

I hadn't deliberately kept my feelings a secret, it was just that when I tried to tell her about him at the time (we were seventeen) she was so scathing I barely mentioned him again. I suppose I was a little resentful that he got so little airtime but she wasn't being deliberately cruel. She'd spent the whole of July in Greece at her dad's hotel, inventing hazardous ouzo cocktails and sending me postcards about a Greek waiter who was very free with his hummus and made her heart go 'pitta-patter'. I expected her to come back all golden and loved up, signing her name Izzy Acropolis, but instead she was sunburnt and man-hating having lost her virginity to a 'Manky Manc' who'd got separated from his 18-30s group one night. He left before she even woke up.

For the rest of the summer she shuddered every

time she heard a Mancunian accent and had to give up watching *Coronation Street* altogether. How could I possibly tell her my heart had inflated to the size of a dinghy and that I was in love with someone other than a pop star for the first time in my life?

She did ask about the drama course I'd been on, but when I said, 'There was this one guy . . .' she just rolled her eyes.

Ignoring her blatant lack of interest, I told her his name was CJ and he had ultra-shiny shoulder-length hair and was carrying the collected works of W.B. Yeats when we met.

She shot me down by tagging him the 'Pantene Poet'.

'Let's hear it! Let's hear his line!' she crowed.

I couldn't do it. His 'lines' were too precious and too open to ridicule.

'Did you shag him?' she asked.

'No, but —'

'Thank God one of us has been spared the violation!' she huffed. 'Bastards. Lousy cherry-nicking bastards.'

Within a week of being back at school, she was having a full-on affair with the supply teacher. He was entirely at her mercy so her confidence was restored and she was back to her gregarious self. She salivated over their clandestine encounters and when she described the way he kissed, I found myself picturing CJ's lips. I tentatively tried to include him in the conversations, 'Oooh, I know what your mean . . . You know that bloke I met on the drama course? Sometimes his mouth

19

would just hover over mine and we'd breathe each other's breath before kissing and . . .'

I never got more than a 'hmmmm' or a 'yeah' in response. One day she did ask, 'Where's the Pantene Poet now? Floating downstream with the Lady of Shalot, I suppose . . .' but even if I'd wanted to, I couldn't answer her. CJ's parents had moved up north, taking him away from me, and I'd never heard from him again. Not one letter. I rang my mum every lunchbreak to check if there was anything in the second post but nothing ever came. So I made a million excuses for him and secretly planned pilgrimages across the Scottish highlands, dreaming of a passionate reunion amid the heather. I never even got to the Edinburgh Festival.

It still feels like unfinished business. No one else has ever come close to having such an impact on me. My heart started pounding before I even saw his face. I remember walking into class and despite all the new faces in the room I just couldn't take my eyes off the back of his head. Admittedly I do have a weakness for hippy hair but when he turned round, revealing an aquiline nose (my personal favourite), olive skin and the palest green eyes, I was entranced.

I remember Linda Evans saying that when she met Yanni it was as if he had been invented purely for her eyes. Okay, they've split up now but I related to the sentiment. I couldn't stop looking at him. He wasn't model-perfect but he had a face I felt I could look at for the rest of my life.

The improv tutor – Mr Reise – came in to the room

and told everyone to take a seat. CJ sat right next to me and I was busily trying not to hyperventilate when Mr Reise pointed straight at us and said, 'You two are falling in love!'

CJ just smiled and said, 'Excellent!'

Then Mr Reise pointed to another couple and said, 'You two have been rivals since childhood.' Then another and said, 'You have a guilty secret you are finally about to confess to your neighbour.'

It was just an acting exercise. He told us that most of the class would consist of quick-changing improvisations but that we would keep coming back to the characters he'd assigned that day so that we could experiment with going deeper.

When the bell rang Eloise from school pounced and insisted I go into town shopping with her. I couldn't help but turn back for another look at CJ. He was right behind me.

'Darling!' he said, all mock-angst. *'When will I see you again, sweet, sweet love?'*

'Tomorrow, tomorrow, I'll love ya, tomorrow – it's only a day away . . .' I replied.

'Ah well, *I can dream about you, if I can't hold you tonight . . .'*

And so it went on. Being consummate professionals, we never stepped out of character. I could barely concentrate through the play critiquing and mime and Alexander Technique lessons, I just counted the minutes till Mr Reise's class. I saw our pairing as an act of fate. It was as if we had been given official permission to fall in love. In class, we got a taste of how it could be with no limits and no caution required. It was amazing to be coached on how to express emotions that I was genuinely feeling but that we only joked about in the real world.

'Now let's see you aching for that first kiss – stop distracting him with the chatter, Jamie, be brave and just look at each other. . .' And then, 'Okay . . . you can stop now . . . that's enough . . . Jamie . . .?'

Within the week we had moved on from exchanging song lyrics to lines from classic poems. He definitely had the upper hand here, poetry being his passion. I had to pack in some intensive research, speed-reading poetry anthologies in break times, but it gave me such a buzz when I found the perfect words to reflect our situation.

The day after our first kiss – in front of a class of twenty-two whooping students – he asked me, 'How was it for you?'

I took a deep breath and replied:

> '*I felt the while a pleasing kind of smart,*
> *The kiss went tingling to my panting heart*:
> *When it was gone, the sense of it did stay,*
> *The sweetness cling'd upon my lips all day.*'

The look in his eyes made my knees go weak. I was relieved that he pushed me against the wall to kiss me again because I needed something to prop me up. I'd never experienced such a surge of passion. I was a gonner – plunging from a plane with no parachute and loving it.

CJ took my hand and led me out of the college

building, our pace quickening as we crossed the grounds and ran down to the river. We trampled through delicate jasmine and robust cowslips until we reached a grassy rest under a weeping willow tree. We kissed for about five hours, barely coming up for air. From then on all our free time was spent at that spot by the river. It became our secret world.

Warmed by the sunlight, our nest was as nuzzly as peach fuzz by day, even before we started bringing an old dog blanket along with us. After dark (when we snuck away from the dormitories), it became our own enchanting scene from *A Midsummer Night's Dream*. My hair may have been cropped and erect with gel but, lying there, I felt I had Rapunzel ringlets entwined with exquisite buds and vines. My Miss Selfridge T-shirt dress was a diaphanous gown. My face entirely blemish-free.

Sometimes we would sit in perfect silence, and I'd nestle in his arms, utterly content, almost floating. Other times we were playful and teasing – on one particular scorcher, I was waiting for him by the river as usual and he stumbled up, kissed me and then said:

> *I saw her stretched upon a flow'ry bank*
> *With her soft sorrows lulled into a slumber*
> *The summer's heat had to her nat'ral blush*
> *Added a brighter and more tempting red . . .*

In other words, you're burning. Here!' he grinned, slinging some factor 30 at me.

'What are your plans for this afternoon?' I asked.

'I think I'll just sit here and count your freckles!' he beamed.

'As opposed to counting the ways you love me . . .?'

'I can do that too.'

'Or, if I may just channel Eliza Dolittle: "*Haven't your lips longed for my touch? Don't say how much – SHOW ME!*"'

'Show you?' He laughed. 'I'll give you grass stains no dry cleaner in the land can remove!'

'Promises, promises . . .'

And we rolled down the bank squealing, wrestling in the reeds, trying to dunk the other's head in the blanket weed.

No doubt we made all the other students nauseous.

The stars were so bright on our last night together they gave me a kind of hope and I didn't feel sad. I didn't really believe tomorrow could exist without him anyway. At one point he stood up and paced a little.

'My own words seem inadequate to describe how I feel about you, Jamie,' he said, swatting at the willow leaves. 'I've found this poem. I want to read it to you.'

His hands were shaking as he unfolded the sheet . . .

> '*There's not a fibre in my trembling frame*
> *That does not vibrate when thy step draws near,*
> *There's not a pulse that throbs not when I hear*
> *Thy voice, thy breathing, nay thy very name.*
> *When thou art with me every sense seems dim,*
> *And all I am, or know, or feel is thee.*'

He looked down at me nervously. I reached over and tugged at his trouser leg to bring him closer to me.

As he dropped down beside me, he whispered, 'Jamie, I love you!' and before I could speak pressed a tiny tissue package into my hand. Inside was a dainty silver charm – a mask showing the two faces of the theatre.

'The smile shows how happy you've made me,' he explained. 'The frown is for how sad I am that we have to part.'

Is it any wonder I felt like screaming when my life was reduced to mindlessly watching game shows on the sofa with Travis? I once insisted he write me a poem, convinced that all the drugs he took should give him some access to creativity.

This is what he wrote:

There was a young girl called Jamie
Whose smile could positively slay me
But the best thing of all
Was her wake-up call
Because of the two cups of tea that she made me

To CJ I had been the sun, the moon and the stars. to Travis I was, essentially, a Teasmade.

I wished sometimes I'd never met CJ because he raised my romantic expectations so high. He showed me how it could be, what I could feel. And every other man seemed so crude and dull by comparison. Not to mention utterly unaware of what my heart was capable of. It's as if he took me for a walk in this magical garden, then shut me outside, leaving me slumped against the mossy gate aching to get back inside. Mentally I was still there, waiting for him to turn up with the key.

For years I had weepy tantrums about it. 'Why would I feel so much for someone and not be able to follow it through? What was the point?' It had felt like such a beginning with him, such an invincible bond. It was a criminal waste of love that we couldn't be together. And then, when the disappointment of losing him got too much to bear, I got angry. Then I got cynical. Then I started to make incredibly bad choices with boyfriends. I am not one of those women who can say, 'No regrets' and mean it. I've got plenty. I don't even know some of their names. It was like I peaked romantically at seventeen and my liaisons got steadily worse from then on.

You know how episodes of *Friends* are called things like, 'The One Where Monica Shags Magnum?' Well, my 'series' of boyfriends would go something like this:

1. The one who was paranoid every girl he dated was really in love with his gay brother (quite rightly so).
2. The one who insisted on tailing his ex-wife of an evening, returning apoplectic that she had a boyfriend, even though he had a girlfriend – i.e. me.
3. The one who insisted on paying for my ride home after our date – and then handed me my bus fare.

4. The one whose parents considered me to be some kind of corrupting Mrs Robinson figure.
5. The one I let go in favour of a git, who then joined a boy band and became a superstar pin-up.
6. The one who dismissed me with a pitying, 'You're never going to be Mrs Michael Cheney!' (Pur-*lease*!)
7. The one who told me that he was so glad we'd slept together because it made him realise how much he still loved his ex-girlfriend.
8. The one who told me that, in his country, only the really attractive women had moustaches. (Thank God for facial strip wax.)
9. The one who bragged about having the smallest willy in the south-west. (And then confessed that women's curiosity/sympathy had netted him over 100 shags.)
10. The four who are now gay. Four!!! (I *am* a gay man trapped in a woman's body.)

I could go on. And on. But there's little point because as different as they all sound, I basically make the same mistake over and over again.

I tell myself this one can't possibly be like the rest because he has short hair and bathes regularly and then one day he pulls off one of those stretchy prosthetic masks and reveals the face of the basket case that prompted my emotional breakdown, aged twenty. And Izzy wonders why I've stayed obsessed with CJ for so long.

I read this book that says if you've felt true love once it means it's always inside you. And that means it can happen again. I think I'd be better off accepting that my idyllic three weeks with CJ was all I was meant to have. Hope is a terrible thing – you bounce back like one of those targets on a fairground shooting game only to get thwarted by the next round of ammunition. You keep thinking: 'This time, this man.' And they are all crap.

It doesn't help that my sister has segued smoothly from one long-term relationship to the next. We don't have intimate girlie conversations (I've never even told her about CJ), and yet she seems to learn from all my men mistakes, making none of her own. The way she tells it, each ex-boyfriend was the perfect 'growth partner' for that phase of her life, nurturing her and helping her to the next level of her evolvement. (Of course they also happen to have progressively higher status jobs and cars.) Unlike me, she's not one for getting giddy with love, instead she maintains a cool upper hand. I didn't really expect her to get married until androids were perfected but a year ago Mum started getting letters from her rapturizing about this dream man and how she'd never felt this way before. (Mum would summarise the letters for me as 'More of the same – only worse.') She stayed in Glasgow with him over Christmas (they both got jobs up there after university – her as an accountant, him as an architect) and he proposed in June. Shortly after, Nadine announced she was bringing him home to meet the family. I tried to wriggle out of the rendezvous – she's three years younger than me, can you imagine the gloating about getting married first? – but Mum said, 'He's going to be part of the family: your brother-in-law. And besides, it'll be amusing to see if she'll let him make one single decision for himself.'

My one condition was that Izzy be present. She always managed to protect me from Nadine's hooded claw, keep the vampires from my door, etc.

Izzy! I look at my watch – I've been gone half an hour. This is ridiculous. I didn't come all the way to Vegas to sit in a toilet cubicle and mope over lost loves. My eyelids may look like thick slices of ham from all the sobbing but I'm ready to brave the casino again.

Who knows, Izzy may have hit the jackpot and we can embark on a new life as Sugar Mummies.

4

'There you are!' Izzy cries, pouncing on me from out of nowhere. 'Oh God! Have you been crying?'

'No! Yes! I don't want to talk about it!'

'Okay,' she says, happy to let it go. 'You'll never guess what!'

My heart starts pounding. 'How much did you win?'

She looks confused for a second, then says, 'No! Nothing – I've met a man! Well, three actually!'

'Always wise to carry a spare,' I say, covering my disappointment. I hadn't realised how much I wanted to bounce on a bed littered with $100 bills.

'I was asking this dealer where the high rollers were and these guys heard my accent and asked me if I was a Spice Girl!' she recounts gleefully. 'Anyway, they're having a flutter and then going on to check out a band at the Desert Inn which – correct me if I'm wrong – is a high-roller haven, so I said we'd meet them there for drinks.'

'How old are they?' I ask, immediately suspicious.

'Hard to say really.'

Great. At least forty.

'But they've got that sexy southern drawl like the men on *Savannah*,' she wheedles, trying to win me over.

'What do they do?'

'Um . . .'

'The truth!' I say sternly.

'They're in town for a consumer electronics convention,' she cringes.

'Suits,' I sigh.

Izzy looks mildly defensive but can't hide her lust – she loves any suit from a Clark Kent city gent to a photocopier salesman, whereas I find boardroom fashion a major turn-off. There are only two types of suit I find acceptable – vintage on a deft-footed swing dancer and Versace on a Backstreet Boy (preferably Kevin). It's not so very surprising – we've had polar opposite tastes in men ever since our teens. While I made myself miserable pursuing tortured souls with pretty boy faces, she was going to fancy restaurants with men most women her age would simply call Dad. And looking back, I'd say she made the tactically smarter choice. Can you imagine how mid-life crisis merchants feel when a busty young blonde lets them buy her a cocktail? How pitifully grateful they are?

I don't know whether this fetish for Receding Romeos originated with genuine feelings of lust, or whether once she realised the power she could wield, she didn't look back. Either way, it works. She has a near enough 100 per cent success rate with her targets. The fact that they may well be married doesn't bother her at all. Au contraire: I remember when we filled out a dating agency form as a dare on our twenty-fifth birthday, she misinterpreted the category enquiring into our marital status and next to the box marked MARRIED she scribbled 'Preferably'.

I realise this makes her sound like a home-wrecking harlot but when you know her like I do, you can see it's actually more about her insecurities than anything else. I have a theory that she prefers her men to have another woman because in a warped way her ego gets a double boost – not only is he attracted to her but he's attracted to her *more* than the woman he's already with. I certainly don't condone her behaviour and if I heard of anyone else deliberately going after married men I'd think it was despicable, but with Izzy it's not her fault – she was born without a conscience.

'Think of it as a warm-up exercise,' urges Izzy, now in the hotel room and busily pulling so many skimpy tops from her suitcase she looks like a magician doing the endless-hankies trick. 'We can always dump the conventioneers if they're dull!'

Other than a minor delay getting in the lifts servicing only the even floor numbers, finding our room wasn't quite the pilgrimage we were dreading. As for the decor, well, the primary colour scheme with its balloon motif wall frieze is a bit too reminiscent of the kiddy play area at McDonald's for my taste but the two beds are indeed whoppers and come complete with ketchup-coloured counterpanes. Overall it's fun and functional: there's a table with two chairs by the window where I can do my writing, a dresser with an ice bucket which will become our bar, and a bright white en suite bathroom which will see a fair amount of miracle-working over the next few weeks.

While Izzy organises the wardrobe, I busy myself arranging an alarming array of potions around the sink and fill a plastic cup with make-up brushes, lipliners and eyebrow shapers. All done, I crack open the Duty Free vodka and turn it pink with a splash of cranberry juice. It's obviously been some time since I've had brand-name spirits because after one sip I feel a rush of sentimentality for my best mate, coupled with remorse at being a party pooper on our first night in Las Vegas.

'It'll be a laugh!' I assure Izzy. 'Whatever happens it'll be an improvement on Tiffany's.'

'Ya think?' she deadpans.

'I wonder if Amanda missed us tonight?' I ponder. Amanda works in the art department of the *Express & Echo* – she's the little gem that kick-started my occasional contributions to the paper – and we go dancing every Friday night. Izzy joins us if a better offer is not forthcoming.

'Do you think she'll give in to Awful Alan without us there to protect her?' I ask.

Izzy shrugs. I get the feeling she doesn't want to think about home right now. 'Ready for a voddy?' I ask, changing the subject.

'Yeah, mine's a double and I don't mean my chin!' she grins, pepping up.

I pour her a drink and we chink glasses, chorusing: 'Project Presley!'

Saying it out loud gives me the chills. Suddenly I can't wait to get on my glad rags and hit the town. 'D'you wanna go in the bathroom first?' I offer.

'No, you go – I'm just gonna leave a message for Dave to let him know we got here safely.'

So much for not thinking about home. Despite this prime opportunity to cut the chord after four years of mediocrity with Dave, Izzy decided against breaking up with her fiancé. Her reasoning? 'I don't want guilt and suicide notes ruining my pulling technique!'

Dave's a nice enough fellow but I find him rather passive. Ask his opinion on anything and he gets a panicky look. Some people can come off brooding and wise in their silence, but Dave has so little presence I often forget he's in the room. He's made me jump more than once, usually with some incisive comment like, 'Cuppa tea, anyone?'

Sometimes I watch him running around after Izzy and I feel like I'm in the presence of a dutiful courtier and his demanding monarch, rather than a boyfriend and girlfriend. So what's the attraction? I ask almost daily. He's not even Izzy's type physically. Two years younger than her and a gangly 6ft 5' in his stocking feet, he hardly matches her Blake Carrington ideal, and he has disappointingly few flecks of grey. (Mind you, she's doing everything in her power to give him a few more of those.)

The biggest problem is their lack of sexual compatibility – he's a limp lettuce-nibbler, she's positively carnivorous in that department. She always presumed she could train him up to her standards but I don't think he'll buck up until the makers of *South Park* bring out an animated version of the *Kama Sutra*.

Her frustration peaked last summer when they went to Spain for a week. After the third sex-free night, she decided to try to jumpstart Dave's hormones. It was an idyllic setting – their room was colonial style with those big revolving ceiling fans, slatted shutters and wicker furniture. She lit every available candle and gave him a large glass of orange liqueur before disappearing into the bathroom with her Ladyshave and a tube of mango body butter.

Ten minutes later she emerged, confident she could get away with a striptease in the flattering flickering light. Stepping up on to the bed where he lay, she let her silk dressing gown drop, flicked her hair back . . . and started screeching like a banshee. The ends of her hair had tangled in the fan and as it whizzed round, it was reeling her up to the ceiling. A startled Dave leapt to his feet, sliced his hand stopping the fan blades, then managed to stretch his leg to the wall and flick off the fan switch with a nimble toe. Then, without a word, he gently wrapped Izzy in her dressing gown and set about freeing her mangled tendrils with nail scissors.

She was so grateful he hadn't just lain there crying with laughter as she got a naked scalping that she accepted the engagement ring he'd bought earlier that day in a jeweller's in the old part of town.

He told her he'd handpicked the sapphires to match her unusually dark blue eyes. She told him she'd leave him if he ever repeated a word about The Fan Incident.

Izzy's mum was delighted at the engagement because Dave fulfilled her most important criteria for a son-in-law: solvent. (That was the one thing Izzy's dad couldn't manage and the main reason for their divorce when Izzy was twelve.) Dave has always been sensible with his money – other than volunteering to fund Izzy's seasonal excursions to River Island – and is working his way up in an IT company. He's a man with prospects, if you can call computer tedium at Deskbound & Snoring prospects.

The thing is, it's just not happening fast enough for Izzy. His current yearly income of £30,000 sounds perfectly respectable, especially for the West Country, until you consider she has no desire to contribute a salary herself and simply won't last another year without a swimming pool and convertible BMW. Before we left, Amanda asked me why Izzy had to go all the way to Las Vegas to find a rich man when there's plenty of local ones bobbing around on yachts in Salcombe and I told her I think it's because Izzy first needs to free herself from her mother's stifling influence. Iris has relentlessly drummed into Izzy the value of security and stability – if you get a Dave, you don't let him go. She can't seem to accept that Izzy is more of the 'hard man is good to find' persuasion.

Since her husband left, Iris has scared off all her suitors with her eagerness to settle down and is now attempting to live vicariously through Izzy. She's always dropping round to Dave's house with his favourite dinner or taking his suits to the cleaner's, as if she can somehow compensate for her daughter's lack of domesticity.

Though she's been close many times, Izzy feels that to dump Dave would be to trash everything her mother holds dear. (Her mother does a great line in emotional blackmail.) But she is also her father's daughter and he brought her up to believe that life could live up to your dreams, if you were prepared to go to the distance. By settling for Dave she feels she is betraying his spirit. She doesn't see her dad so often – he's still running his hotel in Greece – but the pull of a glamorous 'like-it-is-in-the-movies' life is still strong.

She has tried to be happy with just Dave but Just Dave isn't enough. She loves him but she isn't *in* love with him. But why leave until something better comes along? Infidelity seems the ideal compromise – a necessity, even. That way she gets to keep Dave and keep her dreams alive by continuing to search for her (incredibly wealthy) soulmate. She justifies her behaviour in part by insisting that her flings do not in any way affect how she feels about Dave, and strangely enough I believe her there. It's as though she has a surplus of emotions that must be explored and sated and these rather more extreme feelings run on a different level to her core affection for her Rock.

I feel sorry for Dave in some ways. I can't help thinking it would be better if she just released him back to his own kind so he could find a nice homely gal with plenty of Catholic guilt who prefers Hoovering to sex. I'd never actually say that to Izzy though. To

37

judge her is to lose her and I don't want to risk that. She wouldn't listen to me anyway and besides, its her life.

'Whoa! Hoochy mama! I laugh as Izzy steps out of the bathroom looking bustier and wenchier than ever. 'I take it you are ready to paint the town fluorescent pink!'

'Yup!' she says, giving her hair a final upside-down rumple and then throwing back her head. 'Let the groom-grabbing commence!'

5

The Desert Inn is the closest thing Vegas has to understated elegance. The Grand Lobby is five stories high with a crystal chandelier so vast that every one of the immaculately attired staff could probably swing from it at the same time. No one pushes or hurries here. They just glide. It's refined. Tasteful. Classy. We immediately feel out of place.

'Imagine how far you could skid in your socks on that marble,' slurs a vodka-adled Izzy. I'm already knee-high in carpet, creeping towards the high rollers as if they are rare birds that will scatter if they sense our presence.

We move in on a Baccarat table with a $100-dollar minimum bet notice attended by men with manicured nails and flashy watches. None of whom asks us to blow on their dice. Realizing we could be naked bar a few strategically placed four leaf clovers and they still wouldn't look up, we head for the bar and down a pair of vodka cranberries. They're mixed to perfection and easily triple the strength of what we're used to. It's not long before our conversation gets a little surreal:

'You know how at home we call off-licences "offies" . . . ?' says Izzy, swaying slightly. 'Do you think Americans call liquor stores, "lickies"?'

We dissolve into giggles and summon the barman again. This time he tells us our drinks are free if we're gambling. It's only then that we notice that the bartop is cunningly inlaid with slot machines. We waste an indeterminate number of quarters (no doubt more than our bar bill) cluelessly playing poker and listening to the barman's chatter.

'I know you kids in England have a stack of history but this hotel is one of the oldest in Las Vegas – it opened in 1950!'

'Someone call the National Trust!' mugs Izzy.

He looks confused but continues: 'Three years ago they gave us a $200m face lift.'

'Don't tell me,' Izzy giggles, 'you chose the nose job!'

Mercifully she's barely audible because she's sucking an ice cube. I give her a 'Don't be mean!' nudge and encourage him to continue by asking about the Rat Pack.

'Well, Frank Sinatra used to appear in our Crystal Room but when he was with Dino and the boys he performed at the Sands Hotel.'

'That's where I wanna go!' I enthuse.

'No can do, honey,' he laments. 'They blew it up and the Venetian was built in its place.'

'That's sacrilege!' I cry.

'Same story with Bugsy Seigel's suite at the Flamingo, it's all gone . . .'

I'm just in the mood to get morose about the

decimation of Vegas history when a trio of front-pleated – forgive me, I have to use the word – *slacks* appears before us. Don't look now, it's The Three Conventioneers!

'This is Mitchell,' purrs Izzy, signifying, *'And he's mine.'* 'And these are his friends,' as in *'Take your pick!'*

'I'm Jamie!' I say, torn between shaking the hand of The Flick with his nasty frosted highlights and The Moustache who's already laughing loudly at his own Austin Powers impressions.

They seem just as dismayed by me. Presumably they were expecting Izzy: The Sequel and here I am: short dark hair with zero flesh on display. They obviously don't get the Natalie Imbruglia look and talk amongst themselves. Philistines. Why, when I don't even *want* them to like me, do I feel like the booby prize? Bad choice of words.

We move through to the lounge area and take a seat at one of the candlelit tables. I'm silently willing the ruched curtains to raise up and reveal the band when I hear The Flick mutter, 'Do you think we could swap her for the waitress?' This is all I need after my earlier blubfest. Perhaps I should get one of those Chinese character tattoos that usually have some spiritual meaning like 'honesty' or 'friendship' only mine would say 'ugly friend'.

I know we've come to Vegas to get married but I can't help wondering if I've got it in me to pull off being a bride. I seem to have been in training for the 'always the bridesmaid' cliché most of my life – I was that archetypal teenager staring at her shoes on a street corner as her friend gets into a panting embrace with some guy, it was me sent into Top Man to find out if the cute Saturday boy fancies my mate and if so, to negotiate a date, me digging my nails into my palm as my friend excitedly tells me that the boy I've been mooning over for the past year has just asked *her* out.

Ironically it was also me the boys would come to when they wanted to break up with my mates. They'd say how they felt they could talk to me, how they wished they'd gone out with me instead. How I was much prettier than Izzy/Lisa/Justine or whoever. But it always came too late.

I suddenly feel remarkably sorry for myself and profoundly alone. Not to mention horribly dismayed that these feelings have managed to track me down in Las Vegas of all places.

'You all right?' asks Izzy, extracting herself from Mitchell's personal space.

'Yeah, I'm just a bit pissed!' I smile wanly.

'What are you pissed about?' asks The Moustache, eavesdropping.

'Not pissed *off*,' I explain. 'Pissed as in drunk!'

How ladylike. The language barrier is worse than I thought.

'Ladies and gentlemen!' roars a disembodied voice as the lights dim, 'Please welcome tonight's entertainment in the Starlight Lounge – Kid Creole and the Coconuts . . .!'

'Oh my God, Izzy! Did you hear that?' I cry joyously.

'Didn't we see them at the Bristol Hippodrome?' she gasps.

'Year, *years* ago! Remember, "Annie I'm Not Your Daddy"? I love them!'

The Flick seems unimpressed – until the Coconuts shimmy on in stretchy satin hotpants. The Kid – aka August Darnell – steps forward in a dapper banana-yellow suit with black shirt and matching kerchief peeking from his pocket. Izzy takes a moment to admire his sharp threads but they are no match for the furry chest hair trying to escape over Mitchell's starched collar.

I don't remember the drummer from the original line-up – he's gorgeous and as he thrashes his cymbals his dreadlocks take on a life of their own. Things are looking up. I'm sitting in his line of vision so with any luck I should manage to establish eye contact. Rather annoyingly The Flick has his arm slung proprietarily across the back of my chair. I jig the chair forward but this causes The Moustache's eyes to light up and he, too, pulls forward, moving his thigh so that it's aligned with mine. I don't know what was in his last drink but apparently I'm starting to look good.

Even though the Kid is only halfway through the brilliant 'Gina, Gina (He's Just a Ski-Instructor)', the conventioneer claustrophobia gets too much and I announce I need to go to the loo.

'The loo!' the men hoot.

'What do you want me to call it? The *john*?' I grouch, getting to my feet.

I stop the passing waitress and ask directions to the nearest ladies'.

'Which ladies?' she asks, clearly baffled.

'Um, I'm looking for the toilet . . .'

'Ahhh, the *restroom*! It's down that corridor on the left.'

'Thanks!'

'You're *so* welcome!' she gushes. It's amazing just how American Americans can be.

Turning the corner I see an EXIT sign and think of my big red bed back at Circus Circus. But I can't just leave. Can I? Perhaps I just need some air. I step out on to the street and enjoy the caress of the warm breeze and the rustle of the gangly palm trees. An elegant older couple pass me, flicking through a brochure and humming show tunes. Across the street a drunken fellow attempts to steady himself by grabbing a lamp post but ends up doing a Gene Kelly twirl and hitting the floor. I hear shouting in German and watch intrigued as a multi-pierced wedding party approaches. Even the mother-of-the-bride has tattoos. What would Miss Broderie Anglaise make of this?

I can still picture the sneer on Nadine's face when Izzy and I announced we were leaving for Las Vegas. To someone who's subscribed to *Wedding & Home* since the age of eighteen, Vegas is the devil's work and as far as she's concerned every wedding that takes place here involves a bride with a bouquet of fake flowers and a dishevelled man lurching up the aisle in a burgundy velvet Tavares-style tuxedo.

I've since become quite attached to that image. Nadine can keep her organic lily bouquets. I'm going to carry my wipe-clean gladioli with pride.

6

I'll never forget the day I first saw the 'to-be-weds'
together.

Nadine came down to Devon a few days ahead of her
fiancé to prime Mum and Dad and check the house for
any interior design faux pas. I was summoned the
night before and discovered Mum's pair of rearing
bronze horses had been removed from either side of
the fireplace and re-stabled in the cupboard under the
stairs, along with a photograph of Nadine with braces
and pre-Frizz-Ease hair, the kitten reminder board
from the kitchen and an 'oil on canvas' salmon-pink
sunset scene from the hall. As disgusted as I was with
her censorship, I was with her on the sunset painting.

At 8 p.m. the four of us – Mum, Dad, Nadine and
myself – sat down to a dinner of chilli con carne and
salad. (Only I had a wedge of quiche because I'm the
lone vegetarian, something which Nadine still claims is
all attention-seeking on my part.) It was more like a
business strategy meeting than a family meal.

'Now, I've laid out the outfits I'd like you to wear,'
Nadine began her briefing for the next day.

'Don't you think your father will look a bit overdone in a suit?' worried Mum. 'I mean, we are having a barbecue.'

'But he looks so handsome in that pale grey one,' whined Nadine, reaching out for Dad's hand. 'And it is summer-weight. You don't mind, do you, Daddy?'

'If it makes you happy, of course I'll wear it.'

I felt a pang of jealousy. Dad wouldn't put a plaster on a bleeding cut if I asked him to.

'And, Mummy, you know your tummy sticks out in that lilac dress, you'll be much better off in the two-piece I selected. Just don't put any of your cheap jewellery with it.'

Mum sighed heavily and I gave her hand a squeeze. 'You always look beautiful in whatever you wear,' I reassured her, then turned to Nadine, telling her: 'You're pretty much stuck with the one outfit I brought with me!'

'Oh, it doesn't matter what you wear, I've already warned him about you.'

'What does that mean?' I snapped.

'Jamie, don't raise your voice to your sister,' Dad scolded.

I pouted at the injustice and sucked up my last dribble of wine, making a mental note to buy Mum and Dad some decent-size wine glasses for Christmas. Their 'special occasion' cut glass jobs barely hold a gulp and Dad is slow to top up – no use at all when you're trying to blot out a droning family member.

For a good twenty minutes I didn't join in the conversation and no one asked me to, then talk turned from Nadine's relationship to my own. Or rather my lack of one. I hated feeling under family scrutiny. I was such an easy target.

'So, there's been no one since Travis dumped you?' Nadine revelled.

'No,' I replied, prodding my quiche crust.

'Not that he was exactly up to much, was he?' Nadine tinkled.

I couldn't argue with her there. Mum used to complain she could smell him before she could see him, once Dad asked if he was a squatter and Nadine took one look at him and said, 'I think you're taking this down-dating trend too far.'

As Dad speared the last cherry tomato he muttered something about how I always choose losers. As if there is some *Usual Suspects*-style line-up of gorgeous, eligible men for me to choose from and I opt for the one loser!

'The perfect man for you is out there somewhere,' my mum soothed, only for Nadine to add: 'Yeah, he should be out of Borstal in a year or two.'

Why does Dad always laugh so hard at her jibes? And how does she always find such effective ways to put me down? It's as if she can sense my brewing paranoias before I've even had a chance to claim them for my own. Recently she latched on to my fresh fear that every man I met was thinking, 'Nearly thirty and not even got a boyfriend. Must be something wrong with her.' Of course only one man has actually said this out loud to me. But like I say, my dad and I have never been close.

In the rare event that we do the father/daughter bit, we always have the same conversation: he opens with fairly innocuous, 'Don't you want to be happy, like your sister?' and on particularly whisky-soused occasions ends with 'Are you a lesbian?'

Even when I try to appease him and say, 'I'm not averse to supplying you with grandchildren, it's just that I'm waiting until I meet the right person to make them with!' he makes dismissive comments like, 'I don't think I'm going to live that long.'

Mum tells me he doesn't mean to be cruel but it hurts nonetheless. You'd think he'd ease up on me now that Nadine is bringing him one step closer towards grandfatherdom, but actually her success seems only to heighten my failure. It's as though he thinks I'm being deliberately awkward to spite him. He never considers how hard it is for me that I haven't found anyone to love and love me back. He never says, 'You deserve someone wonderful!' He just looks at me like I'm disappointing him. Again.

It's not just my love life he despairs over. He's never really recovered from the day I told him I wanted to be an actress. That was far too flighty for him. His motto is 'ten per cent inspiration, ninety per cent perspiration!' Work, work, work. In an office. Get a decent pension. Well, the actress thing didn't work out, I got myself into debt and that just seemed to prove him right. Then I decided I wanted to go to journalism college because everyone was always telling me how good I was with words, but Dad obviously sees me more as a dreamer than a career girl and told me that the eternal student syndrome was just another name for being lazy and irresponsible.

He then offered me a loan to sort myself out, provided I got a proper 9–5 job. Hence my now being cooped up in a call centre getting moaned at all day by dissatisfied customers. Not exactly rewarding work but try telling that to a man who has unquestioningly devoted his whole life to a plastic drainage company. Worse still, I think he actually likes his job – many was the Sunday afternoon he'd drive us miles out of the way of whatever fête or park we were visiting, to eye up somebody's U-bend. We were trained to differentiate between his company's guttering and the opposition's at twenty paces.

How he ever pulled my mum is a mystery. Everyone used to say she looked like Cyd Charisse – dark movie star looks and long ballerina pins – but she was always more than just a pouty face. She was the first girl in her family to go to university and went on to teach English. There's no doubt she's cleverer than my dad and I think that's always irked him. He's the type who has to prove himself. She doesn't need to.

When Izzy and I were younger we used to wish we could re-pair our parents – my dad was so much better suited to her mum with their penny-pinching, 'you can't have your cake and eat it' ways and that would leave my mum free to lead a romantic, gypsy existence with Izzy's dad. Mum never complains about Dad's stubborn refusal to go abroad but I sometimes felt she used Izzy and Dave's relationship as a metaphor for her own.

'You don't want to end up like them,' she'd say. 'Why rush into anything? Wait for the man you can't wait to be with!'

Part of me admires her indifference to Dad's increasingly anal behaviour, but mostly I just find it depressing. I know he's not really a bad person but he's so critical and inflexible. Surely she feels she's missing out? Surely she wants more? I look at her and see all the things she could have been and then blame Dad for none of them happening. And I'm so afraid that will happen to me. Ever since I saw *Shirley Valentine* I've had an abject fear of turning into a Liverpudlian housewife that talks to the wall. It could happen to you! When we rented the video, I remember complaining to Mum about Shirley inviting her husband out to Greece after he'd been such an insensitive pig and she just gave me a knowing look and said, 'You don't give up on your husband that easily.'

According to Mum, if you understand someone, really know and understand them, then they can't hurt you because you know exactly why they are doing what they are doing. I tried to apply this to Nadine but I couldn't think of a single motive for her meanness so it didn't work.

That night especially I wasn't in the mood for Nadine's gloating, so after shovelling down a double portion of trifle (Nadine had a nectarine), I made my excuses and retired to my room on the pretence of an early night. I couldn't get a decent picture on my portable TV so I started rooting through my old things. Everything was just as I had left it when I moved out to share with Izzy five years ago and as I pulled open one drawer, a book snarled up and jammed it half-open. I prised it out, careful not to tear the pages. The *Wordsworth Book of Love Poetry*. Was there no escaping mush tonight? I flung it on the dressing table and burrowed further.

What's this? I pulled out a candle Izzy had given me years ago. It was called a 'Catch a New Love' candle. Her aunt had brought a stack of them back from LA. The idea was that you lit one after sundown on a Friday night, whispered a brief 'spell' to summon your ideal mate, and then let the candle burn all the way down for seven days and seven nights. It was entirely safe to leave it unattended because it was in a protective thick glass tube. The pink candle was dressed in aroma-therapy oils and spangled with glitter. Izzy had burned hers and then met Dave and I guess that's what had put me off lighting mine – I didn't want to get lumbered with a dullard of my own. I didn't really even want a 'new' love. I still wanted my old one. But that night I felt different. As repulsed as I was by Nadine's behaviour, I wanted to feel what she was feeling.

Did I dare light it? I felt around my desktop for some matches. A red box from the Ay Carumba salsa club met my fingertips. I pushed a chair over to secure the door and dimmed the lights. The yellow flame sprung up from the wick and I watched it dance until I fell asleep.

When I woke the next morning the wax had sunk but the flame was still burning. I felt unusually serene, still partly experiencing the dream I'd been having about a wonderful man who'd made me feel completely happy and wanted. His face had been hidden and I lay there trying to think who he might be. He felt so familiar but every face I tried to match with him conjured up a different feeling in me. It didn't seem to be CJ. It certainly wasn't Travis. In fact, I didn't think it was any of my ex's, which was probably a good thing. For a while I just revelled in his warmth – like being wrapped in a dressing gown straight from the radiator.

Then I reached a hand out from under my duvet, felt for the phone and dialled Izzy. She was staying over at Dave's and he'd just brought her breakfast in bed. Judging by the string of dancemix cover versions playing in the background she was watching the chart rundown on Saturday morning TV, which she dutifully put on mute to hear about my dream.

'Maybe it's someone you haven't met yet,' she suggested.

'Then why did he feel so familiar?' I asked.

'Because it's right with him. That's all I'm saying. It's too early for any of this premonition stuff. What time do you want me over?'

'Well, he's arriving at one so any time before then.'

'Permission to humiliate Nadine in front of the man of her dreams?'

'Granted. See you later!'

At 12.30 p.m. the doorbell rang. Nadine was still in the bathroom (no doubt plucking away what little there was left of her eyebrows), Dad was enveloped in black smoke trying to start the barbecue and Mum was down the shop buying limes for the kebabs. That left me. I ignored it. It rang again. I skulked out of my room and banged on the bathroom door.

'Nadine! Door!'

'WHAT?!' she shrieked. 'He can't be this early.'

'Okay, I'll just leave it then.'

'No, no! Get him a drink but keep him out of the kitchen.'

Even Nadine in full *Changing Rooms* mode hadn't been able to do anything to hide the offending Formica table and plastic chairs. She'd tried to buy a new set the day before but Ikea couldn't deliver for several weeks.

I lollopped down the stairs and swung open the front door. Flowers. Rustling paper. Green eyes. Suit. No tie. Olive skin. Bottle of wine. Beautiful pale green eyes. Confusion. Recognition. A weird swimming feeling in my head and an eruption in my heart.

'CJ!'

'Jamie? Is that you? What . . .?'

'What are you doing here?' I asked, delighted but dazed.

'What do you think he's doing here?' jibed Nadine, transferring freshly-applied mulberry glaze on to his lips. 'He's come to meet the love of his life's family. May as well start somewhere – Christian, this is Jamie!'

7

Horror. Absolute horror. I fell back against the door.

'She has a small drinking problem but it means she mixes fabulous drinks. Fancy a Pimms, darling?'

No reply. Nadine inspected his furrowed brow.

'Or would you rather a cold beer?'

He tried to speak, nothing came out.

'Surely it's not that hard to choose?' she laughed, then shrugged. 'He'll have a Pimms.'

Snaking an arm around his waist she set him in motion. 'Come through to the garden and meet Daddy.'

I was still leaning against the open door when Mum arrived back with her limes.

'What's the matter with you?'

I swallowed. 'He's here!'

'That bad, eh? Well, we musn't interfere. She's the one that's marrying him.'

I buckled.

'Are you all right?' asked Mum.

'Fine!' I fled up the stairs and threw myself on the bed. Searing pain shot through my hand and through my tears I saw the blood and scrambled to my feet. The candle had exploded, sending shards of glass and molten wax across the room. Looking at my horror movie hand, I thought I was going to faint but instead I pressed a wodge of tissues to my wound and huddled in a corner of the room.

A tap at the door.

'Don't come in!' I yelped.

'Jamie, do you not feel well? Nadine says you've been drinking Pimms since breakfast. Is that true?'

'No, Mum! I just feel a bit sick. I think it was the smell of the raw minced meat. I'll be down in a minute.'

I heard her footsteps get fainter and exhaled, trying to get my head together enough to make sense of the situation. Christian was CJ. My CJ. Her Christian Johnson. All this time and no clues? I tried to remember what Nadine had told me about him but my brain offered nothing – I had always switched off at any mention of her love life.

Suddenly I remembered the letters she had written to Mum. Heart hammering, I got to my feet and crept along the corridor to my parents' bedroom. Inside the top drawer of the beside table was a neatly stacked bundle of envelopes postmarked Edinburgh. I ran back to my room and pushed the chair against the door again. With shaking hands I opened the pages. My eyes raced over the tidy ink letters.

On Valentine's Day he had this poem handprinted in gold lettering on a pillowcase for my bed:

> Let us vie kisses, till our eyelids cover,
> And if I sleep, count me an idle lover;
> Admit I sleep, I'll still pursue the theme.
> And eagerly I'll kiss thee in a dream . . .

It was perfect, Mum – it totally co-ordinated with my Ralph Lauren Egyptian cotton collection.

I skimmed a chunk on her promotion, then found an earlier letter from when they had only just met.

Christian took me out to dinner last night at Mont Blanc and gave me a really expensive antique bracelet! Bless him, it was so not my taste. I explained that I only wear pure gold and we're going to swap it for something lovely tomorrow. Anyway, before he gave it to me, he told me that when he first saw me it was like finding something precious he thought he had lost years ago. He said I made him feel all the intensity of first love again and that now he'd found me I would be his everlasting love. Can you believe it? Romantic words and lovely presents – finally a man who truly deserves me!

I felt as though barbed wire was being ripped through my heart. His first love? I was his first love! How could Nadine make him feel like I did? Maybe he could see something of me in her? I knew some people considered her a younger, prettier, thinner version of me. Travis had helpfully told me that once when he was tripping. Had CJ unconsciously homed in on a family resemblance? How could he love her? Why hadn't he waited for me? Why hadn't he found me until now? I had found him and lost him in the same moment.

I was crippled by the unfairness of the situation. All the dreams CJ and I had talked about, he was now sharing with Nadine. That thieving witch – she's living *my* love life.

I was distracted from my surge of outrage by the unmistakable sound of Izzy doing Elvis: '*Bright light city gonna set my soul, gonna set my soul on fire . . .*'

'Open up!' she yelled, pummelling my door.

I crawled over and let her in.

'Jesus!' she gasped, surveying the broken glass, bloodied tissues and my angst-ridden face.

'It's not what it looks like,' I said, half-heartedly. 'But now I come to think of it . . .'

'What the hell has happened? What are you reading?' she demanded, making a grab for the letters.

'Nothing!' I said, shoving them under the bed.

'Well, what's going on? Is that your Catch a New Love candle?'

'What's left of it . . .'

'Those things are explosion-proof!' she insisted, picking up a jagged chunk which begged to differ.

I took a deep breath. 'Izzy, CJ is here.'

'CJ who? What are you talking about?' she frowned.

'Remember the boy I met on that drama course ten years ago?'

'Vaguely.'

'The Pantene Poet?'

'Oh God, yes! What do you mean he's here?'

'The doorbell rang and he was standing there.'

'I take it you weren't pleased to see him,' she said, crouching down to inspect my cut hand. I could tell she thought I'd entirely lost the plot.

'I know this is going to sound absurd but Nadine's fiancé . . .'

'Christian . . .' she said, helping me through my sobbing sentence.

' . . . is CJ, the Pantene Poet.'

For a moment she just stared at me. Then she shot out the door with a firm, 'Don't move.'

Five minutes later she was back with a bottle of Jose Cuervo and boundless sympathy.

'I can't bloody believe it! It IS him! I introduced myself and then said, "Gosh, you really remind me of an actor," and Nadine butted in: "Oh, that's all in his past now. Christian is an architect now." He looked all shifty and I said, "Nadine's sister Jamie used to act, you know. Got her first taste of it at a drama course in Guildford about ten years ago."'

'Izzy! You didn't!'

'I did. He went bright red. Anyway, naturally they're all asking after you so I said we had something important to do and then we'd join them. The barbecue's gone out anyway.'

She sat beside me and poured me a huge glug of tequila. As I downed it I winced but the warmth felt good.

'What am I going to do Izzy? He's the only man I've ever really loved. He's The One for me.'

'But you're not The One for him.'

'How can you say that?' I cried.

'He's spent a year with Nadine! He's wearing a suit. He has short hair. He can't be the same person you got all soppy over Shelley with.'

We took another slug each. My brain was beginning to feel woolly.

'I think the burst candle is a sign,' she said, feeling for my Achilles' heel. I was big on signs.

She reached for the tequila again, brushing a book to the floor. It was the collection of love poetry I'd rescued yesterday.

'I thought you were poetry-free these days?' she said accusingly. She'd never approved because she said it always made me misty and morose.

'I am, I just –'

'Pick a page,' she interrupted.

I looked up at her. We hadn't done this for years. In the past, whenever we had to make a tricky decision we'd grab a book, pick a page and however we interpreted the words would decide our fate. Winnie-the-Pooh books proved particularly profound.

'Ninety-five!' I said defiantly.

'Bloody hell! Listen to this:

> *My love? alas! I must not call you mine,*
> *But to your envied bride that name resign:*
> *I must forget your lovely melting charms,*
> *And be forever banished from your arms!'*

'Stop!' I insisted. I must have registered that in my subconscious from years ago. 'Let me pick again – just hold out the book!'

Izzy just looked at me. Then she touched my hand and quietly said, 'This can't go on.'

Izzy was in a heightened state herself, having just received the latest pleading proposal from Dave. Every time he got down on bended knee she'd bolt like she was being chased by the child-catcher in *Chitty Chitty Bang Bang* and we'd end up on some bender.

Until now, the longest we'd been missing in action was a week and it had been all hysterical shrieking and giggling as we sped off in her Golf. This time was different. As she knelt beside me I saw misery morph into absolute determination. It could only mean one thing: Project Presley.

'This can't go on, Jamie,' she repeated. 'If we keep doing what we're doing, we're going to keep getting what we're getting. Something major has to change.'

'Epiphany?' I whimpered, sensing hope.

'The name's Izzy,' she grinned. 'How do you feel about your life at the moment?'

I gave her a 'Do you really need to ask?' look and wailed the expected, 'What life?' line.

'You know I feel the same way and every time Dave tries to set the date I just see my life shrinking before my eyes. Basically, if I marry him I have to say good-bye to any chance of a celebrity wedding, being a kept woman, Jennifer Aniston hair . . . I know it's no picnic for you being single but at least there's that possibility that a prince could walk into your life and change everything. If I marry Dave I'm accepting that will never happen and one day I'll wake up and actually know how to change a fuse and which cleaner works best on ceramic tiles and I can't tell you how depressing that is.'

She took a breath and continued: 'I can't go on wondering if there is someone better out there. And you can't go on believing you've had your only taste of true love. We have to find out if any of the dreams we use to get through the day can come true. I say we give it a shot and put our plan to the test.'

Still gasping from my exhaustive sobbing I managed to form the words: 'The Marry a Millionaire plan?'

'I always liked it so much better than our Work Really Hard & Get a Promotion plan.'

'Me too,' I smiled.

'Is it too late to accept that writing assignment?'

'No,' I said, eyes widening with the realisation that we were really going to do this.

'Okay. Make that call.'

8

All I had ever wanted was the chance to see CJ again. Suddenly I was one floor up and two rooms along from him. Ten years too late. And in a right mess. Izzy was busily trying to bandage up my 'exploding candle' wounds, aware that we had been upstairs a conspicuously anti-social length of time and needed to go and face the music. Andrea Bocelli to be precise. My mum always likes a bit of cheesy opera when we have guests.

'Don't wrap it around my wrist,' I squawked. 'They'll start thinking *razor blades*.'

'Ugh! Stop!' she grimaced.

I looked down at my hand. The cuts were too big for plasters but hardly worthy of this level of mummification.

'Okay, that should do it,' she frowned, snipping the fabric and securing the end with a safety pin. 'Now for your eyes.'

'Bandage away – nothing else is going to disguise how bloodshot they are,' I humphed. 'Glad I'm looking my best for the reunion with CJ.'

'It's not a reunion, Jamie. It's a hideous ordeal that you are merely required to survive.'

I reached for the eyedrops.

'You might want to put a few drops on your cheeks, they're kind of blotchy,' she advised.

'Don't look at me like that – Pam at work swears the "get-the-red-out" works for beacon-like spots too.' And with that Izzy nipped to the bathroom leaving me staring at the forlorn figure in the dressing-table mirror. It wasn't meant to be like this.

Suddenly voices penetrated my room as if I'd switched on a baby listening device. The 'meet my fiancé' party had congregated in the hall, looking at the cluster of kiddy pictures by the telephone desk. There was my dad's booming, patronising laugh and Mum's subsequent 'Oh Ivan!'s. CJ must have kept zoning out because Nadine kept calling, 'Christian, Christian!' to bring him back from his reverie.

Izzy returned just as Nadine began a cautionary tale about having toddlers at weddings.

'God, I thought they'd have exhausted all that wedding talk by now,' she moaned. 'I'm buggered if I'm listening to people discuss how many centimetres deep the icing should be on the cake. Let's go and shake things up a bit!'

We waited for them to move back into the lounge, then made our descent into hell. The tequila was still humming around my body and thumping in my head and I started to worry about what I might blurt out when I came face to face with CJ again.

'Better let me do the talking,' suggested Izzy.

I should have known I was in trouble because, at the time, this seemed a sensible thing to do.

'Here's the sister we've all been waiting for!' Izzy piped, ushering me into the lounge with a highly inappropriate flourish. I stood swaying in the door-way, trying to suss the safest place to position myself in the room. There was a space on the sofa next to CJ . . . I thought perhaps I'd give that a miss. Nadine and Mum were chatting by the fireplace, looking like they were posing for a sixties cardigan catalogue. I'd never seen Nadine look so stiff and awkward, then I realised she was trying to surreptitiously nudge an onyx tortoise along the mantelpiece to a hiding place behind the candlesticks.

'The wall is your friend! whispered Izzy from behind.

I headed for Dad, who was trying to chat to CJ and keep an eye on the barbecue from inside the patio doors.

I leaned heavily on one and fell into the garden.

'The door, however, is not!' said Izzy, stifling a giggle as she helped me to my feet.

'What have you done to your hand?' asked Dad in an exasperated tone.

'Her love magic candle exploded,' said Izzy matter-of-factly. 'Glass everywhere!'

I cursed Izzy for making me sound like a wannabe Eastwick witch – what was I thinking letting her do the talking? Duct tape across her mouth would have been a wiser move. In a trice Mum was beside me, cradling

my hand and brushing my hair away from my forehead in a 'poor baby' way. 'Jamie, you're really hot! Do
you think you're getting a temperature?'

Claustrophobia swamped me. 'Perhaps I could do
with some fresh air . . .' I stumbled back into the
garden only to be engulfed by kebab fumes. Nauseous
and disoriented I ran and buried myself in the
bougainvillea.

'Jamie!' hissed Nadine, scuttling after me. 'Will you
stop behaving like a complete freak! Christian will
think it runs in the family. You'll scare him off.'

It started to spit with rain. 'Perfect!' Nadine
scowled, as if I'd summoned the rainclouds personally.
I could almost feel the droplets sizzle as they hit my
skin. It felt like a blessed relief. I would have stood
there through the ensuing downpour had Mum not
ushered me in with a concerned expression and
handed me a glass of water bobbing with dolphin ice
cubes. The touching detail nearly set me off again. The
slightest hint of sympathy and I'd be ruined.

I reluctantly joined the others at the table where
Dad was dividing up too few cooked kebabs on to too
many plates of pitta and shredded salad.

'I'm sorry you're not feeling well,' said CJ softly, his
green eyes soothing me.

Before I could reply Nadine butted in, 'Don't worry
about her. She's a big drama queen!'

'Speaking of drama,' Izzy began. I kicked her under
the table. She shot me a look and began again, even
more deliberately, 'Speaking of drama – we have some
dramatic news of our own!'

'Oh? What's that then?' said Dad with a conspiratorial wink at CJ as if to say, 'You'll have to forgive my crazy daughter and her wayward friend – just humour them like I do!'

Izzy paused to make sure everyone was paying attention and then blurted out: 'We're chucking in our jobs and going to Las Vegas!'

Silence.

'Chucking in your jobs,' repeated Dad.

'Yes!' whooped Izzy.

'Izzy, you're a temp.'

'I know, but I'll still have to tell the agency.'

'Jamie – what's this all about?'

Fine time to ask me for a clear and convincing case for the defence. This was one of my more irrational life choices.

'Well, you know I told you that the *Express & Echo* offered me that story investigating the use of animals in shows and exhibits in Las Vegas?' Dad looked blank. 'It's just the most amazing opportunity in my life, why would you remember,' I sighed.

'It was because she did such a good piece on Paignton Zoo, you remember that, Ivan?' Mum prompted.

'Yes, yes, but what has this got to do with leaving your job?'

'Well, the trip is booked for the middle of July and I asked my boss if I could get time off and she said no. I tried to explain how important this was to me and what an amazing chance it was but she said if I took a week off during their peak summer period they would fire me.'

'So she quit!' beamed Izzy triumphantly. 'About fifteen minutes ago!'

'It's quite an opportunity really, Ivan,' Mum soothed.

'One story! You give up a job with prospects so you can write one story! And you'll be gone, what, a week?'

'Well, er, actually, I got to thinking that if I was going to go all that way I may as well stay a bit longer. Like a month. This is such a great chance for me to get some really different stories that would make my cuttings stand out and, you know, it could lead to me working as a journalist full time.'

Hey! I sound pretty convincing, I congratulated myself. And it wasn't a bad plan – I could fit in the writing around the husband-hunting with Izzy. Emboldened, I added: 'They've offered us a free room at Circus Circus for the first week and then we get a press rate.'

'I hardly think sending in the odd story about Devon's "heart-throb vets" and seagulls that "talk as well as squawk" qualifies you as press!' snorted Nadine.

'This is ridiculous!' Dad announced. 'You've got a perfectly good job at that call centre. It may not be all glamour now but you'll work your way up.'

'This is something I really want to do, Dad,' I pleaded, suddenly really wanting him to understand. 'You know how I feel about Las Vegas . . .'

'So go on holiday like everyone else! You don't have to chuck in your job to go there!'

'I can always get another job.'

'You were unemployed for six months before you got this one! Anyway, neither of you can work out there without a green card, what will you live on?'

'We'll have the deposit from the flat and the holiday money we've put by,' explained Izzy. 'An hour at the roulette wheel and we should be able to triple that . . .'

'Don't joke like that, Izzy, you'll give Ivan a coronary,' said Mum.

Dad put down his knife and fork, indicating he was about to launch into a heavy duty lecture.

'You know, I have an uncle out there, perhaps he could help out in some way,' Christian offered, trying to derail the rant.

'Is he rich?' Izzy asked.

'I think he's done pretty well for himself. He runs a big gift shop and I know he has a high turnover of staff. Maybe you could do a bit of work for him – he's always looking for new girls.'

'Is he single?'

'Izzy!' I cried, on behalf of the whole table.

'I'm not sure,' Christian answered, looking a little disconcerted. He's got to be fifty though, wouldn't that—'

'Do we have to talk about his now?' Nadine cut in, looking imploringly at Mum.

'I just thought, seeing as everyone was together, you might like to toast our new life as well as Nadine and CJ's,' said Izzy, all innocence.

'CJ?' frowned Dad.

'Um, Christian! Nadine and *Christian*'s new life,' I corrected.

'You're quite right, Izzy,' said Mum, trailing off with an 'In fact . . .' as she disappeared into the kitchen.

I was half-listening to Izzy baiting my dad when I heard Nadine hiss at Christian, 'Will you stop staring at Jamie!'

My ears were suddenly bionic.

'I'm sitting opposite her, Nadine,' he sighed. 'It's hard not to. Besides, she's nothing like you described. I'm just a bit surprised, that's all.'

'I'll bet,' I thought.

Mum reappeared brandishing her prized bottle of Veuve Clicquot.

'I've been saving this for just such an occasion!'

'Anna!' said Dad, startled.

'Yes, Ivan?' Her look was pure defiance.

'I'll get the glasses . . .'

9

Now I understand what Dean Martin said about being so hungover your hair hurts. I fumble for the glass on the bedside table and take a sip of Ribena.

'Pwah!' I spit, face shrivelling in disgust. Vodka cranberry. Lukewarm. Gross.

Suddenly excitement leapfrogs my grogginess and I spring to the curtains, ripping them back to let in the retina-scorching light. Welcome to our first day in Las Vegas!

The Strip has slipped off its Shirley Bassey evening dress and thrown on casual daywear. It's a much less glamorous look but still quite a sight with its overgrown buildings and palm trees. In the distance, I can see ranges of russet mountains but the panorama is dominated by a vast expanse of blue sky. I feel overwhelmed with optimism. Despite yesterday's tearfest, this is the first day in ages I haven't woken up with a sinking feeling. Could I be cured?

Afraid I'll fall back to thinking about my poor puréed heart I creep over to Izzy's bed, trying to make out if there is one lump or two beneath the duvet.

'What time is it?' she croaks, struggling solo to the surface.

I smile. 'Nine forty-eight a.m. Which is actually not bad cos everyone said that the jet lag would have us waking up at four a.m.'

'I didn't go to bed until five!' she wails, attempting to get upright.

'Well? I want the details.'

'Water,' she husks.

I bring two plastic cups through from the bathroom and clamber across her to the free side of her bed. There's nothing I like better than a morning-after story from Izzy. Even if they all come to the same inevitable conclusion. Probably *because* they all come to the same inevitable conclusion. However, it's tradition that I get my boring narrative out of the way before we get stuck into Izzy's tabloid tales so I hark back to last night first.

Despite my desperate urge to do a runner from the Desert Inn, I couldn't leave Izzy with three suits in a strange town so I returned to the bar where Kid Creole was taking his final bow. Izzy's work at securing her fella for the night was done, so she was happy to head back to Circus Circus. Only The Flick remained because he fancied his chances with the waitress.

There was a familiar awkwardness to the walk home – Izzy wrapped around some guy as I skulk behind with his reject friend, both of us trying not to appear embarrassed by their snogging. In the rare event that such a situation is reversed, Izzy makes far more effort than me to accommodate the reject mate. I remember

71

one time we took these two guys back to our flat and then promptly disappeared into our respective rooms with our respective blokes. The next day she quizzed me for sex tales and when I dreamily announced that we'd stayed up all night talking she look peeved and grumped. 'Great! I only shagged his lardy compadre cos I didn't want him to go home the next day feeling like he got the raw deal!'

'Was it dreadful?' I asked.

'It was okay – I just closed my eyes and thought of Phil Collins,' she explained. Not everyone's idea of a fantasy man but, like I say, she has unusual taste.

I tell Izzy that I got away with a snail-slick kiss from The Moustache's liquor-lubricated lips, fell into bed and dreamt I was being forced to teeter along a tightrope juggling coconuts.

Meanwhile, Izzy went back to Mitchell's room and discovered just how deep his Anglophile tendencies ran.

'He's got some sort of British Royalty fetish,' she frowns. 'He kept trying to get me to say, "My husband and I!" and "You may rise!" – as if he needed the encouragement!'

'Details!' I cry.

'I don't have the strength!' she groans, flumping back on the pillows. 'He's off the list anyway. Their flight left for Georgia at 6 a.m. so I won't be seeing him again.'

'Would you want to, if he was still here?'

'Well, he was lovely and hairy. When I closed my eyes I kept getting images of Chewbacca.'

'And?' I can't believe she's holding out on me with the most vital info.

'I have only one word for you.'

'Yes?'

'BUFFET!'

'Yarrr! I'm in the bathroom first!' My fascination with Izzy's conquest is usurped by thoughts of food glorious food.

'Let me just have a wee!' Izzy pleads, swinging herself out of bed, only mildly surprised to find she's still in the outfit she'd worn last night. 'Ooh, something's not right,' she grimaces as she hobbles to the loo. Halting, she gives me a wide-eyed look. 'You should have seen the size of his—'

I raise a knowing eyebrow.

'I didn't mean to,' she says sheepishly.

'Can I just ask,' I interrupt, 'why you decided to bring a 72-pack of condoms to Vegas when you swore you were going to put your nymphette ways behind you and only sleep with your future husband?'

She thinks for a moment and then says, 'Well, when I meet The One . . .'

'Yes?'

'. . . he might need a bit of persuading!'

We splutter raucously.

In fact we don't stop giggling until we see the queue for the buffet.

For what seems like days we inch along, sniffing the air like Bisto kids, eyes straining for a glimpse of bacon. And I'm vegetarian. According to our leaflet, Circus Circus has the busiest buffet on the Strip, feeding 10,000 people a day. We could be here for some time. The couple in front of us start bickering.

'I thought you were gonna run out on me at the Court House,' she says accusingly.

He says nothing.

'What was it? Did the serious, sombreness of the occasion finally hit you? Is that it?' she needles.

He just looks stunned. 'No.'

'What then? You don't want to get married do you? Do you?' she hisses. 'You'd better say now! Everyone is arriving tomorrow. They'll all see it in your face.'

He sighs wearily and tries to put his arm around her. She pushes him away. We all take a step forward.

'It's not like I bullied you into coming here!' she grumbles.

We find that hard to believe.

'I know, I want to be here,' he says flatly.

'But not with me – I know what you're thinking.'

His patience is astounding. He's obviously heard it all before. Perhaps she's just hypo-glycaemic.

'I don't suppose you booked the Johnny Mathis tickets either.'

'Yes, I did. We just have to pick them up before 7 p.m.'

'What row?'

'Q I think.'

'Q??? I told you to book earlier. There's no point in going now, we won't see a thing.'

'Okay, we won't go.'

'And you've got that kind of money to throw away,

have you? You know how much I love him and you deliberately got bad seats to spite me.'

'You're right,' he concedes.

'What?'

'I can't bear the way you look at him when he's singing. That night in New Jersey when he gave you the rose – I wanted to punch him.'

'You never said.'

'I go and see him because you want to go but I don't like it.'

'Oh, baby!' she snuggles into him. The wedding is back on. They are clearly a match made in heaven.

Finally the cordon is lifted and we're escorted to our table next to a wall painting of a giraffe. Sunday means champagne brunch and seeing as we've had to cough up $6.49 instead of the usual $4.49 (that's about three quid – *how* cheap?!) it seems churlish to turn down the offer of a Bucks Fizz, or rather a Mimosa as they call it in America. One glug and we charge for the food, greedily darting between the school canteen-style serving stations, filling our plates with infinite mismatched items. Apparently you can actually go on a course to learn the art of buffet eating and avoid stomach-curdling combinations. The sooner we sign up for that the better. Back at the table I realise I've loaded on three types of potato (hash browns, chips and a baked spud), two types of egg (scrambled and poached), half a plate of red cabbage and a dollop of butterscotch Instant Whip. My hunger doesn't discriminate – I practically swallow the lot whole.

Izzy has a more delicate arrangement of salad items (which remain untouched), corn beef hash (which smells like dog food) and a dozen prawns (drowning in Thousand Island dressing).

Trip two she opts for a mound of mashed potato, a mystery pork disk and some spring rolls. I have curried lentil soup, a wodge of spinach lasagne and some sliced beetroot. Eating is getting painful at this point but we persevere. Trip three tempts us with bread and butter pudding, cheesecake and the prettiest lemon meringue pie. We succumb to all three. Finally, like athletes straining for the finishing line, we stagger back for frozen yoghurt covered in 'sprinkles'. They don't call them 'hundreds and thousands' here. This is an education as well as an exercise in gluttony. Just when we think it's all over, we go back for cookies and bananas to stuff in our bags for when we get peckish later.

Sometime in 2009.

We had intended to go over our Vegas masterplan while gorging but our conversation hasn't got much further than 'Try *that* dipped in *this*!' Now all we want to do is lie down for a very long time.

'Perhaps it's a reaction to having to eat what you're given as a kid,' reasons Izzy, eyeing a passing plate to make sure she hasn't missed anything good.

'We should have been born in medieval times when it was de rigueur for wenches to dribble their food and have cake crumbs lodged in their belly button!' I suggest.

76

'Yeah! Food used to be such a celebration in those days – all hearty feasting at banquets. Now it's eat, drink and be miserable,' she sighs. 'That's such a downer when you consider people generally consume three meals a day – can you really be bothered to feel bad that frequently for the rest of your life?'

'I can't. But I know a woman who can . . .'

'Nadine and her bloody diet diatribes,' groans Izzy.

Despite inheriting my father's trim physique, Nadine has always been terrified her figure could take a sudden turn for the worse. 'Look what happened to you,' she'd say, eyeing my lumpen thighs.

So from her early teens she resigned herself to fat-free martyrdom. There was a time when she would give me a daily rundown of every nodule of cottage cheese, flake of bran or strand of celery that had passed her lips, all in such a worthy voice it sounded like Hail Marys. Things came to a head one day at a Sainsbury's checkout – she was queuing with her apple and Ryvitas, I had my microwave macaroni cheese and syrup sponge pud and she started the old 'I really need to lose some weight' routine.

Exasperated, I said, 'Nadine, why do you keep going on about how huge you are when I'm clearly twice the size of you? How do you think it makes me feel?'

She just gave me a withering look and said, 'Yes, but the difference is that you don't mind!'

As crushed as I was, she had a point. I don't turn into a heap of self-loathing when I eat a Malteser. And I feel having a bottom that gets wedged in the bath is a small price to pay for the luxury of eating what you want.

Soon I even got used to Nadine telling people I had a special kind of bulimia – one that didn't involve throwing up after you'd swallowed the larder.

Izzy has more of a love/hate relationship with food. She alternates chocolate thickshakes with diet pills to keep her weight steady. She actually has a fabulous figure but having been a chubby child still thinks of herself as overweight. It's like that scene in *Absolutely Fabulous* where Jennifer Saunders pouts: 'Inside me there's a thin person trying to get out!' to which June Whitfield replies: 'Just the one, dear?'

But despite our bloated bellies, there was one thing guaranteed to get us moving – shopping. We'd heard the Forum shops at Caesar's Palace were sufficiently out of our price range to make actually buying anything out of the question. Just as well. Besides, just being around Gucci and Prada would get us in the right frame of mind for millionaire men. We'd try on hundreds of pairs of shoes and – if anyone asked – introduce ourselves as Ivana and Marla. 'I'm just going to nip up to the room and get my sunglasses – do you need anything?' asks Izzy.

'Just a stomach pump and a coupla grand spending money,' I reply.

10

'I don't think I can make it!'

'Yes, you can,' Izzy assures me. 'I believe in you.'

'I'm DYING!' I wail.

'It's a dry heat!'

'That just means that instead of getting huge wet sweat patches, we're actually involved in a subtle cremation process,' I groan.

Caesar's Palace is only five hotels along on our map but we've totally underestimated the scale of things in Vegas. It's like walking in a dream: you see your destination in the distance and walk and walk but the pavement is like a treadmill – as far as you pace, you don't get any closer.

'Can't we get a taxi?' I whine.

'Look, we're nearly at Treasure Island!' encourages Izzy.

The wooden footbridge overlooking what is known as Buccaneer Bay is crammed with tourists watching the dramatic sea battle between a pirate galleon and a British frigate. Cannons boom, smoke billows and costumed actors yelp as they plunge into the choppy water below.

'Hello sailor!' mutters Izzy in her best Leslie Phillips voice as we squeeze through the crowd. I'm all set to surrender to sunstroke when a sexy scent arouses my senses. I glance back as a pair of softly fraying jeans passes me. Denim – for men who don't have to try too hard. My pace quickens to keep up.

Izzy titters at my renewed vigour. 'That's some carrot!'

'Did you see his face?' I ask anxiously. I've already had several nasty surprises today checking out guys with long hair. Promising from behind, the majority have turned out to be fifty-plus with bald crowns, hook noses, chewing on tobacco with Steve Buscemi teeth. But this one I have high hopes for. His dark hair is still wet from the shower, dripping crystal splashes an inch from his broad shoulders. The sun streams through his loose shirt to reveal the silhouette of a lithe body. As I gain on him I catch a glimpse of long, black eyelashes and an angular cheekbone.

'If I could just see his face,' I pant.

'It's like that dream you had a month ago – you met the man of your dreams but you couldn't see his face,' Izzy goads me.

'The lengths you'll go to keep me walking!' I grin.

Suddenly he steps on to the moving pavement that transports you, like something out of *Gattaca*, to the Mirage. Izzy turns to find me gone, waving frantically from behind him on the conveyor belt.

'Sorry, my feet made the decision before I could

speak,' I explain as she catches me up.

He's just a couple of people ahead of us and seems lost in thought as he runs a slo-mo sensual hand through his wet hair. No wedding ring. We inch closer. I notice a chain glinting around the silken slope at the back of his neck. Closer still we hear him let out a heavy sigh as he steps off the conveyor belt and enters the casino.

Dodging through the crowds we catch his picture perfect profile and I grin triumphantly at Izzy.

'Provided the left-hand side of his face doesn't require a Phantom of the Opera mask, it looks like we're in business,' she observes.

Following his scent around the corner, we find him dallying by Siegfried and Roy's legendary white tiger exhibit. The whitewashed rocks and turquoise pool look like the backdrop for a Fox's Glacier Mint ad but instead of polar bears we're looking at a rare breed of cat. There are two tigers on display and their fur is indeed white, though one has liquorice stripes and the other chocolate brown, as if he singed himself leaning against a radiator. They seem so magical and unreal, I could be looking at a pair of unicorns. The liquorice-striped one is out for the count, splayed out in front of a vast birds-of-paradise mural, twitching occasionally as he sleeps. We watch as the other leaps on to a ledge and then doubles back on himself, restlessly repeating his circuit.

'He doesn't look very happy!' says Izzy sadly.

'Well, this sounds a bit weird but a woman at the

Born Free Foundation told me that when they manically repeat circuits like that they go into a kind of trance and it actually causes them to release adrenalin.'

Izzy frowns. 'So it's their way of getting drunk?'

'Kind of. Oh wow – look at his eyes!'

The chocolate-striped tiger breaks his *Groundhog Day* routine and pads over to the crowd, glaring out at us with startling ice-blue eyes.

'Beautiful!' I sigh.

Our man with the wet hair looks on and smiles.

Overhead, a video shows white tiger cubs frolicking and explains how these rare species would be extinct were it not for the pioneering preservation efforts of Siegfried and Roy.

'Nature is our roots and our heritage. We must treasure it,' they insist.

I jot down notes for my feature as we learn that Siegfried (the blond with the magic touch) and Roy (the brunette with the amazing affinity with animals) have notched up over 16,000 performances in Las Vegas, to audiences including Barbra Streisand, President Clinton, Michael Jackson and Robin Williams – one of Izzy's favourites.

'They are two of the richest men in the world,' a man reads from his guidebook next to us. 'Easily Las Vegas' most infamous residents and – listen to this, honey – they're *German*!'

Suddenly wet-look man makes a move and the chase is back on. We weave through the casino with its rainforest atrium and Polynesian-style Lagoon Saloon, dodging Asian gamblers and foxy temptresses. I feel like we're location scouting for a Bond movie!' Izzy grins.

Halfway along the ritzy shopping boulevard, he turns back. We spin round, pretending to be enchanted by a bejewelled clutch bag in a boutique window. In the reflection we see him move on again.

'C'mon, Sabrina, let's go!' Izzy giggles.

'I don't want to be the smart one,' I object, following her. 'Let me at least be Kelly!'

Barging through two sets of glass doors, we're met by squeals and splashes from the hotel pool. It looks like an unrealistically idyllic scene from a holiday brochure. He hesitates for a second and then takes the other fork, heading deeper in to the sweating foliage and crossing a humpback bridge.

'Siegfried and Roy's Secret Garden,' Izzy reads the sign before us.

He passes through the barrier after a brief chat with the plump woman at the ticket booth.

I look at Izzy.

'Well, it is on your list of places to investigate for the article.' She shrugs. 'I'm game!'

We hand over our money and then Izzy points to our prey and says loudly, 'Hey, is that Mike? It looks like him.'

The ticket booth woman follows Izzy's gaze and interjects, 'No ma'am, that's Zane.'

'Zane? Are you sure? I could have sworn it was Mike.'

'No, it's definitely him. But if you know a lookylikey I'm all ears,' she grins.

We take our tickets and scamper to catch him up but a perky tour guide named Shereeee halts us and tells us we need to wait for a full group to assemble before she begins her introduction. He's already moved on. I can see him having a 'Hey dude!' moment with a guy by the dolphins. As he leans over to pet one of Flipper's friends, Izzy enquires, 'Do we have ourselves a Dr Dolittle?' This is what we call men who pass the animal-lover test. The next stage is seeing if he can show as much public affection for his girlfriend as he can for his dog.

'Follow me and we'll take a look at the video showing the birth of baby Sprite,' says Sheree, sweeping us down the tunnel to the underwater viewing area, away from Zane. I feel a wave of panic but this is replaced by blissful calm as we're swamped with translucent turquoise light. We watch mesmerised as the dolphins skim by, then Sheree starts the video and we see how the now full-grown Sprite came into the world.

'He's so cute!' coos Izzy. 'He looks like a squeaky bath toy!'

'We don't teach our dolphins tricks here, everything you see them do is what they choose to do naturally,' explains Sheree. Two dolphins flip and dive with perfect synchronicity. 'We reward the positive and ignore the negative.'

I'm in my element. I've had a thing for dolphins since I was a nipper and take a ridiculous amount of pictures even though I already have a boxful at home. I often think that if I didn't look so dumpy in a wetsuit

I might have worked at a dolphinarium.

Sheree hands us batons which play taped information (recorded by Siegfried and Roy themselves) and we are free to roam in the next stage of the garden at our own pace. Meandering through the greenery we discover many of the big cats enjoying a siesta, sleek fur gleaming in the sun, moist Hubba Bubba pink tongues lolling forth. We spend some quality time with Gilda, the fifty-one-year-old elephant, who has her own ruined temple to shelter under. She's rather petite (at three tons) and her crepey skin is in need of some intensive moisturizer, but she's not looking bad considering she disappears twice a night in Siegfried and Roy's show.

Crossing over to where the white lions sprawl in the sun, we marvel at how they manage to look simultaneously lazy and majestic. I'm listening to Roy tell of when he nearly became a Lion Bar when my nostrils flare. Scent of a stud. I glance around. I can smell Zane but I can't see him. He's the gazelle and I'm the predator. An elderly man next to me moves on and there he stands – six foot of gorgeousness, hair still glossy and black even though it's now dry. I lick my lips.

He looks up, I look away, my hand involuntarily shoots to my hair, and I twiddle with a strand using my palm to shield my embarrassed eyes from him.

'I'm half a horse, too!' he rumbles.

Wha . . .? Typical! He's obviously Nevada's best-looking escapee psychiatric patient.

He reaches over and jangles the Sagittarius symbol on my charm bracelet. 'The centaur – half-man, half-horse.'

'Ohhhh! We're both Sag actually,' I say, turning to include Izzy but she's off with a breezy, 'See you in the gift shop!'

'I made this myself,' he says, leaning forward to show me the archer's bow and arrow pendant around his neck. His shirt falls away from his chest and on the pretext of admiring his soldering skills, I sneak a southerly peek at his corrugated stomach. My ears feel very hot.

'So, er,' I blush, 'you're a jewellery-maker?'

'No,' he smiles. 'It's just a hobby, I make stuff as presents, that's all. I work at the Stardust.'

'We haven't been there yet. It's our first day. What's it like?' I babble, praying he won't ask me which hotel we're at.

'Not bad. No live animals there, just parrots on the wallpaper. I come here to watch the big cats chill out. I love how they seem so stress-free,' he says, rubbing a little knot at his temple.

'I hate to tell you this but I just saw the snow leopard on a mobile . . .'

'Bastard!' He laughs.

''Ere, Gary, look at this one – he's taking a dump!' An uncouth English couple ruin our moment.

'Relatives of yours?' he enquires, recognising their accent.

''Fraid so – is it any wonder I prefer the company of animals?'

'Me too,' he grins. 'Some of my best friends are panthers.'

I'm just thinking he looks as sleek and sexy as one

when we get jostled out of the way by two rampaging ten-year-olds. I stumble, thwack my leg and fall backwards on to a bench.

'Good call!' he smiles. 'It's too hot to stand up.'

I wince with pain and surreptitiously rub my shin where a bruise is already planning its purple progress.

'So what else you got on there . . .?' he asks, again touching my bracelet. This time his fingers brush my wrist. I make the dreadful mistake of making eye contact. His eyes are darkest brown with flecks of gold.

'Can I see?' he asks softly.

I lift my hand and rest my elbow on the back of the bench to steady my trembles.

'Er, most of them are from Izzy, my friend . . .'

'The one in the gift shop . . .'

'Yes, um, we gave each other a centaur last birthday. She's the 17th of December and I'm the 20th—'

'No way! *I'm* the 20th!'

'You're kidding!'

'No, Wow! That's *so* cool!' he raves, looking genuinely chuffed.

Inside me there's a party going on to rival the millennium celebrations but outwardly I'm nonchalant.

'So would you say you're a typical Sagittarius?' I immediately regret asking a question that makes me feel like that '*Hi, I'm Barry and I'm a Cancer*' song.

'If you tell me what the traits are, I'll tell you if I've got 'em!' He laughs.

'Well, according to Izzy's aunt, who's quite the expert, Sagittarians need a career that challenges them either physically or intellectually. So are you a books or gym kinda guy?'

'I'd have to say gym but I'm more into extreme sports – skydiving, bungee, that kind of thing. How about you?'

'I'm from England, remember? We're an indoor nation. I've got to go with the book team. Um, would you say you are arrogant?'

'No, but I have every reason to be!' He holds a straight face for a second then cracks up.

'Adventurer?' I giggle.

'Well, I'm really into travelling. I have Argentinian and Apache blood in me, believe it or not!'

I have a million questions I want to ask but simply quaver, 'Romantic?'

He looks sad for a minute. 'Pass.'

'Optimistic?'

'Generally yes, right now no.'

'Extrovert?'

He smiles to himself. 'You have to be in my line of work. You?'

'I used to be but I've kind of lost my nerve.'

He studies me for a second and then says, 'You'll get it back.'

'What makes you say that?'

'We Sagittarians are intuitive folk with a gift for seeing the potential in other people! I read that once. You're not the only one who checks their horoscope!'

I want to freeze-frame the moment and bound over to Izzy, tell her how great things are going and then come back composed, ready to bask in his sexiness once again.

'What's this mask?' he asks.

'Um, that represents the two faces of the theatre – comedy and tragedy.' I say levelly, careful not to say out loud: 'And it was given to me by The Love Of My Life before he decided to marry my *sister*!'

'Are you an actress?'

'Nooo. I used to want to be but I seem destined to be behind the scenes.' I say, looking at my feet. My plaster has worked it's way free of my shoe and is clinging on to my heel by a sticky thread. I tuck my foot under the bench and continue: 'The only spotlight I've been under lately is a pivoting desk lamp!'

What a glamour girl you sound, Jamie.

'Actually, I just gave up my office job,' I add quickly.

'What do you do now?'

'This!' I say, waving my arms around. 'Vegas!' I'd feel silly telling him about the newspaper article because chances are I'll be working in CJ's uncle's gift shop within a week.

'Hence the dice?' he asks.

'And the baby roulette wheel!' I say, jangling my wrist.

'Oh yeah! Wow, it actually spins!' He's moved pretty close to discover this. He smells soooo divine.

He touches the engraved heart-shaped locket. 'Is your boyfriend in here?'

'He's not that small!' I laugh. 'Actually, I don't have one. Right now.'

'I just split up with my girlfriend – she was a lifeguard at the pool here,' he says, rubbing his temple again. 'That's the trouble with this place – everything is so transitory. She lasted three months and then decided there's no place like home.'

Stay in Kansas, Dorothy! I chant to myself.

'Sorry,' I mumble.

'It's okay, life goes on . . .'

I want to hug him, to soothe him, to be his new Dorothy.

'Zane! Sorry, man!' puffs the guy from the dolphin pool. 'We can go now . . .'

'Todd, this is . . . shit! I'm sorry, I don't know your name . . .'

'Jamie, hi!' I shake his hand. It seems so formal after such an intimate moment.

I smile up at Todd. 'What a great job you have!'

'Look at this,' Zane says, extending my arm towards Todd and showing him my dolphin charm. 'I think she was a mermaid in a previous life!'

Finally a man who doesn't think all mermaids have to look like Daryl Hannah. My heart flips – it's the nicest thing anyone's said to me in ages.

'Cool!' says Todd. 'You know, if you want I can give you the special, behind-the-scenes "Todd Tour" of the pool one day – just give Zane a call and we'll set it up,' he winks.

All my Christmases have come at once. I've known Todd under a minute and he's offering to make one of my dreams come true, meanwhile the man of my dreams is writing down his phone number. It must be the desert sun. My chest puffs with bonhomie and I gush, 'Gosh that would be great!'

'Gosh!' Todd mimics. 'That's some accent you got there!'

'There you go,' says Zane, handing me the scrap of paper with a private smile. 'I'm usually around in the day.'

As they turn to leave Zane says, 'You know there's a beautiful aquarium at Caesar's Palace? One of the guys that used to work here feeds the fish there. You should check it out.'

'I will,' I smile. I'm a mermaid, it'll be like coming home.

11

'There's good news and there's bad news . . .'

'Let's hear it!' Izzy nods.

'First the good news: he's from heaven. Officially. I mean, he's just the loveliest man that ever walked the earth. His birthday is the same day as mine. I didn't ask how old he is but he's definitely no teenager. I think he likes me. I made him laugh. His eyes are dreamy. He gave me his phone number and I'm in love. CJ can have twenty-two children with Nadine and I Don't Care.'

'And the bad news?'

'None yet but with my luck there's got to be some soon . . .'

'You old pessimist!'

'*Hello?* With my track record, do you blame me?'

Izzy laughs, and I realise she is propelling me out of the hotel at some speed.

'Where are we going? I ask.

'I went for a wander while you were with Mowgli,' she says with a minx-ish glint, 'and I've got something to show you!'

As we hit the Strip, Izzy insists I keep my eyes fixed

on the pavement. That I can do – it's my feet I can't keep on the ground. I'm so walking on air from meeting Zane I feel like a human hovercraft. I can't believe things are working out so beautifully so soon. It's really going to happen! I'm going to have a brand-new, shiny happy life!

'Keep looking down!' she barks as we cross the street.

'What's all this?' I ask as I notice tattered pages from nasty sex magazines littering the sidewalk. I'm shocked to find a small man thrusting a copy at me. Sneaking a glance back, I see him trying to foist his wares on an equally repulsed middle-aged, middle-class couple. I'm just thinking that he could benefit from a little research into his target audience when Izzy stops and positions me.

'Behold!' she flourishes.

I look up at a row of enormous white G-strings, as taut as wind-filled kites. They appear to be clinging to vast suits of copper armour but on closer inspection I realise these are in fact the hard, tanned, gleaming bodies of six male strippers. Izzy is beaming so proudly you'd think she'd polished them herself. Still, give her time.

'I saw the billboard when I went up in the lift at the Mirage,' she explains. 'They're performing at the Stardust, practically next door to us! It's just too brilliant. Now, I don't have my contacts in but I think I'm going to have to claim the big one with the short blond hair for myself.'

'You're more than welcome to him,' I allow. 'You

know I only have eyes for ones with hair like straggly seaweed. If we're making bids I'll have . . .' I survey the Golden Guys. 'OH NO!'

'What?'

'Here comes the bad news!' I bleat.

What d'you mean?'

'Second from the left . . .'

Izzy squints and then cries, 'No!'

'Yesssss! It's Zane!' I cry, hiding my head in my hands. 'Oh God, he's a stripper!'

Izzy pauses for a second and then says, 'Remind me again why that's bad.'

'He's hardly gonna show any interest in me . . .'

'Jamie!' interrupts Izzy.

'Yes?'

'He just did.'

'Well, he was obviously just being friendly. That's Sagittarians for you, talk to anyone.'

'Two minutes ago you said he really liked you—'

'That was before I new he was a stripper,' I pout.

'He was a stripper when he was talking to you,' Izzy points out. 'He's not the one that's having the change of heart, you are.'

I have no comeback for that.

'You know your problem? As much as you claim you want someone to love your body how it is, cellulite and all, the minute you meet someone truly hot you think you're beneath them.'

'I wish,' I joke feebly.

'Okay, not good enough for them. You think that

you have to be equally good-looking. Well, that's rot. You know I'm twelve times better looking than all the men I date!'

Izzy nudges a giggle out of me.

'You're the one behaving like a body fascist. Maybe it doesn't matter to him,' she reasons. 'You know, just because he's got the body of Adonis doesn't mean he's looking for Aphrodite or Catherine Zeta-Jones or whoever the hot-bodied goddess of the moment is.'

'Oh no! I've just remembered – his last girlfriend was a lifeguard! I don't stand a chance.'

Izzy groans, exasperated. 'What happened to the Jamie who pulled the leading man in the Northcott Theatre's production of *What the Butler Saw*? The Jamie who says everyone is special in their own way? The Jamie who actually quite likes herself?'

'I wouldn't know, I haven't seen her for years,' I sulk.

'Well, it's about time she came back. I'm sick of this Moaning Minnie persona.'

'I know,' I empathise. 'I'm getting on my own nerves.'

'You like Zane,' she says, struggling not to take the piss out of his name.

'Yes.'

'He likes you. He does. It's obvious,' she reassures me.

'But he's so good-looking!' Moaning Minnie is already on her comeback tour.

Izzy rolls her eyes. 'I'm sorry, did I miss the conversation where you told me you were only interested in ugly men?'

I shake my head.

'Anyway, there is an upside to all this.'

'What's that?'

'You get to check out the wares before you buy.'

'I already got an eyeful of his stomach – bloody hell, Iz – it was like six kiwi fruit under a layer of caramel!'

'And you're complaining?'

'We can't just turn up at the show uninvited.'

'$14.95 says we'll be more than welcome.'

'I'd feel silly paying to see him,' I object, concerned he'll think I'm a desperate groupie.

'Okay, ask him for free tickets!'

'No way!' I'd rather drink a gallon of baby oil.

'Look, you want to see him again,' Izzy states firmly.

'Yes.'

'You want to see his kiwi fruit again.'

'Most definitely.'

'That's settled then. We're going tonight!'

Our pilgrimage to Caesar's Palace is swiftly postponed. We now have an urgent appointment at the Stardust box office.

'Hi!' Izzy chirps when we get there. 'Do you have tickets for the Golden Guys tonight?'

'I surely do ladies, what kinda seats y'all looking for?'

'Close enough to see their razor rash!' Izzy grins wickedly.

Mary-Sue (according to her name badge) falters for a moment and then assesses her computer screen. Her nails are as long as emery boards, each one decorated with a flag of the world. Watching her fingers flit across the keyboard is like standing in front of the United Nations on a breezy day.

'I can squeeze y'all on this front table but it's kinda off to the right,' she says, pointing to our seats with Japan. 'Or, if you want something more central, I have seats K3 and 4 right here,' she says, indicating with Italy.

Izzy knows what she wants. 'The front row.'

Freshly-printed tickets in clammy hands, we head back to Circus Circus, trying to decide what to wear tonight.

'You know what it's like at these things,' sighs Izzy. 'You wear your tightest, sexiest outfit and then you get there and the rest of the women in the audience are so provocatively dressed you might as well be a Saudi Arabian woman in a yashmak.'

Speaking of fashion, two things have already struck me about Las Vegas: firstly, the streets appear to be swarming with the 'befores' in a huge makeover challenge. It's as if every piece of clothing you ever went, 'My God – who'd wear *that*?' about is being modelled down the Strip catwalk. Anyone dressed stylishly sticks out like a sore thumb and you find yourself gawping like you just saw Posh and Beckham.

Secondly, with all the millions and millions of dollars spent on the casinos, they appear to have put aside about £20 of the budget for uniforms. They could easily afford to kit the staff out in Dolce & Gabbana but no, they put them in polyester (in this heat, for God's sake) and waistcoats with scratchy, mottled patterns that don't even complement the decor. And don't get me started on the waitresses in their starchy tutus and seven pairs of support tights.

Last night, on the way to the loos, the barman at the Desert Inn told me that when the gangster Bugsy Siegel opened the Flamingo Hilton every employee wore tuxedos – *including the janitors*. Now that's class.

We decide to reward ourselves for all our hard work husband-hunting with a languish by the hotel pool and head back to the room to change. So while Izzy balances with one foot on the bath and the other on the loo seat, trying to get a full-length view of herself in her sheeny bikini, I sit on the bed in my black one-piece and surf shorts, trying to avoid even catching my reflection in the TV screen. One glimpse and it's all over, I'll lose my nerve. My body wasn't designed for viewing under direct sunlight.

'Ready!' says Izzy finally, knotting a wispy sarong around her waist, and I sigh and follow her down to the pool.

It could be worse – there are a few of those teenage girls with flat stomachs, flawless skin and bored expressions copied from their supermodel idols, but for the most part it's families at one with their blubber. I think it's great when people let it all hang out. I always want to cheer, 'Good for you!' rather than 'Put those porridgey thighs away, woman!' but I've never worked up the nerve to be that 'take me as I am' myself. I always feel I should be apologising for the fact that I didn't visit an air-brusher before I shed my clothes. Consequently it's always a relief for me not see anyone I actually fancy when I'm in my cossie.

It doesn't work like that for Izzy. She *has* to fancy someone. Wherever we are. If at first glance no one leaps out at her, she'll scout again. And again until her flirtaholic needs are met. Today it's a lone middle-aged man reading a John Grisham novel.

'Let's go to the other side of the pool – too many divebombing kids this end,' she suggests, heading his way.

We lay out our towels and I drag over a parasol, instantly craving the sanity of shade. A waitress comes by and we order daiquiris – one mango, one strawberry. The icey, pulpy slush is deliciously refreshing but not enough to cool me down so I drop my towel and plop into the pool. Once my body is submerged I feel totally liberated. I swim and splash and float and roll like a seal pup. The water feels so good and I can see Zane's beautiful smiling face every time I close my eyes. Bliss overwhelms me, and I suddenly want to speak to my mum. I always get the urge to call her when I get one of my happy highs – I like to try to balance out all the weeping and moaning she's had to put up with over the years.

Meanwhile Izzy – who was clearly born to lie out on the top of a yacht – reclines on the edge of the pool occasionally swirling her toes in the blue water. I see her flick some water at the Grisham fan and then, when he looks up, she acts all innocent, saying: 'Oh did I splash you? I'm sorry!' I can tell she doesn't really fancy him – it's just something to do while her skin turns brown.

I'm loath to get out of the water but our second round of daiquiris is melting. Along with my concerns for Zane's profession. So it's naff and sleazy! It could be worse. He could have a proper job.

'You know what, I'm gonna get Zane. I am!' I say, suddenly defiant.

'Good girl! And then I think you should marry him!' Izzy announces, entirely matter-of-fact.

'What!' I splutter. 'Why?'

'Well, apart from the fact that that's what we came here to do . . .'

'Ah yes.'

'Picture Nadine's face.'

'Oh my God!' I say as the penny drops.

Izzy props herself up on her elbow and grins. 'Imagine being at one of her perfect dinner parties and one of her stuck-up accountant friends asks, "And what does your husband do, Jamie?" And you reply, "He sticks his naked, waxed bum in strange women's faces of an evening."'

'You know what would really make it rock?' I say, warming to the subject.

'What?'

'If he lived in a trailer park!'

'*Yeah!*' Izzy raves.

'We'd have a big snarling dog tied to the door with a manky old piece of rope and I'd sit on the stoop with my bra straps showing, covered in lovebites, picking at the scabs on my legs!' I fantasise.

'*Gross!* But you'd have a real purdy dress . . .'

'Just the one! And it'd be covered in sick and snot

from our kids who are total malnourished barrels cos we eat nothing but peanut butter and Cheesy Wotsits!'

'What will you call the little darlings?' asks Izzy, egging me on.

'Wendy and Ronald – inspired by our favourite fast-food restaurants!'

'Hahaha!' chortles Izzy. 'And Zane would go back to his real name: Brian!'

'Bitch!' I laugh. 'But I'd love him anyway.'

'Even when he loses his job at the Stardust and has to go back to stealing cars?'

'How could I not love a man reeking of axle grease? Besides, he'd do anything for me – he'd probably have my name tattooed on his neck.'

'Spelt wrong!' adds Izzy.

I fall about cackling, near to tears.

'Of course, I'll be shacked up with some millionaire by then!' she gloats.

'Yeah but every fortnight we'd come and visit Auntie Izzy at the mansion!' I threaten.

'I'll greet you at the door wearing a fuschia velour leeeeizure suit and sunglasses with big Versace lions' heads on the side.'

'Sipping a dirty Martini at 3 in the afternoon.'

'Heeheehee! I may be a drunk but I'm houseproud – I'll put plastic covers on all the sofas when your little brats come round!'

'Yeah, but you'd have a soft spot for li'l miss Wendy.'

'I'd give her all my old cropped tops and PVC miniskirts.'

'And I'd forbid her to wear them! I'd say, "Do you want to end up a slapper like your Auntie Izzy?" And she'd look at you in your *Dynasty* house and me in my tin can and she'd say, "*Yeah!*"'

Izzy looks delighted. 'On your way out I'd run the metal detector over you to make sure you hadn't nicked any of the household silver!'

'Yeah, but you'd let me get away with a few spoons every now and again because you know we're trying to make up a set!'

We screech with laughter at the whole horrific picture until Izzy complains her stomach is hurting from too many laughter spasms.

I can't stop smiling. Still radiant, I whisper, '*I can't wait!*'

12

The last time I felt this level of nervous excitement in a darkened room I was entering a fairground haunted house. I fumble for Izzy's arm in the blackness and give it a squeeze.

'I can't bear the suspense!' she hisses back at me. Dry ice swooshes around us, music bursts from the speakers with a beat so booming our seats vibrate and blinding lights sweep across the room.

As the thunder rumbles to a roar, a figure looms before us. Flashes of lightning afford us tantalising glimpses of a hulk in full Viking regalia.

'Are you feeling horny?' a voice booms.

Every woman in the room screams, 'Yeeeeeeessss!'

'Then please welcome our next Golden Guys' gift to you!'

'Which one it is?' Izzy cries, craning to identify the body.

The Viking pounds forward into the light, striking a series of beefy poses in time to 'Bad to the Bone'.

'Who says the best things come in small packages?' the compère smirks. 'This is our Scandinavian stud

Lars and he's going to unwrap himself for you.'

The squealing in the audience reaches a crescendo as he starts losing the various rabbit pelts slung from his belt and hurls his helmet into the wings. Ruffling his blond hair he pauses to give the audience an 'I'm too sexy for my sword!' look and Izzy pipes, 'It's my one! Look! He's even better-looking than on the poster!'

The heavy rock beat segues into Elvis's saucy rendition of 'One Night with You' and Izzy can barely contain herself. 'That's all I want,' she leers, 'one night!'

He sheds his suede trousers. 'Or maybe a weekend!'

'A bank holiday one!' Izzy squeals as the lights dim and his G-string goes fluorescent.

'Whoa – Lars by name, large by nature!'

'Don't you think he looks like Arnie?' says the sixty-something woman with Cleopatra make-up sitting next to us.

'I wouldn't mind terminating the evening with him!' sniggers her grey-haired mate. They remind me of the joke about the flasher who exposed himself to two elderly ladies in the park – one had a stroke but the other couldn't reach.

The show is slick, the compère funny (at the beginning he teased: 'There are two things you won't be seeing tonight . . . husbands and boyfriends!' to enormous cheers) and the men are stunning – not the usual Tango-tanned types covered in enough grease to be mistaken for a cross-Channel swimmer. And with the exception of Lars (who is HUGE) the guys are normal-size but incredibly defined. I feel quite light-headed at the prospect of seeing Zane strip and impatiently demand, 'Where is he?' as the fourth Golden Guy canters on stage dressed as a cowboy with no jeans under his chaps.

'Which one are you waiting for?' asks Cleopatra, eager to assist.

'Zane, with the shoulder-length black hair—'

'He's the one after next,' she cuts in. 'It's called saving the best to last!'

On closer inspection I see that her bright blonde Babs Windsor hair is in fact a wig and marvel at the amount of jewellery she's managed to laden herself with. Before too long she lays a jangly hand on me and says, 'Here he comes now!'

An Arabian Knight leaps on stage, all lashing whips and fluttering fabric. His dark eyes peek out from beneath the shimmering gold turban, a silk scarf is swathed over his nose and mouth. As he dances to the exotic music his robes swirl around him and then fall to the floor, the brocade waistcoat is shrugged from his shoulders and he spins on the spot ripping open his shirt to reveal that divinely bumpy stomach. I can't believe I was privy to a sneak preview earlier in the day. I can't believe this snake-hipped God sat and discussed bracelet charms with me. I can't believe I can smell his aftershave from here. In one move he whips off his satin pantaloons and stands before us in gold sequinned underpants, wrist cuffs and black boots. He folds his arms in front of his chest and nods his head as 'Genie in a Bottle' strikes up.

The compère announces, 'And now, ladies, Zane is

going to make one of your dreams come true!'

He backflips off the stage and runs into the audience. I try to duck beneath the table while Izzy madly waves her arms above my head.

'Stop it!' I hiss.

'He's coming this way! He's seen you! Oh my God!' squeals Izzy.

I sneak a peek and see an outstretched hand. No way! But Izzy de-limpets me from my chair and shoves me into his arms. Before I know it, I'm sitting on a chair in the middle of the stage, rigid with embarrassment.

'Just relax and enjoy yourself,' he whispers, straddling me and placing my hands on his naked back. I shudder at the sensation of his silken skin. He nuzzles my neck like a cat leaving its scent, only in his case it's Joop. Then he leans back, arching himself into a crab. Certain body parts jut upwards. I look away. The audience howls at the wasted opportunity, screaming, 'Grab it!' But before I can even take a second glance he kicks his legs up around my ears and flips over, ending up kneeling at my feet. He'd better not part my knees like Butch Kissidy did with that poor girl. He reaches forward, I flinch but he takes both my hands and presses them to his soft mouth. My whole body goes slack. Take me now! Instead he hands me the loose end of his turban and as it unwinds from his head he loops it around me and feigns tying me to the chair. As the song fades out he slides up my body and plants a tender kiss on my lips. For a moment I forget where I am and who's watching – I'm in Zane World and it's a beautiful place to be.

I'm walked back to my seat in a trance. Izzy is delirious with excitement. 'How was it? Why didn't you grab him when you had the chance?'

'Wha . . .?' I attempt to reply.

'Are you okay? You look like you've just been dropped back to earth from the mothership.'

I collapse on the table in a giddy, desirous heap. 'I'm ready to die! I've just done what I was put on this earth to do. That's it!'

Izzy rouses me for the finale with all six guys in white shirts, white socks and black Ray Bans à la *Risky Business*. I nearly pass out when Zane winks at me. Cleopatra looks on fondly and sighs: 'I remember the first time I was taken up on stage.'

That's what I love about male strip shows – the camaraderie in the audience. It's all-girls-together having a rollicking good time. As long as you're not too pretty. Izzy has already fixed on some potential rivals and isn't happy.

'Who do they think they are?' she scowls. 'All blonde hair and big boobs!'

'Izzy, you're all blonde hair and big boobs!' I remind her.

The crowd gives the Golden Guys a rowdy standing ovation and then the compère invites us all to stay and get a Polaroid pic with them. At $10 a pop. My legs are too jellified to move just yet so Izzy and I watch the gaggles of women stumble up on stage and lie across the Golden Guys' laps/hang off their necks/give their bums a surreptitious squeeze, etc. Zane humours them but doesn't appear to be flirting back, I'm thrilled to observe.

'We've got to go up and say hi,' Izzy insists. 'He keeps looking over.'

'I don't know what to say to him!' I wail.

'Look, they're just snapping the girls and moving them on, you don't need to prepare a speech, we'll only be up there a few seconds. Just tell him how much you liked his . . .' she pauses naughtily, 'routine.'

I take a deep breath and get to my feet. 'Do I look all right?'

'You look fantastic! Come on, let's do it!'

We join the queue and inch our way up the stairs to the stage. I'm shaking with anticipation. I look everywhere but at him, even now that we're at the front of the queue.

'Jamie! He's trying to get your attention!' says Izzy, jolting me.

'This is on me!' he says, motioning to the compère not to take our $10. Izzy makes a beeline for Lars as Zane pulls me into a hug. 'Did you have fun?' he asks.

'Are you kidding?' I rave, looking up at him. 'It was amazing, you were—'

'Everyone, smile!'

The Polaroid flash pops and I go to move on, aware of the swift operation they've got going, but Zane holds me back. 'Do you want to stick around? Lars and I are hanging out after the show, you could join us if you like.'

Izzy has to say yes for me because all I can do is grin.

We take our piccy and sit back down in the auditorium, watching with glee as the foxy posse are forced to part with hard cash for theirs. Hah! Then I watch our Polaroid develop with dismay – Zane is a rich, nutty brown whereas I'm so pale I look like I'm haunting him.

'Don't worry,' soothes Izzy. 'Opposites attract!'

Twenty minutes later the boys are done snapping and signing and appear in mufty. Zane is in jeans and a sheer pale blue shirt. Lars is rather more worryingly in tracksuit bottoms, one of those gapey bodybuilder vests that show your nipples if not properly aligned and a bumbag. Izzy refuses to be deterred. She knows what's underneath and that's all that matters.

Zane beckons us over. 'This is a shortcut to the outside world,' he explains, holding open a door, then adding: 'Do you two like playing games?' as we pass through.

Izzy and I exchange a look, unsure how to respond.

'Amusement arcade games,' Lars clarifies.

Izzy eyes the former Viking and huskily enquires, 'Is there any pillaging involved?'

'Would you like there to be?' he flirts back.

'Well . . .' she says, toying with him.

He takes her cocked eyebrow as a yes, throws her over his shoulder and charges into the car park.

13

'Sit in the front with me,' invites Zane, unlocking his car. Izzy and Lars pile in the back, still frolicking. For once I don't feel like I'm making do with the duff friend, even if Zane does have Bon Jovi on his CD player. My eyes can't get enough of him and I love that every time we hit a set of traffic lights he turns and gives me a big smile. He doesn't seem to be aware of his looks at all and by the time we get to the Excalibur, I'm more relaxed and chatting (reasonably) normally. As we cross the drawbridge he steers me over to the side and points to where a dragon lies dormant. 'At certain times of the day he rises up and all this fire flares out of his nostrils, it's so cool!' he grins.

'We're looking at a mental age of – what – five?' Izzy whispers to me.

How dare she! Just cos he's got a playful nature. I turn to scold her but she's busy rummaging in Lars's bum bag, supposedly looking for chewing gum. Judging from the look on her face, he carries Extra.

Inside the casino we duck under various coats of

arms and excitedly note that Sir Galahad's Prime Rib House has Yorkshire pud on the menu.

'You've got to write an article about this place!' Izzy snorts as a wandering minstrel crosses her path.

'You didn't tell me you were a writer!' says Zane, looking intrigued.

'I'm just doing a piece on some Las Vegas attractions,' I say vaguely.

'Hope I'll be in there!' jokes Lars.

'Well, she is focusing on the animal kingdom!' giggles Izzy.

'That's so cool,' Zane enthuses. 'Are you including Siegfried and Roy's Secret Garden?'

'Of course, I'll say you meet the nicest people there,' I beam.

Zane smiles back. 'Remember I told you about the aquarium at Caesar's Palace? I could introduce you to my friend Finn if you want to interview someone who works there.'

'Finn? I think I know his brother Gil!' sniggers Izzy.

'He's really the best, I think you'll like him,' Zane continues.

'If you like fish . . .' adds Lars.

'What do you mean?' I ask, suddenly picturing a scaly-skinned man with a down-turned mouth.

'He talks about nothing but nauticals,' groans Lars. 'Personally I think there's a time and a place for that. Plaice, geddit?' He nudges Izzy and they snicker like schoolkids. She has so pulled.

'He only talks about fish when he's nervous or around strangers,' Zane defends. 'Honestly, he's a real laugh when you get to know him.'

'Sounds like a bit of a damp squid to me,' titters Izzy. 'What does he look like?'

Before Zane can answer she adds, 'Has he got a mullet?'

Zane refuses to be baited by their inane punning and continues to address me: 'He's an amazing guy and he really knows his stuff. Maybe I could take you to meet him?'

Things just keep getting better and better. Now he wants me to meet one of his best friends. That has to be a good sign.

'Yeah, I'd love to!'

'When's good for you?' he asks.

I don't want to look overly keen. 'Tomorrow morning?'

'Tomorrow it is. But let's make it 1 p.m. so we can catch him on his lunch break.'

'Brilliant,' I grin. 'And I don't care if he does just talk about fish – I'd find it interesting.'

'You know he never swears?' says Lars, looking serious for a moment. 'Just says, "Oh Cod!" now and again.'

Zane grabs my hand and leads me down the stairs to the amusements, confiding: 'They don't really get on – Finn and Lars.'

I'm hanging on his every word but my brain is reeling from the fact that we're now at the bottom of the stairs and he hasn't let go of my hand yet. It's as though every sensation in my body has been channelled into my fingers and I'm praying my palm doesn't go clammy. As he surveys the amusements, I feel his thumb lightly stroking mine. It's amazing how such an innocent thing can feel so erotic when you fancy someone this much. Better yet, people must be thinking I'm actually with him.

The games flash and ping around us and Zane proudly shows me that he's one of the top three highest scorers on the virtual ski-jump game. I have to admit I was a tad nervous about the prospect of an amusement arcade after last night's teen angel humiliation but look at me now! Suddenly Zane stops and turns to face me. His brown eyes lock on to mine and then his gaze falls to my mouth. My heart starts to pound as he lifts his hand and pushes my hair away from my face. It's such a gentle movement and yet my scalp tingles at his touch. Please let him say something nice. Anything to give me a clue that he likes me too.

'I wonder what our kids would look like?' he broods.

I laugh out loud. Wow! Talk about exceeding expectations! I'm stunned that a man beat me to this thought.

'Well, with any luck they'd have your eyes, your hair, your EVERYTHING!' I blather.

'*Everything*? Not so great if you have a girl!' sniggers Izzy, sneaking up on us and ruining our intimate vibe. 'I mean, what would you call her? Hermione Hermaphrodite?! Sounds like one of Paula Yates' kids!'

Lars falls about laughing even though I doubt he knows what Izzy is talking about.

'Come on, let's do it!' Zane exclaims. Blimey, he's

keen! This is a bit quick even for me. I'm wondering how to respond when Izzy grabs me by the shoulders and spins me round. I am now facing a Photomorph machine offering punters the chance to 'Find out what your children would look like!'

Ah. That'll teach my brain to make Evil Knievil-style leaps.

But before I have a chance to blush Zane pulls me into the booth and swishes the curtain across in front of Izzy's and Lars' nosy faces saying, 'Please excuse us, we're conceiving!' He pulls me on to his lap. Great – you can hold in your stomach but not your bum. I lean heavily on to the side of the booth and lightly on to him. We feed in the dollar bills and wait. His face is required first so we do some human origami to exclude me from the picture. It freeze-frames. What a dish.

I'm next. I blink. It freeze-frames. 'Oh God! Our child is going to have squiffy eyes! Make it do it again!' I cry. The next shot isn't perfect but if I ask for any more tries I'm just going to seem off-puttingly vain so I grin and bear it.

As soon as we're out of the booth, Izzy and Lars leap aboard the swivel seat choosing to face each other, rather than the camera. Over their shrieks and giggles, I ask Zane if he wants kids for real.

'Are you offering?' he laughs.

'Yes,' I think.

'I don't know. I guess I'd have to have a career change before I considered it for real. Being a stripper doesn't sound like much of a "Dad" occupation, does it?'

'Perhaps you could incorporate the kid into your act,' I suggest. 'You know how women go crazy for men with babies!'

'Oh God!' Zane cringes. 'Can you imagine? Changing nappies on stage?'

'What does your dad do?' I ask.

'He's in construction. I used to work for him, actually.'

I imagine a swift role-reversal in wolf-whistling on his building site.

'Not a bad job but then one day I was "discovered" in a gym and I liked the idea of the travel and I guess I always was a bit of a show-off.'

I smile at his false arrogance.

'Were you nervous the first time you went on stage?'

'Terrified!' he admits. 'You know when your rhythm is all out and you can't seem to dance?'

I nod but find it hard to believe he'd ever have that problem.

'I was concentrating so hard on getting the steps right and hitting the beat I wasn't really aware of the audience and it just felt lame. Then "Kiss" struck up and I had to run through the crowd,' he remembers. 'What a charge! It was like slow-motion – I looked into the women's faces, felt their hands on me and it was like this connection – I realised what they wanted.'

'And what was that?' I ask breathlessly.

'Energy! Passion! They don't want some cool, distant, perfect guy. They want heat and intensity. They want to feel that one touch from you could make them melt and writhe.'

115

I gasp involuntarily.

'Most guys these days are lazy with their women. They don't make them feel desired. Women like to feel that a man is on fire for her.'

My chest is heaving so fast you'd think someone was inflating me with a foot pump. And still he continues.

'But they want humour too. They like to be teased. I don't stand on stage going, "Check me out!" I lean over and whisper, "Come play with me! Come play with my fire!"'

I feel his warm breath on my ear and fall against the booth just as our child is born. 'It's a boy! Honey, look!' I coo.

Zane inspects the print-out of our offspring. 'Are you sure he's mine?'

I whallop him. He pulls me into a 'just kidding' hug. His body feels hot. I'm no iceberg myself right now. It doesn't help that Izzy and Lars have fallen silent except for the odd slurp, moan and body slam.

'What shall we call him?' I ask, staring at the full-lipped, jet-haired scruff in the picture.

'I guess it should be a combination of our names – what could we make out of Zane and Jamie?'

I think for a moment, seeing the letters float before me. 'Hmmmmm . . .' I dismiss options like 'Amen' and 'Enime', then offer 'Jaz'.

'Jaz? Yeah, that sounds cool. Well, I guess we'd better go win some toys for his playpen.'

'Hold on a moment!' I turn back to the booth and call to Izzy.

'Yes,' she says, clearly peeved to be interrupted.

'We'll be over by the metal claw grabber thing, see you when you're done. Oh and please bear in mind that the booth curtain is not full-length.'

We walk past a man who claims he can guess anyone's weight within three pounds and if he's wrong, you win a prize. I'm fairly skilled at disguising my weight but I don't feel now is the right time to put that boast to the test. We walk on and Zane challenges me to a game of air hockey. I'm almost afraid to accept because I know this particular game gets me violently competitive, but I can't resist. I slam the disk across the table and flip it into his goal with my first shot. 'Yayyyy!'

'Right! You asked for it!' he says, slashing it back to me, I defend my territory and get hot and screamy as the close-fought match continues. We settle on a 2–2 tie. 'You're pretty good at that!' he concedes, tousling my hair. 'What are you like at the rifle range?'

'Never tried it,' I admit. 'I think I'd rather watch you.'

He topples the tin can in three shots and then tells me to close my eyes. When I open them I find a Little Mermaid soft toy in my arms.

'Oh, thank you!' I sigh, forgetting he's a sex god and throwing my arms around him.

He hugs me back. 'My pleasure!'

This is the best! He's so much fun! So affectionate! He's just suggesting we get something to drink when Izzy catches up with us, looking flushed and not a little sheepish. I peer at her raging red chin.

'I thought he was clean-shaven.' I frown.

117

'Sven stubble.' she shrugs. 'It's so pale it's practically invisible.'

'Where's Lars?' asks Zane, a little mystified by our exchange.

'Um, he had to go . . .'

'That's a bit sudden, isn't it? Why didn't he say goodbye?'

'He didn't feel well.'

Zane looks concerned. 'Maybe I should go and check on him—'

'I don't think there's anything you can do to help him,' Izzy insists with a twisted smile.

'Anyway, I think I might go too, it's late.'

Like that's ever bothered her.

'Oh. Well. I guess we should all be getting back,' Zane shrugs.

My heart sinks. I can't bear for the evening to be over.

'I'll drop you guys back at your hotel. Where are you staying?'

Izzy and I exchange a look. We've grown to love Circus Circus but it doesn't quite project the image we're after.

'The Sahara!' says Izzy. Just as I say Desert Inn.

14

The waitress sets sombrero-size glasses of margarita before us. It's 11 in the morning but everyone else in the casino is at it and we have lined our stomachs with a fat stack of pancakes and syrup (rather intriguingly presented with a garnish of parsley and frazzled bacon rashers).

I'm just asking Izzy to remind me to call CJ's uncle to see if he has any vacancies at the gift shop when she gasps, 'Oh my God, it's that woman from the Golden Guys show!'

I look up and see what's left of Carry On Cleo. 'She's still in the same clothes. Do you think she's just getting in?'

We get a closer look as she passes our table. She seems to have lost her left set of false eyelashes but the right eye still has the full tarantula effect, making her look like the guy from the *Clockwork Orange* posters. Worse still, her Babs wig appears to be on backwards.

'Do you think she had one of them?' I whisper.

'Well, if she did, it certainly wasn't Lars!' Izzy grins.

'He was in no fit state by the time I'd finished with him.'

'You're so lucky! I didn't even get a snog with Zane,' I sigh.

'Yeah, but he did see you home and he knew he was meeting you at the aquarium today so maybe he didn't want to rush things.'

'I hope you're right. You just don't expect strippers to be gentlemen, do you? Ooooh, I can't wait to see him!' I shiver. 'He's so touchy-feely-huggy, I love it!'

'Let's have a toast to your upcoming snog!' says Izzy, needing two hands to raise her glass.

I haven't drunk tequila since the day CJ appeared on my parents' doorstep. Do I dare now? I brush the salt from the rim, take a sip and shudder at the familiar tang. Before I've even sucked the lime my mind starts flashing back to that day . . .

My mum's special bottle of champagne was gone and so was the majority of the drinks cabinet. I looked at the clock – 5 p.m. on the longest day of my life. The 'nice to meet you' pleasantries that first greeted CJ – or Christian as he's now known – were a distant memory. Our slumped bodies testified to the fact that every one of us had been summoned to the spirit world.

Dad topped up his whisky. 'For a minute there I thought you and Izzy were going to announce some kind of lesbian engagement!'

'Dad!' I howled.

'Well, you've always had lousy taste in men.'

'Not always,' I said wistfully, peering at a distorted Christian through my glass.

'No point in looking at the past now, Jamie,' said Izzy sternly. 'It's all about the future.'

'I think it'll be a wonderful adventure for you both,' sighed Mum, looking misty with longing. 'To go somewhere new, a different country, a different culture, different food, different men.'

Izzy made an 'I'll drink to that' gesture and drained her glass. 'You'd better watch out, Nadine – with all those chapels we might beat you to the altar.'

Nadine attempted a derisive snort but rather too much came out of her nose. Izzy cackled to herself as Christian hurriedly handed her a tissue. Regaining her composure Nadine snarled, 'I can't see your Dave getting married in Las Vegas. He's more of a registry office/reception in a curry house type. And as for Jamie, do I really need to give odds on any man falling head over heels with her? America is the land of dreams, not miracles.'

I thought I was imagining it when Christian muttered, 'I think she's easy to fall in love with . . .' but judging by the look on everyone else's faces he really did say it. He seemed to be as taken aback as the rest of us and tried to tone it down by saying, 'I mean, if she's anything like my Nadine.'

Nadine shrugged off his reassuring squeeze in irritation.

Meanwhile I reached a kind of morphine high and mentally smiled up from my hospital bed at the visitors around me.

The evening staggered to a premature close at around 9 p.m. We'd all made a veiled attempt to watch a thriller on TV but Mum was far more engrossed in her secret stash of holiday brochures, elbow-deep in a box of Roses, Dad was busy totting up the cost of replenishing the bar while dosing himself with black coffee and as soon as the credits rolled, Nadine dragged Christian upstairs with the old, 'It's been a long day, travelling is just so exhausting – we're going to bed' line. Izzy pulled gleeful faces as their bickering bounced off the walls and then called Dave to come pick her up.

Finally it was just me sitting in the lounge, unable to move, mindlessly channel-hopping while picking at a loose thread and unravelling one of the embroidered flowers on the armchair. I was numb and grateful for it. Eventually my eyes flickered closed, then opened again. According to the clock, four hours had passed. It was 1.30 a.m. The TV was off and I was in total darkness. I reached out and hoisted a glacé cherry from the bottom of Mum's glass to counter the bitter stickiness in my dehydrated mouth, then I began a stretch. But as I shifted I noticed a figure silhouetted in the doorway. A Christian-shaped figure. I froze, elbows up by my ears as if I was being held up in a robbery.

'You awake?' he whispered.

My heart ricocheted around my internal organs like a pinball machine game. 'Kind of. I've only just opened my eyes.'

He stepped forward and gave me something to look at – a vision of crumpled-sexy in his pyjama bottoms and a white T-shirt. His previously neat hair was deliciously rumpled and tufty. The hall light highlighted his breastbone and the golden hairs on his chunky arms. The boy had become a man.

'Um, I was just going to get a glass of water. Do you want anything?'

'Water would be perfect! But let me get it,' I said, feeling obliged to play hostess. My knees cracked as I tried to get to my feet.

'You stay put. I'll bring it to you.'

I felt my body stiffen and then start shivering with anticipation. I inhaled deeply to try to calm myself. After an excruciating day having to behave like strangers, we could be ourselves again in this Twilight Zone. We could be the way we were. Words could tumble out as we filled in the missing ten years, then we'd comfort each other and heal the pain.

The kitchen door squeaked open, then slowly closed. He was on his way . . .

'If he puts dolphin ice cubes in the water, he'll be mine,' I told myself. 'If there's just normal square ice cubes it could go either way. No ice cubes and he's all Nadine's.'

His footsteps padded nearer on the carpet. I heard the tinkle of ice cubes jangling against the glass and my heart soared.

Suddenly there was a creak from the landing.

'Where are you going with that water?' It was Nadine.

'Um, just thought I'd grab a handful of bar snacks from the lounge. I'm a bit peckish, babe.'

'Babe!' I mouthed in disgust.

I heard Nadine sigh heavily and tramp down the stairs. 'I'll take those. You won't be able to carry it all. Grab me a couple of slices of orange and don't be long. All your tossing and turning is driving me crazy.'

I could see him watching her from the bottom of the stairs. He waited a few seconds to be sure she was gone and then stepped into the lounge.

'I don't know what to tell you – I was mugged! They took all the water,' he whispered.

'It's the ice cubes they were after!' I replied.

'Sorry.'

'It's okay, I've found half a can of tepid Pepsi that'll do the job.'

'No, I mean, sorry about today.'

Emotion washed over me. I was no longer numb but I didn't know where to begin. Neither did he. For a moment we were silent.

'I had no idea . . .'

'Me neither,' I concurred.

'Of course, now that I've seen you together the similarities are quite clear . . .'

'And the differences.'

'Yes. The big differences,' he sighed, rubbing his hands over his face. Then he just looked at me.

'I see you still wear your charm bracelet.'

'Of course. And the mask charm you gave me is still there.'

'I saw it earlier at dinner. I wondered if you'd still remember me.'

'CJ, I . . . or I suppose I should say Christian now.'

He grinned. 'Well, it got to the point where half the people were calling me one thing, half another. Nadine never liked nicknames anyway, and when I got a proper, grown-up job . . .' he trailed off. 'You're even more beautiful now, you know.'

I was grateful for the cover of darkness as my skin began to glow.

'When did you cut your hair?' I said, trying to deflect the compliment but beaming inwardly.

'It's been like this a while. My Lord Byron days are long gone.'

My heart sank. 'Are they?'

'Well, outwardly anyway. There doesn't seem much call for poetry-spouting in the real world. Do you do any acting at all now?'

'No, I reckon Sadie Frost and Jude Law have filled the gaps meant for us!'

He laughed. 'Yeah, it gets you thinking, you know, what might have been . . .'

He knelt by the armchair so our faces were level. The familiarity in his green eyes took my breath away. I longed to touch him.

'I never stopped loving you,' I blurted. I had to say it.

'I hope you never will,' he said, moving forward, closer to me . . . The landing creaked again. We both froze.

'I have to go,' he said, shovelling a handful of cashews and orange slices on to a napkin.

Turning back he bent over me, paused for a second

125

and then kissed me tenderly on the lips. And then he was gone.

For a while I just sat there revelling in the pure pleasure of his touch. The scent of him was still in the air. I didn't want to breathe and risk dispelling the traces of him all around me. Then my mind began its twisted journey. I kicked myself for not getting to the point, 'Why didn't you call me or write to me? Why did you disappear out of my life for all those years?'

Then I started the analysis. What did that kiss mean? It felt like, 'I remember. I still care' but it could have been 'Farewell to the past.'

Or, 'Let's have a shag on the side,' suggested Izzy the next day.

She was having none of it. 'What's the point in even trying to interpret it? Can you imagine the mess you'll get into if you try to get him back?'

'What if he wants to get me back and, and . . . I'm in Las Vegas!'

'Well, absence makes the heart grow fonder.'

'Izzy, this is serious!'

'Yes, it is. That's why we have to go. Do you want another ten years of angst from this man? Anyway, the ball is in his court now. Let's wait and see if he's finally mastered the art of dialling your number . . .'

15

'Oooooh – the telephone light is flashing!'

Izzy makes a dash for the phone but I pounce first, speed-reading the small print that explains how to retrieve messages.

'There's a fax waiting for me at reception and one voicemail,' I announce, then press the relevant buttons. 'It's your mum. She sounds weird.'

Izzy blanches and then shrugs. 'She's probably just asking me to bring back a showgirl costume for her. You listen to it.'

'. . . Las Vegas of all places! I don't know what you think you're playing at, young lady, but I hope you'll get this nonsense out of your system once and for all. Dave won't put up with being given the runaround for much longer and he doesn't deserve to be treated like this. I must say I'm surprised at Jamie for behaving in such a reckless way. Her father seems to be under the impression that she has emigrated but he reckons she'll be back within the week with her tail between her legs. I just hope he's right. For God's sake don't do anything stupid. There are a lot of corrupt, desperate people in those places and I don't want you getting into any more trouble.

'Anyway, this call is costing me a fortune, I have to go. I just want you to know I'm going to the doctor's tomorrow to arrange for you to see someone when you get home. Nothing I say seems to get through to you. Perhaps you'll listen to a professional.

'All right, I've said my piece. The rest is up to you. If you have any consideration for anyone's feelings other than your own you'll come straight back home.'

'Well?' Izzy tries to hide her concern.

'You guessed right – she'd like a gold bodice with red feathers, if you can get it in her size,' I confirm.

Izzy grins in relief and heads for the bathroom. Why subject her to any more maternal abuse than is absolutely necessary?

Iris's bitterness and resentment has been getting more unwieldy with each passing year – sometimes I catch her looking at Izzy with a kind of manic sneer, as if part of her wants to cradle her baby girl and part of her wants to put a pillow over her face and destroy her. She always claims she has Izzy's best interests at heart but ever since she snuck into her room at night when she was thirteen and cut off her much-admired, long silky hair (in a bid to teach her a lesson about the sin of vanity, she claimed), Izzy has had a problem with trusting her. Funny that.

I look at the bathroom door – Izzy takes longer to clean her teeth than anyone I know (horrible fear of dentists) so I have a few minutes to myself. I spend the first ninety seconds trying not to get my hopes up that the fax waiting for me is from Christian, though it's unlikely he'd confess undying love in writing – far too incriminating. But what if he's found a poem that says it all for him? Trying to divert this train of thought, I sneak another look at the morph pic of the child Zane and I created last night and smile fondly. Such are the benefits of being a fickle woman – I can have hardcore yearnings for two men from two different continents in under three minutes.

Izzy appears at the bathroom door with a white frothing mouth and makes some strange sounds which I translate as 'Don't forget to call Uncle Sam!'

I delve in my bag and fish out the note Christian gave me with his uncle's work number, stroking the digits because he penned them. I can't help wondering if they share a family resemblance. What if I fall for Christian's uncle like he fell for my sister? How weird would that be? I take a deep breath and dial the number.

'Sam's Shopping Extravaganza, can I help you?' trills what has to be a gum-chewing broad.

'Hello, can I speak to Sam Johnson, please,' I say in my best phone voice.

'Who's calling?'

'Um, if you could say it's his nephew's fiancé's sister . . .' I frown.

'Huh?'

I can tell she's never going to get such a complex concept so I try: 'My name is Jamie Miller.'

'Does he know you?' she asks suspiciously.

'No, I—'

'Where are you calling from?'

'Just down the road, actually—'

'No! What company are you calling from?' she groans.

'Oh, I'm not with a company, I—'

'So you're not one of the lawyers?' she affirms.

'No,' I reply, mildly concerned but keeping it simple.

'Okay, putting you through.'

'Yello!' says a cheery male voice.

'Hello, is that Sam?'

'Yes it is and who are you with the English accent?'

'I'm Jamie, I think Christian might have mentioned me, he, er, he's marrying my sister . . .'

'Ah yes! So you're the pretty little thing who's run away to Las Vegas!'

'Well—'

'How are you liking this crazy town?'

'I think it's wonderful—'

'But you've run out of money already and you're looking for a job!' he concludes.

'Not quite!' I laugh nervously, unsure how to interpret his tone. 'I've actually got a bit of work to do but Christian said to give you a call and I was wondering if I might drop by to say hi and then if anything came up in the next week or so—'

'Oh things are always coming up here,' he chuckles.

'We'll certainly take a look at you, see if you're up to my high standards!' He pauses. 'I expect Christian has told you all about me?'

'Well . . .' No. Nothing.

'He's such a kidder that one – used to call me the Hugh Hefner of Wolverhampton!'

So that's the accent trace I'm detecting. Interesting mix – Brummie with Yankee drawl.

'I was the first to get a jacuzzi in our cul-de-sac. Caused quite a stir!'

Oh dear.

'Anyway, why don't you come by for lunch, say on . . . (rustling of paper) how does Tuesday sound?'

'Great! I look forward to it!'

'You've got the address?' he checks.

'Yes, Christian gave it to me!'

'I bet he did!'

'Pardon!'

'Nothing,' he says breezily. 'So, Jamie, what do you look like – so I know what to look out for?'

'Um, average height, dark brown hair, freckles, um . . .' I don't know what else to say so I joke: 'Don't worry, I'll find you – I'll just look for the man wearing silk pyjamas!'

'What do you mean by that?'

'Um, just, you said Hugh Hefner and—'

'Oh yes. Very good,' he says dismissively. 'Now Christian said you've got a friend with you?'

'Yes, my best friend – Izzy.'

'Blonde he says . . .'

'Yes, that's right.' What on earth?

'Bring her along if you like. The more the merrier.'

'Okay, well, I have to go.' I try to sound cheery. 'The casino is calling!'

'Good luck and put a dollar on number 69 for me!'

Oh pur-lease! I say goodbye, shuddering as I put the phone down.

'What was all that stuff about pyjamas?' asks a now minty-fresh Izzy. 'Don't tell me you fancy the uncle now!'

'No, I most certainly do not. Oh Izzy, I think he might be an old perve!'

'Really?' she laughs. 'Oh, don't worry – I'll come with you when you go to see him, check him out. You know I've got a way with perves!'

'Now why is that?' I ask.

'I've got something they want!' she winks, grabbing her boobs.

'What are you like?' I shake my head. 'Are you ready to go?'

'Yup, but I think I might need another margarita if all we're going to talk about is fish.'

'Oh, come on, we'll be with Finn an hour max. And the aquarium is right in the middle of the shopping forum. Did I mention the CDs are a third cheaper out here?'

'Talk discount to me, baby!' Izzy giggles as I usher her out the door.

We squeeze into the lift with a bunch of guys looking the worse for wear, still sweating last night's beer.

'$3,000!' sighs the one with the goatee.

'Don't think about it, man!' urges his mate.

'What am I gonna do? She's gonna kill me. I took it out of the joint account! She'll be able to tell straight away.'

Izzy and I exchange a grimace.

'If she asks, you'll have to say you bought her a present.'

'For $3,000?'

'How about a ring?'

'I just bought her one, stupid! That's the only good thing about wedding rings – you just need the one.'

'Well, there is the engagement ring,' offers an unhelpful soul.

Goatee just rolls his eyes. 'The point is, I'm screwed. I've trashed $3,000 of our savings and I've got no way of getting it back.'

'You could try to win it back . . .'

'No way, man, I told you, I'm not gambling.'

'How can you even suggest that after last night?' I blurt without thinking.

All four guys turn and look at me. 'He didn't lose the money on the tables,' says the unhelpful soul as the lift doors open. 'He blew it on hookers!'

Izzy and I stand stunned, watching the lads tumble out and head straight for the bar. Finally we get ourselves together enough to walk over to reception.

'Yes!' snaps the woman behind the counter, clearly gagging for her ciggy break.

'Do you have the fax for room 1409?' I ask.

She sighs testily as she locates it on the system and

then hands over the page, smiling through gritted teeth.

'Who's it from?' asks Izzy.

'My mum. It's kind of long. I'll give you the highlights when I'm done.'

'Okay. Shall we treat ourselves to a cab today?'

'You're my best friend in the world, do you know that?' I grin.

'Right back atcha!' says Izzy as we climb into the air-conditioned sanctuary.

I unfold the page spotting Christian's name immediately but forcing myself to start at the beginning.

My dear, darling daughter,

I know you've only been gone a couple of days but I have been thinking about you non-stop, wondering what you are up to in that magical kingdom of twinkling lights. Thank you for the call letting me know you arrived safely. You sounded so clear, as if you were in the next room. I had no idea jet lag could make you so emotional as well as disorientated. Well, I wouldn't, would I? There's no invisible forcefield to pass through on the way to the Lake District. Anyway, I hope you are feeling back to normal now and that you enjoyed the modern dance production you went to last night.

I know it's expensive to phone for a chat but if you get the chance to fax me every now and again – no pressure – that would be wonderful. I think this is only the second time I've used your father's home office. Which is probably twice more than him, come to think of it.

Las Vegas seems everywhere since you left – we opened the Sunday paper and there was a review of some new themed hotel, switched on the TV tonight and there was a couple on the Holiday *programme getting married in an Elvis chapel! Tomorrow I'm going to rent the video of* Girls' Night *to get a feel for where you are.*

I can't believe Tom Jones is going to be appearing there next month! Do you really think it's a sign that I should come out? It would be my dream come true but you can imagine what your father would say! Even so, I can't stop thinking about it. I wouldn't want to cramp your style but if you are going to be out there a while I will miss you so much I'm just going to have to hop on a plane! Well, an old lady can dream!

The funny thing is that your future brother-in-law might beat me to it! Nadine said Christian seems very keen to visit his uncle in Las Vegas. She's really cursing that he came up in conversation that day. She says Christian hasn't mentioned him in years and now he won't stop talking about him. He's even mentioned having his bachelor weekend in Las Vegas instead of Amsterdam. Bit of a contrast to Nadine's tasteful hen weekend in Tuscany. A month ago she loved the idea of lying by the pool drinking Chianti. Now she's talking about Tenerife! Talk about wedding day jitters! I really thought nothing could faze her – she's been building up to this all her life.

Well, have fun, darling! Make the most of every minute and put a fiver on number 20 at the roulette wheel for me! Good luck!

Your ever-loving Mum (aka Delilah!!!!)

'So, what news from the homefront?' Izzy enquires.

'Well, my mum says . . .'

'Yes?'

'She'd like a silver bodice with purple feathers . . .'

16

A pointy Pinocchio nose spears its way through the water, narrowly avoiding impaling metallic silver Pilot fish, so pancake-flat he looks two-dimensional. Opalescent Rays make their swooping undulations, disturbing shimmering schools in their wake. I've never seen such a dazzling range – copper fish with pale blue stripes, a canary yellow Tweety-Pie, a leopard-spotted barmaid type. They pass before my eyes like floating works of art – abstract splashes of colour on one, an intricate mosaic design on another, a few who appear to have been graffitied with Tippex. One unfortunate has outsize red-rimmed eyes, a stubby tail and body that looks frayed and scorched as if he's survived some radiation experiment.

'There are some real freaks in there,' says Izzy, pointing at the one with a tail like a crab claw. 'Oh my God, look at this one – he looks like he's got miniature sticks of dynamite tied around his tail!' And as absurd as it sounds, it really does look that way.

We chortle at their 'expressions'. There's one with a

bottom jaw jutting out like a sulky child, another with a down-turned Victor Meldrew mouth who appears to be going 'Moan, moan, moan' as his mouth opens and closes.

'There's a shark!' gasps a kiddy in high-pitched alarm.

We watch the foot-long grey form track stealthily along the bottom of the tank.

'How come he doesn't eat the other fish?'

The kid's dad is stumped. 'I don't know, son, maybe there's someone we can ask.'

Right on cue, a woman with a headset microphone appears at Izzy's side.

'Welcome to the Aquarium at Caesar's Forum. You're just in time to see the fish being fed. We have over 500 fish and 100 different species and then there's this fella.'

An alien form enters the tank, lowering himself past the coral sculptures and fauna, down to the shingle. He's carrying a plastic picnic hamper of food. The fish scuttle to him, clamouring for a bite.

'This is Finn, our diver, he's so at home under the water we're convinced he has webbed feet under those flippers!' she jokes.

His head is closely shaved but it's hard to tell what his face looks like with the mask and breathing apparatus distorting it. We watch as he moves gracefully along the tank with his Pied Piper following.

'I bet he's a Pisces!' Izzy laughs.

'He is!' It's Zane, squeezing through the crowd to get to us. He slots in behind me and stands with his hands on my shoulders, fingers dangerously close to my hyper-sensitive neck. I turn around to smile and get a mouthful of his silky black hair and a slight grazing from his stubble. He smells as gorgeous as ever. As the crowd surges forward to watch Finn rub the shark's head, I feel Zane's chest pressed against my back.

'That isn't just affection,' explains the woman with the microphone.

I freeze.

'It's to get the shark used to human touch so that if we suspect he is sick, or something doesn't seem right, we can check him over without alarming him.'

'Or losing your right forearm,' adds Izzy.

Zane takes a step back as the crowd moves around the tank. Shame.

All the other fish are gagging to tuck in but the shark is playing hard to get. Finn is determined to get Jaws Jnr to come to him and waits patiently, leaning on a rock. Izzy has already lost interest but I am utterly absorbed.

'He's probably got a rubber fetish,' Izzy whispers. 'Imagine if you invited him over and he turned up in his wetsuit, expecting to jump off the top of your wardrobe . . .'

'Izzy, shhh,' I hiss. But Zane seems oblivious.

'This marine environment holds 50,000 gallons and the water is kept at 78 degrees,' the woman continues.

I listen, scribbling notes until I notice Izzy's eyes flicker closed one too many times. We free ourselves from the tightly-packed onlookers and just as I'm about to try out some of my pre-rehearsed charm on Zane he announces, 'Okay, I have to run!'

'What?' I cry. 'Why?'

'Lars has groin strain . . .'

'Don't look at me!' says Izzy, throwing up her hands.

Too late. We both are.

'I've got to run through his moves with one of the back-up dancers,' explains Zane. 'I've told Finn you'll be waiting right here. He's seen you now so you shouldn't miss each other.'

'Okay,' I say, somewhat forlorn.

'Remember, he is rather shy so—' he casts a wary look at Izzy – 'go easy on him.'

'Will he be wearing the wetsuit to meet us?'

'Ignore her!' I groan. 'And, er, thanks for setting this up!'

'No problem, I hope you have fun. Oh, and you should try the Cheesecake Factory over there. The menu is like a telephone directory, that'll keep you out of mischief.'

'It'll take more than cheesecake . . .'

'Okay, I'm going to leave you two cats to it!' He laughs, sprinting past many an admiring glance on his way to the exit.

'Say hi to Lars!' Izzy giggles.

'Groin strain, for God's sake. What did you do to him?'

'Well . . .'

'I don't want to know!' I say firmly. 'Not right now, anyway. I need to be in a work mode.'

Izzy looks longingly at the Virgin Megastore. I give her a firm, 'No!'

'But why can't I go shopping while you're doing your interview?'

'Because I want to make a good impression. Zane is bound to ask Finn what he thinks of me and I need you to make sure I'm saying the right things. You're the man expert, after all.'

'I wish he'd hurry up then,' Izzy groans. 'I feel like a stupid teenager waiting to get an autograph hanging around here.'

'Why are you so grouchy?' I ask despairingly.

'I just feel I'm wasting valuable man-hunting time on fish.'

'What if Finn's a cutie?' I ask.

'I refuse even to consider a man who gets up to his elbows in algae. If it wasn't for Zane, I'd say he'd be perfect for you. Your mum told me about all those frights you gave her lying at the bottom of the bath with your eyes open as a kid!'

I was always a 'water baby'. Virtually all the family holiday snaps have me trailing seaweed along the surf, collecting shells. There's one classic shot of Nadine gingerly tiptoeing into the sea while I charge ahead, arms flung wide, embracing the spray. I suddenly feel nostalgic for that feeling of joyous abandonment.

'Here he comes,' Izzy says. 'Nice shirt!'

He's wearing a faded Hawaiian print, fraying slightly at the collar, baggy shorts and open-toe sandals.

141

'Hi, I'm Finn!' he says, a nervous hand on the back of his hedgehog scalp.

'We know who you are!' Izzy laughs. 'You must be like a celebrity round here! Jamie was just saying she felt like a groupie, waiting for you.'

Finn glares at the floor. I glare at Izzy.

'We saw all the lipstick marks left on the tank!' she teases.

'And you thought the sharks were the scariest things round here!' I say, trying to make light of Izzy's assault.

'Actually, it's the Lion fish we have to watch. They're venomous. I could point one out.'

'Yes, do!' I say, matching his eagerness and darting for the tank.

'There's one!' he says, indicating what looks like an offcut of ruched tortoiseshell-print chiffon, rippling delicately in the water. 'Looks pretty but those prongs can be fatal. When we're in the tank we're in constant contact with whoever is on the mike so they can warn us if they're getting too close!'

'Wow!' I gasp. 'Do any of the others bite?'

'The Grunts are pretty aggressive but it's more like pinching – they don't usually break the skin. The silver Pilot fish rub up against us when they need to scratch. It's called flashing!'

Izzy's eyes light up for a brief second.

'So what's the story with Tweety-Pie?' I ask. 'You know, the yellow bumpy one that you fed by hand, where is he . . .?'

'That's the Cow fish. He's real slow. If we didn't put

142

the food right in his mouth the other fish would beat him to it. It's as if he's a rowing boat and all the other guys have outboard motors.'

'He always seems to be by himself. Does he have any friends? You know, hang out with the other fish?' I ask, surprised to find myself worrying about the emotional state of a fish.

'He follows the Porcupine Puffa around sometimes but really he's kind of the outcast.'

'That's so sad!' My eyes glaze over, watching him puttering around as the other fish dart by.

Izzy mimes concussing herself on the tank glass.

Finn tells me the two fish swimming in a circle recreating the 69 Pisces symbol are actually fighting. ('It's a territorial thing.') And the ones who appear to be kissing are actually having a staring contest!

'I tried that once, I got my ass kicked!' he laughs.

I look around to check on Izzy. She's become suspiciously alert. 'Um, I think I might, er, go on ahead and get a table at the Cheesecake Factory,' she says, oh-so-casually. 'It would be nice to get one outside where we could still see the fish.'

I narrow my eyes. 'Which one?' I demand.

'Which one, what?'

'Which waiter are you after?'

'Better than that,' she beams, 'Elvis has entered the building!'

'What?' I laugh.

'He's really tall, too, not some squat little impersonator with a burger belly. This one's Elvis at his prime, which means he's the perfect match for me!'

143

I watch her sashay into the restaurant. Poor guy, he's about to be Priscilla'd to within an inch of his life.

A little boy tugs at Finn's shirt.

'Are you the man from the tank?' he asks.

Finn nods.

'Why did my goldfish die?' he asks plaintively.

Finn looks up at the dad, who explains: 'He was floating at the top of the tank on his side, he couldn't seem to get upright or move. A few days later he died.'

'Sounds like he had a problem with his swim-bladder. When it swells up they can't keep themselves down or move around.'

'I guess there's nothing we could have done?'

'Actually there is, the problem stems from bacteria. You could have set up another little aquarium and medicated him in there.'

'But why was he the only one to get sick?' the little boy quavers. 'The other fish were okay.'

'It's just like people,' explains Finn. 'You know how some of your friends get flu and others are fine? It's the same with fish, some are healthier than others. Anyway, if it happens again, you'll know how to save the little guy, won't you?'

The kid looks chuffed and nods. 'Daddy, I want to do what he does.'

'So do I!' I tell Finn as he turns back to me.

His face takes on a hint of pink and I suddenly feel embarrassed myself. That's the trouble with shy people, they end up making you feel just as awkward and inept as them but you're still left in charge of the

144

conversation. Naturally, I start to babble.

'You know, that little boy has made me remember when my sister and I brought two goldfish home from the fair. We were about seven and four. I kept them on my bedroom window sill and I'd watch them for hours. Nadine's was orange and mine was mostly silver. Anyway, I came home from school one day and hers was floating on the top – dead. Nadine was hysterical. Do you know what my dad did? He told me that it wasn't fair for me to have a fish if Nadine didn't so he was going to send them back to the sea and he flushed them both – one alive, one dead – down the toilet!'

That's a nice cheery story for a fish-lover, I congratulate myself.

'I practically had a marine lab in my bedroom by the time I was ten,' Finn reveals. 'We lived right on the coast so I was always coming home with bits of driftwood and jars of slippery creatures. My dad hated it but my mum used to sneak off with bits of seaweed and make body wraps!'

'A spa in your own home – I bet she has beautiful skin!'

'She did,' he smiles. 'Actually, er, actually, she passed away. It's nearly three years ago now . . .'

'Oh, I'm so sorry,' I gasp, clamping my hand over my mouth.

'It's okay.'

'Er . . .'

'Shall we go eat?' he asks. 'The toffee pecan cheesecake is really good . . .'

145

17

I've seen some curious sights in my life – Izzy in a nun's habit at a fancy dress party for one – but what I'm looking at now takes the entire biscuit barrel. After we left Finn, Izzy was eager to shop and I wanted to do some more research for my animal feature so we agreed to split up for the afternoon. Which is how I ended up here, at the top of an escalator at the MGM Grand looking down on a luridly-carpeted casino with endless gaming tables to the left and a shaggy-maned lion leaping across some ragged rocks to my right. Only a sheet of glass separates the two.

I descend and take a closer look. As I put my hand out to steady myself, a giant paw matches me from the other side of the glass. It seems to be the size of a dustbin lid but with cushiony pads and tufty fur tickling between the toes. From the info on the board, I'm guessing this is Goldie – descendant of MGM Studios' famous signature lion Metro. It's like seeing one of the Redgrave dynasty.

Though her jaws only open in a slack yawn, dramatic pre-recorded roaring causes a few nearby poker players to check over their shoulders. This is no token tribute to Metro. The project cost $9 million, providing a state-of-the-art showcase with over 5,000 square feet of rocks, ravines and acacia trees. I had thought it smacked of the ultimate exploitation – gamblers and lions in the same pen? – but considering the main complaints levied against most zoos are cramped conditions and under-funding, these cats are in the lap of luxury. Keepers hang with the lions, scratching their bellies like domestic kitties or try to engage them in a ball game. I take out my notebook – this is a good sign, the woman at the Born Free Foundation told me animals like to be stimulated. The other good thing is that the lions' appearances are rotated so their entire life is not lived out in public. This way Louie-B, for example, can flick through his diary and think, 'Tuesday: showtime, Wednesday: hang out with mates, sharpen claws, etc.'

I walk through a tunnel with a ten-foot lion prowling directly above me and pass a queue of people waiting to get their picture taken with one of the outrageously cute lion cubs. The cubs are kept in another viewing area, tussling and chomping on each other's ears and shins until the punters are in place. They are then plopped on to a table with a safari background and suckle on a bottle of milk until the photographer gives a signal. They don't seem to mind a bit and blink, brown-eyed and beguiling, at the camera.

Moving into the shop, I scribble down some puns about doing a 'roaring trade' and notice that a percentage of the profits go to organisations actively engaged in the preservation of lions. Nice one. I have an appointment with the head keeper tomorrow (most of my interviews required formal requests on headed paper from the newspaper sent in advance of my trip) so I move on to the Rainforest Cafe to write my questions, perching on a bar stool that gives me the rump, tail and hindlegs of a zebra.

I then visit the Mandalay Bay only to discover they never built the controversial swim-up shark tank they were planning, but instead now have a Shark Reef exhibit. I just have time to drop in on the African penguins, Chilean flamingos, Mandarin ducks and koi fish in their lush surroundings at the Flamingo Hilton on my way back to Circus Circus. I've had a great day and by the bags and tissue paper littering the room, Izzy's had a fab shopping spree.

'Wow! I take it we're going out!' I say, admiring her brand-new shocking-pink tube dress.

'Well, er, EP rang and . . .' She looks embarrassed.

'Oh.'

'EP being . . .'

'The Elvis Presley lookalike, I'm guessing.'

'Yes. You don't mind, do you?' she asks, applying a second coat of lipstick.

'No, no. I've got loads of notes to work through and questions to write for tomorrow. You go ahead.'

I don't see Izzy until 9 a.m. the next morning when she pops back for a change of clothes.

'He's taking me to some kind of Elvis convention!'

she says, wriggling into a pair of denim shorts and a LOVE ME TENDER T-shirt.

'What time will you be back?' I ask, trying not to sound forlorn.

'Not sure,' She shrugs, lacing her pink suede trainers. 'It's in Phoenix.'

'Phoenix?! As in Phoenix, Arizona?'

'It's a really short flight, apparently.'

'Flight? Flight!' I shrill.

'It's okay, I'm only leaving the state, not the country! We'll be back tonight. How's the feature coming?'

I'm thrown by her interest in my writing. She normally avoids any work-related topics. 'Okay,' I reply. 'I've got two interviews set up for this morning and then—'

'That's great!' she cuts in. 'Gotta run!'

'And then . . .' I repeat, talking to myself, 'I'm going to find someone who listens to what I have to say.'

Three p.m. I'm scribbling away, playing back my tapes from the morning's interviews and feeling like I should be wearing a trilby with a little card saying SCOOP! tucked in the band. Look at me! I'm a real-live journalist!

I take a break at 6 p.m., realising I'm already way over the 1,200-word count, and my mind wanders to Zane. I've promised to have the feature faxed to the paper first thing Tuesday morning, which means getting it done by midnight tonight, just about the time Zane will be getting done with the show. Hmmm.

149

I psyche myself up and dial the Stardust. When I say his name the female receptionist lets out a supercilious sigh as if to say, 'Another day, another groupie.' Jealous cow.

Still, he sounds pleased to hear from me: 'Hey darlin'! How did it go with Finn yesterday?'

'Great! I got loads of good stuff from him – thanks for the introduction.'

'No problem. I think he enjoyed it too.' Zane tells me. 'So when are we gonna get a chance to see the article?'

'Well, I should be finished in a few more hours.'

'By tonight?'

'Yes!'

'Wow! It sounds like a celebration is in order. You coming out later?'

'If you insist.' I chirp joyously.

'We could go for something to eat after the show, if you like.'

'Yum! Yes!'

'Okay, see you later!'

Never was dating so easy.

I return to my writing but have to set down my pen almost immediately and dance around the room to expel some of the energy talking to Zane has given me. I think I've just discovered the key to my lacklustre love life – lack of lust. I never fancied any of the boys I've been out with this much. I clearly should have been dating male strippers all these years. What a revelation!

10 p.m. I'm thrilled with what I've written and give it one last read-through.

10.15 p.m. The whole thing is an incoherent mess! I've cut out all the best bits! Help!

11.45 p.m. I'm in the business centre watching the final edit judder through the fax machine. Jamie Miller, reporting from Laaaas Vegas, Nevada!

I grin and head for the Stardust.

Zane takes me to an out-of-the-way Italian restaurant favoured by locals. It's relaxed and buzzing, heaving with meatballs and offers a half-price menu after 11 p.m. Even the wine is 50 per cent off if you buy it by the glass. Fan-bloody-tastic. We toast the completion of my article with Merlot.

'So, Miss Journalist! What's next for you?' Zane grins.

'Well, I'm going to see what the editor thinks of the piece I just sent and then maybe suggest some new ideas, still with a Vegas theme.'

'Sounds great!'

'The only thing is, they won't be able to run a load of Vegas items one after another so I need a Plan B. I'm actually going for a kind of job interview tomorrow, just a bit of temporary shop work to keep me ticking over.'

'What about Izzy?'

'Um, she's okay for money at the moment.'

More to the point, she knows she can always find a

151

man who's willing to pay for her, should she run out. It sounds a precarious way to live but for her it's a tried and tested formula and sure beats working.

'My contract is coming up in a month,' notes Zane. 'I've got to decide whether or not to renew.'

'What would you do if you didn't?' I ask.

Zane sits in silence, chewing a series of olives. He finally shrugs and says, 'No idea. Well, I guess that's just made my mind up for me!'

I laugh. God, I love looking at this man! Tonight he's got a Zorro vibe going with his all-black ensemble. I keep thinking of when he slid up my body on stage at the Golden Guys show and long to be pressed up against him again. Could tonight be the night?

'Would you like another glass of wine?' the waiter asks, noticing my drained glass.

'Yes, please!' I nod.

'And for you, sir?'

'Mineral water will be fine.' Zane smiles.

Darn! Restraint is a bad sign. However, the fact that we're talking relationships before we've even finished our tricolore is a good sign.

'I've pretty much always had a girlfriend,' Zane confesses. 'It's an important part of life to me, I like the sharing, I like the company.'

'So do I,' I think. It's just that some of us don't always have the option.

'I think I'm pretty easy to please, I don't ask for too much. Someone like Finn is more complex, he needs someone pretty special.' Zane wipes up a smudge of avocado with his ciabatta. 'What did you think of him?'

'I thought he was lovely.' I smile noncommittally. 'Very knowledgeable about fish.'

'Would you go out with him?'

What? This must be some kind of test.

'I, er . . . I don't really know him,' I say, trying to be diplomatic.

'But you found him attractive?'

Oh God! Surely Zane can't think I fancy Finn more than him? He couldn't be jealous, could he?

'He seemed really sweet but you know I can't think of other men when I'm with you!' I flutter my eyelashes madly to give the impression that I'm joking and Zane puts me in a headlock. He only releases me because the waiter comes with our main course. I feel deliciously ruffled and jostled and now smell of Zane's aftershave, which today, I believe, is Drakkar Noir.

Over pasta Zane starts spilling forth about Mia (the ex lifeguard chick). He's still woefully hung up on her and it all sounds strangely familiar. It could be me talking about Christian.

'You know, when there's a bond between two people, it can't be broken. Not by time or distance or other people. If you profoundly feel something for someone, you always will,' I tell him.

'You really understand, don't you?'

'Yes,' I say, taking the supportive, 'poor baby' tack – I'll win him over to me nice and slow. No rush.

We chat some more and then he takes my hand. My tagliatelle trembles on the end of my fork. 'You're so easy to talk to, Jamie. I really appreciate you listening to me.'

153

'It's a pleasure,' I sigh, adding, 'well, not a pleasure to hear you're heartbroken but . . .'

'I think it's so important to feel that someone gets you, that you're seen. That's what we all want, isn't it? To find someone who makes you feel like the best you can be!'

That's it – I love him! 'Exactly!' I sigh.

'Actually, it's Finn that said that to me, but I have to agree with him.'

'Oh.'

He leans forward and plants a soft kiss on my cheek. 'I'm so glad we met.'

'Me too,' I breathe, desperate, *desperate* to kiss him back.

'I don't have too many female friends because they always seem to want more.'

'Really?' I try to sound above such things but I daren't say any more on the subject so I simply smile and say, 'shall we get a dessert?'

After coffee I claim I'm still too full to walk so Zane offers me a piggyback to the car. He charges hither and thither making me scream as I jiggle and bump around on his broad back. Finally he lets me down and I lean panting and giggling against his car. He leans alongside me, his beautiful face just millimetres from my own. If I stuck out my tongue I could reach him. 'Jamie, you're the best!' he sighs, turning towards me.

I twist myself around so that I'm in an entirely kiss-friendly position. He moves a fraction closer and then with a kerCHUNK! All the locks on the car pop up. He looks startled and then sheepishly holds up the set of keys he's been fiddling with. I curse the automatic lock/unlock device for ruining the moment but I can't suppress a 'nearly there' grin. He really likes me! He does, he does. It's only a matter of time. I'm just wondering when I'll get to see him again when he says, 'Hey! What are you doing Wednesday, during the day?'

'Nothing in particular. Why?'

'Well, Finn and I are heading up to Red Rock Canyon – it's pretty cool scenery around there, I just thought maybe you and Izzy could come along?'

'We'd love to! Yes! Great!' I rave.

'We're leaving about 11 a.m. so why don't you meet us in the Stardust diner?'

'Okay!'

Back at Circus Circus, he leans across from the driver's seat and gives me a big hug. He feels so good. 'Thanks again for being such a good listener!'

'Any time!' I trill, then skip up to the room tra-la-la-ing like some Disney heroine. I'm dying to relive the evening with Izzy but there's no sign of her.

I can only imagine that she's getting a really good Roustabout.

18

It's now midday on Tuesday and still no Izzy. I guess she's forgotten about our lunch appointment with Uncle Sam. Forgotten or doesn't care. So much for her promise to protect me from his potential perviness. I'd postpone but I could really do with some job prospects now my article is done, and besides, curiosity is getting the better of me: I'm dying to see if Sam has any of Christian's looks or traits and it'll be such a treat to talk to someone who really knows him. I might learn a thing or two. He might even know about me! What if Christian has confided in Sam or asked him to sound me out? Suddenly I can't wait to see the very man that gave me the creeps on the phone two days ago.

I scrawl Izzy a note and get a cab to the address thinking it might be hard to find but with giant letters flashing SAM'S SHOPPING EXTRAVAGANZA along the length of three buildings, it's unmissable.

The girl on the till tells me Sam has just popped out to Burger King and should be back in five minutes so I have a mooch around. The stock is diverse to say the least: I prod a transparent plastic pillow filled with authentic shredded dollar bills, tinker with a natty automatic card shuffler, then stroke a cluster of rabbit's foot key rings with fur dyed every imaginable hue. Over in the Native American corner there's an abundance of turquoise and feathers and next to that an entire section on Elvis offering everything from a mock-up of The King's driving licence to incongruous tapestry cushions. The doorbell jangles and a handsome man strides in. My heart leaps, then a woman calls 'Frank! Over here!' from the purse section. False alarm.

I go back to inspecting ashtrays marked 'John's Butts' and 'Caroline's Butts', etc. and rifle through personalised pens, shot glasses and mugs. I'm just admiring a tin tray depicting a woman in a frilly pinny yelping, 'To hell with the housework – let's go to Las Vegas!' when the doorbell jangles again. This time I know it's him. He's carrying a Burger King bag.

As far as family resemblance goes, Christian could well be adopted. Sam's complexion is oily and overtanned, his hair dyed, and knobbly elbows jut out from his short-sleeved dragon-motif shirt.

The girl on the till alerts him to my presence.

'So let me get this right!' he says, throwing open his stringy arms. 'You're my nephew's fiancé's sister?'

'Yup!' I grunt from deep within his clammy embrace.

'Don't tell me your sister is any prettier than you because I won't believe it!' Before I can speak he rattles on, 'Well, Christian's loss is my gain! You don't have a boyfriend, do you?'

157

'Not exactly—'

'Good, good! That's what I like to hear. You afraid of heights?'

'No, I don't think so . . .' I say, bewildered.

'We might need to get you up a ladder from time to time to reach these top shelves,' he explains, waving his hand in the direction of a ceiling-high stack of T-shirts.

'Oh, I see.'

'Don't want any jelly legs on the team!' he says, jiggling my thighs. 'Worked a cash register before?'

'No, but—' My head is spinning.

'You're a smart girl, I can tell. You'll pick it up in no time,' he jabbers. 'Now, let's eat lunch before it goes cold. I got you a cheeseburger, hope that's okay?'

'Actually, I'm a vegetarian—' I begin.

'Don't apologise – we're an equal opportunity employer!' he chortles, grabbing the bag of food from the counter and leading me into his office. His shoes squeak noisily as he walks.

'I'm really not that hungry,' I tell him as he brushes aside a pile of paperwork to make room for the Styrofoam cartons. 'Why don't you have mine?'

'Well, if you insist,' he says, tucking in with relish. And mustard. And mayonnaise.

'Sit down! Sit down!' he bays, noticing I'm standing awkwardly in the doorway.

I look around for a free chair but they are all crammed with product samples and boxes marked FRAGILE. I end up perching on the sofa beside a crate of snowglobes. 'You've got some fabulous items in your shop!' I observe. 'Very kitsch!'

'Kish?' he says, cheeks bulging with fries.

'Er, trendy.'

'It's a load of cheap crap but it sells,' he grunts, wiping his fingers on a napkin, then missing the bin as he discards it. 'This might look like a downmarket operation but it's got me a big house with a pool, a sports car to run around in and if I see something I like, I buy it.'

'You might want to consider purchasing a few packs of those papier poudre facial blotters from The Body Shop next time you're out,' I think as I admire the glassy sheen on his nose.

'That's great,' I enthuse. 'Must be exciting having your own business.'

I can't keep it in any longer. I have to ask.

'So, how long have you known Christian?'

'How long?' he repeats.

Oh, you complete buffoon! He's his uncle! 'No! Sorry,' I backtrack, 'I mean, how well do you know Christian?'

'How *well* do I know him?' He's still confused.

'No! I mean, well, are you two close, at all?'

'Oh yes,' says Sam, ignoring my nonsense. 'I feel like a surrogate father to that boy. My brother – his dad – he's pretty straight-laced, naive some would say, so I've tried to teach Christian a thing or two about the ways of the world.'

'Does he listen to you?' I ask, vaguely concerned.

'Obviously not or he wouldn't be getting married!' he hoots.

159

I force a laugh, then find myself blurting: 'So do you think this is the real deal – true love and all that?'

'I don't know about that!' He sucks on his Coke straw. 'But I tell you one thing – your sister must be pretty good in the sack!'

'What?' I flush, horrified.

'I'm just saying she must have some pretty good bedroom tricks to keep the Casanova Kid coming back for more!'

'What do you mean? Christian's not—'

The phone rings. 'Excuse me a moment. Yello! Yes, put him through. Hey, stud! We were just talking about you!'

Oh my God! It's Christian!

'Me and Jamie,' Sam continues. 'Yup, she's here right now.'

I feel all flustered. Is this the only building in Vegas without air conditioning?

'Yes, yes. Well, that's up to her, isn't it? Few can resist my charms,' he winks at me.

I want to tear the receiver out of his hands and listen to Christian's beautiful voice. It's not fair!

'So, when are you coming to town? We've got some partying to catch up on! Uh-huh. Well, if you have to – just do whatever it takes! Uncle Sam needs you!' He chuckles. 'Okay, okay, well, we'll talk later. Yup. Bye.'

Sam puts down the phone. 'He sends his love!'

'Does he?' I sigh, eyes lighting up.

'Yeah. In fact he might be able to give it to you in person soon – it looks like he's coming to Vegas.'

My heart stops. 'Really?' Oh my God, I shriek

inwardly. 'Do you really think he will?' I ask, trying to sound casual but failing miserably.

'Looks to me like you might have a little crush on my nephew!' Sam observes with a sleazy grin.

'No! No, no, no!' I protest. Heaven forbid Sam let such thoughts drip from his greasy mouth around Christian.

'No?' He sounds unconvinced.

'Well, ha! Who wouldn't?' I say, trying a different tack. 'I mean, you Johnsons are a pretty irresistible bunch!' Oh my God – I'm channelling Izzy!

'You're not the first to notice!' he smirks. 'So, what do you say, do you want to work here?'

At least we're off the subject of Christian and my nymphette sister. 'Yes, yes. I'd love to!' It's not exactly headlining at Caesar's Palace but my options are limited – who else in Vegas is going to employ me?

'You can start Monday if you like. I'll pay you cash-in-hand, no questions asked.'

'Wow! That's great.' He's not so bad after all.

'I like my girls in dresses,' he continues. 'Shorts are okay but not trousers.'

'Right.' The perve returneth.

'How long are you planning to be in town, by the way?' he asks.

'Until . . . um, I'm not sure.' I shrug.

'Well, that's fine. I'm your flexible friend! We'll just see how we go, shall we?'

'That sounds great, I really do appreciate you taking me on at such short notice.' Let's just hope it's for a short time.

161

'I'll scratch your back, you scratch mine – we can help each other out,' he leers.

There's a knock at the door. The girl from the till sticks her head in and says, 'There's someone out here wants an XL of the gold-embossed T-shirt. Can you hold the ladder?'

Sam leaps eagerly to his feet, then turns back to me: 'Well, it's been good to meet you, Jamie and I'll be seeing you next week!'

Time's up! I give one last longing look at the telephone on his desk – as if Christian particles might still be hovering around it – and then head for the exit. I turn back to give Sam a final wave goodbye but he and the male customer are engrossed in peering up the shopgirl's skirt as she wrestles with a pile of T-shirts from the top rung. Oh dear. Suddenly culottes seem like an essential purchase.

Back at the hotel Izzy has returned, in body if not in mind. Lying prone on the bed she opens one weary eye and croaks, 'All right?'

She looks like she hasn't slept in days so I keep my news simple: 'I got the job!'

'Job?' she enquires drowsily.

'The cash-in-hand job at Uncle Sam's.'

'Hand job? Uncle Sam? Oh Jamie, you didn't!'

I go to clarify myself but she's conked out.

19

Cashmere kisses cover me. The taste of him is as warming and silky to my tongue as Bailey's Irish Cream. He's saying I love you without speaking. His mouth moves tenderly yet intensely. Pausing for a moment, he tilts his head and lets me see the passion and vulnerability in his eyes. He sighs and says, 'Jamie, you're drooling . . .'

My eyes spring open. Izzy is leaning over me. She frowns. 'You're having that "first-kiss-with-Zane" daydream again, aren't you?'

This keeps happening. I seem to lose all control of my saliva when I think of him. I can't help wondering if today will be the day we get to do it for real. Red Rock Canyon sounds like the perfect backdrop for a kissing scene.

I'm just deciding whether to pack my toothbrush when the phone goes. It's Dave. Izzy puts him on speakerphone so she can carry on doing her make-up while she talks. He's on his way to her mum's for dinner and wants to know if Izzy has a message for her. 'She seems pretty concerned, Iz,' he says. 'She

163

hasn't heard from you at all. You know how she worries . . .'

'Ahh, so she's going to try to wheedle information out of you.'

'No. She said she bought a bunch of food expecting your aunt Josie and the kids and they've cancelled.'

'They're in France.'

'Well, I guess that's why they couldn't make it . . .'

'No, they always spend July in France. She's got some ulterior motive.

Just don't bring me up in the conversation when she's wielding the carving knife.'

Dave laughs. 'She's just lonely, Izzy. Anyway, I don't mind going. She's quite a laugh when you're not around to wind her up.'

'Cheers! I miss you too!'

'So what have you been doing?'

They chat amicably for a while, then as soon as Izzy puts down the phone it rings again. 'EP!' she mouths, seguing smoothly from one beau to the next.

I leave her to it and stumble into the bathroom. When I emerge she gives me a cheery, 'See you later!' and heads for the door.

'Wait a minute! Where are you going?'

'EP is meeting me in the lobby . . .'

'What?' I splutter. 'What about our day trip to Red Rock Canyon?'

'I think I'll get my rocks off elsewhere,' she grins without a hint of apology. 'You'll be with Zane, anyway.'

'Yes, but Finn's coming,' I remind her.

'That's not exactly an incentive for me.'

'I can't believe you're dumping me like this!' I say, outraged.

'It's not like I'm leaving you to sit in the room all day. You'll be off on your little excursion.'

'But I want you there, it won't be the same.'

'Look, EP's in Memphis for a convention all next week, I've got to make the most of my hunka hunka burning love while I can,' she shrugs.

I flump back on the bed, stunned, and snap, 'Thanks for the notice,' to the carpet fluff kicked up from Izzy's speedy exit. I should be used to this kind of behaviour from her but it still hurts every time I come second best.

I look at the clock. I should get going. A stomach-churning nervousness descends. Without Izzy on the girls' team my bravado could falter. I worry that I'll feel like a lame girl simpering, 'Hay-elp! Hay-elp!' as the two action men leap across gaping chasms.

Perhaps I should postpone until Izzy can come with me. 'Oh, how pathetic!' I scold myself. It'll be fine and I'm hardly going to turn down the opportunity to spend a whole day basking in Zane's sexiness.

'He's not coming,' says Finn, pushing a note across the counter at the Stardust diner. 'He's had to fly to LA, won't be back until 7 p.m.'

I fight to hide my disappointment but know I look like the recipient of some tragic news in a silent movie – my eyes widen, a hand flies to my mouth and I mentally fall on to the counter and beat my fists. No words come out.

'Where's Izzy?' asks Finn.

I'm still suffocating with disappointment so it takes all my strength to reply: 'She couldn't make it – had to see a man about a Hound Dog . . .'

I force a smile and slide on to one of the cushioned stools.

'So it's just us?' Finn croaks, looking awkward. I can practically see dolphin data darting across his eyes.

'D'you think someone's trying to tell us something?' I joke.

Noticing his instant blush I quickly add, 'Like we should call it off. I mean, the posse are dropping like flies – first there were four, now there's only two – maybe there'll be an avalanche if we go!'

Mercifully, he interrupts my gabbling overcompensation: 'If you want to make it another day, that's fine. I've gotta go anyway, I promised I'd take back the tools I borrowed from the Lodge.'

'Oh.' I'm torn. It's not like I get to see Zane if I stay but I'm not sure I can last a whole day with Finn. Or if he can last a whole day on dry land. He'll probably have to keep throwing cups of water over himself. But of course we will have the scenery to comment on and it might be a good subject for an article. What if I don't get the chance again? I take a deep breath.

'Well, if you're going anyway and you don't mind me tagging along . . .'

'No, I'd like the company.'

'I thought you were supposed to be the ultimate loner!' I tease.

He scuffs the floor with his shoe. 'Um, I'd like *your* company . . .'

Oh God. 'I think I'll get a chocolate maltshake for the journey, do you want anything?'

'No, I'm good, thanks.'

'You sure? Coke Float? Dr Pepper? Cookie? Doughnut? Muffin?' I bluster. 'Um, travelling companion who doesn't waffle so much?'

'No, really, I'm fine.' He laughs. 'But the waffle sounds tempting!'

Oh my God! He made a joke! I'm too shocked to laugh. I give him a suspicious look as the waitress comes over in her fifties gingham and serviette-style hat.

I place my order and intently watch her scoop the ice cream into the metal canister and then squeak across the lino to the mixer machine. I look at the other customers, then the napkin dispenser, anything but look at Finn.

It's amazing how long a milkshake can take to make.

'So, how's the shark-feeding going?' I ask, breaking the silence. Great. This fishtalk-when-nervous thing is catching.

'Pretty good, you know, he has his moods, just like the rest of us.'

'Help yourself to straws!' the waitress interrupts, handing me my giant carton of indulgence. I follow Finn out to the car park, only half listening to his thoughts on a new chlorination report.

'Wow! Look at this car!' I coo, halting beside a metallic-blue convertible with ivory leather seats and polished wood dashboard. 'It's amazing!' I know nothing about car makes or years but I know what I like when I see it.

'Mustang,' says Finn, peering at the logo. 'Yeah, it's pretty cool. Must be a relic of the fifties.'

'Relic indeed! This is my dream car,' I say, putting my shake on the ground so I don't ooze over the gleaming paintwork. I step closer, imagining myself cruising the Californian coastline with Zane beside me. I'd watch the wind whip his long hair into Medusa tendrils from behind my winged shades as Doris Day and Andy Williams serenade us – preferably from the back seat.

'I can definitely see you in it,' says Finn. 'Why don't you jump in and check it out?'

I'm horrified. 'I couldn't! What if the owner came back?'

'There's no one around. Anyway, it's not like you're gonna steal it, you just want to sit in it. Do it while you have the chance!'

I step away. 'I couldn't!'

'Well, if you don't I will!'

He opens the driver door and slides in. 'It's in pretty good condition. Seats have still got some spring in them.'

'Finn! Get out! There's somebody coming!' I panic.

'Jesus! They left the keys in the ignition. Shall I . . .?'

I spin around. The man is heading right for us. 'Finn, please!' I dart behind a jeep and screech under

168

my breath, 'Get out! Get out!'

My heart freezes as I hear him switch on the ignition.

'Come on! Get in!' he grins.

I have a sudden vision of us being on the run – and our first casualty will be the innocent car owner that we mow down while reversing out of the parking space at 70 mph.

Finn revvs the engine and then leans over. 'Jamie. It's my car. Get in.'

The man passes us and hops into a bright red sports car.

I'm still not convinced.

'Well, it is blue . . .' I reason.

'What do you want? Dolphins painted on the side?' he laughs. Then, switching off the engine, he jumps out, walks round to the boot and opens it to reveal a wetsuit and a clanking box of tools. 'Satisfied?'

'Okay, yes,' I concede, my heart still pounding. 'I suppose, in a way, I expected you to be driving a converted submarine or something.'

He just groans. My eyes narrow.

'I can't believe you own my dream car! You bastard!'

I experience a pang as we pull away from the Stardust but tell myself it's okay about Zane – I'll see him soon. In the meantime, I'll get my fix by talking about him.

'So, how did you and Zane meet?'

'Well, I went in to audition for the Golden Guys . . .'

'What?!'

169

'Kidding! God, you're easy to get!'

I'm puff with exasperation. 'Who are you and what did you do with the Finn the Fish Man?'

He just smiles to himself and concentrates on weaving through the traffic along the Strip.

I'm not normally comfortable with silences but now seems like a good time to start adjusting.

Within minutes we're on the freeway and as we pick up speed I get the sense I'm embarking on an adventure. Probably the first one I've had without Izzy. I feel all the more daring for not having her with me.

The buildings soon fade out leaving only flat, scrubby desert and distant unreal-looking mountains. I think of Devon and squeezing down twisty-turny lanes with hedgerow crowding in on me. In comparison, everything here seems exaggerated – the sky is bigger, the land stretches further. There's even scratchy tumbleweed skidding along the roadside. I feel so far from home and it feels so good. Strictly speaking I'm in a car with a relative stranger heading for an unfamiliar destination and yet I feel safe. Soaring, even. I close my eyes and let the sun fill my face, absorbing the glow to power me internally. A fanfare of horns startles me as they launch Dean Martin into 'Ain't That a Kick in the Head?' Finn adjusts the volume on the stereo with a sheepish, 'Sorry!'

'That's okay, I love this song!' I say, dueting with Dean to prove the point.

Singing in cars is one of my favourite things. I find it strangely uplifting – the more people the better and it doesn't matter how bad you are, as long as you are loud.

Izzy and I once sang along to Abba all the way back from a weekend in Blackpool. Our version of 'SOS' was particularly heart-rendering. But of course this kind of cathartic shouting/singing is not always appreciated. My dad used to prefer it when I was choreographing dance routines in my head.

Next up is Frank Sinatra with 'I Get a Kick Out of You'. I drain the last molten slurp of shake and sigh contentedly. For forty-five minutes we croon along to various Rat Pack toons, unashamed of our unharmonious harmonies.

The mountains rise up before us – craggy rust-red rocks roaring their presence in the eerie quiet. We roll up and climb out of the car. Finn steps back to let me have a moment lost in wonder. I scrabble for my notebook but my pen stays poised. What words? I look around me again and then scribble 'prehistoric', 'radioactive' and 'terracotta'. Finn hands me a bottle of water.

'You writing about this place too?'

'I might,' I shrug, wanting to make light of it. 'I thought I'd make some notes, just in case.'

'Did you bring boots?' he asks.

'What do you mean? I can walk in these.' I stare down at my trainers, already dusted with the earth's natural rouge.

'Yes, but can you climb in them?'

'Very funny. You won't catch me clinging to cliff faces . . .'

'Have you ever tried?'

'Look, we have red rocks in Teignmouth, you know. It doesn't mean we have to climb them.'

'How red?'

'As red as these. Maybe a bit pinker. The sand on the beaches is a kind of a dark, gritty . . . well, *rhubarb* colour. This is more intense, I suppose . . .'

For a minute he just smiles at me. Most disconcerting. But he can smile all he likes, I'm not climbing. No way.

'Can't we just walk?' I suggest. 'I'd only slow you down if we try anything vertical. Isn't there a nice gentle incline with a fabulous view you could show me?'

'Sure,' he shrugs, 'But I don't think you'll want to mess up your clothes. I've got some overalls in the trunk.'

What am I? A car mechanic?

He unravels a roll of clothes and throws a ball of denim at me.

'They're clean,' he says.

'They're dungarees,' I say.

'Is that what you call them? Funny. You can put them on in that restroom there. And you should probably wear a hat.'

I emerge in my farmer-cum-trucker ensemble and stand there waiting for Finn to crack up. He doesn't. He just nods and busies himself lacing his hiking boots.

I can feel a line of sweat beading beneath the peak of the baseball hat already. A dent will be forming at the back of my blown-straight hair and I just know my bum looks like its been slung in some vast saggy denim nappy.

'Don't suppose you've got any mirrored sunglasses and a spare tyre I could hold?' I ask, rolling up the ankles so I can walk without tripping.

'You look great as you are,' Finn says, looking up and smiling.

'Just call me Chuck.'

'Okay, Chuck – let's go get ourselves a view!'

20

Thank God Zane didn't come, I console myself as I wipe away a sweat moustache. I'd die if he saw me like this. Years of coming to terms with my body shape and learning how to disguise my flaws have been undone in a matter of minutes. And what was I thinking spending the morning giving myself a manicure? I approach the first set of rocks like I'm in a dilemma at the Pick 'n' Mix stand, reaching out, then changing my mind, trying to find a rock without too much scratchy gravel around it.

Finn scampers ahead, then turns and offers me a hand. When our two clammy palms meet we create a paste from the red dust. Within minutes we're like the *Red and White Minstrel Show*. Where's Nadine and her wet wipes when you need her?

Finn springs from rock to rock like a sure-footed goat – which doesn't really do justice to the elegance in his agility or the flex in his calf muscles. As trekkers go (and I haven't known many – make that any), he's pretty considerate, always turning back to offer encourage-ment and make sure I haven't fallen to my death.

I attempt to straighten up and take in the view but nearly lose my balance when I see how far we've climbed. It's dizzying. I go back to fixating on his boots.

'Here,' he says, stopping suddenly and surveying the kingdom before him. 'Are you happy to sit here for a while?'

'More than you'll ever know!' I say, collapsing on to the ground with an audible splintering of bones. After a few minutes adjusting to the ecstasy of being stationary, I look up and realise that the view requires I switch my eyes to their panoramic setting. It's stunning. To our right a gap in the rock formation acts like a jagged picture frame for the multi-hued blue sky. I take a photo knowing it won't do justice to the vivid colours.

'This is amazing,' I sigh.

'Worth the climb?' asks Finn.

'I don't know about that . . .' I laugh, foraging in my rucksack for the water bottle.

Finn takes a swig from his. I watch a trickle of water escape his mouth and make a glistening slick down his neck. I bet he would taste salty if I licked him. And fishy, I remind myself. The altitude is obviously affecting my brain.

'You know, I did try to go climbing at home once,' I confess. 'It was a complete disaster! I wanted to get to the top of this cliff overlooking the sea and although there were paths winding around I thought I could get there more directly if I just went upwards. I made a good start, grabbing hanks of shrubbery to pull myself up and enjoying the whole Indiana Jones thing, but about three-quarters of the way up I felt a horrible sense of dread. I was practically upright, the cliff face was so sheer and there was no way I could boost myself on to the next level. Walkers were passing on the paths and I was desperate to appear casual about being pinned to the side of the cliff so I inched my camera out of my bag and started snapping the scene before me. Can you imagine how silly I must have looked? Anyway, the rubble gave way and I skidded all the way down, my trousers got pushed up as I slipped and I grazed my shins and hands. I was a mess by the time I got to the bottom!' I'm surprised I've told Finn this so I say, 'It's not that I'm a wuss. I just had a bit of a fright.'

'I wouldn't let you fall,' he says simply.

I look up, startled by the pure romance in his words. Then I realise he just means he won't be encouraging me to do any high-risk stuntwork today. Relief all round. I turn away and squint into the sun. 'I wouldn't let you fall.' Hmm, I guess there are just some things you wait your whole life to hear and that's one of them. It promises both gentleness and protection.

Often found on deodorant labels, rarely in men.

When I turn back Finn has opened an old tin paintbox and is splashing a drop of water from his bottle into a dip in the lid. He loosens the bristles of a dry paintbrush between his fingers and then dips it in the water.

'I thought I'd do a bit of painting while you write,' he says as if it's the most logical thing in the world.

'Oh. Okay.' I'd forgotten my notes already. I sit cross-legged and get out my notebook and pen. I stare at the three words on my otherwise blank page. I stare some more. I look at Finn swooping colour across the dimpled sheet of his art pad. Ten minutes later he looks up to find me mindlessly tapping my pen on the rock.

'Lost for words?'

I nod.

'Izzy told me you're into poetry, I thought this place would inspire you.'

'When did she tell you that?'

'When you went to the ladies' room at the Cheesecake Factory, if you want me to be precise.'

'Oh. I'm surprised she brought that up. I don't really write poems. Well, not since I was a teenager. I got into reading all these genius works and all my stuff seemed so feeble by comparison it hardly seemed worth trying.'

'That's a dumb attitude!'

'Thank you.'

'No, really! Do you think I'd be sitting here if I compared myself to any of the great artists? It's crazy even to contemplate. You don't have to be the best at something to enjoy it!'

'I know but . . .' Oh, spare us the pep talk, Finn. I can't bear people who don't get the British self-deprecating humour.

'You know, I have an older brother and he was

177

really good at art so I always thought he had it covered and I didn't want to seem to be copying him so I tried to be good at everything he was weak at. I got into sport and science and that's how I ended up becoming an aquarist and you know I love it, but this is like my secret pleasure. I don't have to earn a living from it or show anyone else. It's just something I do when I feel like it. It soothes me.'

I look at his mouth. For someone who spends so much time talking about fish, he certainly does more than blow bubbles. I feel rather foolish. I don't like it. Things would be so different if Izzy and Zane were here. She would have pissed herself laughing at him painting for one. There are no moments of contemplation and reflection with her around. Izzy and I reserve our heart-to-hearts for ten minutes before closing time over a tableful of empty cocktail glasses, so unsurprisingly 99 per cent of our revelations are regarding men and how much better we could do. It's a hell of a lot more fun than this. Or maybe it's just more familiar. I feel most unsettled. And irritated.

'Are you doing this to show off?' I ask, motioning at his paintbox.

He looks up. Was that a flicker of hurt? Then he smiles, 'No, I'm not doing it to show off.'

I feel horrible for accusing him and I try to think of something nice to say but nothing seems appropriate. Besides, within seconds he's totally absorbed in his painting again. Now I feel ignored. And what's this one? Envy.

I remember feeling lost in the moment. Having something that doesn't require anyone else's permission or approval. I really did get a kick out of my poetry. It made me study my emotions and enhanced them in a way. I always felt so much better when everything was out on the page instead of stewing in my head. And my heart. Somehow it made it okay to be a hysterical female.

I shuffle over to Finn.

'Can I see?'

'Sure!' he replies. I watch him smudge real red dirt on to the mountains. 'I like to put something from where I am into each picture, so you can touch it and know it's real. That way you've got illusion and reality.'

'Which is better, do you think? Illusion or reality?' I ask without thinking.

'What do you think?' he replies.

'Don't get deep, Dolly,' I caution myself. 'I don't know. Probably illusion – reality is such a let-down. Except in Las Vegas where illusion is reality.' I grin.

'But this painting is an illusion,' he counters. 'It's creating the effect of looking at rocks. The rocks are the reality. Would you rather experience a piece of paper or all this.'

It's a beautiful painting but there is no comparison with the majesty around us. He notes my reaction.

'And where do you think illusions come from?'

I shrug. Uh-oh, what have I started?

'Illusions are based in reality,' he tells me. 'All your dreams are just the best possible outcome for your reality. When you are in love with someone you dream of being with them all the time, don't you? You don't want to be on a spaceship or on a magic carpet, you just want to be with them. If you had the choice between dreaming about someone or actually being with them, touching them, feeling them in your arms, which would you choose?'

'Point taken,' I nod, feeling out of my depth.

'Which would you choose?' he asks again, not letting me off the hook.

'Reality, I guess. Maybe it's not so bad after all, I smile. That's quite enough of that kind of talk.

'Jamie . . .'

'Shhh! What was that?' I interrupt.

Finn stops and listens. 'Nothing. I don't hear anything.'

'Oh my God! It's inspiration! It's creeping over me!' I titter.

'About time!' he laughs.

'Be quiet and let me write!' I scold.

As the sun sinks, the sky becomes even more dramatic – streaked with colour like a Mexican blanket. It's as if nature is saying, 'You think those neon lights are cool? Check this out!'

I've been so absorbed with my scribbling I hadn't noticed how much the temperature has dropped until Finn tells me I'm shivering.

'I guess we should head back, we'll warm up with the hike,' he says, helping me to my feet and leading the way back down to the car.

'Do you miss living by the sea?' I ask when we pause to catch our breath.

'Of course. I reckon I'll probably be back home by the winter. I get pretty bad cravings for the surf.'

'Why did you leave?'

'Well, I was pretty lost after my mum died. It was hard being surrounded by so many reminders of her. Every time I looked at the sea . . .' He pauses. I wonder how she died but I daren't ask.

'Anyway,' he recovers. 'I got offered the job at the Caesar's Palace and I thought it was like a sign that I should have a change of scene and move on. There were just too many memories at home.'

'Where are you from, exactly?' I ask softly, aware I've jabbed the wound again.

'California, so it's not so very far away. It's a cute little town called San Luis Obispo, you should check it out if you get the chance.'

'Yeah, I'd like to see more of America. Vegas is the only place I've been to. Are you glad you moved here?'

'Yeah, I've seen some sights!'

'I'll bet!'

'Made some good friends.'

'Like Zane?' I ask.

'I was talking about the fish!' he deadpans. 'No, Zane's great. A little heavy on the cupid stuff sometimes . . .'

'How do you mean?'

'You know, always trying to set people up.'

'Oh, yeah, I noticed!'

'You did?'

181

'Yeah, he really seemed to be trying to get Lars and Izzy together the other night!'

Finn pulls a face. 'I wouldn't have thought either of them needed much encouragement. Did it work out?'

'Well, he's got groin strain and now the rest of the troupe are scared to go near her!'

'See what I mean? That's the risk you take when Zane gets into matchmaking mode.'

'Do you ever matchmake for him? You know, try to set him up with girls?' I ask.

Finn laughs. 'Do you really think he needs any help in that department?'

Oh no. 'Is he a philanderer?'

'Not at all. He was totally faithful to Mia.'

'The lifeguardess?'

'Yeah. He was pretty cut up when they split. He's the kind of guy who likes having someone around. He really thinks we were all meant to live in pairs.'

'And what do you think about that?'

'I think it suits some people and not others.'

'Oooh, Mr Cryptic!'

'What about you, do you think there is just one perfect person out there for each of us?'

An image of Christian and Nadine snuggled in bed together flashes into my head. Swiftly followed by one of Mia giving Zane *Baywatch*-style mouth-to-mouth.

'God, I hope not.'

21

Back at the car, Finn hands me my clothes. I've grown strangely attached to the dungarees but I don't want to scare the other diners at the restaurant we're going to.

'I'll just be a minute!' I say. 'Give you time to comb your hair . . .'

He rubs his shaved scalp and smiles. 'I like the messy look!'

I take off the baseball hat and attempt to rumple my flattened hair back to life. But so what if it's not groomed? This is the Great Outdoors. And I feel great, positively revelling in being so dishevelled . . . until I reach the ladies'.

I stare in disbelief at the face in the mirror. My transition to 'outdoor girl' has not been smooth. I was expecting flushed radiance and the kind of all-over bronzing the dirt gave Susan Sarandon and Geena Davis in *Thelma and Louise*. Instead my souped-up freckle count, underlying pink blotches and patchy foundation make me look like I've contracted a skin disease. My eye make-up has disappeared bar a crinkle of brown at the outer corner of my left eye and my bottom lip is peeling. I'm so disappointed.

'What does it matter anyway?' I ask myself. 'Who am I trying to impress?' But I suppose old clichés die hard – sunset plus man equals romance, even if it is the wrong man. And, for that matter, the wrong woman. I see Finn with some nymphy oceanographer or seaweed specialist who wanders around in flip-flops, a baby T-shirt and bikini bottoms. All glowing make-up-free complexion and Wash 'n' Go hair. It's all right for those natural beauties – they're not fazed by their boyfriend dropping by unexpectedly on a Sunday afternoon. They can just chirrup, 'How lovely to see you, honey! I'll be ready in five minutes!' The last time I got caught like that I retreated into my hooded top like a turtle and screeched, 'Don't look at me – my hair's all fluffy and I've got no eyes!'

I look at myself in the mirror and wonder who Finn would put me with? I've got a horrible feeling it wouldn't be Zane.

I'm always trying to picture people's other halves. I even have a nasty habit of fixing my boyfriends up with other 'more appropriate' women in my mind. When I was with Travis I'd see some foxy pierced chick in the street and think how good they'd look together and then feel all jealous and rejected when he hadn't even laid eyes on this 'perfect' passer-by.

I've always wanted to 'look good' with someone. You know how people say, 'They look good together.' It seems the ultimate confirmation that you are meant to be together. You were designed to fit. You are an aesthetically pleasing combination. If a stranger saw me and Travis together they'd probably think I'd just stopped to buy a copy of the *Big Issue* on the way home from work. I could never match his muso grunge, however hard I tried.

In a way, the more extreme your dress code the easier it is to find a partner. It's like zebras going for other zebras. They are not going to get confused and run off with a chestnut pony. Elephants can look at hippos and go, 'I dunno, there's something about the nose that just ain't right.' Similarly, a white-faced, black-lipped Goth isn't going to go falling in love with some city suit, and a *Wallpaper*-reading chick isn't going to wrap her pashmina around a Marine with tassled loafers. It's us inbetweenies that can have problems. If you are not part of a distinct group, your markings are not clearly displayed and all too often you end up dating outside your species and all sorts of trouble begins. But the toughest thing of all is when you can't identify your own species. When you wonder if – like that poor little yellow Cowfish in the tank – you are the only one like you. And whoever you are with, you just keep noticing the differences, not the similarities.

'Finn! Good to see you, man!'

'Hey, Joe!' Finn gives a robust-looking man an appropriately hearty handshake. 'This is Jamie. She's over from the UK.'

'Is that right?' he smiles. 'Well, young lady you're gonna make all the waitresses jealous tonight. I don't know how they're gonna take seeing Finn with a pretty thing like you!'

I can't believe he called me pretty. What a nice man.

'I gotta cosy booth available if you want it,' he adds. Steady . . .

'Great!' says Finn, indicating for me to follow Joe. 'I'm just going to drop the tools round the back and I'll be right in.'

Joe hands me a menu as I slide along the red leather booth seat.

'This do you?'

'Yes, it's lovely,' I grin, smoothing the red and white tablecloth. 'It's like a Swiss chalet with all the carved wood and little lanterns!'

'The wife's influence. It's something different, I guess,' he smiles. Leaning over to light the candle he adds, 'You know, it's funny, I always knew it would be a special girl to capture Finn's heart, but British? Who knew?'

I'm about to correct his assumption when Finn returns and I decide it would create too much fuss. Besides, being the envy of the waitresses does have its appeal. Especially if it means snubbing that sassy, brassy thing giving me the evil eye from behind the bar. 'This is great!' I tell Finn. 'I can't believe we're in the middle of the desert!'

My stomach growls like a coyote. 'Menu!'

'Menu!' he agrees.

Sassy Brassy glowers over us with pen poised. I wonder how many other waitresses she has slain to make this her table. Listing the 'specials' purely for Finn's benefit, she can't even bring herself to acknowledge me. It must be particularly galling to her that I look so rough.

We both opt for the vegetarian goulash but it'll be easy to tell the orders apart because mine will come with extra spit.

An hour later, a pregnant woman and a pregnant man waddle towards the fireplace. At least that's how we must look. Finn and I ordered an additional side of mashed potato boosted with roasted garlic and exploded cherry tomatoes, followed by hefty wedges of Key lime pie and now we're paying the price.

'You think you're safe if you avoid the buffets, but greed can get you just like that!' Finn moans.

I wish my mum was here to smell the charcoaled cedar wood and listen to the whisper of the ashes. Okay, we've had a few. Joe gave us complimentary sambuca to round off the meal. It scores a direct hit with Finn which I find rather endearing because I can't bear men who can hold their booze.

Part of the pleasure of us getting on well is the knowledge that this will all get back to Zane. Getting the thumbs up about a 'chick' from one of your best mates has got to be the best recommendation going. I toy with the idea of telling Finn about my feelings for Zane, he might be able to offer me some advice, especially now his tongue is loosened.

I look at his mouth again. And his tongue. What is this sambuca like? My heart is hammering and my loins are doing a passable impression of the flaming coffee bean. How I wish Zane were here to ravage. Poor Finn – little does he know how close he is to becoming a substitute snog.

We sit and watch the glowing embers, too full to talk, happy to eavesdrop on other conversations and sway to the background music. Meanwhile, Sassy Brassy uses any prop she can lay her hands on as an excuse to come over – first coffee refills, then complimentary chocolates and finally condoms. Well, not literally condoms, but her last look was so blatantly seductive Finn started describing the exact dimensions of the mackerel chunks he feeds to the sharks.

'I think we'd better go!' he says, heaving himself to his feet and accidentally jostling the youngest waitress. She makes the most of steadying him. You go, girl!

I look at my watch. Eleven p.m. I wonder if Izzy will be cuddled up with her 'Teddy Bear' when I get back.

As we leave, Finn collides with the doorpost and claims he can actually see cartoon stars circling his head. Joe offers us a room but I just know Sassy Brassy would be waiting for me behind the shower curtain, so I reassure him I'll be driving and we step out into the cool night.

Finn opens the passenger door to the car and then has an extended feline stretch which lifts his shirt to reveal lowslung shorts and a small turquoise dolphin tattoo leaping his belly button. I turn on the ignition to drown out the purring growl that escapes my lips. Blinking hard to dispel the image of his stomach, I turn on the headlights. As I swing on to the road I get a thrill, as if this really is my car. As if this really is my life.

'*The look . . . of love, is in . . . your eyes . . .*' croons Izzy in her best Dusty-does-karaoke voice. 'You must have had a good day with Zane, you're all a-glow!'

'Zane wasn't there. He had to go to LA. It was just Finn and me and I'm not glowing, that's either sunburn or red rock dust.'

There's no need for her to know I had a good time. I want her to feel as guilty as possible for abandoning me this morning.

'Oh,' says Izzy, nonplussed.

I tip out the contents of my bag trying to find my lip balm.

'So, how did he cope being on dry land all day?'

I sit down on the bed. 'It's weird. He was like a different person. He even took the piss a couple of times.'

'No!' gasps Izzy. 'He seemed so wet – pardon the pun.'

'Not at all. It's like he's got this playful streak but he's also . . . well, pure!' I find myself saying.

'Pure?' she hoots. 'A pure man. Isn't that what they call an oxymoron?'

'He's no moron, believe me!'

'Boom boom!' groans Izzy.

'He's really quite wise.'

'So would you be if you only talked about your specialised *Mastermind* subject all day. Though in our case I'm not quite sure what that would be.'

'Exactly!' I say triumphantly. 'What do you and I really know about? We don't have a specialised subject. I used to like poetry, you like seducing men. We don't have any hobbies.'

'Hobbies? What are we – anoraks? Personally, I don't have time for hobbies,' Izzy announces proudly.

'I'm just talking about adding a new dimension to our lives.'

'If you want to explore a new dimension, check out the Star Trek Experience. Personally I'm going to celebrate my 3-D ness – or should that be 34D-ness – while I'm still young.'

'You know he hardly mentioned fish at all, in fact—'

The phone rings. It's Zane apologising for missing our day out. What a babe he is. He sounds elated and says he's got something he wants to show me and to meet him tomorrow lunchtime. I come off the phone on a high, Finn, fish and the value of hobbies completely forgotten.

'Now you can sing to me!' I command.

Izzy gives me a knowing look and sings, *'The look . . . of LUST . . .'*

22

I'm awake but I keep my eyes closed. I'm longing to shift and stretch but I don't want Izzy to know I'm conscious yet. I need some time to myself to think.

Today I'm going to tell Zane how I feel. But I don't want it to be a big scary love confessional – I'm thinking more of a gentle invitation for him to forget Mia and be mine for all eternity.

I run through infinite scenarios: in one visualisation he looks relieved and says, 'Oh my God, I've been hoping you were feeling the same way but I just couldn't tell if you really liked me because I don't know you very well and you seem so friendly to everyone . . .' and I silence his babblings with a kiss. Then I realise it's me who babbles, not him, so I alter the fantasy so that he just smiles sexily and says, 'I was hoping you'd say that!' In the chick flick version he shyly squeezes my hand and looks at me with pure love. In my favourite scenario we just run, tumbling and giggling to his room and—

Izzy stirs, I realise I've dragged my pillow into an

191

embrace. I keep perfectly still for the next five minutes but my mind is still racing . . .

I wish I had the nerve to say something really romantic but I know my delivery would ruin the sentiment. Only a chosen few can pedal mush convincingly. Most of them live in Hollywood. Mind you, Christian certainly knew how to speak from the heart. That reminds me, I brought my poetry book with me. Could I get away with a surreptitious flick-through without Izzy noticing? I roll over and move my hand towards the bedside table drawer.

'Jamie? You awake?' asks Izzy.

I pause for a moment, loath to leave imaginings of Zane whispering beautiful clichés like, 'I knew the moment I saw you . . .' 'I never thought I could feel this way again . . .' and 'Fellow Sagittarian be mine!'

'Jamie?'

'Mmm-yeah . . .'

'I've been awake for an hour. Just couldn't get up,' Izzy informs me.

'Mmm-ohh . . .'

'So,' she sighs, clearly restless. 'Have you got your love ammo ready for the showdown at high noon?'

Here we go.

'No chickening out now. If you leave it any longer you'll just end up friends and you'll never get to squeeze his kiwis,' she warns.

'I know. I'm going to do it. I'm just thinking about how to word it—'

'It's not about words, Jamie. It's about stirring his loins,' says Izzy, pulling herself upright in bed. 'You've already got the chat, you get on well, you're trying to take this to the next level and the only way to get there is by arousing his interest physically. If you just talk about feelings that's not going to get the results you want, you'll just panic him or make him go, "Ahh, bless her!"'

'Oh. Well. Teach me, oh master,' I yawn.

'What you need to do is kiss him on the lips when you first say hello. You always hug and there's the odd brush of the cheek but a full kiss on the lips will get his attention straight away. Do it all cheery and perky as if it's perfectly normal but leave a hand on the back of his neck or on his arm to keep the physical link there. Stand closer than normal – let some of your pheromones wake up some of his.' She pauses for breath. 'This would be so much easier if you've both had a few. Are you sure you don't want to do this at night?'

'I don't want this to be a drunken scenario, Izzy. I want to see what he really feels. I want to be honest and get an honest reaction.'

'Blimey – one whiff of fresh air and scenery and you're all born again!'

'It's not that. If I did the drinking advance I'd just wake up the next day wondering if he meant it, presume he didn't and then get all paranoid and ignore him. At least this way I'll know straight away.'

'Well don't expect too much. If the idea hasn't crossed his mind then he won't be able to switch into boyfriend mode instantly. You know what men are like – they have to think everything is their idea . . .'

'Oh God, relationships are just the biggest design

193

fault in the universe!' I wail, suddenly daunted. 'It's like freak weather conditions when two people actually feel the same way about each other. I remember I wrote this poem about how the clouds represent unrequited love and the raindrops are the tears of frustration and disappointment . . .'

'Cheery!' Izzy groans.

'Well, I also had rainbows as the symbol for happy ever after but you know how rare they are . . .'

'Do you think you might be dehydrated?'

'Could be,' I croak. 'Let's get room service.'

I've got to stop having margaritas for breakfast. Izzy's theory that 'the more flesh you have on display the better' started to make sense and she talked me into one of her skimpy halterneck tops with a strapless push-up bra. I have never felt so trussed up and yet so precarious. I can't stop my hands doing sporadic checks to make sure everything is still in place – no peeking labels, gaping necklines or squidges of X-rated flesh. What I can barely bring myself to acknowledge is the disturbing presence of Izzy's 'instant cleavage' secret weapons – two uncooked chicken breasts. At least that's what they look like. Have you seen those things? They are pale pink gel-filled sacks that warm to your body temperature and mould to boost your inadequate boobs. I can just see one of them plopping on to the floor during a frantic embrace and some poor bloke thinking he's dislodged an implant. What a turn-on that would be.

Initially I liked the effect the chicken breasts created

but now I'm away from the safety and hilarity of our hotel room I just feel ridiculous. It doesn't help that Izzy's strawberry motif halter top bears an invitation to 'Scratch 'n' sniff!' Not that I'd notice if anyone did – my boobs are so numb beneath gel pouches and foam padding I wouldn't feel a thing.

I do a final check as I enter the Mirage and try not to make any sudden movements as I head for Kokomo's bar. Sitting unusually straight of spine, I try to find a casual way to fold my arms across my bulgy new cleavage and then start to shiver. How could I have forgotten how chilling the air conditioning would be? What I wouldn't do for an outsize M&S men's cardi like I used to wear when I was fifteen. I'm toying with the idea of buying one of the canary-yellow, hotel-emblem sweatshirts from the gift shop when I hear Zane's voice. I shiver all the more. His hands on my naked back make me spasm and I remember too late to aim for his lips and suck on his aftershave-drenched neck. Convinced his boisterous hug has dislodged a chicken breast I involuntarily grab my boobs the second he pulls away. He gives me a quizzical look.

'You're freezing!' he notices, rubbing my goosebumped arms and causing undue undulation.

'Jamie . . .' he says, strong brown fingers holding my arms steady now, 'I'd like you to meet Mia!'

Stepping out from behind him is something far worse than any *Baywatch* blonde. She's gorgeous – dark and exotic with lustrous chestnut hair to her waist and skin like sheeny butterscotch. She's wearing a tiny tan suede bikini top over small but perfectly formed boobs with a gold, shimmery sarong knotted over narrow hips. I had a Pippa doll just like her once and spent my whole childhood wishing I had her colouring. But I've never felt more pasty and lumpy and foolish than I do right now.

'Mia, honey, this is Jamie!'

I struggle to maintain control of my facial expressions as she extends a petite hand to me. Then Zane enthuses: 'Jamie is like the sister I never had, I love her!'

I go to speak – my mouth twitches but nothing comes out. Just as well because what I'm thinking is 'I love you too!'

'I thought we might have lunch together, I really want you two to get to know each other,' beams Zane, caressing Mia's silky shoulder.

I feel a sickening pang of jealousy. I have to get away. What was I thinking mixing with these genetically elite people? How did I get separated from my own species?

'I just need to make a call!' I shrill. 'I'll be back in a second.' I realise I'm behaving like a woman possessed but I can't contain my scream of horror a second longer and bolt before Zane can speak.

'He's reunited with Mia!' I howl as soon as Izzy picks up the phone. 'I've just met her. I didn't even say hello! I just ran! What do I do?'

'What does she look like?'

'A cross between Guam's entry for Miss World and Pocahontas!' I blub. 'I can't bear it!'

'I can be there in fifteen minutes,' soothes Izzy. 'Just

survive the appetizers and I'll get you through the rest.'

I quaver my gratitude and insist she brings my black bra and baggy Indian print shirt.

So that's what Zane went to LA for! I pout as I hang up the phone, suddenly feeling ridiculous for even thinking I was in with a chance. Thank God he introduced her before I started my 'let's get together' speech. I blanch at how the situation could have been even more dire. At least this way the humiliation is my own private burden. If I can get through the meal without crying or skewering anyone with a fork, Zane need never know.

But before I face the lovecats again I need to lose the chicken fillets. I daren't visit the loos because I know the worst thing I can do right now is look in the mirror. There's only a little old lady on the house phone near me so I reckon I can get away with a quick breast reduction right here. I lean into my phone booth, forage efficiently and shove the pouches into my bag in disgust.

Bolting back to Kokomo's I'm dazzled by a bright light and collide with a hunk with tufty bleached blond hair. He smiles in response to my apology and I realise the glare came from his teeth – so white they have an alarming fluorescence. I blink and hurry on my way.

'Excuse me, ma'am!' he calls after me.

I turn round. He has something pink and fleshy in his hand. Dear God, no! I keep walking.

'Ma'am!' The voice gains on me. 'I think you dropped this!'

The Grin hands me my still-warm breast.

'You didn't see any broccoli, did you?' I say, squinting at his teeth.

'What?'

'It's my lunch, you know! Bit of chicken, steamed broccoli, rice . . .'

He starts to laugh. I just turn and run.

Back at Kokomo's the strapless bra has worked its way down to my waist, giving me a padded stomach. Like I needed any help there. Darting behind the maître d's desk-cum-palm tree I swivel it round, unhook the clasp and shove that in my bag, taking care to zip it this time.

At the table both Zane and Mia try not to stare at my deflated chest. I take my seat and make full use of the big white napkin and grin. 'Sooooo!'

They smile gormlessly back at me.

'Sorry I had to rush off like that! Had to catch Izzy before she left. She's coming here. Then we have to leave. Which is a shame cos I would have loved to have stayed and chatted with Poca . . . *Mia*!' I correct myself.

'Jamie, are you okay? You seem kind of flustered,' asks Zane.

'Do I? You know, I think I may have got a teeny bit of sunstroke yesterday at Mount Charleston.'

'Yeah, sorry I couldn't make it but my baby called . . .'

'You have a *child*?' I howl.

'No,' he laughs. 'My baby Mia.'

Of course. What was I thinking?

'So, Mia, I take it you're moving back to Vegas?' I ask,

realising I haven't yet spoken one word to the vision.

'Oh yeah, like, Miami was just, like, too intense for me and when I heard my baby's voice on the phone I just had to run to him.'

For a moment I just look at her. A half-chewed piece of papaya sits in my mouth. I expected a gentle breeze of a voice but hers is the most squeaky, nerve-shrivelling thing I have ever heard. She's got to be putting it on.

'Um, and will you be getting your old lifeguard job back?'

'Oh yeah, natch! My boss has just been the coolest about that. I start back tomorrow!' she squawks.

'Gee, that's just great! We should celebrate!' I grin. 'Can I have a pitcher of pina colada?' I ask a passing waiter.

'Sure thing!'

'You guys want anything?' I address Zane and Mia. They look stunned. 'Kidding!'

Mia pushes her glossy hair behind her dainty little ear and peers at me. 'You know, I think you're really brave to wear your hair that short!'

What the hell does that mean? I've hardly got a skinhead. Somehow the remark seems to imply I look less than feminine. I smile sweetly. 'Don't tell me – you've never had yours cut and that's your baby hair on the ends.'

'How did you know?' she gasps, delighted.

For some masochistic reason I ask how they first met and get the whole soppy, kissy-kissy story. Consequently the pina colada goes down a treat and by the time Izzy arrives, I'm wearing a flamingo feather in my hair and a pink orchid where my cleavage used to be. She looks mortified at the saggy strawberry that greets her.

'Where did it all go?' she gasps.

I hold up my bag and shrug.

'Izzy, this is Mia!'

'Wow! I mean, hi! What a great outfit!' she says, taking the seat beside me.

'Thanks!' coos Mia.

Izzy orders a coconut stir-fry and prepares to dominate the conversation to spare me. I have a better idea.

'Mia, do tell Izzy about the time you were rescuing that old man in the pool and he tried to untie your bikini,' I suggest.

She just shakes her head shyly.

Speak, damn you!

'Come on, it was great. I want Izzy to hear it.'

'Go on, baby,' urges Zane.

'She doesn't wanna hear about that, she just got here!'

There it is again – the voice that would make a screeching cockatoo sound as mellifluous as Joanna Lumley.

Izzy's eyes light up. 'I think I do. It sounds really funny!' She gives my knee a squeeze under the table. And squeezes even harder with every syllable Mia slaughters, disguising her wincing by chewing on a lime segment.

By the end of Mia's story we're all in tears, tummies aching from laughing so much.

'I knew you girls would get along,' says Zane triumphantly.

Hysteria numbs my pain for the next couple of hours – as soon as the loving couple are out of earshot Izzy and I mimic Mia wherever we go, daring each other to order drinks and place bets in her scratchy tones – but after a while the fact that a pretty girl has a horrific voice ceases to make everything all right. At the end of the day, she has Zane and I have to face the fact that he's out of the picture, romantically at least. The frustrating thing is that I can't even dismiss him as a bastard – he hasn't done anything wrong. He never made me any promises, it's all been wishful thinking on my part. He's just as lovely as he ever was, and I even have the oddest feeling we'll still be friends but I can't escape the feeling of 'here I am again, devastated with disappointment' and the worst part is I don't even feel that surprised any more. I even know I'll get over it. I guess it gets quicker every time. The hardest part is having to let go of the hope.

Every time you get a crush on someone you get a bit of hope, a flash of future, something to look forward to, something to live for. When you get dumped or rejected that's all taken away. You survived perfectly well before you met that person but when they are removed from the equation you sense a much greater loss. And that's because the loss is greater than the person. You are not just mourning their passing, you are mourning the death of possibility. Zane represented something that could take me out of myself and make me different, make my life different. Now he's gone it's just boring old me again.

'Never mind, sweetie,' says Izzy, handing me her Starbucks latte so she can rummage for the room key. 'There are so many other gorgeous men in this town. Forget Zane. We have to move on!'

Just like that?

I hate how quickly he's become past tense, indistinguishable from all the other failed relationships in my life. Suddenly I'm supposed to feel nothing for him? My emotions are all crying out in confusion – 'Hey! Could you try and give us a bit more notice? This morning you got us all worked up thinking we had a big love scene ahead.' I try to explain that Zane is no longer the potential saviour or hero or Romeo or soulmate. I can't help but regret that I never even had the chance to find out how good we could have been together. Me and the male stripper. Perhaps I should take some of the blame for not seeing this coming. I tied *myself* to the railroad tracks. Still, I miss that feeling of being 'connected' and I can't believe how quickly it's gone. It's like going back to work after being on holiday – an hour at the photocopier and it's as if you never went. All those vivid, sangria-soaked memories evaporate and everything is underwhelmingly, mind-numbingly ordinary again.

23

It's only 4 p.m. but I've had it with today, however Izzy says we still have time to 'regroup'. To get ourselves back on track. To come up with a plan to divert the depression that is threatening to descend on this inappropriately beautiful afternoon. I find I do this best with the duvet over my head.

'Now I don't want you to think I'm turning into you,' Izzy begins.

'Heaven forbid!'

'But, I read this article in *Cosmo* – the kind of thing I'd normally dismiss as mumbo-jumbo . . .'

'No spells, Izzy!' I plead from beneath my padded shroud.

'No, this is just your average spiritual clap-trap but I liked the sound of it.'

'Let's hear it!' I feign enthusiasm and reveal one eye.

Izzy pulls her chair over to face me, like a counsellor trying to reach her patient. 'It's called "Acting As If",' she starts slowly. 'Apparently, the best way to achieve any goal is to act like you've already succeeded. You talk about it in the present tense as if it's already happened. Like, instead of saying, "When I get my promotion . . ." you say, "Since getting my promotion . . ."'

'And everyone thinks you're nuts or lying?' I offer.

'Noooo! Well, I suppose you mostly talk to yourself about it. But we could talk to each other.' She looks confused. 'It made sense when I read it.'

'Keep going . . .'

'The idea is that if you completely believe that this thing, whatever you really want, has already happened, then it most likely will because one of the hardest things is believing that good things can really happen to you.'

'I can't believe you're into this!'

'I can't believe you're not, it's so up your street!' Izzy suddenly looks sad, which is really my bag. 'I just figured we needed a boost. A new tactic.'

'What's the matter?'

'Oh, you know, I've got to face facts: it's not going to work out with EP.'

'What makes you say that?' I ask, revealing my other eye. 'I thought you couldn't get enough of each other.'

'He was never destined to be more than a gap-filler. I can see that now,' she sighs. 'The problem is that it's all too easy to get distracted in a place like this. I think we need to restate our original goals: we came here to get married, not shilly-shally around with strippers and Elvis impersonators. We've strayed from the path. What we need to do before we do anything else is write down exactly what kind of man we want to proposition us.'

'You mean, propose,' I correct her.

'Whatever,' she shrugs, jumping to her feet and looking around the room. 'Have you got any paper?'

'Just notebooks,' I reply. 'But there should be some headed paper in the desk drawer.'

'Perfect! Okay, pen for you, pen for me. Let's do it!'

I watch Izzy scribbling busily and then stare at my blank piece of paper with furrows so deep in my brow you'd think my forehead was made of kneaded dough. I've given this subject enough thought over the years, why am I finding this so hard? I've gone right off Zane. Should I just describe Christian and throw in a kiwi/caramel stomach? That doesn't seem right. I press my pen to the page, hoping my hand will be guided by a higher force. Nothing.

'I just want to say,' I say, sighing heavily, 'for every magazine quiz and questionnaire I've made you fill out, for every self-help book exercise, automatic writing experiment, dream analysis diary and psychometric test I've ever made you do, *I'm sorry*.'

Izzy chuckles and motions for me to get on with my list.

'I just can't do it!' I humph finally, throwing down the pen.

'Yes you can. You have to,' she says, retrieving the Circus Circus biro. 'How are you going to know when you meet Him if you don't have some signs to look out for?'

'But I only seem to know what I *don't* want – you know, my usual unreliable, unfaithful, unhygienic teenagers. I can't seem to put into words what I do want. Partly because what I want doesn't seem like a terribly good idea.'

'What are you talking about?' I've obviously lost her.

'Well, I'm wondering if I should really be writing a list of qualities for a man that would be good for me instead. I mean, what I want is a spontaneous, passionate, impulsive ball of fire, but how exhausting would that be? And what would be good for me would be someone who could temper my flightiness with a bit of stability. Someone calm and wise and mature. Someone I could trust and rely on. And yet, if I write that down I want to kill myself because that just sounds so predictable and dull.'

'Can't you find a happy balance?'

I humph again. 'It's like, I like the idea of someone glamorous but that would make me feel inferior. I'd like someone to snuggle up and watch TV with but I'm worried about that getting too cosy and addictive and slipping into a coma. I'd like someone funny but if they were japing and joking the whole time that would get on my nerves. And I'd like to be proud of someone, watch them holding court in a room, but often those people don't function without an audience and their one-on-one performance is lacking.

'I want someone attentive but I don't want someone who suffocates me. I want someone I'm comfortable with but you can't have that and feel ignited by someone, can you? I want a real man who's also sensitive and considerate. I want him to be outrageously sexy but not remotely flirtatious with

206

other women. I want him to have a mysterious allure but not be distant. I want him to be affectionate but never, EVER call me bunny.'

I pace the room. 'Do you know what my mum said once? That all we really want is someone who makes us feel good about ourselves. Does that mean relation-ships are all a big ego trip?'

Izzy rolls her eyes. 'Okay, I'm writing yours for you. You want someone a little bit off-the-wall and unconventional with a heart of gold and a touch that makes your heart do somersaults. Someone who'll still surprise you and hold your hand when you're seventy. Most of all he has to be someone you can have deep conversations with so you don't have to bother me with meaning of life stuff!' She grins. 'There!'

'Okay.' Sounds good to me. 'What did you put?'

'Rich. Older. Obsessed!'

'It's really that simple for you, isn't it?'

'I just know what I need to make me happy. Now, we act as if these dream lovers have popped the question and get on with the best bit of getting married.'

She reaches behind her and then throws the Vegas *Yellow Pages* down on the bed.

'Choosing a wedding dress!'

'Marion's Faithful Bride Boutique.'

'Gown and Out Rentals.'

'Altar-Ations.'

We've read so many absurd shop names, we're now making up our own and giggling wildly. I keep getting that plummeting lift-shaft feeling in my stomach when I think about Zane and can't help but wonder if going to look at wedding dresses isn't like dumping ten pounds of salt on my open-heart surgery, but Izzy is so convinced it's a constructive thing to do and I don't want to knock her first foray into spirituality. Mustering all available fake enthusiasm I tell her, 'This is a great idea – it's like a visualisation exercise: if we see ourselves in our wedding dresses we'll really be able to picture the wedding scene.'

Izzy's face brightens. 'We're going to do it, you know – get married. We're going to shock everyone.'

And no one will be as shocked as me if this actually works.

'There it is!' I alert the cab driver. He pulls up in front of Dress for Excess, a look of misty pleasure filling his eyes. As we hand over the $10 bill he says, 'If you see Cindy, tell her Derek the cab driver said hi, would ya?'

'Okay!' we chirrup, surveying the shop front before us.

'Could there BE any more Cupids?' asks Izzy with Chandler intonation.

There are gold ones, rosy-cheeked porcelain ones, plump Cabbage Patch Doll-style ones, painted ones, pop-up ones and plaster-of-Paris ones. All clustered around one solitary dress bearing a sash printed with the words, 'This month's special!' and a small card saying, 'Enquire inside for details.'

'Fight you for it!' says Izzy, eyeing the organza extravaganza.

'Isn't it funny how you only see leg o' mutton sleeves in wedding dress shops and Oxfam,' I muse.

'Well, are we going in or what?'

As Izzy pushes the door open I suddenly feel nervous, as if even trying on dresses is too big a step, too scary a commitment. And what an admission! What if someone I know sees me? I'd feel like a transvestite husband caught rummaging in his wife's undies drawer.

Am I really bold enough to confess 'I want to get married' for all the world to see? Walking down Exeter High Street alone after the shops closed, I'd often find myself gazing at wedding dress window displays with furtive wonder. Even then I was convinced I'd be moved on if I lingered too long. By day I didn't even allow my eyes to flick in the direction of the Berketex sign and would never have considered going in for a mooch. I presumed they must have some kind of membership policy, like entry wasn't 'allowed' unless you had hard proof of a wedding-to-be.

'Can we see your papers?' a Gestapo-esque guard would say.

'Papers?'

'Yes we need the marriage licence, the receipt from the reception booking and the fingerprints of the vicar intending to perform the ceremony before you can proceed.'

To me, wedding dress shops have always been the domain of others, the chosen few. As the bell announces our entrance, I feel embarrassed and self-conscious, not to say entirely fraudulent. What are we doing here? This is ridiculous! No doubt the woman in the bridal shop will be able to tell instantly that we're groom-free fakes. We'll be hustled out of the shop and told to go back to watching *Muriel's Wedding* on video.

'I'll be with you girls in a minute!' says a voice from beneath a cascade of veils. She's bound to be some matronly dame with a pincushion strapped to her wrist and a tape measure slung like a silk scarf around her neck. She'll take one look at Izzy and say wearing white would be in poor taste. And one look at me and presume I'm the bridesmaid.

I run my hand along an alarming array of man-made fibres. 'Just what I always wanted – a dress that will fuse to my skin in the 100-degree heat,' I murmur.

'Hello, Krystal Carrington!' Izzy giggles, pointing to a heavily-beaded drape of fabric slung between two imposing shoulder pads.

'Look! This one comes with a lacy parasol and big hat like the woman on the Quality Street boxes!' I flick to the next one on the rack. 'This one's not bad . . .'

'If you're going flamenco dancing.' Izzy grimaces.

'Do you remember Paula Yates married Bob Geldof in a scarlet dress?' I ask, noticing a dress embroidered with red roses. 'Nadine was scandalised! I thought it was so daring but I just wouldn't have the nerve, would you?'

'Nah, I wouldn't feel wedding-ish in anything but white or cream,' she admits.

'My mum always says white looks cheap but then cream can look dirty,' I muse.

'Ivory is the answer,' Izzy concludes, then looks up and gasps: 'I can't believe we're having this conversation!'

We move through to the designer section of the shop and I'm instantly drawn to a tight white satin corset with a full net skirt sprinkled with diamanté studs. All my suppressed girlish longings come swirling to the surface.

'I want to take his breath away. I want tears to spring to his eyes when he sees me walking down the aisle,' I sigh.

Izzy grins. 'I want him to get an enormous—'

'Sorry to keep you!'

We spin around. A perky blonde with top-of-the-range silicone boobs clomps over to us on stacked raffia platforms.

'Hi, my name is Cinderella but you can call me Cindy!'

This is definitely an *FHM* version of the fairytale. Dazzled by Cinderella's breasts we morph into a couple of blokes, fnarr-ing into our stubble. 'See anything you like? she asks, obviously used to the reaction. We gulp and try to regain our composure.

'Which one of you girls is the bride-to-be?'

'We both are!' asserts Izzy.

'Yes, that's right!' I add, boldly Acting As If. 'We're having a double wedding!'

'How fun is that!' whoops Cindy. 'Are the guys friends too?'

'Umm . . . actually, no. They haven't met yet!' I find myself saying.

'No,' confirms Izzy. 'Our schedules have been crazy! It's going to be a surprise on the big day!'

'And when is that?' asks Cindy, twiddling a dangly Cupid earring.

Izzy and I look at each other. 'Sometime in the next two weeks.'

'So you haven't fixed a date just yet?'

'No, we've got one or two details to sort out before then.'

There's a brief, awkward silence.

'Well, take a look around and if there's anything I can do to make your wedding dress quest more enjoyable, just let me know.'

We watch agog as Cindy wiggles away from us in her taut baby-pink mini-dress.

'Do you think she's had Jennifer Lopez bottom implants too?' Izzy giggles.

'What was that?' she turns back.

I try to look like a serious shopper. 'Um, I was just wondering if, um, do you have any period dresses?'

'What, like when you're feeling all bloated?'

Izzy's chewing gum flies out of her mouth.

'Um,' I falter.

'She's kind of into the whole Kate Winslet corset thing,' Izzy rescues.

'Oh! Right! Sorry!' she flushes a pretty pink to match what little there is of her dress.

'Something like this?' She holds out a petite antique dress with exposed shoulders and gold shimmer underlying the lace. Cher does Jane Austen.

'Perfect.' I nod. 'I don't suppose you have that in a UK size 14?'

'Let me see what I can lay my hands on . . .'

She flicks expertly along the rails, occasionally turning back to me to assess whether it would suit or fit.

'I think this would go great with your colouring. It's got an apricot glow to it.'

'It might be okay . . .' I hadn't considered apricot.

'Feel like trying it on?'

Cindy has such a naturally flirtatious tone, her every suggestion sounds improper.

'There's an awful lot of hooks and eyes there,' I observe.

'Don't worry – we'll get it on!'

'I think she's in training for a Miss Innuendo contest!' whispers Izzy.

I hold out my arms and Cindy fills it with apricot chiffon.

'That's you started. Now, what about you, Miss Thing!'

Cindy obviously recognises a fellow exhibitionist when she sees one.

'Where do you keep the sexy stuff?' Izzy growls.

Cindy's face lights up.

'Do you want modern or girly?'

'Modern, definitely.'

'I know just the thing for you. It's actually over at our showgirl shop. Have you seen *The Fifth Element*?'

'Not the bandage bondage outfit?' Izzy's eyes widen gleefully.

Cindy and Izzy are having a 'separated at birth' moment.

'It's basically straps of white leather encircling your body. It's more secure than it looks. You won't fall out but everyone around you will be on pins expecting a nipple to peek out or the butt sash to gape! They won't be able to take their eyes off you!'

I get a shuddering flashback to chicken breasts and halterneck tops but Izzy is getting more excited by the second.

'When can I try it?'

'Well, my friend Layla is headed over there now. I could get her to bring it by if you can hang around for half an hour.'

'Yeah!' enthuses Izzy.

'Okay, let's measure you up and I'll give her a call.'

'Great!' she whoops.

Cindy wheels a bare clothes rail over to me, transfers the abundance of apricot on to it and adds, 'If you see anything you'd like to try, just hang it on here. We won't be long. Have fun!'

Oh, to have a body that only requires you to cover up the naughty bits.

I dismiss endless sleeveless, backless, strapless, tasteless numbers praying for something with old-fashioned glamour that will disguise my faults but still make a husband-to-be hanker for the inevitable après-reception four-poster bed scene. An elegant slim-cut satin number reminds me of my mother's wedding dress. I coveted it for years as a child, slinking around in the matching over-the-elbow gloves, straining at the seams on me because they had been custom-made to fit my mother's dainty digits. I longed for the day I would be tall and busty enough to fill the dress. My dressing up games lapsed in my teenage years and then suddenly I was too chunky – I'd missed my chance. Of course it fitted Nadine perfectly. After Christian's reappearance in my life I found this oddly symbolic.

If visualisation is a valid technique, Nadine's wedding is long overdue. While I was papering my room with life-size pop posters, Nadine refused to let one blob of Blu-Tak near her pretty pastel walls. The first thing you noticed walking into her room were the endless bridal magazines taking pride of place on her shelves as if they were classic first editions. If you happened to pull one down from its chronological position you'd find it littered with Post-it Notes and annotated pages – a jewelled cuff circled here, a taffeta toe there. She photocopied the pages she really liked and would insert a cut-out photo of her face over the model to get a proper idea of how the dress would look on her. If there was a groom in the shot she'd slot in a picture of a current boyfriend or her fantasy man Gary Barlow. (Need I say more?)

As you can imagine, there was never any question that Nadine would get married. That was a sure thing. What was totally unexpected was me giving a damn. Quite a large damn, as it turned out.

I look over at the Groom annex of the shop. Christian could be getting measured up for his morning suit as we speak. Would it be so very wrong to visualise him walking up the aisle with me instead? Perhaps things didn't pan out with Zane because I truly am destined to be with Christian. I guess I really do need a dress, just in case.

I go back to the white diamanté-studded designer number, ignore the price tag and after five minutes wrestling with the netting, swoosh it over to the mirror. I hold it up in front of me and sigh. Wedding dresses really do possess a magical quality. I find my spirits strangely lifted. Izzy was right – this is a good pep-up activity. I only wish it wasn't entirely founded in fantasy. If only someone could convince me this could happen for real.

Out of nowhere, Cinderella appears by my side and whispers, 'You shall go to the ball!'

24

Cindy and Izzy have spent the last half an hour hoisting and hoiking me into a series of dresses ranging from what Cindy politely described as a 'snug' fit to a laced corset that caused me to pass out.

Did you ever play that passing out 'game' at parties? You'd take a breath, someone would squeeze all the air out of you in a bear hug from behind and everything would go black. You'd regain consciousness a minute or two later. Where I come from that was considered A Laugh. Anyway, I suppose the same principle applied to the rib-crushing dress. I'm just thankful I didn't fall on any of Cupid's arrows.

'How do you feel now?' asks Cindy.

'Fine!' I say, draining my last sip of Sprite. Lemonade is the ultimate cure-all in my book. I always drink it if I've got a dodgy stomach. My friend Amanda's mum told me the best thing is to boil all the bubbles out in a saucepan and then drink it lukewarm, but ice-cold from a vending machine would do for now.

'Layla should be here any minute,' says Cindy,

replacing the final rejected dress. 'She must have had trouble getting a ride.'

'Oh!' Izzy jumps in. 'We had a message for you: Derek the cabbie says hi!'

'Oh God! Whatta creep!' Cindy grimaces. 'Did he try it on with either of you?'

'No, but he *was* driving us to a wedding dress shop, so . . .!'

'That's never stopped him before!' she groans. 'When he was a limo driver he'd hit on the brides on the way to the chapel! Got lucky a few times. Wedding day nerves can really mess with your head,' she sighs. 'I was so annoyed when he found I worked here. He used to stop by all the time until we told him the shop had a new women-only policy.'

'Where do you know him from?'

'My other job. He was a former client.'

Izzy and I exchange an 'Oh my God she's a hooker!' glance.

'It's not what you think,' Cindy assures us. 'I work at this lap dance club three nights a week. It's all above board – no sex.'

'Just stripping and groin-grinding?' asks Izzy matter-of-factly.

'Pretty much. It's a classy joint. Really. And the pay's good.'

'Why do you work here, then?' asks Izzy.

'It's a family business. I came out here from Maryland for this job and my folks would ask too many questions if I left. It's all good though. I'm saving up to go travelling for six months. I want to see the rest of

America. Live a little,' she shrugs.

'I've always wondered what those lap dance clubs are like,' Izzy confesses.

'Why don't you come along?'

'Oh no! We couldn't!' I protest.

'Why not?' chorus Izzy and Cindy.

'Wouldn't it look weird? I mean, do they let women in without men?' I ask.

'Oh sure!' Cindy reassures us. 'You can even get a lap dance! A lot of the girls prefer doing women.'

Fascination has gripped Izzy. I'm surprised to find that I'm mildly curious myself.

'I'm working there later tonight if you're not doing anything,' Cindy continues. 'I'll write down directions for you, it's not far from where you're staying. Club Lap and Tickle. Just come along after 10 p.m., ask for Cinderella and they'll come find me.'

'Do people really call you that?' asks Izzy, intrigued.

'It's my real name, believe it or not. Cindy is just a lot less bother for daytime use.'

'But tonight, Matthew . . .' Izzy giggles.

'Well, you've gotta have a gimmick,' Cinderella smiles. 'I've got these fantastic Perspex stilettos for my glass slipper routine.'

The doorbell announces Layla's entrance. Judging by her red leather hotpants and flame-motif bra top, it's just possible that she, too, is a lap dancer.

'What do you think?' she asks, pirouetting on a spiked boot heel. 'I kept it on to show you! Totally got stuck to the car seat on the way over!' she says, rubbing at the indents on the back of her muscular thighs.

'It's hot!' Cindy gives her approval. 'Functional zips?'

On cue Layla unzips her hips, rips open a couple of poppers between her legs and wiggles until she's only in a sequinned G-string.

'Ta-daaa!'

We turn round in time to see a horrified mother and daughter scurrying away from the entrance of the shop.

'Oh man! Not again! Sorry, Cindy!' Layla apologises.

Cindy just giggles and introduces us.

'This is Izzy who's into the bondage and her girl friend Jamie.'

We shake hands wishing Layla would put some clothes on. Instead she bends over and rummages in her bag. Her bottom is incredible, as firm and round as two crash helmets. I see Izzy's hand go to her own, wondering if it can cope with anything as risqué as a 'butt sash'.

Layla holds up The Outfit. It looks like an unravelled mummy's bandage with buckles. 'Looks better on!' Cindy assures us, ushering Izzy to the changing room.

Apparently Layla has no need for a cubicle and a curtain. She unpings her bra top, shakes a forties-style print dress from her bag and slips on a pair of flat pumps. Tying her braided hair into a high ponytail she looks all set to go swing dancing.

'That's better!' she smiles, perching on a stool by the till.

'So, do you work at the same club as Cindy?' I ask, somewhat stumped for conversation.

'Yeah! It's a blast!'

'Have you, er, always been a, er . . .'

'Stripper? No! I came to Vegas as a dancer for one of the big production shows—'

'You were a showgirl!' I interrupt, enthralled.

'Yeah, I had plumes that dusted the ceilings, sequinned turbans, Joan Collins make-up – the works!'

'How fab!' I gush. 'Why did you leave?'

'Money. Not that the showgirls are badly paid, it's just I can make $1,000 a night at Lap and Tickle. There's only one other black girl there – we've kind of got a niche market going.'

'But . . .' I can't find the words.

'Don't I find it degrading? Not really. I've always been a bit of a deviant, so it suits me fine!'

'Is it hard to find a boyfriend who doesn't mind your job?' I ask, then apologise. 'You must get sick of people asking this kind of question.'

'No, I don't mind. I'm not really looking for a boy-friend right now. I've been married once. I don't think I'll do it again.'

'Has Cindy been married?'

'Nooo. She drives the guys crazy – that body, cutie voice saying all those naughty things. They all reckon she's a real home-cooking girl at heart. She must get proposed to once a month by guys who want to take her away from it all.'

'Is she ever tempted to take them up on their offer?'

'She doesn't trust them,' says Layla, lighting a

menthol cigarette. 'She thinks they'll lock her in a box or have her pumping out a kid every year. She's more independent than she looks.'

Searching for an ashtray, Layla continues, 'Cindy hasn't had much of an education but she wants to learn. She's always telling me she wants more. She just doesn't know what that is yet. Nobody believes that she'll really go travelling but I know she will. One day she'll just take off. I've seen the maps she's got at home, heaps of travel guides. She wants a suitcase with stickers from every state. That's her dream, not some picket fence and a guy. No offence.'

'What do you mean?'

'No offence, what with you and your friend getting married and all. Different strokes for different folks.'

I smile weakly. Getting married seems like a drag compared to Cindy's road trip. I flashback to the glorious feeling of liberation driving to Red Rock Canyon in Finn's car. Is that what Cindy is craving? Could I really have something in common with a bubblegum Bunny girl?

'I see you don't have a ring yet,' observes Layla.

'Er, no . . .' Has she sussed me?

'They do those too. Engagement rings and wedding bands. Has Cindy shown you the cabinet?'

I shake my head.

Layla dips beneath the desk and reappears with a key. 'Follow me!'

We walk behind a screen to a hidden part of the shop and she opens a Chinese-style display case. Hundreds of jewels sparkle back at us. 'The left-hand side are pretty affordable. This side gets pricey. The ruby is my favourite. It's practically heart-shaped, look!' She admires it on her hand. 'Go ahead, try one!'

I slowly trace my fingers along the velvet casing. I stop at a ring with five small diamonds in a row and intricate gold swirls cut into the band. I pluck it and place it on my wedding finger. Layla follows it with a plain gold band. I hardly recognise my hand. 'How does that make you feel?' she asks, taking a long draw on her cigarette.

I find myself adjusting my posture, standing straighter yet cockier, taking on a more knowing look. I feel smug, truth be told. The last time I did this was for a method acting exercise – I wore my granny's wedding ring for a whole day. It seemed to throb on my hand, sending the message, 'Someone wanted me so much they married me! I am loved!' The ring was like a visible seal of approval. Men would look at me and know that another man had road-tested me and given me the thumbs up.

I felt strangely assured in public places, as if the ring was a physical symbol that I was protected, that I didn't stand alone, that if you messed with me you'd be accountable to another person. I went to a bar in the evening and felt almost brazen. You can't hurt me! See! I'm not interested in you! I don't need you to like me to make me feel good. You can't trick me into wanting you and then abandon me. If you smile at me, I have the confidence to look you right in the eye. No implications, no complications. I have a safety net. If you don't smile back I just stroke the jewels on my finger and summon up the love genie in my heart. Sorted!

If I could have got away with wearing it all the time, I probably would. But I went back to my bare-fingered ways soon enough. And since then I've found that I might be yakking to some girl at a party or a work 'do' thinking how alike we are and what a riot she is and then notice a wedding ring and it would change everything. Suddenly she's not the person I thought she was. She's not like me. She's one of them. She knows something I don't. She *has* something I don't. She's on a different level and I can't see what it's all about however much I crane my neck and stand on tiptoe.

Layla's one of 'them' even though she's divorced now. But she's also a stripper, for God's sake. Talk about a different species. Men touting their wares is funny but lap dancers are lowlife slags, right? I'm not so sure. I've met two in one day and I like them both. What's going on?

'Jamie! Where are you?' It's Izzy.

We dart back to the main shop. Goosebumps aside, she looks great. Every strip of fabric is matched by a strip of flesh. She looks wild and provocative and about as unvirginal as you can get.

'It's so me!' she giggles. 'Can you put it aside?'

'Sure!' says Cindy. 'I knew it would suit you!'

'And you've got all that hair to use as a cover up if you feel too exposed,' confirms Layla, fluffing her blonde straggles. 'What's that joke I saw today? Group of guys in a tavern in olden times, one is keeping an eye out the door and he spots a naked woman approaching on a horse so he yelps, "Lady Godiva's coming!"

'And the fella behind the bar says, "Must be all those cobbled streets!"'

On that note, we head back to the hotel to face a new dress code dilemma: what to wear to a lap dance club.

'I knew I should have packed my nipple tassels,' Izzy sighs.

I only wish I could be sure she's joking.

25

Club Lap and Tickle: we pull up a chair at one of the five circular 'bigger than a podium/smaller than a dancefloor' stages dotted around the room. All eyes are on Venus, who certainly looks like she's trapped a few flies in her time. She snaps and splits and bounces in whatever direction the dollar bills are most plentiful. Izzy dares to tuck a cluster of notes in her G-string but I just peer into my drink when she comes our way. Yikes! Here she comes again . . .

She stoops down and addresses the rather nervous, besuited man sitting beside us.

'Sir, can I dirty your glasses?'

He looks down at the empty gin and tonic tumblers before him, shrugs and pushes them in her direction. 'Sure, help yourself!'

'No, I mean these glasses,' she says pointing at his black-framed spectacles. He looks bemused as she breathes heavily on the right lens and then goes cross-eyed as she lunges at him and presses her breast against it. She pulls away, winks and carries on gyrating. For a moment he just sits there. Then he removes his glasses, takes out a small cloth and, trembling slightly, holds them up to the light. A nipple print is clearly visible. He goes to wipe them clean but hesitates, looks again, shifts in his seat and puts them back on his face – another satisfied customer.

There are a good many boobs shoved in faces over the course of the evening. I didn't realise it was such an in-demand act. To be honest I hadn't really expected the punters to have that much physical contact. Although the term lap dance is fairly self-explanatory, I didn't think the girls literally sat in the blokes' laps. Call me naive, I thought a lap dance just meant a personal dance – one-*to*-one not one-*on*-one. I certainly wasn't prepared for the two-on-one option some fellas were treating themselves to.

I look around the dimly-lit but plushly decorated room swarming with nearly nude women, some of whom even have real boobs. There are several lap dances taking place right by us which is highly disconcerting. I find myself more fascinated with the men and watch their faces as they revel in erotica, embarrassingly catching a punter's eye from time to time. Then I feel bad. They didn't come here expecting to get filthy looks from women. Well, not my kind of filthy look. A lot of them are good-looking, normal guys and that depresses me. These are men with wives and girlfriends. I feel I'm spying on them being shamelessly unfaithful and I'm quietly disgusted with every man in the place. I realise this is hypocritical in view of my male stripper lustings but there really does

seem to be a distinct difference. At the Golden Guys'
show the atmosphere was euphoric, it brought out the
rowdy, giggly side in the women. I looked around the
audience and liked what I saw. Here the men seem to
be taking it far too seriously and I can't help thinking,
'You sad gits!'

One guy in particular stands out, mostly because since
we arrived, not even the women with breasts the size of
beach balls can get his attention. If anyone offers him
a lap dance he hurriedly sends them on their way so
they don't block his view. He only has eyes for Izzy.

'Is he still looking?' she asks me.

'Yup, and a big gob of saliva has just splashed on to
his shirt. It picks out the dark sweat stains under his
arms quite nicely,' I observe.

'I think he's kinda cute!' says Izzy, seductively
sucking on a straw.

'Oh God, don't encourage him!'

'Why not?' she giggles, flicking her hair back to
reveal a bare shoulder. 'He might be rich.'

'He could never be rich enough to justify that belt,'
I object. 'Or the belly that's hanging over it.'

'Look, just because you wouldn't touch him with a
deodorant stick doesn't mean he's not the man for
me!'

'You're winding me up, aren't you?' I beg. I've seen
her pick some duff guys in her time but this is a bald
patch too far.

A waitress leans between us and sets down an ice
bucket of champagne and two glasses. 'The gentleman

over there—' we don't even need to look – 'sends this over with his compliments,' she announces, sounding bored.

'Don't drink it!' I beg Izzy.

'He's harmless,' says the waitress, popping the cork. 'Enjoy!'

Izzy raises her glass at Señor Sweat and urges me to get guzzling.

'I've always wanted a man to send over champagne, how classy is that?'

'Izzy,' I say, exasperated, 'we're in a strip joint. There's nothing classy about what he's just done. A classy guy wouldn't be in here in the first place.'

Right on cue a well-respected Academy-award-winning actor and his entourage walk past our table. He is swiftly swept through to the VIP area and the girls are all a-flutter at the prospect of straddling his Armani suit.

'Yeah, it's just riff-raff in here,' Izzy smirks.

'You're actually flattered that some old guy can't take his eyes off your cleavage, aren't you?'

'With this level of competition, *yes!*' she grins, pouring herself a second glass.

Aw heck. It seems criminal to let good champagne go to waste – God knows how much they mark up a bottle of Taittinger in this joint. I take a morally-challenged sip.

'I wonder why he doesn't come over,' muses Izzy. 'I don't suppose he wants to intrude. That's nice, isn't it? Show a little respect.'

I'm just about to wonder aloud about the chances of

him having one of those spindly little director ponytails when the waitress comes back. This time with a note. Here we go . . .

'To the girl with spun gold hair!' reads Izzy. 'Well, I've got to marry him now!' she laughs, holding out the note so we both can read.

I realise you are not working tonight but I am transfixed by your beauty and your glowing presence and would like to know if you would consider just one lap dance with me. Naturally I'd be willing to pay above the going rate.
  Your devoted admirer,
  Reed Mahoney.

I finish before Izzy and watch her face for a reaction. First she looks confused, then her mouth falls open. Then she grins uncontrollably. 'Ohmigod! He thinks I'm a lap dancer!'

You'd think someone had just mistaken her for Jennifer Aniston.

As Layla sashays by, Izzy grabs her and demands to know the 'going' rate.

'For a lap dance? $20 for one song.'

'Do you ever get tips on top?'

'Oh sure. That's how they try to impress you.'

Izzy's eyes turn to saucers. 'Like, how much?'

'Sky's the limit if they like you, baby!' she grins. 'Thinking of taking it up?'

Izzy shows her the note. 'Whoa! You've got a good one there. He pays big.'

'Does he often fixate on one girl in particular?' I ask,

trying to bring a modicum of caution to the brewing insanity.

'Nope, he doesn't really have a type. He's not grabby or anything. Mostly he likes to chat. I think he's just lonesome. He's always in town on business. I've never done him so I don't know more than that. If you want to take him up on the offer, let me know. You can't do it public view because you're not an employee but I could sort something out if you like . . .'

'Okay,' Izzy nods.

'I've gotta run, I'm up on stage three next.'

Izzy ponders her predicament for some time and I can feel us sinking deeper into the underworld with every second that passes. Pammy lookalikes sidle by in pairs. A group of men get raucous and security has to retrieve one girl from an impromptu rugby scrum. We watch Layla do an erotic fire-eating act from a safe distance and then Izzy turns to me and says, 'Jamie, would you liaise with him for me?'

'Liaise as in pimp?' I clarify.

'Look, you've never judged me. Don't start now. I want to do this.'

'If my mother could see me now,' I can't help thinking. I'm even walking like Huggy Bear. Do I call her a 'ho' or a 'bitch', I wonder. Do I use her real name or go for something like Goldilocks? I try to look tough as I face him. It's hard, he has a kind face for a sad bastard.

'I've come to make the arrangements,' I sound ridiculously stilted and more Mafia than pimp.

A huge smile lights up his face. 'Then she'll do it?'

I nod.

'I haven't seen her before. Is she new?'

I nod again. The less said the better, I figure. 'If you'd like to follow me . . .'

I lead him, according to Layla's instructions, to a backroom. Not a pervy backroom, just a disused office. All the same, I feel like I'll never be clean again.

Supervised by Layla, he takes his place on the chair. Now his collar has darkened with sweat. Delicious.

Izzy slinks from the shadows like Jessica Rabbit and stands in front of him. For what seems like hours they just look into each other's eyes.

Layla shrugs when I look to her for an explanation.

I continue to watch, feeling increasingly anxious and then breathe a sigh of relief when Izzy breaks the interrogation scene pose and takes a step closer to him. Placing her hands on his quivering shoulders, she sweeps her long hair across his moist face and in return he lets out a moan that contains a strange mixture of pleasure and confusion. She's just about to straddle him when he grabs her at the elbows and blurts, 'I can't do it! I don't want you like this!'

Stumbling to his feet he stammers, 'Here take the money, I'm sorry I've inconvenienced you.'

Izzy is stunned. She looks down at the $100 bill he's crumpled into her hand and then rushes to stop him before he reaches the door.

'I don't want your money!' she says softly. Uncharacteristically.

He looks even more dismayed.

'Unless it's to buy us a drink!' she suggests.

He turns to face her, a look of hope in his eyes. She smiles kindly, taking his arm and whispering, 'Let's find a nice cosy booth.'

Layla and I are left gawping after them. 'What was *that*?' I ask.

'I don't know. Strategy?'

Back in the club, Izzy and Reed have already cracked open a fresh bottle of Taittinger so Layla suggests I hang at the bar and leave them to it.

'There is SO much I don't know about men!' I sigh, looking around the room.

'You don't want to know, believe me!' Layla groans.

'It's so weird how they have all this small talk after such an intimate act,' I marvel as a lap dancer and punter near us chat about the roadworks on the 15 freeway. 'That would just ruin the illusion for me, if some sex god started chatting about the weather or the spiralling costs of car insurance.'

'Well, like I say, a lot of them are just lonesome or don't know anyone in town so they come here for the company as much as anything.'

'Do you feel sorry for them?' I ask.

'Sometimes, but I try not to get too involved, it's just not worth the hassle.'

'Look! That guy has brought his girlfriend!' I watch a man with a beard and a stunning blonde woman with an elfin crop settle into their seats.

'Oh yeah, they're regulars. He gets a kick out of watching her get a lap dance.'

'I could never do that,' I say, horrified.

'Oh, she loves it.'

'Really?'

'Yeah, she's Danish.'

'Riiight!' I watch them for a bit and then conclude that they've probably got the best set-up in the place – they both get turned on and then they can go home and shag each other stupid, whereas all the other men here wind up skint and profoundly frustrated. Layla lights up a menthol ciggie and asks me to hold it in between puffs in case her boss catches her.

'So, I take it Izzy has a pretty open relationship with her fiancé . . .' she smirks, exhaling in the direction of Izzy, who is currently covering Reed's bald patch in kisses.

It takes me a second to realise that Layla is talking about Izzy's phantom fiancé and not Dave. Then I remember that I also claimed to have a fiancé of my own earlier in the day. I can't face further deceit so I come clean about Project Presley. When I'm done, Layla shakes her head. 'You've come all this way to find your dream guy?' I nod. 'Well, more power to ya! I hope you find him. Personally, I'm hanging out for Denzel.'

Cinderella joins us and Layla brings her up to speed, but she still looks a bit confused: 'I don't understand why you'd want an American man when you could have an English gentleman like Jeremy Northam. He was sooo debonair in *Emma*.'

I explain that Jeremy Northam is tragically not the norm and that compared to the lads and losers Izzy and I have dated, Americans seem far more glamorous and well-mannered.

'Well-mannered? You're kidding – you Brits are all tea time and minding your Ps and Qs,' Cindy informs me.

'That's like saying all Yanks gorge on hamburgers and carry handguns,' I reason, a little sorry to disillusion her. 'And anyway, we've had enough of lukewarm pints of beer, now we're after an ice-cold Bud!'

'You guys are crazy!' Layla grins. 'Let's meet up again!'

'Yeah, I'd love to hear more about living in Europe,' Cinderella sighs. 'Have you ever been to London?'

'Of course! And I'll tell you all about it, provided you trade some secrets on how to entice men!' I barter.

'Deal!' they chorus.

Numbers exchanged, the girls go back to their 'and then all my clothes fell off' routines and I persuade Reed and Izzy to make a move. Once outside it's a relief to see fully-clothed people again.

As we step out on to the pavement a limo glides up and stops directly in front of us. This is typically one of those moments where you joke, 'That'll be my ride!' Only this time it's for real. The driver tips his hat at Reed as he opens the door and invites us to get inside.

'You're sweet, Reed, but we're only around the corner, we could easily get a cab,' simpers Izzy.

'I wouldn't be able to sleep tonight if I didn't see you safely home,' he replies, helping her in. 'There are a lot of crazy people in this town.'

'But only a few of them have limos,' I think to myself

as I slide along the supple leather. It appears to be even longer on the inside and I end up so far from Izzy and Reed they look like dolls from where I'm sitting. Giving them a silly wave, I take in the luxury mahogany interior, desperate to tinker with the cut glass decanters and rattle the ice bucket. If Reed wasn't here we'd no doubt be sticking our heads through the sun roof screaming, but I'm following Izzy's nonchalant lead and stretch my arm along the smoked glass window ledge. Behind me, I sense the partition between us and the chauffeur sliding down.

'Yes, Mr Mahoney?' says the driver.

'Oh, Jamie, I think you must have accidentally pressed the call button,' Reed surmises. 'Just reach behind you and press it again, would you?'

'Oh, sorry!' I say, finding myself confronted with an array of knobs and switches. 'Um, is this it?'

We're suddenly deafened by Mariah Carey.

'Sorry!'

I try again. This time a panel rotates to reveal an elaborate computer system.

'It's on the left,' says Reed patiently.

My finger hovers nervously, if I press the wrong one the limo will probably turn into a Batmobile or I'll nuke some Eastern Bloc country. I close my eyes and press. The partition slides back into place. Phew. I sit on my hands to avoid further incident.

'Even I get confused.' Reed smiles. 'So, Jamie, Izzy says you're starting a new job next week. Sales, isn't it?'

Knowing Izzy, she's probably told him I'm chief buyer at Tiffany's so I settle for a simple, 'Yes, that's right' and shift the focus back to him with an innocuous, 'Are you based in Las Vegas?'

'No, but a lot of my work is here and I'm actually looking to buy a place at the moment. It's not a bad commute from Denver but I thought if I had my own pad here with a full wardrobe I could travel with just my briefcase!'

'It's like he's got a place in Barbados with a wardrobe full of beach clothes!' Izzy adds, trying to sound like the idea merely tickles her when I know inside she's doing a celebratory 'He's rich!' pogo.

'I'd love to take you there one day,' he says, gazing at Izzy with the kind of googly eyes usually reserved for peering into cots.

Fortunately I only have to endure this for a few minutes before we pull up outside Circus Circus. I clamber out first to let them have a private farewell exchange. The chauffeur is not a chatty fellow so I stand alongside him in silence. After ten minutes I feel like a long-suffering lady-in-waiting. Eventually Izzy emerges, realigning her clothes as she steps on to the pavement. Classy bird. Reed gives her hand a last lingering kiss and sighs, 'Until tomorrow!'

As the limo slips away into the night I turn to Izzy and say, 'We need to talk!'

'No,' she says, shimmering with excitement, 'we need to *pack*!'

26

'Welcome to the Bellagio!' says the doorman with a flourish.

You'd flourish too if you worked this entrance. It's exquisite. Above us is a canopy of green oxidised copper with filigree trimmings, beneath us a shimmering mosaic floor, and to our left is a vast pine-lined lake with fountains whooshing so high into the sky they could hose down passing aircraft. Everyone is dressed to the elevens, *at least*, and there is an excited buzz in the air.

'I feel like we're arriving at the opera!' Izzy marvels.

We push the heavy wooden rotating doors and discover an even more lavish interior. You can smell the money. And the Chanel No. 5. After Circus Circus it's intoxicating. Previously we'd been shabby wannabes coveting the glamour of others, like those imitation designer perfumes – 'If you like Elizabeth Taylor's Diamonds you'll love Cubic Zirconia' or 'If you like Estée Lauder's Beautiful you'll love She's No Oil Painting'.

I'm ashamed to acknowledge that I actually have a

mini 95-cent Confession! about my person because my bona fide bottle of Obsession! is too weighty for handbag usage. Mind you, I don't think that excuse will cut it in the Bellagio powder rooms. I can see sniffer dogs chomping into my ankles and security forced to confiscate Izzy's knock-off Prada purse.

We pause to admire the women reclining by a grand piano in full-length evening gowns and gaudy jewels. It's tea time but for every cup of lapsang souchong there's at least two glasses of champagne being guzzled.

'This is just *so* Ferrero Rocher!' Izzy giggles.

'What happens now?' I ask, momentarily distracted by a roar from the casino. A group of well-heeled men dance idiotically around the craps table and give each other high fives.

'We just check in like normal. Reed's sorted it all,' Izzy says proudly.

'And it's definitely free?'

'Don't worry, he's the real deal! He'd be here now but he's got a meeting he couldn't change cos this guy has flown in from Asia and he's only scheduled to be in Vegas for three hours.'

It's curious to hear Izzy talking so assuredly about a relative stranger, particularly because it's not just the money she's getting a kick out of. It seems there is already a bond between her and Reed.

'What does he do again?' I ask.

'Business stuff.'

'What kind of business?'

'Does it matter?' she groans, propelling me towards the check-in desk.

I can't help be suspicious – Reed does appear to be entirely guileless but what kind of man sets you up in a sumptuous suite just hours after meeting you? Last night when Izzy told me we were changing hotels I humoured her because I was fairly certain everything would be different in the cold light of day. But then Reed called at 10 a.m., just as he said he would, wanting to know what time to send the limo to pick us up.

That's when I knew we were in trouble. At first I told Izzy I was staying put and the whole thing was far too dodgy but she just carried on packing, pointing out things like 'a discounted room is great but free is better' and 'we came to Vegas for adventure and this more than qualifies' and concluding that if he is a gangster, few women are better suited to being a moll than her bad self.

There seemed unlimited pros and the only cons I could come up with were that we didn't know him well enough to trust him and that we'd feel beholden to him. Such concerns don't hold up too well somewhere as surreal as Vegas and ultimately the thought of waving her off in the limo so I could sit alone in a room with clown-motif decor seemed profoundly unappealing. Izzy threw the word 'suite' out there one more time, I caved and here we are.

Back at check-in everything is going smoothly. Baby oil smooth. When Reed's name comes up on the screen ('Ahhh, you're guests of Mr Mahoney') there seems to

240

be a rush of subservience from the staff – much clicking of fingers, a bow here, a scrape there . . .

'You don't get this kind of service at the Holiday Inn,' says Izzy, eyeing our handsome young bellman as we wait by the lifts. She then spots a white china ashtray embossed with a gold 'B' beside the house phone and sweeps it into her bag.

'From now on I'm only staying in hotels where there's stuff worth nicking,' she whispers, delighted.

'You'll need to use your key to gain access to the penthouse floor,' instructs the bellman, swiping our credit card-style room key. Our chests swell with new-found prestige. First the limo, now this. Once again screaming is inappropriate so as we soar to our giddy penthouse heights we settle for leaning into each other so hard we practically merge into Siamese twins.

'After you, ladies,' says the bellman as the lift doors open. Corridors flare off from the circular reception unit like exits from a ring road. The bellman marches on. We scurry to keep up. 'This is your suite right here!'

Your! Suite! Oh how I've longed to hear those words linked together!

He opens the door and motions for us to enter ahead of him.

Suite my arse. This is a mansion. It just happens to be on the 36th floor of a hotel.

'I'll just show you where everything is—' begins the bellman.

Izzy stops him in his tracks. 'No need!' she says, voice quavering, hand shaking as she pressed $5 into his palm. As soon as the door clicks behind him Izzy lets out the most almighty howl of victory. It would be rude not to join her.

'Look what we've got!' she says, spinning round. We hug each other and then career around the penthouse like dogs so ecstatic their owner has come home they don't know which direction to run in next.

There's a sunken cream dream lounge with a seventeen-seat sofa and fluffy papyrus reeds in a five foot vase, a full bar area in dark wood and burgundy leather, a sparkling chrome kitchen and a vast balcony with a jacuzzi and a spectacular view of the Strip. Dear God, there's even an elevator to take you to the second floor if you can't manage the sweeping shagpile staircase.

The first bedroom is warm Tuscan orange with an orgy-accommodating bed, Roman-themed antiques and a DVD player.

'Do you want this one?' Izzy enquires.

'You betcha!'

'Check out the en suite!'

'You can do laps in that bath!'

I gaze in delight at the marble-topped sink – no more cheap bottles of shampoo which barely create a froth or flat tablets of soak that flake as soon as you remove the wrapper. Here we have a full range of gorgeously-packaged goodies including dinky hair-sprays the size of Gold Spot breath sprays and a nail file in a Bellagio-emblemed sheath.

'Oooh, there's extract of clove and violet in this mouthwash!' I observe.

I'm getting far too involved in the minutiae for Izzy.

She's already screaming, 'Nooo!' from another room.

'What?'

'Nooo!' I echo when I see a fitness room stocked with exercise bikes and running machines.

Another bedroom, another bathroom and on to the master bedroom. I freeze.

'What's that? Ohmigod! Someone's left their stuff here!'

I fling open the wardrobe and my heart sinks. There's a row of hideously garish suits and a rainbow array of silk shirts. They may be lacking tell-tale sweat marks but I think I can guess who they belong to.

I turn around. Izzy is standing nervously in the doorway.

'I didn't think you'd come if I told you,' she says sheepishly.

'Told me what, Izzy?' I want to hear her say it.

'That we'd be sharing with Reed.' she grimaces.

I close the wardrobe doors. The lime and lilac number is hurting my eyes.

Izzy senses my burgeoning fury and babbles: 'It's not like we're all stacked on bunk beds together – there's three bedrooms, three bathrooms, two different lounge areas – we'll have the run of the place . . .'

'But it just ever so slightly changes *everything*, doesn't it?' I roar.

'Isn't that what we wanted? Things to change,' she says defensively.

'Yes, but that's hardly the point, is it? We're supposed to be in this together. You only told me half the story!'

'Would you have come if I'd told you the truth?'

'No way!' I bark.

'Well, then I'm glad I lied,' she pouts. 'Look at what you'd be missing! This isn't the kind of upgrade you get every day.'

She's not kidding. I never thought I'd experience this level of luxury in my life. But I don't know if I want it like this. I feel totally tricked and betrayed. Izzy has altered the entire dynamic of our holiday without even discussing it with me and though it hurts me to admit it, I'm getting a strong sense that if I walked out the door right now, she wouldn't follow. I have to try to convince her to see sense: 'It's one thing Reed getting us a room, but moving in with him . . .' I sigh. 'Come on, Izzy, this is crazy.'

'Oh for God's sake! It's not like we're on a remote island with him! If he gets weird we'll just leave!' Izzy is now as exasperated as me and snaps, 'It's not like you have to sleep with him!'

'But you will, you know that, don't you?' I warn her.

She gives me a big, filthy grin. Apparently that wouldn't be a problem.

'At least let's stay a couple of nights,' she reasons.

I feel like I'm ankle-deep in quicksand. How can I be considering staying? Then again, how can I leave her here? What is up with this town?

'The words "gifthorse" and "mouth" keep springing to mind,' I sigh, giving in. 'And like you say, if it goes pear-shaped we'll just check out.'

'Yayyyy!' Izzy cheers, giving me a hug. 'Let's make the most of every minute!'

We spend the next half an hour exploring our new pad, opening every drawer, flicking every switch, turning every tap. We're just seeing whether I can run down the spiral staircase quicker than Izzy can descend in the lift when the phone rings. We both freeze as we've been found out and our time is up.

'What do you think?' asks Izzy.

'Answer it – it could be Reed.'

It is. Izzy falls back into the velvety caress of the sofa and breathes into the receiver. I decide to start unpacking but I've only just released the fasteners on my suitcase when Izzy appears in the doorway.

'He'll be up in five minutes!'

'Where was he calling from?'

'The lobby! He didn't want to burst in on us! Isn't that sweet?'

I can't help but smile. 'If I didn't know you were just a conniving little gold-digger I'd think you actually liked him!'

'Gotta put some make-up on!' she trills, scooting to her room.

I'd love to know what's really going on in Izzy's mind, but she rarely expresses her feelings for men. I'm always in on the plotting to get whoever she's after and she doesn't usually shy away from graphic sex details but there's scarcely ever any sentiment on show. I think this is mostly because she drops out of my life during the initial intense three or four weeks of her relationships. I don't take it personally. If someone is really ambitious you don't begrudge them putting in extra hours at work, you accept that you'll see less of them while they are angling for a promotion. It's the same with Izzy, only men are her career. When a good one comes along she stops clockwatching and really loses herself in her work. I just hope she knows what she's getting herself into with this one.

Reed rings the doorbell before entering. We run to greet him but instead we're confronted with a vast bouquet of flowers with legs. I accept them graciously. Kidding! Izzy squeals in delight and kisses his bald patch.

'Have you got everything you need?' he asks earnestly. 'If you want anything at all just say the word, I'll arrange it.'

We've come from a room that didn't even have tea-and coffee-making facilities. Does he really think we'll be lacking anything here?

Izzy takes one of the long-stemmed roses, snaps and twists it below the bud and carefully feeds it through Reed's buttonhole. He looks on the verge of tears but manages to offer, 'Champagne?'

'Ooooooh! Mmmm!' we reply.

He walks to the bar and opens a fridge entirely stocked with bottles of Bollinger. Pouring two glasses he walks Izzy's up to her, rapt in her gaze. He extends one hand holding the other glass in my vague direction, never taking his eyes off her. To be a gooseberry I believe you have to feel in the way. Right now I'm not sure I even exist.

'Mind if I drink this while I unpack?' I ask.

No uproarious objections are raised so I return to

my room, which is so beautiful it hurts. That's the trouble with luxurious hotel suites – it's too much bliss for one person and you start wishing the fluffy white robe came with a gorgeous man inside. I flick on the TV to stop my thoughts turning back to Christian and mindlessly channel hop until I'm all out of champagne. Before you can say Kir Royale Izzy arrives with reinforcements.

'You may as well finish the bottle – plenty more where that came from!' she grins. 'Reed is just taking a shower and then he's booked a table for an early dinner at a swanky place called Aureole. It's meant to be fantastic. All the wine is stacked on this tower in the middle of the restaurant and when you order this person in a catsuit abseils on a rope to get your order, like something out of *Mission Impossible*!'

It sounds fantastic but I feel the need to be alone. Alone by myself that is, not alone at a dinner table with Reed and Izzy.

'Would you be really pissed off if I didn't go?' I ask.

'What's the matter? Is it the Zane situation?'

'Partly, but it's also that we've been out every night and this place is so gorgeous I can't bear to leave. I really fancy just hanging out here.'

I can see Izzy weighing up the situation – should she bully me into coming or grab the quality time with Reed.

'Well, if you're sure. You can order anything you like from room service. Reed said . . .'

'Okay. Don't worry about me, I'll be fine!'

I feel myself putting on a brave face even though my

circumstances are hardly tragic. Turns out you can't sit in a bubble bath sipping champagne and think, 'Poor me!' no matter how hard you try.

I wait with a simmering sense of anticipation for two voices to call, 'Bye, Jamie! Have fun!' and then rise up from the tub. Wrapping myself in the long robe I romp around the penthouse with newfound awe, leaving a trail of gently popping bubbles behind me. For one night all this is mine.

I turn on the stereo and dance over to the fridge. '*Just help yourself*,' I sing, merrily popping the cork and taking a ceremonial swig from the bottle! I swirl around the room toasting every arabesque and archetrave and then swan out to the balcony. In the distance I can see Excalibur's fairytale castle, but it is I who feels like a princess in a turret.

I sigh, misty-eyed. So this is what money can buy? Wow! Finally I see what all the fuss is about. I feel more refined just by association with this level of wealth. What if it were really mine? I close my eyes and imagine this is my penthouse, my furnishings, my champagne. I feel more glamorous, more composed, more powerful instantly.

I always thought I would be rich. But then I turned twenty-five and found myself still shopping at New Look and realised things weren't going quite according to plan. Probably because I never actually had one. I thought it would somehow just happen, and I suppose that in a way it has. Not that any of this is mine. It's just an illusion. I don't even have a credit card at the moment and yet look at me! I've really gone and done it now. I've had a taste of the dream.

Staring down the Strip I feel a rush of senti-mentality. Look at this place, would you? All those gorgeous shimmering lights, all these gorgeous once-in-a-lifetime memories being formed. I feel alive. This is what life should be about – champagne, excess and falling in love. I'm suddenly gripped with impatient determination to share this with as many people as possible. I've got to get Amanda and Colin over. And my mum! She has to come this very instant! I can just imagine the rapture on her face.

I rush back in the room and fall upon the desk. I'm going to write to her right now! The words spill out on to the page. As does my champagne. Bugger.

To my beautiful beautiful mother! We've left Butlins and now we're at the Ritz! (new address and phone/fax numbers at the top of the page!). I feel so at home here! So right! Are you sure I'm not the product of an illicit affair with a billionaire playboy?! If you're wondering how we got so sumptuously upgraded I just want to say that Pretty Woman *was based on a perfectly acceptable premise! Girls really do get plucked from the street and set up in hotel suites bigger than our house. Although you've just got to leave any expectations of him looking like Richard Gere at the check-in desk! I was wary at first but if you could see this place! Let me rephrase that – if you could see this palace!*

I can so picture you sipping a pre-dinner cocktail in your gold crêpe dress! They have fountains here that would make you cry. They sway and spray in time to the music, great powerful bursts rocketing into the sky. It's magnificent! We loved the Pavarotti routine but what got me was Lionel Ritchie's 'All Night Long'. Do you remember dancing to that in the living room and Dad came home and told us to turn 'that racket' down and you just put the needle back to the beginning of the record because you said he'd ruined it for us? Reckless woman! Be that brave again! Come to Vegas! Please!! I don't care what excuse you use to drag Dad over. Tell him anything! Tell him I'M GETTING MARRIED!

I stop suddenly and look at the words dominating the page: I'M GETTING MARRIED! Would that be so hard for the folks back home to believe? Marriage runs in the family, after all. And Acting As If worked for Izzy. (Rich? Check. Older? Check. Obsessed? Does the phrase 'love slave' mean anything to you?) It couldn't hurt to try. And if it got my mum to Vegas . . .

There's this wonderful boy. No – man. *There's this wonderful man.* Better already. I duck and dive as clichés fly at me. How can I make this sound authentic? How can I convince myself? *He's simply the best. Better than all the rest. Better than anyone I've ever met.* I realise I'm just transcribing the Tina Turner lyrics serenading me from the stereo. *I really hope you like him. He's so unlike all my other boyfriends* (with the exception of Christian he'd have to be or I'd never consider marrying him!). I hark back to Izzy's list: *a little bit off-the-wall and unconventional with a heart of gold.* I smile. He sounds lovely. *I can't wait for you to meet him.* (I can't wait to meet him myself!) *I realise this is sudden, I've only been gone a week, but apparently you can hurry love after all!*

The words continue to flow though I can no longer focus on them. When I reach the end of the page I squiggle a signature, grab the keycard and rush out the door. I'm at reception before I realise I'm still in the bathrobe. The two male (wouldn't they be?) staff don't bat an eyelid.

'I need thish faxed!' God, I sound drunk.

'Certainly ma'am.'

'The number is on the back of the page,' I say, gripping the countertop.

'Thank you. Is there anything else we can do for you this evening?'

I ponder for a second and then say, 'I need chocolate. Quite urgently.'

'Just around here . . .'

He leads me to a display unit. Five exquisitely piped gourmet chocolates sit on a doily.

'I may need more than this,' I gravely inform him.

'Let me see what I can do.' He nods to his second in command who instantly reappears holding a beautifully packaged, two-tiered box of chocolates. Bliss. I slur my appreciation and turn to leave. All the corridors look alike and I feel like Alice in Wonderland after too many Drink Me potions.

'Ma'am?'

'Um, I can't remember where I came from . . .'

27

I awake groaning. Is it any wonder? Only a handful of praline truffles and violet cremes to soak up two bottles of Bollinger. I hear another groan but this time it's not from me. I whip my head to the right, half-expecting to see a groggy naked receptionist, but the bed is empty. There it is again. Louder and more urgent. It's coming from across the hall. It must be Reed. He seems to be suffering badly. To many *Mission Impossible* bottles of wine, I suppose. I get up to clean my teeth. And now that I'm closer to the door I realise that's no groan of suffering.

As the erotic soundtrack coming from the bedroom reaches Scandinavian porn level, I try not to listen but there's something about sexual sound effects that make one's ears prick up like an extra alert guard dog. Worse still, pheromones begin seeping around me like insidious curls of smoke from a Marlboro. Passive sex – it may not be as bad for your lungs as passive smoking but it sure messes with your head. At least this time I'm not trying to get to sleep alongside the belly to belly trampolining – all too often I've found myself involved in a bizarre game of tug-of-war over the bedsheet and Izzy always has an extra member yanking on her team.

The worst time was when we were crashing at our friend Tony's place in London – he had stayed in working while we partied and was already asleep when we staggered back to the bedroom with a guy named Phil in tow. At this point it wasn't absolutely clear which of us was destined for a night of sin and believe me if it had been a question of who had abstained so long they couldn't even identify His 'n' Her sexual organs then he would have chosen me. But it soon became apparent that Izzy's superior cleavage had won the day and – seeing as Tony was already occupying the sofa – the gracious loser thing to do was to feign instant exhaustion and fall into a Rumpelstiltskin deep sleep.

Only Mr Sandman wasn't interested in my company either so I just lay there, eyes wide shut, cringing and dejected.

Remember that word game where you alternate fortunately/unfortunately clauses? The situation went something like this:

Fortunately there's a double bed.

Unfortunately there's three of us.

Fortunately only two of the three will be having sex.

Unfortunately I am not one of the two.

Fortunately I really need my sleep.

Unfortunately I don't stand a chance of getting any.

Fortunately she's not a screamer.

Unfortunately the bed is not the type with

individually pocketed springs they demonstrate on TV by dropping a bowling ball on one side of the mattress leaving the skittles upright on the other.

Fortunately there are no bowling balls or skittles in bed with us (I'm grasping at straws now).

Unfortunately his elbow or some angular body part is digging rhythmically in my back.

Fortunately my friend now owes me Big Time. Especially when, the morning after, our host Tony finds our three-in-a-bed body collage and the not-so-great-now-he's-sated Phil has to be passed off as my conquest on account of my mate fancying Tony.

There are few things worse than people thinking you've had the best sex in the history of bouncing bedsprings when you in fact spent all night performing a balancing trick perched on the very edge of the mattress with one hand on the bedside table for support. You can't even pick up any good performance tips this way.

I climb back into bed to peruse the room service menu. Breakfast. Let me see . . .

Waffles? On no, I couldn't stomach the syrup. *Grits?* As appetising as it sounds, I think not. *Heuvos Ranchos.* If I only knew what it was . . . I lean across to the phone and punch in the extension. I hear a woman's voice say my name. That's efficiency for you.

'Yes, hello, I'd like the Spanish omelette with hash browns and a glass of orange juice, please.'

'What size orange juice?' the voice giggles.

'Oh! You're English! Large, please.'

'Jamie, it's your mother! Are you all right?'

It takes me a good minute to realise my mum is on the phone from England and not working in the Bellagio kitchens.

'Mummm! Hiiii!' I squeal. 'Sorry about that – I've only just woken up!'

'I suppose there was lots of champagne last night!'

'Yes, there was!' How does she know?

'Well, you had reason to celebrate!'

'I know, isn't it amazing!'

'I always knew he'd find you in the end! I just never thought it would happen this fast!'

What's she talking about? She can't mean Reed.

'So what's his name? This miracle fiancé of yours?'

Fiancé? Oh no. Oh NO! I scrunch my eyes in horror. The fax. *I'm Getting Married. This wonderful man.* I can't even remember what else I wrote and the incriminating page is nowhere in sight.

'Darling, are you there? I just asked his name!'

When people in films are put on the spot like this they always look around frantically and fall on the first brand name or newspaper headline they see. Before you know it you're calling yourself Mrs Doubtfire.

'Hold on, Mum, let me just get my water . . .' I lunge for the remote and flick on the TV. Kermit? That'll never fly. Hulk Hogan? This isn't helping . . . Come on! Come on! All these channels have got to be useful for something . . .

'Jamie?' I hear my mother's voice just as I hit an old episode of *Joni Loves Chachi*. That'll have to do.

'Scott. His name is Scott.' (What, did you think I was going to say Chachi?)

'Scott what?'

'Yes.'

'What's his surname?'

'All in good time!' I laugh in what I hope is an easy-going, what's-the-rush? manner.

'Will his parents be attending the wedding? Where's he from? What does he do?'

My mum quite understandably has a million questions and all I'm capable of is Acting As If I have amnesia.

'He must be terribly rich if he's putting you up in such a posh hotel!'

'Actually,' I interrupt. On second thoughts I better not explain about Reed in case my dad feeds the info back to Izzy's mum. Instead I just make a non-committal noise. I feel terrible. Deceiving my poor mum. Not that she seems to mind too much – she's busily chatting away despite my lack of input.

'. . . and who'd have thought both my daughters would get married in one year!'

'You haven't told Nadine, have you?' I panic.

'I haven't spoken to anyone yet – I just got in from shopping and found your fax.'

It's not too late to stop the rot. Speak now! the rational side of my brain urges.

'Your father will have to eat his words. Your trip has been a success after all.'

Uh-oh. Wavering.

'And what will Nadine say? She's not in the best

spirits at the moment – she's having all sorts of problems with her wedding dress – ripped one of the seams in a trying-on session the other day. Says it's shoddy workmanship but I think she's put on some weight. It's all those wedding cake samples she's been trying . . .'

'Mum . . .'

'Yes, love?'

'If I do get married, um, here, would you come over?'

'Just try to stop me! I'd have to give them a week's notice at work but you weren't planning anything for at least ten days, were you?'

I can't answer. All I know is that I want my mum here more than anything else in the world. I mean, really, what's the worst that could happen if she did come? She arrives and I tell her my 'fiancé' has dumped me and run off to Niagara Falls with a showgirl and then she has the holiday of a lifetime. Dad will never treat her to this kind of luxury but I can.

'Book your flight now!' I insist.

'Well, you know the travel section in the *Sunday Times* has all sorts of flights listed, I'll look tomorAAAGH!' She suddenly screams.

'Mum, what is it?'

'I forgot to tell you! Yesterday's *Express & Echo* – your feature was in it!'

'Really?' I cry, delighted. 'How did it look?'

'Just wonderful. They used the picture of the MGM lions really big and the headline said: "The Mane Attraction in Las Vegas!"'

'I wrote that! That's my line!' I beam.

'Amanda phoned to get your address so she could send you some copies but I guess now she can just bring them out with her – I presume she's invited . . .'

'Not yet, but she will be.' Uh-oh – back to the phantom wedding – can't we just talk about the article some more?

'Oh darling! I can't wait to see you! All in white! That's if they wear white in Las Vegas . . .'

'They do!' I do! Oh God!

'And what does Izzy think of all this?'

'She thinks it's a great idea!'

'So do I! Everyone is too cautious by half these days. If you love each other why the hell not? And you do, don't you?'

'What?'

'Love each other . . .'

I take a breath but Mum gasps, 'Oh! That's your father coming in the door! Listen, big kiss and hug to you both. I'll give you an update tomorrow, sweetheart.'

'Love you, Mum!'

'And I love you, darling. Bye!'

I replace the receiver. What a mess. All I wanted was an omelette.

I don't end up eating until 2 p.m. (I fell back to sleep after talking to Mum and had frantic dreams of The Fonz breaking up a fight between Scott Baio and Christian.) Reed has been out since midday at another mysterious meeting and I join Izzy on the balcony for some eggs – sunny side up in 90-degree heat.

258

'You can't beat wearing sunglasses to breakfast. Isn't this unbelievable?' she says, admiring the white linen tablecloth adorned with fresh flowers and silver cutlery.

'Oh my God!' she suddenly grabs my arm. 'You'll never guess what Reed said this morning!'

'What?'

'That he'd willingly pay me whatever I was earning as a lap dancer if I promised never to go back to Club Lap and Tickle!' she grins.

'No!' I laugh.

'What do you think about that – I'm going to be paid to stop doing something I never did in the first place!'

'You're going to take the money?' I cry incredulously.

'I'd be a fool not to – it's a drop in the ocean to him anyway.'

'Yes, but, isn't it like him paying you to sleep with him?' I suggest, concern mounting.

'Not really. I made it clear to him I'd do that anyway. I think he sees it as a kind of business transaction. As far as he's concerned, he's asking me to give up a salary so he's compensating me financially.'

'Excuse me for stating the obvious, but you're *not* giving up a salary.'

'You know that and I know that,' she winks. 'Anyway, he's used to making deals with money. It's no big thing.'

'Don't you think it would be better to come clean with him?'

'I thought about that but I think he likes the idea of rescuing me from sin. Don't look at me like that! What would you do if Enrique Iglesias asked you to accompany him on a world tour?'

'I can't see the connection!'

'Well, you'd have to give up your job to go with him and there would be no way you could work being in a different city every night. He's rich, you're poor. It would be perfectly natural for him to pay.'

'I see you've given this some thought,' I sigh. There's no point in discussing it further. Sometimes I think Izzy should have been a lawyer.

I watch her blob a dollop of ketchup on to her plate. 'He's completely self-made, you know – brought up in a rough part of Philadelphia, parents dirt poor, lived off economy vats of sloppy peanut butter. But he has always been a bit of an entrepreneur – started selling revamped cars he rescued from the scrapyard from the age of fourteen. Started work in an office at sixteen. It was always his dream to be a flash business-man in a suit. He didn't have a good education but he's read all these books on manners and creating a polished image and it's paid off. Now he's bought his parents a big house in the posh part of town and he flies all round the world doing deals,' sighs Izzy. 'The only thing that's missing is a woman to share all his wealth with. Do you know, he thinks having an English wife is the epitome of class? I know I'm no Natasha Richardson but I don't think he can tell the difference. Do you think they make bustiers in tweed?'

Some people might think Izzy is only into Reed for his

money – no really! But she deserves more credit than that. Her men may not be good-looking but they have good hearts and she's really come up trumps with Reed – she can see that he will slavishly adore her, elevate her to goddess status and probably commission portraits of her. You can't knock her knack for finding men who are looking to love one woman for the rest of their life. Men who will always put her as their number one priority. If only the feeling were mutual.

Anyway, I'm in no position to criticise anyone. I take a deep breath and tell Izzy about the drunken 'I'm getting married!' fax and the following dig-myself-deeper conversation with my mum. She just wrinkles her tanned nose and laughs.

'You always say you work better under pressure. Your hubby-finding deadline has just been brought forward, that's all.'

'Did I mention that he has to be called Scott?'

'What?'

'I told her my fiancé's name was Scott.'

'Please tell me you didn't also say he had one green eye, one blue and could speak seventeen languages?'

'No,' I say sheepishly. 'All I said was Scott.'

'Ah, it could be worse. Scott Baio. Scott Bakula. Who was that surfy boy from *Neighbours*?'

'Scott Michaels?'

'That's it. Um, Scott of the Antarctic. Great Scott . . .'

I look at Izzy. Other than the mascara she never seems to remove, she's make-up free and never looked so pretty. This heat would give anyone rosy cheeks but she's shimmering rather than sweating.

'Perhaps Scott could be his last name – Ridley Scott, George C. Scott, Douglas Scott . . .'

'Who on earth is Douglas Scott?' I ask.

'Inventor of the double-decker bus.'

'Oh. Right.'

'I wouldn't worry,' she smiles contentedly. 'With any luck you'll be as lucky as me.'

And with that Reed lumbers on to the balcony, causing the sun to recoil at the dazzling yellow suit he's sporting. He casts a buttery glow upon Izzy as he leans over and drops an envelope on to her lap. She scrabbles to open it and then whoops, 'Guess what we've got tickets to!'

'What?' I ask.

'Cirque du Soleil!'

Izzy and I shriek girlishly and exchange a hug. Reed looks pleased but bemused.

'I guess they must be good, I'd never heard of them until yesterday.'

'We were walking past the theatre downstairs and I told Reed about when we went to see them perform at the Albert Hall on our twenty-third birthday!' explains Izzy. 'Remember how mind-blowing it was?'

How could I forget? John Cleese was in the audience and got picked on during a brilliant comedy mime sketch. My favourite thing was the bungee trapeze. It made my heart soar and my stomach flip. I'd never seen such bendy people in my life! Or such strong arms – there was a group of gymnasts who could hold themselves out from a pole in a horizontal line and then hoik themselves upwards, bodies still erect. The show made me feel that there was real magic in the world and revived all those childhood dreams of running away to join the circus. I can't think of a better pep-up so I'm thrilled.

'I bought a fourth so you could bring a friend,' Reed smiles.

'A friend?' I repeat. What am I going to do? Call up David Cassidy and see if he can get a night off from serenading Sheena Easton at the Copa?

Izzy senses I'm about to make an excuse and hisses, '$100 a pop, non-refundable. Don't even think it.'

'Thank you! Gosh! I'm just not sure who I'll bring . . .' I mutter.

'What about one of the Golden Guys?' she suggests.

'On a Saturday night? They're working.'

'Oh yeah. I suppose Cindy and Layla will be too,' she adds.

'Yup.' I nod.

'Finn?'

'I thought you hated him?'

'It's a show. It's not like we have to talk to him. Besides it's called *O* as in "*eau*" – "a show on, above and under water",' she quotes from the leaflet. 'Right up his stream!'

'I don't know,' I sigh. Finn seems inexorably connected to Zane and is thus a source of pain and embarrassment to me.

'It would be the perfect thank you for taking you to Red Rock Canyon,' Izzy suggests.

Oh that's low, selling it as simple good manners.

'Caesar's Palace is next door, you know,' she

continues. 'You could go to the aquarium and ask him right now.'

The thought of the tranquil fish tank certainly appeals. And I guess I wouldn't mind seeing him again. I got quite a boost from being with him last time, perhaps he can help me get back on track again. Let's face it, anything is better than watching Izzy feed Reed. She just licked a dribble of ketchup from his chin, for God's sake.

'I'll be back in an hour,' I tell them.

'No rush. The show's at 7.30 p.m. so as long as you're ready to go downstairs at 7 p.m . . .'

'Okay! Bye!'

No reply. I turn back to where they are staring googly-eyed at each other.

'Have a good afternoon,' I call.

Nothing.

'Hey, Izzy – why not show Reed that trick where you make a bikini out of two grapefruit halves . . .'

Nothing again. It must be love.

I feel a little nervous as I approach the aquarium. It's only been three days since I was in Finn's dungarees but so much has happened I feel like a different person – and a very confused, hungover one at that. Mercifully the dappled light of the aquarium has a soothing effect and I stand for a moment, watching the sway of the plantlife.

Suddenly there's a surge of interest inside and outside the tank as Finn eases into the water. Feeding time! I move closer to the glass. As Finn swims over in my direction he looks up and his eyes flash blue like searchlights in the water. I hadn't noticed how bright and clear they were until now. He waves. All the little kiddies wave back.

All the little kiddies and me.

I motion that I'll be in the Cheesecake Factory, and he gives me the okay signal. I watch for another ten minutes, wanting to check on the stubby loner Cowfish. He's still puttering around doing his impressions of a nubbly yellow gourd, bless him.

Over at the restaurant I opt for a booth, a piece of cheesecake and a steamed almond milk. When the waitress returns with my order she tells me she loves my accent and begs me to say something else to her. In my best Queen's English I ask her if she thinks I'm the kind of girl she could imagine marrying a man named Scott. She looks perplexed but is spared having to answer by Finn's arrival.

'I thought you'd gone!' he beams, sliding alongside me.

'Gone where?' I ask.

'Home, I guess. I rang Circus Circus and they said you'd checked out.'

'Yeah, we've moved. To the Bellagio!'

'Oooh! Get you!' he laughs. 'Did you get lucky at the tables?'

'We just got lucky, full stop! Well, Izzy did. She met this rich guy . . .'

'The Elvis impersonator?'

'Oh no, this one looks more like The Colonel! His name is Reed. He's about fifty. We met him at, um,

265

oh! a club and he invited us to stay in his penthouse.'

Finn raises an eyebrow.

'Whatever way I tell this Izzy and I are going to sound like prostitutes, aren't we?'

'Yup!' he laughs. 'I've long suspected your newspaper article was just a smokescreen.'

I giggle. 'Actually I'm here to offer you a chance to get in on the act too!'

'Group sex isn't really my bag,' he smiles ruefully.

'Boy, did I misread you!' I joke. 'No, really, what are you doing tonight?'

'What exactly are you proposing, Miss Miller?'

'Well, Reed has bought tickets to see *O* and he's got a spare and I was wondering if you wanted to join us? For free. Well, that's to say the ticket is free but you'll have to pay if you expect me to talk to you!'

'Naturally!' he laughs. 'What is the current word rate?'

'I'll do you a discount if you order whole conversations in advance!'

'Do I get my money back if you bore me?' he teases.

'You don't need to worry about that – satisfaction is guaranteed!'

'That's what all the hookers say!'

I flick half a forkful of cheesecake at him and he catches it in his mouth like a sealion.

'Mmm, Kahlua Almond Fudge, if I'm not mistaken!'

I smile at him for a second. Maybe those waitresses at Red Rock Canyon were on to something – he's quite a cutie even with those scuba mask indents on his face. At least I wouldn't be turning up with a complete trog on my arm.

'So what do you think?' I ask.

'I still prefer the Chocolate Mocha Java.'

I roll my eyes. 'About tonight!'

'Hmmmm,' he muses.

'Don't worry if you can't,' I say breezily, 'there's plenty more aquarists in the sea!'

'I'd love to!' he grins. 'It's really sweet of you to invite me.'

'It is, isn't it?' I sigh.

'So, what have you been up to since I saw you last?'

Just trying on wedding dresses, getting drunk and lying to my mother, I think.

'Not a lot,' I reply. 'I met Mia . . .'

He nods. 'I was out with her and Zane last night. Sickening, aren't they?'

I smile and carefully form the words, 'She's very pretty.'

'If you like that kind of thing.'

God I love it when men dismiss goddesses in that way!

'Do you want anything?' I ask as the waitress glides by, eyeing me strangely.

'No, I'm fine. I can't stay. I've got a hot date to get ready for!'

I smile, surprised at how delighted I am.

'Where shall I meet you?' he asks, getting up to leave.

'Come to the box office at 7 p.m. I'll be wearing a pink carnation.'

'In your teeth or behind your ear – I have to know.'

'I haven't decided yet, I may just leave you a trail of petals to follow!'

'On a casino carpet? I don't stand a chance!'

Finn is no Zane but at least he's a laugh. I'm still grinning when the waitress returns, looking deadly serious.

'You know, I got a couple of the other girls to look you over and we see you more with a Ben than a Scott. Or maybe a Nick.'

I look at her in wonder. 'Thank you, that's been most insightful.'

'No problem!' she says, handing me the bill.

28

It's about 6 p.m. when I get back to the room and
discover that Reed has been well and truly Izzied. The
wispy strands of hair at the side of his head have been
shorn into a buzzcut and gone are his beloved
radioactive colour combinations, leaving him top to
toe in classic navy.

'Wow! Reed! You look great!' Not something I ever
expected to hear myself say, let alone mean.

'I would never have thought of wearing a tie the
same colour as the shirt but if you're sure, angel . . .'

'You look a million dollars!' Izzy reassures him,
casting a subversive wink at me. 'We went shopping . .
.'

'What are you wearing?' I ask. She's still in her
bathrobe though her hair has been tonged into spirals.

'I need you to help me get into it!' she says, leading
me to the bedroom. Draped over a chair is the most
exquisite periwinkle satin dress.

'I don't want to mess up my hair. It took me bloody
hours.'

She reaches her arms upwards as I stand on the bed

and ease the dress over her head. It's cut on the bias and slinks seductively to a diagonal hem. The straps are blue-hued jewels. And to top it all she's wearing girl's shoes.

'I can't believe it!' I gasp as she tiptoes into a pair of strappy silver heels.

'This is a man who likes to shop. He also likes toes – don't laugh. My days of clompy boots may be over!'

'Izzy, you look beautiful, really. You'll have to put a sheet over yourself during the show or Reed will miss the whole thing.'

Izzy beams at me. 'What are you going to put on?'

I suddenly feel at a slight disadvantage, not having been shopping with someone else's platinum AmEx this afternoon. If I wear my usual matt black I'll just feel like a scene-shifter next to iridescent Izzy.

'I'm not sure. I'd better go and have a look,' I say, as if it's perfectly possible that I've overlooked some utterly stunning outfit in my wardrobe.

Cheap. Cheap. Cheap. I've laid out all my clothes and the bedspread is the only piece of quality material in sight. My outfits all smack of Girls' Night Out. The only item that doesn't require dancing round a handbag is my vintage dress. It's ruched red chiffon with black polka dots. I bought it to go to a *Grease* party but I got flu and I've never had occasion to wear it since. In my mind it is essentially fancy dress. Would I look a total fool in it? I tip out my toilet bag. If I brought the matching nail varnish I'll go for it. Uh-oh. Here it is. Scarlet Woman. Well, this is Vegas – anything goes . . .

I'm thinking old-fashioned glamour. I'm thinking Liz Taylor in *Cat on a Hot Tin Roof*. But the mirror refuses to lie to me no matter how much I asphyxiate myself with hairspray. I remember someone once saying they thought Joan Collins must comb her hair with an egg whisk. I can relate to that now. In a bid to distract onlookers from my hair, I twist up the bright red lipstick. Do I dare? I always find bright colours such high maintenance – they either fray or smudge and one sip of anything and I'm left with nothing but a hard lipline. Oh well. I've done my nails now and it is a perfect match . . . I paint and blot, paint and blot just as the magazines advise, and then stand back and look at my reflection. Collagen smollagen! My already marshmallowy mouth now looks as big and squishy as a bouncy castle. No time to change anything now, I squeeze into my mum's first-time-round black kitten heels and scurry into the lounge.

'Oh my God! It's Rizzo!' Izzy rushes over and rotates me by the cinched-in waist. 'Isn't this the *Grease* dress?'

'Yes, but I don't want to look like a reject extra – is my hair too retro buffy?' I ask.

'No, it's fine. I like it big. The person sitting behind you won't thank you but hey, *there are worst things you could do* . . .' she says, breaking into song.

'If I've gone too far, just say it,' I plead with her to be honest. Finn may be just a friend but he's still a heterosexual male and I don't want to look completely unfanciable.

'No, really, for someone with short hair you look good!' Izzy teases.

'We really should go, girls, it's after 7 p.m.,' hurries the new, improved Reed. 'Your friend will be waiting.'

As we descend in the busy lift I look at the outfits the other women are sporting – a frilly blouse that reminds me of my New Romantic days, a Pucci print dress, a sequinned boob tube and a young girl in combats and a tank top. If we shuffled around we could do a fashion-through-the-ages spread starting with me in the fifties and concluding with Izzy as Millennium Babe. Or at least Millionaire's Babe.

Walking to the theatre I feel even more self-conscious. Everyone else looks so sophisticated. Is it my imagination or are people whispering and giggling to their friends as I walk by? I'm sure I hear, 'What, no Kenickie?'

Izzy, on the other hand, is prompting the lust of men and the wrath of their girlfriends as they turn back to gawp at the satin clinging to the curve of her bum. Reed doesn't know whether to be proud or jealous. I see at least three other Izzy/Reed combos as we walk through the casino, but most of the other Reeds seem to be keen to dispel the notion that it's a father/daughter thing by groping the Izzy in between hands of blackjack.

As we near the box office I spot Finn and get a nervous fluttering in my stomach. He's leaning against a pillar in a slim-cut bottle-green suit and seems to be getting a lot of looks himself. Could this be because he has a pink carnation tucked behind his ear?

'Hey, you look—'

'Don't!' I beg.

'But—'

'Please don't say anything. No, it's not a wig. Yes, I should be at the Rydell High Dancethon. Okay?'

He chuckles, shaking his head and offers me his arm. We walk over to Reed and Izzy. Introductions are made. Tickets are taken. Bums are seated.

As I flick through the programme, Finn points to a male performer in a red frock coat and white suspenders and tells me, 'I'm so glad I didn't wear that tonight – could you imagine the embarrassment of seeing someone on stage in the same outfit as you?'

It's still a little too raw for me to laugh about clothing but I appreciate the attempt at humour.

'I haven't seen that ring before,' I say, pointing to Finn's hand.

'I don't wear it during the day, I'm afraid one of the fish will suck it off my finger. Zane made it for my last birthday.'

I inspect the mermaid curling around his middle finger. 'How unusual, she has short hair.'

'Well, yeah, that's because we had this drunken conversation one night when I was arguing that as pretty as long hair is, it could easily strangle you underwater and I thought it would be more practical for mermaids to have cropped hair.'

'Like Madonna in the "Cherish" video?'

'The one at the beach with the mermen?'

'And the little merboy! Yes! I love that video.'

'I guess Zane saw it too cos when he made this, he gave her a tomboy crop.'

I have a pang for Zane. He's such a good guy. And that beautiful bumpy body . . . I can't believe I didn't even get one night of sin with him.

'Are you trying to summon a genie or something?'

Oh God! I hadn't noticed I was still stroking the ring.

The show is mesmerising, surreal and so creatively stimulating you can feel fuses blowing in your brain as you watch. The guy in the red frock coat parades around sedately swinging an incense lantern one minute, then grabs what looks like a giant ribbon dropped from the ceiling, binds it round his wrist, and runs off the stage, swirling high over the audience in an arch. I gasp in delight. He makes it look so effortless when it would no doubt dislocate your average shoulder. Then the entire stage drowns in water and hyperactive synchronised swimmers appear. Finn tells me that stagehands in wetsuits wait underwater to guide the performers to their exit tunnels or breathing stations. Amazing. The cast are part-human, part colourful fantasy figures. My favourite bit is the see-saw diving scene. Endless performers fly into the air – some graceful, some acrobatic, some comedic – before plunging into the chlorine depths. The female divers are in Victorian underwear or wedding dresses and at one point chase a solitary stud across the stage. How poignant!

Throughout, Reed looks stunned but faintly confused, as if he's searching for a plot. Izzy's pupils dilate at all the ripped athletic physiques, I feel like a four-year-old who believes in Santa all over again and Finn looks like he's died and gone to Atlantis. Overall it's a unifying experience – it's as if we've all witnessed a miracle.

'To the bar?' suggests a culture-shocked Reed when the spectacle is over. He guides us to a lavish setting complete with harpist then settles into a throne-like armchair and orders champagne. Izzy, Finn and I fall on to the sofa equivalent of a four-poster bed – it's sumptuously deep, covered in heavy gold embroidery, trimmed with infinite tassels and scattered with an abundance of hug-me, stroke-me cushions. We babble about the amazing boat-shaped trapeze in the show and I wonder out loud about the people behind the masks. Reed, who has been knocking back his champagne with gusto, takes this as a cue to shed a layer.

'Reed isn't my real name. It's Ray!' he blurts, hurriedly explaining how he felt 'Raymond' lacked the yuppie clout needed to seal megabuck business deals. Two more glass-size gulps of champagne and he confesses that he's never really liked the taste, just the decadent feeling of ordering it. I expect Izzy to be disillusioned but she simply beckons over the waitress and says, 'Can we get this man a beer?'

Finn raises a mermaid-clad finger. 'Make that two!'

As we toast Reed's alter ego Ray, his eyes well up and he announces that he's never felt happier in his life. I feel the same way but that could just be the champagne and the fact that I'm in sofa heaven.

'See those two girls there . . .' observes Finn.

We look over at two slender, elegant young women with perfect postures and low-key but expensive necklaces glinting across their dainty collar bones. They are sitting with two ageing businessmen hunched over them like vultures.

'How did two society girls like that end up with such creepy-looking men?' I wonder.

'They're hookers!' says Finn.

'No!' Izzy and I chorus, looking back at their sleek designer dresses and groomed hair.

'Whatever happened to fishnet stockings and the leather miniskirts? What a swizz!' cries Izzy.

'These are the high-class call girls. They are costing those guys a fortune,' notes Finn.

'They don't seem to be having any fun,' says Izzy, staring at their uniform polite-yet-bored expressions. 'There's not even any flirting . . .'

Suddenly the honey blonde leaps to her feet with a howl. One of the vultures has knocked a triple Bailey's down her cream satin skirt and the gloopy fluid is seeping into a big dark stain. She struggles to maintain composure as the vulture mutters feeble placatory remarks about dry-cleaning bills and dabs at her thigh with a napkin. She bats him away and marches off frosty-faced and dripping. He scurries behind, pink with apologies. I've seen more promising foreplay but if the price is right I guess she's still a sure thing. Naturally we four find this episode hysterically funny and snuffle and giggle into our drinks and cushions.

Izzy and I are still laughing as we roll into the loos.

Then we look in the mirror. It's as sobering an experience as ever.

'Oh God! I was hoping my hair might have wilted a bit,' I say, trying to press down the springy backcombed nest.

'All the ends of my spirals have gone tufty!' moans Izzy. 'You haven't got any wax in your bag, have you?'

'Sorry! You haven't got a hat in yours by any chance?'

Izzy giggles, making do with water to pinch her hair ends together.

'Tonight has been brilliant,' I sigh. 'I can't believe everyone has got on so well!'

'Are you going to shag him?' Izzy blurts.

'Who?'

'The guy swinging the incense lantern!' she groans. 'Who do you think? Finn, of course.'

'Oh no, I couldn't,' I shudder.

'Well, it's been a while and you're drunk enough,' reasons Izzy, ever the romantic.

No, I couldn't. Could I? I picture myself kissing the dolphin tattoo that leaps over his belly button and . . . Oh, look at me, would you? I'm more than just rebound girl, I'm ricocheting around a flipping pin-ball machine. B-doing! Pelted downwards by druggy Travis dumping me, ker-ching! catapulted up at seeing Christian again, BAM! nearly losing my life when I discover he's engaged to Nadine, ching-ching-ching – pinging around joyfully during the Zane crush, uh-oh! dropping again, meeting Mia and now after a few laughs with Finn and a prompt from Izzy

277

the lights are flashing and I feel like I've won an extra go. I try to get a grip.

'We'll just see how tonight goes,' I tell myself. Nice and relaxed. What's the hurry? 'Come on!' I urge Izzy, still tweaking her tendrils. Suddenly I'm gagging to see if I really could fancy him.

Back in the bar, Finn is staring sulkily into his beer and Reed is humming absently along to the harpist.

'God, we leave them alone for a minute . . . Let's get some more drinks in,' suggests Izzy, eagerly ordering another round. Finn declines and gets to his feet.

'I think I should be going . . .'

'No,' coos Izzy, trying to grab hold of his jacket tail.

'I've got to get up early, we've got a delivery of grunts and . . .'

My heart sinks. Fish talk. Something's wrong. But what has brought on this change? He shakes Reed's hand and thanks him for the show ticket and then issues a general goodnight. I get up to give him a hug goodbye and throw a few pheromones his way but he leaves without even looking in my direction. Izzy gives me a mystified look and we turn to face Reed. He looks blankly back at us. I'm feeling increasingly panicky so Izzy takes over the interrogation.

'Reed, can you remember what you talked about when we left for the loo?'

'It's so cute when you say loo!'

'Reed, sweetie, it's important . . .'

'Well, obviously we talked about you gorgeous girls!'

'And what exactly did you say?'

'I just said that you have transformed my world since I met you. That I've never felt so happy or so alive. That you are an angel sent down from heaven just for me . . .'

I look beseechingly at Izzy.

'Nothing about Jamie?' she asks.

'Just how glad I was to see her looking so happy after the heartbreak of being spurned by that dumbass stripper guy.'

Izzy gulps. 'Did you actually call him that?'

'Oh pardon me, should I have said exotic dancer?'

I flump on to the sofa in despair.

'Did he ask any questions?'

'He just asked if the stripper's name was Zane. I guess the guy must have a real reputation if he's heard of him.'

'And what did you say?'

'Zane, Duane, Blane, they're all the same . . .'

'And he said . . .'

'Well, he just went kinda quiet. I told him it was kinda sad because Jamie had even worked out names for their kids . . .'

'Enough!' I cry. I don't want to hear any more. Izzy moves to comfort me but I dodge her and run to the lift. She must have shown Reed the Photomorph picture. I wondered where that had got to. I lean heavily on the call button. Well, the Finn fantasy was shortlived. He looked really pissed off when he left but he's probably laughing about it all with Zane right now. And Mia. And the rest of the Golden Guys. All of them laughing at me. I can't bear the humiliation.

I tear off my dress the second I'm in the suite and trample it into the carpet. Normally I would throw myself into bed with my make-up on but this time I want to feel as bad as possible so I take it all off, rubbing vigorously and then peering and prodding and squeezing every imperfection until I'm a blotchy wreck. I try to brush out my hair but I just end up looking like a gonk doll. I feel ugly and angry inside and out.

'It's all Nadine's fault!' I cry irrationally. I'm losing everyone – first Christian to her, Zane to Mia, Izzy to Reed. Big blabbermouth Reed. That's the last I'll see of Finn thanks to him. I'm surprised at how much of a downer that thought is. Finn has turned out to be pretty good company and just as I start to relax and actually like him – bam! Gone! I feel like I have no one. Perhaps I should just go home before there's any more wreckage. I have to stop my mum buying her ticket. I pick up the phone and notice the message light is flashing. It's her.

'Hello, darling! I expect you're out enjoying yourself! I just wanted to let you know that I've done it – I've booked my flight! I arrive at McCarran Airport at 3.15 p.m. next Sunday – that's only a week away, can you believe it? I'm so excited! I can't wait to make plans with you but if you do call back and I'm not here, don't mention the ticket to your father just yet. We had a bit of a ding-dong about it all but nothing for you to worry about, sweetheart. He'll come round. I'll send you a fax a bit later with all the other news. Well, lots of love and don't forget to take your make-up off before bed. You want your skin to look lovely on your special day! Bye, darling.'

I play the message again and then have a good cry in a bid to make my eyes as red and puffy and pitiful as possible.

Finally I believe that people who live in luxurious penthouse suites can be miserable too.

29

I'm lying in bed with the curtains closed. The drapes are so heavy and effective the room is entirely black. I could be back home in Devon at my parents' house. It could be the morning after the night that Christian kissed me in the lounge and then climbed into bed with my sister. I didn't get up for breakfast that day either. I felt nauseous enough as it was. I certainly didn't need to watch Nadine feeding Christian toast soldiers and then look down and discover that my egg had one of those nasty slimy veiny bits in it.

So I claimed I was too queasy to come downstairs, accepted a cup of tea from my mum and watched Christian and Nadine leave from my bedroom window. He looked up. I knew he would. If I had hair as long as Mia's I would have draped it out of the window and invited him to climb up. That's my problem, I realise in a flash – having short hair. I'm never cutting it again! And I'm never getting up again. Too many things go wrong when I interact with the outside world.

I really thought I was going to break my pattern of

bad luck by coming to Vegas. Right now things seem to hurt more than ever. At least when my life seemed dull or wretched back home I could tell myself, 'Things would be different if I were in Las Vegas!' Now I'm here, what do I tell myself? Do I pick another city to obsess about – Sydney might be an option – or do I accept that I cannot escape myself wherever I go? Now that is a depressing thought.

Last night I was ready to admit defeat and go back home. But to what? I don't remember getting sentimental about anything in the month leading up to us leaving. Everything that happened – every rainy day, delayed bus, nag from my boss, gripe from my dad, dig from Nadine and thought of Christian – seemed to prove my leaving was way overdue.

When I handed in my notice at work my decision was met with disbelief from some: 'Las Vegas? You're kidding!' but for the most part people reacted as if the final part of a puzzle had fallen into place. 'Ohhh, right!' They'd nod knowingly. 'I thought you might do something like this!'

I remember the girl in the booth next to me at work said, 'If anyone can get out of here and make it, you can!' I felt such a pioneer! Such a hero! I was doing it for my people! They believed in me but I have failed them. I've managed to turn all my dreams sour in just over a week. Everyone thought Izzy was just hanging on my coat-tails but look at her – she's managed to velcro herself to a new life and I'm magnetically repelling mine.

I roll myself out of bed and drag my suitcase out of

the wardrobe. In the front zip pocket I stuffed a pack of photos (from our leaving do) that Amanda gave me at the airport. We skimmed through them but I haven't given them a proper look. Perhaps I'm just homesick. Seeing some familiar faces might make me feel better. I jump back into bed and switch on the side light. I smile straight away. The first shot is of Izzy sucking a tequila lime from between the teeth of the sexy barman.

My ultra-camp friend Colin arranged the whole thing with characteristic flamboyance, booking an American-style diner in Exeter and insisting everyone dress up as a Vegas icon. Because Colin works at the Northcott Theatre and thus has access to the costume trunk, we all presumed he'd come as Liberace, but he double-bluffed us by shaking off a sequinned cape to reveal a bushy chest wig and trousers strewn with infinite ladies' knickers (attached with tiny safety pins). From the screaming you'd have thought he was the real Tom Jones. I giggle at the picture of him doing a bit of karaoke with a convincing Liza Minelli (aka Amanda), then flick through a series of shots charting the progress of Sammy Davis Jr (the *Express & Echo*'s pint-size postroom cutie in a feathercut wig) with *Casino* Sharon Stone (the blonde sex kitten from the call centre). Oh God! I look so drunk in this one – my headdress is all skew-whiff.

So many people seemed convinced Izzy and I were going to Vegas to become showgirls we went mad at the haberdashery stall at the market and adorned ourselves with plumage and twinkles. We weren't the only ones – the place was heaving with so many feather boas and sequinned butterfly tops it looked like a low-budget remake of *Showgirls*. I think that's the excuse Izzy used when Dave caught her giving the barman a lap dance.

Mind you, he spent most of the night secreted in a corner with his ex-girlfriend – a mousey little work colleague called Elaine, no threat to Izzy. Here she is gazing at Dave all lovelorn. What did she say she'd come as? Oh, a croupier! Dressed in black holding a pack of cards – really, she shouldn't have gone to so much trouble. Hmmm, I wish there weren't so many pictures of Dave topless – he and his mate Pete turned up in silk shorts and boxing gloves pretending to be Mike Tyson and Evander Holyfield – one wearing vampire teeth, the other with a plasticine appendage stuck to his earlobe, complete with bite mark. Pretty original. Naturally it was Pete's idea and Dave just went along with it.

We had one Hunter S. Thompson – here he is, still don't know his true identity – but most of the other men were in gangster suits carrying big plastic machine-guns. One wise guy turned up reeking of salt and vinegar and held out a paper bag saying, 'I bought some chips to gamble with!' Ooh – there's a classic shot of Amanda discovering she's just sat in them. She was upset for about thirty seconds, then found it hysterical and started begging some poor girl she (mistakenly) presumed was impersonating Barbra Streisand to give us a tune.

Halfway through the night Amanda took me to one

side and presented me with a Mafia Kit (a bag of penis-shaped pasta and a Frank Sinatra CD) and then got all misty-eyed telling me how brave she thought I was. 'I'm so proud of you, Jamie. I know your dad isn't speaking to you at the moment but it's your life – you've got to do what's right for you. If it goes wrong you can always come back but at least you've tried!'

'Do you think it *will* go wrong?' I had asked her, suddenly nervous.

'Not if you keep believing,' she told me. I'd forgotten that until now. I asked her what she meant and she said, 'Don't be fazed if things aren't quite as you imagined them to be. If things don't quite go according to plan, change your plan but don't give up.'

I distinctly remember that. Don't give up! And what am I doing? 6 p.m. and I've wasted a whole day in bed feeling sorry for myself. What a cop-out! If my dad could see me now he'd be saying, 'I told you it would end in tears!' I feel a surge of retaliation – since he refused to come to the airport to see me off I've almost been thriving on his disapproval. I can't let him win. I mean, where would I be now if I listened to him? Back in Devon with my entirely predictable humdrum life.

Setting the photos to one side I climb out of bed and throw back the curtains so I can take in the wild possibilities all around me. I catch sight of Caesar's Palace and feel a weird pang for Finn but push it away. I will not be blue. I have to look forward. I'll imagine I've just arrived in town. I take a deep breath, feeling like I've been given a second chance. Yes, there's the wedding mess to resolve but for every problem there's a solution. I'm just too light-headed to think of one right now.

Food. I need food. All I have in my drawer is a half-eaten Hershey bar – yuk! American chocolate totally tastes of soap. As much as I feel I could devour a family-size bar of Imperial Leather right now, I decide there's probably something more appetising in the kitchen. Uh-oh, the odd couple have beaten me to it.

Izzy eyes me nervously and hands me a packet of biscuits. Reed takes a deep breath. 'Jamie, I'm so sorry about last night . . .'

'It's okay,' I mutter, mouth full of Oreo cookie.

'I didn't know Finn knew Zane and—'

'It doesn't matter,' I insist.

'Well, obviously it does and I'd like to try to apologise by taking you out tonight.'

'Oh no, I don't think . . .' I protest. I'm not as ready for the outside world as I thought I was.

'Come on now,' he coaxes. 'You need to get out. It'll give you a lift. I was thinking of the *Tournament of the Kings* over at the Excalibur hotel. You eat dinner as you watch the show so we'd be killing two birds with one stone.'

'I appreciate you asking but I really don't feel up to it,' I tell him.

'It might be fun,' tries Izzy. 'All those men in tights, and you are a damsel in distress.'

'Yes, but the Excalibur . . .' I say, remembering Zane and I conceiving baby Jaz. 'You two go, you don't need a gooseberry tagging along.'

'What if we asked Cindy and Layla?' suggests Izzy. 'Sunday night – they should be free.'

I'm fairly convinced the girls will say no so I grudgingly allow, 'Okay, I'll go if they go.'

Izzy trots off to the phone and returns five minutes later with a 'Gotcha!' look. Oh no. Please don't make me leave the suite! It's not safe – anything could happen!

'They're meeting us there,' she tells me. 'They have to shoot off to a private do at 9 but they're looking forward to seeing us! You'd better start getting ready!'

Foiled again. I take a couple more cookies hoping to induce a sugar rush and tell them, 'I'm going to put on my hairpiece so I don't get mistaken for a stable boy.'

'Okay,' Izzy grins. 'I'm going to try to talk Reed out of wearing his curly-toed shoes.'

I haven't got much hair (ask Mia) but I can just about scrape it together at the back, disguise the tufty bits with the hairpiece and – in theory – create a long sleek ponytail. I've only ever worn it once before and I lost a good few inches – and a few cat lives – when Amanda accidentally set light to it with her ciggie. Anyway, I've trimmed off the singed bits and I think the length is more realistic now. I decide to dress head to toe in black, in mourning for the death of all hope in my life. That and I feel fat in everything else I put on.

As I step out of my room Izzy sticks her head into the corridor and stage whispers: 'Reed, sweetie, you'll make too much noise in that suit of armour, please just put on the dark grey outfit I picked out for you!'

She skips over to me. 'I love teasing him. He takes everything I dish out!'

'And that's not easy.'

'So, ready to "have a good knight"?' she puns.

'You're perky, aren't you?'

'I am, aren't I? I'm sorry, I know it's in bad taste cos you're so miserable and heartbroken but I can't squish it down. I'm *really* happy. Stupidly happy.'

'Then I'm happy for you, in a jealous, I-want-some kind of way!'

'Thank you. And don't worry, you will get some. Keep the faith!'

Reed appears looking dapper for the second night running. Izzy takes his arm and nuzzles his chubby chops. 'Don't think I don't know that you're still wearing the chainmail underpants!'

Reed sighs, loving the abuse. 'Shall we?'

30

It's not every hotel that has its own sawdust-strewn jousting arena. This one is vast – plenty long enough for the horses to get up a good hoof-clattering canter – and feels authentically dangerous. The seating sections are divided into 'teams' to support the various knights in combat and we're obliged to cheer for the Blue Knight no matter how hot we think the baddie Black Knight looks.

Serving wenches attempt to goad us into banging goblets of Diet Coke and stamping our feet but Layla doesn't need any encouragement and it's amazing how quickly the rest of us go from disdain to whole-hearted yelling and carousing. As the tale of King Arthur unfolds, food is served. It didn't occur to me to pre-order a vegetarian meal and now I'm confronted with a pewter platter with my very own Cornish hen. I'm famished. Something about the flaring nostrils of the horses and the testosterone of their riders makes me lose my senses and before I know it I'm ripping the flesh from the bone and gnawing at the carcass like the rest of the savages around me. Don't look now but I might actually be having a good time.

'I never knew they'd have such long poles!' gasps Cindy, as the jousting begins.

'Take that, sucker!' yells Layla as one knight is rammed off his horse.

Our heroic Blue Knight survives the ruckus and trots up to greet his minions. We roar our approval. I'm trying to master Cindy and Layla's 'Go Blue Knight!' cheerleader routine when he beckons me over. I have no choice but to go to him – all our section is egging me on and wolf-whistling madly. I don't get a proper look at him until I'm hanging over the bar so he can kiss my hand. There's something familiar about his face. He smiles. I'm dazzled by his dentistry. He takes off his hat to bow to me and reveals tufty bleached blond hair. Oh no. It's The Grin. The Grin who so kindly returned my chicken breast at the Mirage. Will the humiliation never end? Perhaps he won't recognise me.

'What beautiful hair you have, my lady.'

He reaches his hand up and I jerk my head back, afraid he'll realise over half of it is synthetic. When I look back at him he has my entire ponytail in his hand. I gasp and feel the back of my head – nothing but pins and tufts of hair. I freeze. I hear laughter. Lots of it. But not from him.

'Thank you for the lock of your hair, my lady,' he booms over the mirth. 'It will bring me luck in battle. I will return triumphant!'

And with that his horse rears up and he's off, tucking my unfortunate hairpiece in his belt.

'She's a plant!' sneers a wise-ass teenage boy.

'Yeah!' his family agree.

I turn around. Cindy and Layla look sympathetic. Reed looks fretful but Izzy is nowhere to be seen. It's only when I get back up level with our table I see she's hunched on the floor, convulsed with laughter.

I raise her to her knees. 'Remember the guy who found the chicken breast on the floor?'

'This is worse!' she wails, tears rolling down her cheeks.

'No, this is the same guy.'

Her eyes widen for a second and then she's gone. Back on the floor. You wouldn't know she was there except for the shaking and the odd screech. She misses the whole sketch with Merlin.

Meanwhile Cindy daintily removes the now redundant clips from the back of my head and Reed shyly informs me that I look better without the ponytail. Poor guy, he must be wishing he'd left me in bed.

As the show stampedes to its grand finale, the girls tell me they have to scoot.

'But we'll come and meet you for lunch one day next week, if you like,' offers Cindy. 'Sam's Shopping Extravaganza isn't far from the wedding shop.'

'And we want to hear all about what's going on with those cats!' says Layla, eyeing Reed and Izzy.

I hug them goodbye, grateful for the boost just seeing them has given me. Neither of them has a boyfriend and they are doing fine. Mind you, they get enough man action at work, I suppose.

Reed and I clap vigorously as the performers take

their bows, then watch nearly all the auditorium file out before Izzy is in a fit state to get to her feet.

'Sorry!' she whimpers, still twitching. 'I couldn't help it.'

Reed's mobile phone bleats urgently as soon as he switches it on and he darts off ahead of us to get a better signal. As Izzy and I make our way to the exit, my eye is drawn to a torchlight moving in the shadows. It appears to be flashing morse code. It's getting closer. Whaddayaknow? It's the human glow-worm aka The Grin aka the Blue Knight.

He is chatting busily to a fellow knight but breaks out into the most spectacular smile when he spots me.

'Hey!' He trots over. 'I was hoping to catch you. I didn't mean to run off with your hair!'

I roll my eyes. 'That's okay. I have lots of spare parts!'

'Kinda like the Bionic Woman, huh?'

I can't help but smile. Just a mere 30 watts to his 100.

'Do you know her name is Jamie,' says Izzy, excitedly joining in. 'You know, as in Jamie Summers!'

'Really, that's your name?'

'Yes. Well, Jamie is. Not Summers.'

'Well, you can't have everything.' he laughs. 'I'm not a natural blond!'

'Tell me about it!' Izzy giggles.

'So listen, do you want to wait a second and I'll grab your hair from the dressing room?'

'Okay,' I say even though I have no intention of wearing the cursed hank *ever* again.

'I should catch up with Reed, really . . .' says Izzy, in a quandary. 'Do you want to meet us at the bar by the main entrance?'

'Yeah, I'll catch you up.'

'You may as well come with me then, Jamie,' he says. 'We won't be long!'

I feel Izzy is about to make some lewd quip so I give her a little push to send her on her way.

The door to the backstage area is right behind us. The Grin shows me to his assigned dressing table and says, 'Take a seat, I'll just be a minute . . .'

The light bulbs around his mirror have photos and postcards tucked behind them and I take a closer look as he changes into civvies – here's The Grin messing around with a group of knights half in costume, half in baseball hats; a portrait of him as a teenager with what must be his mother, looking devoted; him with his arms around another good-looking guy, possibly his brother; him posing by a pick-up truck in the desert . . . and then a strangely familiar scene: a harbour leading to a beach, surrounded by pinky-red cliffs. Rhubarb-coloured cliffs. He returns just as recognition strikes.

'This is Teignmouth in Devon!' I gasp.

'Yeah! Do you know it? My mom used to live there.'

'My mum lives there now!' I splutter.

'Are you serious?'

'Yes! That's amazing!' I marvel. 'So your mum's English?'

'Yeah, my dad was at a marine base in Lympstone during the war – I guess he packed her up in his ole kit bag when he went back to Florida.'

'Is that where they live now?'

'Just my mom, my dad's long gone.'

'Oh. So, have you ever been to Devon?'

'Just once when I was six. I remember this great ice cream we had . . .'

'. . . with a dollop of clotted cream on top?'

'Yes!' He laughs, looking delighted. 'Isn't it good?'

'And yet so bad . . .'

We reminisce some more, gazing at each other with bright-eyed fondness and a newfound familiarity. It's funny how having such a small thing in common can send a fledgling friendship into warp drive. With Izzy it was as simple as sharing the same birthday. With Amanda it was a mutual despair of hair removal products. (We once even sent used wax strips back to the manufacturer to illustrate our letter of complaint! We got a refund but we're still waiting for the miracle that will give us hairless inner thighs without pimples or pain.) With Colin it was something he said at our first social gathering. I'd only been working at the Northcott Theatre box office for two days when I was invited to a house party at the costume girl's house. We were playing a game using the 'If this person were a colour, what would they be?' idea and I was the mystery person Izzy was trying to guess. She asked Colin, 'If this person were a film, which film would he/she be?' And he, without hesitation, said '*Roman Holiday*!' I then totally ruined the game by squealing, 'Oh my God! That's my favourite movie ever! How did you know?'

He'd only met me briefly before but I felt like he'd seen into my very soul – and seen me as I wanted to be seen. Suddenly I was as pure and joyful as Audrey Hepburn, scootering around Rome with Gregory Peck.

Consequently I take the Devon connection as a sign that The Blue Knight and I were meant to meet . . .

'So, how long have you been a knight of the Round Table?' I ask as he hangs up his costume.

'About six months. This actor friend of mine from Orlando was working here and I stepped in when he went back home. It beats bar work – I'm way too clumsy for that cocktail shaker stuff!'

'Are you an actor too?' He's certainly got the movie star looks.

'No!' he laughs. 'I'm studying to be a psychotherapist.'

'Really?'

'Yup! I know I don't look the part . . .'

I study him for a second. He's your basic Brad Pitt. I imagine having a couch in his consultancy room would be quite a liability.

'I think I'm pretty good at helping people emotionally.'

'Could you help me?' I ask, surprised at my own bluntness. And the quaver in my voice – I meant to sound jokey.

He smiles kindly and says, 'I think so. What seems to be the problem?'

I furrow my brow and go to speak but nothing comes out.

'You've got that "Where do I begin?" look,' he observes.

My eyes well up. Still no words.

'Perhaps we should go somewhere more comfortable to talk.'

I hesitate for a second and then ask, 'Do you mean that?'

'Of course! You need to talk and I'm trained to listen – we'll make a great team!'

The sense of relief at someone impartial prepared to listen to my woes warms my heart. I smudge away an escaped tear and try to get a grip. If he can help me, great. If not, at least I'll have a lovely view.

'Okay,' he says, grabbing my hair (the detached portion, that is) and his rucksack. 'Let's go!'

As we march through the casino I worry that I've come off too desperate and troubled. 'I'm not a complete basket case you know!' I say, feeling the opposite.

'Don't you worry, Jamie – we have the power to rebuild you!'

We approach the bar. Reed and Izzy are entwined and if I'm not mistaken she's dribbling beer from her mouth to his. She looks up and winks. 'Here's Jamie and her knight in shining armour!'

'This is Reed,' I say, turning to my newfound therapist. 'And this is . . .' I look blank. 'Oh! I don't know your name!'

'Oh, yeah, sorry about that!' he grins dazzlingly. 'I'm Scott!'

31

'Scott!' says Reed, giving his hand a hearty shake. 'Nice to meet you. Great show.'

'Scott!' coos Izzy, giving me a prime rib elbow dig.

'Scott!' I sigh, looking at his face in a whole new, potential-husband way. If we could just tone down those teeth I think we could be in business. Perhaps he could take up smoking to yellow them up a bit, or gargle with red wine for that oh-so-attractive burgundy stain. Alternatively, if we could exfoliate away some of that tan the contrast wouldn't be so great.

The rest of him will do nicely. A slim figure with no intimidating Popeye bulges, standard jeans and T-shirt. Of course I don't normally go for blonds but what's a packet of hair dye between husband and wife?

'Well, there's a Caesar salad with my name on it down at the Peppermill,' Scott nudges me. 'Do you mind if we get going, Jamie?'

'Of course not,' I beam.

'Do you guys want a lift?' offers Reed.

'No, that's cool. I've got my trusty steed valet-parked!'

'I bet you've got really firm thighs from all that horse-riding.' Izzy leers.

Reed coughs and hurries us on our way. 'See you back at the ranch!'

Scott holds open the door as we leave the casino, then the door to his Jeep Cherokee and finally the door to the Peppermill. My mum's gonna love him.

'I getta little sick of casino food,' he explains as we enter the bungalow-style restaurant. 'This place is open 24 hours and ideal for hay fever sufferers!'

After my eyes have adjusted to the cave-like blackness I realise every surface is brimming with artificial flowers, most of which look like they could do with a good clean. We are led through the sticky darkness to a plum booth framed by nobbly plastic branches drooping with faded silk acacia blossoms. A waitress with an award-winning smoker's cough hands us a menu. What we really need is a torch. I make a joke and speed-read the dessert list by the light of Scott's bared teeth.

Service is swift and as Scott tucks into his chicken Caesar he says: 'Okay – time to spill!'

Suddenly I'm not so sure revealing all my woes and weaknesses will be the best start to our lifelong partnership. I mean, I know that I flit from man to man out of necessity and self-preservation, but to the untrained eye I look like the Queen of Fickle. However, when you put together an open book with a semi-professional therapist few secrets remain. Within three hours I've told him *everything*. He listens

299

patiently, emitting the odd incisive comment like, 'Honey, you've been holding a torch for Christian so long you could get mistaken for the Statue of Liberty!' and – as regards my comparing myself physically with Izzy – 'Forget it! You can't out-blonde a blonde!'

He seems suitably awed by the mess I've got myself into and I'm feeling utterly understood. Then he says, 'Oprah Winfrey once asked Madonna what would be the most important thing she could teach her daughter Lourdes, and she said, "self-respect". Then she asked her what she would tell her about men and Madonna said, "If she had self-respect, then I wouldn't have to tell her anything."'

Scott gives me a sweet smile. 'You think all your problems are about men. Not true.'

I narrow my eyes. 'It's Nadine, isn't it? I knew it!'

'Your sister is not your main concern right now.'

I insist that she is the bane of my existence and remind him that it is she who has stolen my one true love.

'He wasn't yours to steal, Jamie. And besides, she doesn't even know you two dated, does she?'

'No, but she has spent her every waking moment putting me down and trying to outdo me and now she's going to marry the only man—'

'So she's a little competitive,' Scott cuts in. 'You should really feel sorry for her for being so envious.'

'Envious? What has she got to feel envious about? She's got everything!'

'Except the one thing she wants!'

'Oh and what is that?'

'Well, I'd have a better idea if I actually met her but I suspect it's something you've got.'

I snort. 'Something I've got? I don't think so. She's *Elle Decoration*, I'm car boot sale leftovers.'

'I don't mean anything material. I think she envies you your spirit.'

'My spirit? No way, if it doesn't have a Nicole Fahri label she's not interested. Anyway, if Nadine isn't my problem, then who is? Apart from myself, obviously?'

'Izzy.'

'Izzy?' I repeat incredulously. That's what you get for confessing all to amateurs. I doubt Dr Frasier Crane would have come to the same conclusion.

'Izzy is my lifeline. My party pal. My Thelma.'

'You use her as a prop and you let what she wants dominate your life choices.' He takes a breath. 'And she's also morally corrupt!'

'Well, I know that's not true,' I say confidently. 'She doesn't have any morals.'

Scott takes a big swig of his cloudy lemonade.

'You've spent twenty years under her spell. I don't expect you to be able to see clearly straight away.'

'Well, this is a novel experience. You've got to be the first guy who's not desperate to shag her.'

'She's not my type, believe me.'

'Mind you, I don't think Finn is too keen either. Next you'll be telling me he's the man of my dreams.'

'I don't think you're ready to hear that yet.'

We hold each other's gaze for a moment and then I sigh.

'You're wrong about Izzy. We've been through a lot together.'

'And virtually everything has been to her advantage.'

'She's just luckier than me. Things happen to her.'

'That's because she's got two people working on her life – you and her. That doesn't leave much time for you to work on your own.'

He leaves these ominous words hanging in the air for a while and then adds, 'I know this sounds harsh but if you don't address the issue you'll wake up a few years from now wondering why she got the starring role and you're still waiting in the wings.'

'You don't understand,' I insist, 'my life is never more eventful than when I'm with Izzy. She's so fearless and daring.'

'Why can't you be as daring on your own? Take your own risks?'

'Well, it's not as much fun,' I pout.

'Have you tried?'

I think for a moment. Going to Red Rock Canyon without Izzy was by default. The last time I made a bold solo step of my own volition was probably attending the drama summer school ten years ago.

'And when Christian let you down you lost your nerve and you clung to her all the more. And when all the romance had been knocked out of you by your crappy choices of boyfriend you started to treat men like she does because it doesn't hurt so much – if you ridicule them you diminish their power.'

I say nothing.

'You're not being true to yourself because the True You, the Untainted You, believes in love. The Pure You could find love. But the You you've become to suit Izzy won't.'

'How many Me's are there exactly?'

'Let me ask you, what do you do with your time when she's having some semblance of a relationship?'

'I don't know, see other friends, catch up on my washing, watch BBC period dramas . . .'

'Exactly. You wait. Like an army wife. She gets practice having relationships, you just get really good at waiting. You push possible relationships away because you are afraid it will rock the boat. You'd rather keep your friendship with her just so. You don't feel it's your place to be the one with the boyfriend.'

He moves his plate to one side. 'You wait while she loves.'

This is all incredibly depressing. I look up at Scott with watery eyes. 'I thought you were going to make me feel better. This is horrible.'

'Stick with it kiddo, we're having a breakthrough.'

'I don't want one.'

He smiles kindly and takes my hand. 'Tell me how it is when you meet someone you like. How does she react?'

'Well, it doesn't happen very often.'

'Think.'

'Well, there was this one time, this guy was a bit special. Everyone fancied him but he liked me.'

'Don't sound so surprised!'

'He was a chef and when I told him I was vegetarian

he offered to cook me this amazing meal at his house – smoky sweetcorn soup with lime butter, beetroot ravioli with dill cream, tomato and coriander salad and Amaretti fruit gratin for dessert.'

'Sounds great.'

'I'm sure it was. I didn't go.'

'Why not?'

'Well,' I scrunch my brow. 'Izzy got all grumpy about being abandoned on a Saturday night . . .'

'. . . making you feel guilty and responsible for her,' Scott finishes for me, then adds: 'You could have arranged to see him another night.'

'Well, Izzy said she saw him holding hands with another girl in town so . . .'

'You let it go. Just like that. And yet, like with those creepy conventioneers, she expects you to go along with her conquests. With her it's a fait accompli – she tells you how things are going to be, she doesn't ask. You meekly request permission and give in at the first obstacle.'

I am officially pathetic.

'I hate myself,' I wail.

Scott grins. 'Isn't therapy great?'

32

It's nearly 1 a.m. when Scott drops me back at the Bellagio and seven hours later, when I have to get up for my first day at work, my head is still throbbing with the disturbing new slant he has put on my friendship with Izzy. I feel like I'm in one of those war movies where the close-knit squadron suddenly discover the traitor is one of them.

I'm not sure what I'm supposed to do about it so I concentrate my mind on what to wear to work. I settle on a precautionary ankle-length skirt but as it happens, no requests are made for me to scale the ladder. In fact Sam is out for most of the day leaving Nikki to show me the ropes. She explains how to work the till and gives me tips on how to do the minimum work but still look busy and soon we're chewing gum in unison. I think I'm going to like it here. The mindlessness is quite soothing.

I'm back at the hotel by 6.30 p.m. (no sign of Izzy) and get a call from Zane asking if I want to hang out with him and Mia, but I explain I've already made arrangements (to see Scott). I feel awkward at first, but

Zane seems blissfully unaware of the revelation about my former crush on him, so it looks like Finn kept quiet after all. We chat for a bit – he tells me about the new Cossack routine he's working on and I tell him about finding my vocation as a shopgirl. I come off the phone in a pretty good mood. I can see why he's not for me but he's such a sweetie and I'm flattered that he's so keen on being friends. It's funny, I was never in this much demand in England – I'm beginning to think all Americans are part of an Adopt-a-Foreigner scheme. It's like they can't get enough of you. Here's Scott at the door now . . .

He takes me on a tour of Downtown, where all the hardcore neon is, including the infamous waving cowboy (known as Vegas Vic) and the squelchily-named girliebar Glitter Gulch. When we reach the Four Queens Casino, Scott tells me to lie flat on my back on the pavement. The streets are buzzing but I can see other people risking getting a trainer-print on their forehead, so I do as he says. Suddenly the overhead canopy (that runs for about five blocks) is transformed from a white lattice tunnel to a trippy computer-programmed light show. Images of Vegas icons cavort above us by virtue of two million pulsating lightbulbs and music swirls around us. I turn to Scott and grin. 'This is my second favourite attraction in Vegas after the Bellagio fountains! I love it!'

He pulls me to my feet, discreetly removing a gob of chewing gum from my elbow and says: 'Now we're going to gamble with the big guys!'

We hit the Gold Spike Casino for a hedonistic hour playing penny slots and dime roulette and I'm reminded of the classic scene in *Vegas Vacation* where a down-on-his-luck Chevy Chase is reduced to playing scissors-paper-stone in crummy, low minimum-bet casinos in a bid to win back his fortune. Afterwards we have drinks and watch a tacky lounge band and I thank my lucky stars that Scott has slotted smoothly into the vacant role of my constant companion. We're having a blast, even if he does have a tendency to therapise everything. Earlier when I was lamenting that Izzy gets all the guys, he said: 'Izzy is not more attractive than you. You are just very different types who attract different kinds of men. And the type she attracts is the type who is more likely to bowl up and buy a girl a drink and the type you attract is more likely to sit there thinking, "She's hot!" but not know what to do about it.'

'Even if that were true, what good does it do me if they're not going to come up to me?' I replied. 'How am I supposed to find someone? Do you even think I will?'

'Of course you will. You're kind, you're fun, you're open-minded, you have an appetite for life, you have a radiance!'

At which point I rolled my eyes.

'You do. You're sensitive . . .'

'Well, that's got to go.'

'No! You've just become afraid of your feelings.'

'Well, they seem to get me into so much trouble,' I

complained. 'Sometimes I wish I could just unplug my emotions and get some peace.'

'Well, they're not going to go away. You have to learn to accept that you're going to have a pretty intense experience on this planet and if you swapped places with one of the placid, just-ticking-over people, you'd realise you wouldn't want it any other way.'

'Is that so?'

'Yes it is. Trust me.'

Back at the Bellagio, I conclude that this modern, resort hotel end of town is like food-shopping at Marks & Spencer's compared to Downtown's Somerfield.

Apart from a small boy setting fire to his fringe with a lighter with his name on it, Day Two at Sam's Shopping Extravaganza passes uneventfully. Cindy and Layla wanted to come in and meet me for lunch but I was concerned they'd set Sam a-perving so I told them I'd see them for a drink after work at the Holy Cow. By the time I'd brought them up-to-date on Izzy and Reed and convinced them I'd never met the Queen, it was time for them to leave for Lap and Tickle. I talked to the barman for an hour and then Scott tracked me down and came up with his best therapy suggestion yet: dancing.

It's nearly 11 o'clock when we pull up outside a backstreet nightclub called Gypsy. Scott is still in the process of parking when a TinTin-haired chap sticks his head through the driver window and kisses him.

'Where have you been, you naughty boy? You've been neglecting us!'

'Jimmy, this is Jamie!'

'So this is your guilty secret! Well, isn't she a cutie!'

'Jimmy's a cruise ship dancer. He'll do the splits if you ask nicely.' Scott smirks.

The club is small and swirling with dry ice. I squeeze past a series of bare torsos with T-shirts tucked in their jean pockets like window cleaner rags and nudge my way to the bar. I'm halfway through a drink I've ordered from a chiselled barman with pierced nipples when I realise I am the only woman in the place.

I don't know why it hadn't occurred to me before that Scott would be gay. I always knew my soulmate would be. I suppose the whole guru/grasshopper thing threw me off the scent. Anyway, I'm not even disappointed because at least this way I can't muck up our relationship and in theory I get Scott for life.

Jimmy pulls us on to the dancefloor and there's nothing to do but surrender to the sweat. For the next two hours we're lost to the music. I wish Colin were here, we've got some classic home-made routines and the boyband shapes he throws would go down a storm with this crowd. Finally the hi-energy sucks all of ours. Jimmy and I fall upon a pair of just-vacated seats, dispatching Scott to the bar.

'So, has Scott been psycho-analysing you like crazy?'

'Until I can't take any more!' I laugh.

'It's all very well in theory – everyone knows what they *should* do in life. It's all the other stuff that makes it fun.'

Scott returns and hands us each a bottle of water. We down them in one glug and smile in rehydrated relief. Then Jimmy goes back on the dancefloor for more.

'No way!' I scream as he tries to get me back on my pulsating feet.

Scott and I remain firmly seated and do our bit by singing along to 'I Am What I Am'.

'So, when did you know You Were What You Are?' I frown.

Scott grins. 'I had girlfriends when I was at college but really I think I knew since I was a kid. I just didn't do anything about it until recently.'

'How recently?'

'Well, I've only been openly gay since I got to Vegas.'

'Did your parents react badly or something?'

'Or something. It's a long story.'

'I've got all the time in the world, honey!' I smile. 'Hot chocolate?'

'Now you're talking!'

We relocate to Paris (the hotel) for a bit of late-night patisserie action. Scott toys with his lemon torte and then reveals: 'I've never told my parents that I'm gay.'

I ask why and he softly explains how his father left his mother for another man eight years ago.

'Even though he told her he was gay she begged him to stay. She just wouldn't accept it. She never has. Every year she's just got more and more bitter and resentful and hard. It's so sad. I can't remember the last time she laughed. She never goes out. She says she's too ashamed. She shuts down at the mention of

310

any kind of homosexuality – she stopped watching *Ellen* when she came out and that was her favourite programme.'

'But surely you can talk to your dad about it?'

'I don't know where he is. Mum told him she didn't want him influencing me and that he should stay out of my life. We never heard from him again.'

'Oh God.'

'I know. It's a mess, isn't it? I had to move away in the end because I couldn't bear lying to my mum about what I was doing and who I was doing it with. She was always enquiring about girlfriends with this desperate kind of hope in her voice. I've barely spoken to her since I've been out here because I know I can't tell her the one thing that would make her happy.'

'Which is . . .'

'That I'm getting married.'

'Have you ever thought of telling her the truth? You could counsel her afterwards.'

Scott shakes his head. 'I couldn't risk the effect it would have on her. She had me pretty late in life, she's nearly seventy now, not in the best of health. Her life isn't so very fabulous as it is – she's always saying I'm the only thing she lives for.'

'I take it you're the only child?'

'But of course! And for the record, she's a Taurus which is as stubborn and anti-change as they come.'

'There's only one thing for it then,' I tell him.

'What's that?'

'You'll have to marry me!'

Scott smiles.

'I told my mum I was marrying a Scott so really you've got very little choice in the matter,' I insist.

Scott squidges a blob of cream out of my eclair with his fork and muses, 'What a wild party we'd have!'

'I'd beat Nadine down the aisle *and* keep my teenage wedding pact with Izzy!' I say, warming to the idea.

'Maybe it wouldn't be such a bad idea for you psychologically – you might be able to get on with your life if you got this stupid obsession with getting married out of the way.'

'My mum would love you!'

'My mum would love you, too! Oh my God – just to see that look on her face . . .' He trails off. 'I can just see her standing there in the chapel, beaming, little lacey hanky dabbing her eye. Wow! It would really make her . . . well, her life.'

He pauses again and then asks, 'Are you serious about this?'

'Almost,' I say. 'Are you?'

33

Went to lunch with Nikki today and had a laugh at Sam's expense. Turns out he's tried it on with her a few times but she's managed to keep him at bay.

'What's his problem?' I say, shaking my head.

'Just lonely, I guess.'

'Don't you get grossed out by him?'

'There are a lot of men in my family,' she shrugs. 'It takes a lot to upset me.'

Back at the shop, Nikki's endeavouring to teach me a trick with a pack of 'As Used In A Real Las Vegas Casino' playing cards and I say, 'What's that lovely smell?' just as she says, 'Phwoargh!'

I look up. 'Jamie! What a surprise!'

'Zane, wha . . .?' What does he mean, surprise? We had a whole conversation about me working at Sam's Shopping Extravaganza just two nights ago.

'Finn, look who it is!' says Zane, maintaining his 'well, whaddayaknow' tone. Finn steps out from behind him looking sheepish. 'Hi.'

'Hi,' I reply with equal reserve.

'Aren't you going to introduce me?' says Nikki, chewing furiously on her gum.

'Hi, I'm Zane. My friend Finn here is looking for a Dashboard Hulagirl for his car, do you have any?'

'Sure, sure!' she nods. 'My name's Nikki. We have two styles, I'll go get them.'

Nikki is transported from her usual despondency to Shopgirl of the Year.

'Great, I'll help you,' he says swiftly following her.

Finn shuffles closer, rubbing his shorn head. 'Listen, I'm sorry I left so abruptly the other night.'

'That's okay!' I say, reddening. 'It was a good show, wasn't it? Those divers were amazing . . .'

'Amazing,' he agrees.

I find myself turning all the dice on the counter so that six is face up, just for something to do with my hands.

'So, what are you doing working here?' he asks.

'Just making some extra cash. The owner is a kind of relative.'

'Oh, I see. How do you like it?'

'It's okay. No stress.'

'Done any more writing?'

I daren't look up. 'Well, I've sent some ideas off, we'll see what the magazines say . . .'

'I'd like to read something of yours sometime.'

I pull a face.

'Really,' he says softly.

I find myself looking into his magical blue eyes, feeling as soothed as when I'm gazing at the aquarium.

'Do you want a lay?'

314

'What?' I gasp.

'A lay,' Zane repeats. 'You can have this one with the straw skirt and detachable bikini top or this one with the floral garland, known in Hawaii as a lay.'

'Jamie, whatever were you thinking!' Nikki cackles.

I duck behind the counter pretending to burrow for wrapping paper. How excruciating.

'Now what else did we have to do today?' Zane ponders, consulting his list. 'Ah yes! Get film developed.'

'There's a camera shop two doors up,' says Nikki, eyeing his bronzed forearms.

'Great, just one more shot to use up,' he notes, inspecting his camera. 'Hey, Finn! Jump behind the counter so I can get you with Jamie.'

Finn gives Zane a 'Don't push it' look. Poor bloke. He's hating every minute of Zane's mismatched matchmaking.

'Go on, it'll just take a second. That's it. Bit closer. Put your arm around her. Excellent!'

Blinded by the flash, I put a hand out to steady myself, accidentally pressing down on the till button – the cash drawer shoots out, jolting me into Finn.

He says, 'You okay?' but I hear the words 'I wouldn't let you fall!' echo from our trip to Red Rock. I lean on to his warm body and feel his heartbeat.

'What's going on out here?' a voice booms. 'What's that bloke doing behind the counter?' It's Sam on the warpath.

'Oh, Mr Johnson! He was just, we were just . . .'

315

Nikki blusters.

'It's just that you have such attractive staff here,' Zane interrupts. 'I wanted to get a picture of my friend with them. I hope that's okay.'

'Yes, yes, well, come away from the till,' he orders.

'Yes, sir.'

'Hmmm,' he says, eyeing Finn and Zane. 'Don't suppose you're interested in buying any T-shirts? We've got a huge range . . .'

'No, no!' I insist, still disorientated, 'they've got their Dashboard Hula and now they're leaving.'

'Oh,' he says, dismayed. 'Another time perhaps . . .'

'Yes, well, nice to meet you, sir,' says Zane, shaking Sam's hand. 'We'd better be on our way.'

I look at Finn. He goes to speak but nothing comes out.

'Thanks for your help, sweet thing,' Zane winks at Nikki.

'Any time,' she says, blowing an obscenely big bubble as they walk out the door.

Through the glass I see Zane mouthing 'call me'. I nod and wave back, trying to catch Finn's eye but he's already in the car.

'What's up with you and that guy?' asks Nikki, following my gaze.

'Nothing. I don't know,' I sigh.

'Looks like some unfinished business to me,' she says, returning the rejected Hulagirl to the shelf, then going off to the kitchen to make us both a coffee.

*

'You *still* mooning?' she says, handing me a cup bearing the words, 'When the chips are down, drink up!'

'Me?' I say, returning from Finn-land to accept my milky-one-sugar. 'What about you, all over Zane. I take it you fancied him?' I tease.

'Zane? Nah! Too cheesy.'

'What?' I laugh.

'That hair? That tan? That *body*? Looks like one of those Golden Guys!'

I smile to myself. 'He does, doesn't he?'

'Couldn't be though.'

'Oh no?'

'No. They're all gay,' she asserts.

'Really?'

'Oh yes. For sure,' she says. 'Right, back to our card trick!'

34

It's been a long time since anyone used my bed as a trampoline, but Izzy is pogo-ing joyously with no regard for the fact that I'm trying to sleep. Lucky the Bellagio bedrooms have high ceilings. We were once on a nightclub stage dancing to Van Halen and decided to take the 'Might as well JUMP!' chorus literally. Gravity did its thing with me but Izzy soared upward, smacked her head on a beam and dropped unconscious to the floor. I thought her Tigger days were over but apparently not.

'WHAT?!' I scream as she bounces dangerously close to my legs.

She drops panting to my side. 'He proposed! I'm going to be Mrs Reed Mahoney! I'm going to be rich!' She hisses that last bit. 'He loves me, Jamie. He said he'd do anything for me, buy me anything I want!'

I haul myself up in bed and switch on the bedside lamp. 'Did you accept?'

'Yes! Of course! This has been the best week of my life. I want more of it! I can have more of it! We've been looking at condos here. You should see them –

pools with their own fountains! Double staircases! Spa bathrooms! Walk-in closets with shoe carousels . . .'

She flumps on to her back and stamps her feet into the mattress, squeaking delight.

'Looks like I'm going to get my velour leeeeeizure suit for real!'

'Oh my God, you're getting married!' I say as if the penny just dropped.

Izzy scoots up on to her knees and repeats, 'I'm getting married!'

I give her a hug trying to figure out what on earth I'm feeling. 'Left behind' seems to be the dominant emotion. Scott's proposal doesn't seem to compare.

'I hate to be a downer but what about Dave?'

She shoots me a conspiratorial look. 'I have a cunning plan! I reckon if I play my cards right I can keep both of them.'

'What?' I can't have heard right.

'Really, I think it could work. Reed travels a lot on business so I reckon I could have three months here with him and then three months back in Devon with Dave. Reed would understand that I want to see my family and friends . . .'

'But how would you explain spending three-month stretches here to Dave?'

'I don't know, I'd invent some amazing job that has a flexitime option or something. Dave won't question it, you know what he's like.'

'Izzy, you've got to be joking!'

'Why would I be? I think it'll be perfect. Who says everything in life has got to be either/or?'

I think for a moment. Normally I let her scams slide or laugh along with them but Scott has acted like smelling salts on me, reviving my senses. I take a deep breath and tell her firmly: 'You can't do this.'

She gives me a petulant look.

'I'm serious, it isn't fair to anyone.'

'Life isn't fair, Jamie. You have to do what's best for you at the end of the day.'

'But you don't need them both. You've barely given Dave a thought since you've been out here.'

'I've been busy! It doesn't mean I'm not looking forward to seeing him again. It's reassuring to know that he's at home, waiting for me. Anyway, convention aside, the truth for most people is that one person isn't enough.'

'Don't you think you're being a little bit greedy?'

The look on her face chills me. 'In all these years you've never judged me. I thought you understood how I lived. I won't make any apologies for it. Accept me as I am or not at all.'

Her words hang in the air like an ultimatum.

'Your way or no way, huh?' I say, feeling my nervousness at crossing her gather some anger as remember something Scott said: 'Do you know why she behaves in such a selfish way? I'll tell you – because people like you let her get away with it!' It stung me then and it's stinging me now.

'I won't let you do it, Izzy, it's not right.'

'Won't *let* me? Who are you that I need your permission?' she spits.

'Who am I?' I reel in despair. 'I've been your best

friend for twenty years! And it's not a question of permission, I just think you've lost all sense of what is acceptable behaviour.'

'Says the woman about to marry a gay man.'

I glare back at her. This is getting nasty. Izzy sighs impatiently. 'Can't you just be happy for me?'

'I'm happy that Reed has proposed but I don't think you'll be happy if you're messing up other people's lives,' I say, standing firm.

'Don't give me that karma crap!'

'I'm not! I'm just saying you won't feel good about yourself if you play with people like this. Why can't you let Dave go?'

'He's my rock! What if this all goes wrong?'

'Then you'll deal with it. You can't keep him hanging round like a safety net in case you fall.'

'He loves me. It'll break his heart if I dump him. This way he gets to keep me – how is that bad?' she demands, attempting to sound rational but pulsing with fury.

'It's bad because he just gets half of you,' I reason.

'Maybe half is all he needs. He's never had more than that anyway. You know that.'

'I always thought you were just keeping him on until you met someone you really liked. And now you have. Do you really need him any more? You haven't even bothered returning his calls lately.'

'I love him, Jamie,' she insists.

'If you loved him you wouldn't be marrying someone else,' I counter.

'Oh please, like, monogamy is really working out for

you!' she snaps, jumping off the bed and walking to the window. 'You're just jealous because I've got two men when all you can manage to attract is a gay guy. At least mine are proper relationships! What's your excuse?'

She's looking at me with such contempt I'm stunned into silence. And she's not even done yet. 'Look at you with Scott! Walking around loving the fact that people must think you're together. Total illusion. I may not be perfect but I'm not afraid to get involved. You never do! You'd rather waste your life believing that Christian will come back to you, dreaming of some pathetic hearts and flowers existence – anything rather than take the chance of really getting in deep with anyone else.'

She glowers at me as I shrink back into the pillow. 'I know you better than you know yourself – running a mile from Finn because you sense there could be something real there. It's such a cop-out. You think you're picky, you're just a coward.'

And with that she storms out of the room, leaving me smarting from her attack. Wasn't it supposed to be me disapproving of her? My God, how long has this been brewing? All those years of supposed support and encouragement . . . Have we just been papering over disapproval for how the other one lived? My initial outrage gives way to hurt. Scott would say that means there must be something in what she said. Am I really such an emotional wimp? 'Perhaps she's right,' I think forlornly, at least she's bold with her loving. And in a way she's making two men happy.

Look at my life, how much love have I actually dished out? There was Christian, of course, but that was ten years ago and since then all the love I've felt for him has just been sent out into the ether, not doing anyone any good. Very few of my crushes have ever amounted to anything – I've stood there with my heart on a platter and they've politely declined, 'Oooh, no thank you. I'm a bit full. But thanks for offering.' And most of my actual boyfriends have had a 'Does it hurt when I do this?' attitude to my heart so I never gave them full access.

All the while I've been holding on to these big ambitions, eagerly awaiting a man who I deem worthy enough for my love. Perhaps I've carefully chosen undeserving boyfriends as the perfect excuse to be miserly with my affections and emotions. Perhaps I should have given more freely like Izzy does. Perhaps I've enjoyed being scandalised by her supposedly mercenary behaviour because by comparison to her I've looked normal. Romantic, even. But what good has it done me? I can sit here and say that she's doing it wrong. I can say I'd never do what she's doing. But she must be doing something right because her cup runneth over and mine is bone dry.

I hear the doorbell ring and Izzy acknowledge a delivery boy. A few minutes later she bursts into my room, tears streaming down her face, hurls a piece of paper at me and screams, 'There, that should make you happy!'

For a second I just stare at the angrily scrumpled

paper. What the hell is going on in the world tonight? Then I pick it up, smooth out the paper and sit back down beside my lamp.

It's a fax. From Dave.

Dear Izzy,

I feel a real heel for not telling you this in person or at least on the phone but you haven't returned my calls so here goes.

Since you've been gone I've been working closely with Elaine on a marketing project and we've come to realise that we never stopped loving each other. I've been dazzled by you ever since we met and I will never love her like I love you but the significant difference is that she needs me. And it feels good to be needed and depended upon. I have been happy to take a back seat in your life and grateful for your occasional glances in the rearview mirror but with Elaine I feel like I get to drive.

You know I would never deliberately set out to hurt you but she has asked me to move in with her and I have accepted. As sudden as this is, it feels right and I hope that in time you can find it in your heart to forgive us and wish us well.

Dave.

Oh God. How can this be? Talk about having to watch out for the quiet ones. Where did a metaphorical mute like Dave get the gumption to leave Izzy? I can't believe he's done it. He was always such a fixture, indistinguishable from any other household object. Him leaving is akin to coming home and finding your sofa gone because it's decided it would prefer to be sat on by some people further down the street.

I re-read the fax this time feeling partly to blame, like I willed it to happen. Only I didn't want it to happen like this. Izzy always thought she could trust Dave, and this is going to hit her hard. Despite the bitter clash we've just had, it kills me to see her crying and I hurry to her room. I can hear sobbing but I can't see its source. A loud sniff from the wardrobe halts the hide and seek.

'Izzy?' I say as I prise open the door. There she is, sitting awkwardly amid Reed's loafers and golf shoes. All the defiance has gone out of her eyes and her face is dribbling with tears. I crawl in beside her and perch on a shoe horn.

'What was all that rearview mirror crap?' she snorts. 'Now he gets to *drive*?' she gasps as her chugging tears get the better of her. I give her hand a squeeze.

'Yeah, but let's face it, it's never gonna be anything more glamorous than a Ford Cortina.'

She smiles for a second and then falls, snot and all, into my arms. I start crying too, creating a big damp patch in her candyfloss hair. Just look at us! One minute we're on top of the world, the next minute we're in a heap of Odour Eaters.

'How could he, Jamie?'

I catch my breath and wipe my eyes on a dangling shirt cuff. 'I don't know. I guess he just wanted to feel like the number one guy and . . .'

She looks at me mournfully.

'I'm not saying you didn't love him but . . .'

'Bitch! Moving in on him the minute I leave the country!' she howls.

'Well, you did steal him off her in the first place . . .' I'm not helping so I shut up.

'I knew I wouldn't really be able to keep both men stringing along,' she admits. 'I just didn't know how I was going to break up with Dave – he's been so good to me, I didn't want to hurt him. Talk about role reversal!' she snivels.

'Perhaps it's a sign.'

'Oh here we go!'

'Well, look at the timing. You've got the chance of a brand-new life here but you wanted to cling on to Dave and not commit to either man or either country. Maybe this has happened now to tell you to go for it here, 100 per cent, whole-heartedly.'

'My heart doesn't feel whole.'

I smile sadly. 'I think I've always underestimated your feelings for Dave so this probably hurts more than I can imagine, but in my mind all that's happened is that your stabilisers have come off your kiddy bicycle. Dave isn't going to be your safety mechanism any more. You may be a bit nervous at first but think of the triumph of pedalling your big bike for the first time.'

'Is this Scott-speak?'

'Maybe!' I concede.

Izzy takes a deep breath. 'About what I said to you before . . .'

'It's all right. It's mostly true.'

'It's not. I was just mad because you were challenging me. I didn't expect it.'

'Neither did I!' I smile. 'Anyway, I probably am jealous of you.'

'That's ridiculous. You've got it all!'

'Hardly.'

'You have – everyone loves you, you're gonna be an award-winning roving reporter, your adventure is just beginning.'

'But will I ever get the guy?' I ask in a small voice.

'You're nearly there, I know it.'

I wish I could believe her. Then again, she is speaking from personal experience, having just got the guy herself. 'You really love Reed, don't you?'

'Don't say that!'

'Why not?'

'Because if I really love him then I'm in big trouble.'

'Why?' I laugh. 'What do you mean?'

'Because then he could hurt me.'

'You big softy!' I tease.

'I am not!'

'Yes, you are! And you call me the coward. I don't get involved at all and you only get involved with people you don't care about enough to hurt you.'

'Yeah, well, I'm not stupid.'

'Anyway, Reed would never hurt you,' I assure her.

'But without Dave as back-up I feel . . .'

'Vulnerable?'

She can't bring herself to agree to such a weakness so I tell her: 'You know, Scott has a theory that you're not as wild and mercenary as you think you are.'

'Bastard!'

'Yeah, but imagine if he were right . . .'

I know there's going to be tough times ahead and that our relationship needs some adjustments but at least we're back on the same team.

'I missed being your friend for a while there!' I tell her.

She smiles affectionately. 'Me too.'

We sit in silence for a minute then Izzy picks up a pair of size 11 red patent lace-ups and grimaces. 'These have got to go.'

35

I've got a road map, a full tank of 'gas', a bottle of water and a giant packet of Gummi Bears. I've been driving for less than twenty minutes and I've already eaten all the green ones. Today I'm going to do exactly as I please. All day. All by myself.

I wanted to make the most of my day off work. It only took a few calls to find a car rental company that would accept a cash deposit instead of a credit card. I may never see my passport again and it's a cronky old tin can but I don't care – it's all I need to get away.

I woke at 6 a.m. this morning, desperate to talk to Izzy, but when I crept into her room I found her candy panto bracelet on Reed's bedside table. His gnawing had turned half the 'beads' to pastel dust and exposed the grey, withered elastic. So much for us wearing our matching set on our wedding day. It was no doubt just an innocent case of Midnight Munchies on his part but it seemed more symbolic than that and it led me to question our devotion to keeping pacts we made in our teenage years. Should they have so much power and significance? It's funny – you feel like you are failing to be true to yourself if you let your youthful ambitions slide and yet you don't take into account how much the years change your ideas about what you want and what makes you happy. I'm not the same person now I was when I was eighteen. And yet a eighteen-year-old me is ruling my life, still insisting on a double wedding in Las Vegas. I wish I knew what the twenty-seven-year-old me wanted. I wish I could be as sure about anything as I was when I was at school. Why does life play such twisted tricks? Before we came to America all I wanted was excitement and romance. Today, I'd just settle for a bit of peace.

Lake Mead became the day's destination after an early morning conversation with Scott. He'd already been on a six-mile run and downed a pint of wheatgrass so was feeling nauseatingly perky and positive. He suggested I try breaking my muzzy-headed fug by coming out of my comfort zone. Seeing as this basically means doing something that seems to require too much effort, is unfamiliar or makes you feel a bit nervous, I wasn't convinced. But then I knew cocooning in my duvet for all eternity wouldn't bring on the changes I so desperately crave. Scott reckoned that seeing as Lake Mead is only half an hour's drive from Vegas, it wouldn't push me too hard. And so far so good . . .

I wind down the window and let the warm air ruffle my hair. It feels wonderful to be on the road again. Viggo Mortensen wrote in a poem that 'motion is sanctuary', and I can relate to that. Increasing the pressure on the accelerator I wonder whether it might be possible to outrun my problems.

I come off the main freeway and relax on to the windy roads leading to the lake. It's a rocky, dusty terrain, more bleached and sprawling than Red Rock Canyon but striking nonetheless, especially when you consider that the 550 miles of shoreline is entirely man-made. I pass families unloading cars, slopping on suncream and loading up their youngest sprog with so much beach gear he can't see to walk, and find a suitable place to park.

Down at the lake, I see gangs of friends deciding which boat best suits their need for speed and I can't help wishing I had a playmate with me. If Finn were here I'd probably find myself astride a jet ski, clinging on to him for dear life. Mind you, if I did fall in the water, who better to rescue me? I smile thinking of his strong hand helping me across the crevices at Red Rock Canyon and remember his words: 'I wouldn't let you fall!'

A man hands me a leaflet offering a nice, leisurely cruise across the lake on the Desert Princess paddle steamer. Perfect! I amble over to the ticket office. Nice and safe. Nice and familiar. I can hear Scott tutting from here. I shuffle forward. What if . . .? No. I couldn't. I'm nearly at the desk. Could I? Dare I?

'How many?' asks the girl behind the counter.

'Er, one. No, sorry!' I stop her. She looks up. 'I'm in the wrong line!' I apologise, turning to leave. 'I want to hire a jet ski!'

I can't believe I've said it out loud! I move fast before I change my mind and feel a rush of pride as I strap on a life jacket. Contemplating the sleek machine bobbing at the water's edge I wonder what on earth I've done. This is so not me.

I'm tentative at first, wary of even the tiniest ripple, trying to pootle along at one mile an hour and letting go of the handlebars every few seconds to reassure myself that the power will cut instantaneously. Everyone else is bouncing around, flying through the air and crashing into tidal wave turns. I curse myself for being such a wuss but continue my Sunday driver behaviour until I find a stretch of lake all of my own. I turn the handles slightly and grip tightly as I speed up to two miles an hour then stop again and catch my breath. Gradually I get bolder and discover that the faster I go the smoother the ride. I dare myself to accelerate to full power and feel a rush of exhilaration as the motor roars in approval. Faster! Faster! My heart breaks out of the miserable dungeon where it's been lurking in a dank corner and embraces the sun and spray. I'm smiling – a true, natural smile. Suddenly I feel grateful for everything, not bogged down. I've got a new perspective. I feel defiantly independent. Look at me! I don't have to cling to Izzy or to Christian for my happiness. There is pleasure to be found in things I've never even dreamt of, things I've never tried.

The breeze strokes my face and ruffles my hair as I take a more gentle pace around a corner and discover a deserted bay. I cruise closer and then run the jet ski up on to the shore. The sun is blinding and the sand too hot to endure with bare feet. There's no one around to offend with my blubber so I whip off my T-shirt and shorts and splash back into the water in my cossie. Bliss. I tip my head back to wet my hair and then swim around, swirling and dancing. Instead of searching out the warm bits like I used to do in the sea back home in Teignmouth, I'm trying to find cool patches of water. I let my body relax and float on my back with my eyes closed. There's not a soul in the world that knows where I am.

At this moment in time I'm not wrong, I'm not the ugly friend, I'm not the irresponsible daughter or the reject sister. What do I want to get married for anyway? There is so much more to life! There is so much more to me!

I stride out of the water feeling as fabulous as Ursula Andress in *Dr No* and stretch out on my towel. I wish I had the money to rent a houseboat and stay overnight. Or maybe even for ever. I could become a floating hermit. Actually I think I'd prefer to be a nomad if it came to it. You get to travel more that way. Now I think of it I've still got a couple more months on my visa. If only I could come up with a way of funding a journey across America. I'd love to go to Montana and whisper to some horses. Or mambo in Miami. Or get mugged in Manhattan. Anywhere that begins with an M – Massachusetts, Milwaukee, Madison . . . I'm overwhelmed with options. Maybe I could set myself up as a kind of Vegas correspondent and send stories back to some national newspaper as well as the *Express & Echo*? Or better yet, write for some magazines. I've heard about a legal brothel based about an hour away in a place called Pahrump, that would be great for *FHM*. And what about getting a group of showgirls to do a Tried & Tested on fake eyelashes for *Looks*? And I'm sure *more!* would do something on the Golden Guys, they can't get enough naked men. Even for the younger magazines like *Mizz*, I could do an 'I go to school in Las Vegas' piece – picture a girl in her uniform with all the glitzy lights behind her. Yeah! I'm buzzing now! I'd probably have to write the pieces on spec, seeing as they don't know my work but it would be fun to do, even if they didn't get published. It would give me a purpose, something for myself. It might take a bit of time to establish myself but it's got to be worth a try. I'll work on a game plan when it's quiet in the shop. Anything feels possible right now. Optimism – welcome back! I've missed you!

I stay until the light dims and then drive back with the sunset changing all around me. It's magnificent company. When I get to Vegas, great purpley-yellow swirls loom overhead. The clouds look like bruises. Maybe it's a fight night.

Back in the (empty) suite I put off having a bath – I'm still relishing the sensation of having gritty sand between my toes, lightly scorched skin and ratty, tangled hair. I look relaxed but rough. It's like Red Rock Canyon all over again and suddenly it occurs to me that both my forages into the Great Outdoors have

334

been great successes. I'm not sure where this newfound infatuation with nature has come from – I guess it's an acquired taste, like olives.

I listen to my three voicemail messages: one jokey one from Scott, 'call me' from Layla and finally Sam asking if I would stay until 11 p.m. for a stock-check tomorrow. Not exactly my idea of a fun Friday night but he is offering double pay and I haven't got any better offers – Izzy will be out with Reed entertaining one of his Asian business associates, Scott has his show and then a drag queen's pal's birthday party to go to and Cindy and Layla are working at Lap and Tickle. Counting mugs and ashtrays it is then.

As I forage under my pillow for my pyjamas I spot an envelope on the bedside table. There's a message scribbled from Izzy on the back.

Gone to dinner. Hope you had a good day. These faxes came for you. I haven't read them – it's probably just Dave realising how paralysingly boring Elaine is, asking if you think I'll take him back. If so, the answer's no! Big kiss! Iz.

'Well, she's perked up,' I think as I remove two sheets from the envelope. I squint at the first with one eye. It's from my mum. I have a pang of guilt and look at the second. Nadine! That can't be good. Perhaps Christian has confessed his everlasting love for me and she's raging. Yeah, right. I shove them both back in the envelope and rush to the kitchen. Nice cup of herbal tea and bed. Don't read them. Not yet. You don't want to spoil this good mood. Don't want to get sucked back down. Stay away from the light.

I bluster around turning on the stereo, then the TV, then the extractor fan, then the ice-maker. Nothing can drown out the sound of the faxes waiting to be read. I take a deep breath. Nadine's first. Two paragraphs. How much damage can she do in two paragraphs?

Hello big sister! Or should that be huge sister with all those buffets out there?

Excellent start.

I never thought I'd ever have to go anywhere as vulgar as Las Vegas but Christian says his uncle is most unwell and I can't abandon him at such a difficult time.

Sam sick? He sounded fine on the machine. What could have happened? Fast-food overdose? I'll check on him first thing tomorrow.

Of course he wanted to spare me – what with so much still to organise for our wedding – but seeing as you now claim to be getting married I feel obliged to keep an eye on Mother. I can't believe she is travelling alone to such a corrupt place. (Father is categorically refusing to condone such a fiasco – his words.) I hope you know what you are doing.

By all accounts you are being pretty cagey about your 'fiancé'. Having seen Leaving Las Vegas *(and all your*

previous boyfriends) I fear the worst. Anyway, I'll be able to see for myself in two days' time. I just hope the weather is good. It's raining here and if I can top up my tan before my wedding at least the trip won't be totally wasted. Sam is sending someone to meet us but for your reference we're staying at some bastardised version of a European city – Paris, Las Vegas. Sounds ghastly. Still, I'm sure we'll laugh about it all when we get back to England.
Nadine.

Cow! I flick to my mother's letter before I get too steamed up.

Just a quickie to let you know to expect a fax from Nadine. I gave her your details because she'll be with you in a couple of days! I did ask if she would fly out with me but she doesn't seem to want to let Christian out of her sight at the moment. Poor darling, I'm sure it's just wedding jitters again but she got quite hysterical on the phone the other night. She has convinced herself he's got another woman, silly girl. She's got no evidence as far as I can see – no lipstick on the collar. It's just that he's been reading old poetry books. I don't see how that could be incriminating, do you? He's probably trying to find some nice words to surprise her for the wedding day.

My heart starts pounding. It's quite possible I've been reading the same poems as Christian at the same time. Are we thinking the same thing? Reliving the same precious memories? Dreaming of the same willow tree?

Anyway, the good news is that I've been busy liaising with Colin and Amanda and it looks like they'll be on the same flight as me! Colin is a hoot, isn't he? Apparently he really has a thing for air stewards. Am I too old to become a fag hag, what do you think?

Like daughter, like mother is what I think. I slump on the sofa. No amount of camomile tea will soothe this away. My earlier confidence and clarity has become muddled and muzzy again. Why is it so hard to hold on to those breakthrough moments? How can a whole day's euphoria evaporate just like that? I may as well forget Michigan, Minneapolis and Maryland – another more pertinent M-word has come back to haunt me: MARRIAGE.

What the hell do I do now? I grab one of the tasselled cushions and squeeze it tight. If Christian is coming for me – and I have no proof of that – I don't want to put him off by wafting around with a fake fiancé. On the other hand, he thinks I'm engaged for real and he's coming anyway. Maybe his uncle really is sick. But then there's the poetry – our poetry . . . Izzy would say that the best way to get him back would be to get him jealous. She's old-fashioned like that. Maybe she's right. In which case I'd have to take Scott up on his offer. Then Christian would challenge him to a duel and win back my hand and I'll get my Vegas wedding with the man of my dreams after all.

Of course every silver lining has a cloud, i.e.: Nadine. She's not going to roll over easily. I could get Scott to lend me his spikiest jousting pole but if

Christian truly loves her and has no intention of leaving her, I'll have to let her live.

Either way there's no way she's going to beat me to the altar. Oh no, she's not going to win this race. And she's not going to come here and find me groomless. I promised a Scott and I shall deliver a Scott. It's not like most heterosexual males are any great cop anyway. I really couldn't think of nicer husband material than The Grin. And I would be doing a good deed as far as his mum goes. And Amanda and Colin would get a kick out of it. Did I mention I've swapped my herbal tea for Bailey's? With an extra splash of whisky.

I feverishly dial Scott's number.

'Sin City Sinners!' he chirrups.

'It's me.'

'Hey, you.'

'So, do you want a wife or what?'

36

I wake before the alarm goes off and lie in bed trying to identify the cause of the heavy feeling in my stomach. Then I remember what Nadine said about Uncle Sam's health and dial his number. He answers in two rings and says he's never felt better – until I tell him that Nadine is under the impression he's chronically ill, then he says he had a 'nasty scare' yesterday and was putting on a brave face for me. Ho hum.

'See you in an hour!' I tell him.

It's another scorcher and I'm running out of outfits. Maybe I'll get a chance to go to the mall tomorrow. What I really need is something new to blow Christian away at the engagement party. He dresses a lot smarter than when I knew him and Nadine is always so well turned out, I've got to look immaculate. I seem to remember him liking me in blue . . .

The morning passes uneventfully with me spending most of my time trying to picture the perfect outfit, and the look of rapture on Christian's face when he first sees me. Nikki is not in the best of moods, complaining that

Sam is in a heightened state of perviness today. I don't get any details because we're suddenly swamped by coachloads of Japanese tourists buying infinite tacky items, a good deal of which were Made in Japan.

At 1 o'clock I nip over to the Holy Cow for a veggie burger and when I return Sam is shouting at the till.

'Where's Nikki?' I ask, calmly replacing the till roll for him.

'Oh, she had an emergency. She had to go home,' he says, looking even more flustered.

'What kind of emergency?' I say, immediately suspicious.

'Her mother fell down the stairs,' he says. 'Worst day to leave us short what with the stock-check tonight.'

Heartless bastard. Nikki did say she was worried leaving her mother in the house alone. Apparently she was always having accidents and making claims on their medical insurance.

The afternoon is thankfully pretty quiet and at about 5 o'clock Sam says he's going to the post office and asks me to woman the phones. He's barely out the door when it rings.

'Sam's Shopping Extravaganza!' I chirrup.

'Lo? Sam? Cana speak to Sam?' a male voice slurs.

'I'm afraid Mr Johnson isn't here right now, can I take a message?'

'Jamie?'

'Yes! Who's that?'

'Jamieee, iss Christian!'

My heart flips. 'Are you . . . Have you been . . .?'

'Drunk asah skunk! How diju guess?'

I can't help smiling. I look at my watch and add eight hours – it's just gone 1 a.m. in the UK.

'Don't you have to be up early for your flight tomorrow?'

'Yup! Sixsh a.m. Not goen t'bed. Gunna havvanuvva drink.'

'Are you sure you should?' I ask, concerned.

'God! Slike talking t'yer sister!'

I'm outraged! 'Drink what you like!'

'Thankoo. Churrrs!' I hear a ringpull get torn back followed by a pssssht sound.

'Ahhh! Thash better!' He smacks his lips. 'So! Yur gettin marreeed!'

Oh my God! Is he drunk on my account? Is he drowning his sorrows? I turn away from the couple of tourists that have just entered the shop.

'Christian – are you okay?' I hiss down the phone.

'Yesh, yesh. Why wooddin I be? Yur getting marreeeed, I'm gettin mareeed . . .'

Oh God! Shall I tell him the truth? No, he's too drunk to understand me, there's no point. I'll have to try to talk to him when he gets here. But what do I say now?

'Jamieee?'

'Yes?' I say, holding my breath.

'Beeeeeautiful Jamieeee . . .'

'Um, hold on, yes everything's a dollar in the basket. Yes, yes, EVERYTHING!' I bark at the tourists.

I place my ear back to the receiver. Christian's voice has lowered and his slur softened. 'Look in my face; my name is Might-have been; I am also called No-

342

more, Too-late, Farewell.'

Oh God, now he's quoting Rossetti.

'Christian, I . . .'

'Farewell,' he sighs. 'Farewell . . .'

I hear a click and the phone goes dead. Now what? I can't call back, I'll wake Nadine. I pace around behind the counter, fretting. Customers come and go, all getting consistently appalling service from me. My mind is elsewhere, somewhere at the bottom of Christian's can of beer, I suspect. By 7 p.m. I'm ready for a large alcoholic beverage myself but instead I get a clipboard.

'Right, you start with the purses and handbags. I'm going to do the glassware,' Sam announces.

I find the monotony of counting the stock both calming and absorbing and the first two hours pass quickly. I'm about to move on to the belts when Sam comes over to check on me.

'How are you getting on? Oooh, aren't you the little eager beaver! We should be finished early if you keep up this pace,' he says, patting my bum as he moves on to the game section.

I give him a dark look and go back to my counting. At least this isn't the kind of job that invites chit-chat. Eleven p.m. and my eyes are going all swirly from the concentration and the strip lighting. I move on to my final shelf – Dashboard Hulas. Hmmmm, 12, 13, 14 . . . I straighten up and wave my clipboard at Sam. 'I'm done!'

'Good job, Jamie,' he says, flicking through the completed sheets. 'Come through to the office.'

I'm exhausted and lean on the doorframe to support myself.

'We pay on a Friday so here's your money for four days plus tonight's overtime.'

'Thank you,' I say, taking the envelope of cash.

'Now, how about a drop of whisky? I'm having one myself.'

I would never have guessed from his breath.

'No, I'm okay.'

'Can of something?' he says, opening the fridge.

I'm gasping.

'I wouldn't mind a Dr Pepper, thanks.'

'Why don't you take a seat?' he says, indicating the sofa. Seconds later he's by my side, arm stretching out along the back of the sofa. I sit forward to avoid merging our personal spaces. He knocks back shot after shot as he talks me through supply and demand for the Native American moccasin.

'You know, Jamie, you strike me as a stylish woman. I'm wondering if I might be able to get your advice about this T-shirt sample we've been sent.'

He gets up, using my knee as a prop, then rummages behind his desk and pulls out a pale pink top with raised lettering.

'I'd love to get your opinion. Would you try it on for me?'

Uh-oh. Please don't let this be a perve. I'm too tired to do any vigorous self-defence moves. 'It looks a bit small, are you sure it's adult's?'

'It's meant to be tight. That's the idea,' he says, handing it to me. 'Here, pop it on and we'll see how it looks.'

I can't tell if he's being weird but decide to give him

the benefit of the doubt as he's behaved himself all week. I nip into the loos to change. It's quite a squeeze but I get it on.

'Ooh, that looks great! How does it feel?' he asks when I emerge.

'Okay,' I say.

He walks up to me and inspects the seam. 'Not too tight here?' he says, touching under the arms.

'No, it's fine,' I say, eyes narrowing.

'What size are you?'

'UK 14 usually. But it depends on the shop.'

'I mean, what bra size?'

This is definitely creeping me out. 'Um, 36B. I think I'll change back now.'

'Hold on a second,' he says, moving closer. 'You know what's special about this T-shirt? It responds to body heat. Say if I put my hands here . . .'

I bat them away. 'What are you doing?'

'I'm just trying to demonstrate the T-shirt . . .'

'I can see the different colours fine,' I say, noticing panic-induced splodges of peach and purple.

'You seem to be getting rather hot!' he observes, licking his lips.

An image of Little Red Riding Hood and a salivating wolf spring to mind so I dart past him to the loos and rip off the T-shirt in such a hurry I get in a right tangle – my arms are twisted up over my face leaving my body exposed. I grunt in exasperation.

'Do you need any help?'

'No! Stay where you are,' I cry.

I finally tug the neck free, smearing it with a fair

portion of my foundation while I'm at it. Fortunately it just looks like another smudge of colour. I hand it back and try to ignore Sam's 'Mmm, still warm' comment.

'I think I'd better go.'

'You're still on my time, I've paid you up until midnight,' he says, closing the office door and leaning back on it with a leer.

Oh no you don't.

'You know, I was just thinking,' I begin, 'perhaps we should call Nikki and see how she's coping with her emergency . . .'

He looks nervously at the phone. I make a move towards it and he leaps across the room, grabbing it off the desk.

'Only I really am quite concerned,' I say, staring into his murky khaki eyes, 'you said her mother fell down the stairs and what with Nikki living in a bungalow . . .'

'Get out!' he spits.

As soon as I'm out of Sam's sight I run and run and run, pounding down the street on trembling legs. Poor Christian. He obviously doesn't know what his uncle has become. I feel dirty just from trying on the T-shirt. I wonder how many other girls have been tricked into wearing it. Pausing to catch my breath I shudder at what could have happened. If he'd been bigger or stronger or just more drunk . . . I dread to think. I won't be going back to the shop but I will be checking on Nikki. In the meantime, I don't want to be alone in the hotel. If only I knew where Scott's friend's birthday party was. What would he suggest I do now? He'd tell me to try to get centred. To fill myself with something good to push away the bad. The aquarium would be ideal but Caesar's shopping forum will be closed at this time of night. Hold on, didn't Finn say there was a tank at the Mirage?

The pavement is chock-a-block with weekend party people so it's a relief to get off the street and into the relative calm of the hotel. I ask one of the girls pushing a trolley of change where the aquarium is and she points to her right. I'm instantly enraptured by the flitting fish and brightly-coloured corals. I move closer. The tank stretches the length of the reception area, set back behind the staff and their computers. What an ingenious way of soothing guests queuing to check in. How could anyone maintain any impatience confronted with this bliss?

Seconds ago I felt freaked out and tense, now I feel my shoulders drop and my fist unscrunch. This is my kind of hydrotherapy.

Suddenly someone grabs me from behind.

'GET OFF ME!' I screech, swinging round to face my attacker. 'Oh! Finn! I'm sorry. I thought . . .'

'Are you okay?'

'Yes, yes. I just had a horrible day at the shop.'

'Sticker gun jam or something?'

'Or something . . .' I shrug, no desire to relive the experience. 'What are you doing here?'

'I've just been hanging out with Splash and Sprite.'

'The dolphins?'

He nods.

'Really? Oh wow! Were you in the water with them?'

'Of course,' he smiles, pausing for a moment and then adding: 'Would you like to try it?'

'Oh yeah, it's my dream. That guy Todd that works here said he might give me a backstage tour one day.'

'I can do better than that right now. If you can keep a secret,' he says playfully.

'What do you mean?'

'Well, it's after hours. No one is around.' He lowers his voice, 'I've got the key.'

'You mean, now – we could go there now?' I say, excitement swirling up through my fatigue. 'Will you get into trouble?'

'Only if we get caught,' he deadpans.

'Is it worth the risk?'

'Would it make your day better?'

'Are you kidding? It would transform it!' I laugh.

'Then it's worth it. Come on . . .'

The dolphins scuttle over to Finn and chatter their welcome. He rubs their heads affectionately.

'Will they be freaked out by me, you know, being a stranger?' I ask.

'No, it's cool. They trust me.'

'Any friend of Finn's . . .?' I smile.

'Exactly.'

I kneel at the side of the pool and swoosh my hand through the water.

'Talk about midnight at the oasis!' I say, gazing

around at the moonlit palm trees. 'It's so peaceful here after dark.'

'Are you going to get in?' he asks.

'In this?' I say, pulling at my dress.

'Here, you can put on my wetsuit. I've got swim-shorts.'

'I always seem to be wearing your clothes!' I say, then suddenly feel embarrassed.

He smiles. 'You can change in here . . .'

Easier said than done. The wetsuit is such an incredibly tight fit I feel like I'm trying to stretch a tube of liquorice over my body. My knees bulge unappealingly and I dread to think what I look like from behind. I peek my head around the door. Finn is already in the water, flipping and ducking and rolling with the dolphins.

I scamper to the water's edge and swiftly submerge myself.

He swims over to my side. 'Okay, Jamie meet Splash . . . and Sprite.'

I blink at their shiny black eyes.

'What should I do?'

'Let them come to you, then you can touch them but don't wave your arms around too much and keep your movements as fluid as possible.'

As they brush up against me I gingerly extend my hand and rub their squeaky sleek skin, chuckling at their grinning faces.

'We'll give them a chance to get used to you and then maybe go for a ride.'

'Does it hurt them, holding on to their fin?' I ask, concerned.

'It can if you're not careful. There are no bones in the dorsal fin, just fibrous tissue.'

Finn shows me exactly how to hold on. He looks completely at one with the dolphins. It's amazing to behold. I feel strangely proud of him.

'Okay,' he says, returning to me. 'Your turn now, you might feel the urge to squeal but remember we have to keep quiet.'

'Okay,' I whisper. And then we're off, rushing through the water like a torpedo. It's exhilarating. And I thought jet skis were cool.

'That was incredible!' I gasp. 'Can I go again?'

'Ask Splash!'

I reach out my hand, no sooner is it on his fin than he shoots off again. My body gets pummelled by the waves as we arch our way back to Finn.

'You're a natural!' he laughs. 'Now try this.'

Finn floats flat out on his back and Splash and Sprite put a nose to each of his feet and push him head first through the water. Brilliant! Now it's my turn.

'You might find it easier holding this float,' he suggests as he levels me out, putting one hand on the small of my back and one under my head. I feel so secure with him holding me, I don't want him ever to let go.

'Okay?' he asks.

'Yes,' I sigh, savouring the moment. Then he motions to Splash and Sprite, their noses nudge me and back I go! Whoosh!

'I love it!' I enthuse. 'God, I envy you! What a job!'

I dip my head back in the water and look up at the

stars. 'This is heaven,' I sigh. I turn to face Finn. 'You've turned an ugly day into a beautiful one,' I tell him. 'Thank you so much.'

'My pleasure,' he glows.

For a second we just smile at each other and then I ask a thousand and one dolphin questions. Finn illustrates his answers with the help of his two gorgeous assistants.

'Now can I ask you something?' he says, moving closer to me.

I nod.

'Do you still have feelings for Zane?'

My face falls. 'God! I'm so embarrassed! Reed got the wrong end of the stick and . . . you know, I like him as a friend but . . .' I splutter.

'It's okay,' he says softly. 'I just wondered if you . . . and if you don't . . . well, um, what are you doing tomorrow night?'

'God, Saturday, I know there's something – oh my God! My sister and her fiancé arrive in town.'

'Oh.' he looks crestfallen. 'Special occasion?'

'Yes. Well . . .'

He tilts his head expectantly.

'It's . . . you know Izzy and Reed?'

'Yes,' he says patiently.

'They got engaged. We're having a joint engagement party.'

His brow furrows. 'Joint?'

'That's right. I got engaged last night. To Scott. You don't know him. It happened kind of fast . . .'

Finn looks confused. 'You're kidding, right?'

351

I shake my head.

'You're getting married?'

'Yes,' I say, watching his disbelief morph into anger. I feel a sense of dread. What have I done? Suddenly he disappears below the water, stays there for a few seconds, then hauls himself out of the pool in one move. Looking down on me he glowers. 'You're a fast worker, aren't you? Didn't work out with Zane so you're on to the next. Well, good luck.'

'Finn, it's not like that!' I protest, scrambling out of the water with far less expertise.

'How is it then?' he asks, wet face level with mine. 'Is it a green card you're after?'

'No!'

'What, then?' he barks.

'It's complicated . . .' I flounder.

'Oh, I get it,' he says, a strange look in his eyes. 'Izzy isn't the only one out here to hook a Sugar Daddy!'

'What? No!'

'Boy, did I read you wrong!' he snorts, tugging on his jeans and bowling shirt without even drying himself. 'We have to go.'

I just stand forlornly not knowing what to say.

'NOW!' he snaps.

I feel his eyes boring into me as I struggle to peel off the wetsuit.

'Where shall I hang it?' I quaver, finally back in my dress.

He snatches the wetsuit out of my hand and shoves it in his locker. I feel all teary and told off.

'Finn,' I begin nervously.

'Ready?' he growls.

'Yes,' I say, meekly following him back to the hotel.

The second we're in the casino he vanishes. I look all around me but the crowds have swallowed him up. I feel overcome with panic and loss.

'Finn!' I call into the crowd. No reply.

I push my wet hair away from my face and try to fight off the horrible nauseous sinking feeling. I don't want to feel like this. I haven't done anything wrong. Have I? Talk about an overreaction. What's his problem anyway?

'I hate him!' I decide. 'Who does he think he is, accusing me of marrying for a green card! I'm marrying for . . . I'm marrying for . . .'

I let out a low rumble of frustration. I realise I sound like Doris Day shortly after being insulted by Rock Hudson in one of those movies like *Pillow Talk*. See! See! He was gay and they lived happily ever after. I know what I'm doing! Everything is going to work out just fine.

After gourmet pizza room service back at the hotel I'm still haunted by an empty feeling and I can't seem to stay with the conversation Reed and Izzy are having. I'm not even interested in talking about Christian.

'I think I'll go to bed,' I volunteer finally.

'Quite right – we've got a big day ahead of us,' says Reed ominously.

I climb into bed with my new book on dolphins. Just one more chapter then I'll turn out the light . . .

37

The sky is an opulent, optimistic blue and hovering somewhere up above me is Christian. His plane lands in under an hour. I feel like I'm waiting for an angel to descend. I close my eyes, squeezing the hot metal of the balcony bar. Rescue me. Rescue me. Rescue me . . .

Suddenly I feel guilty. Five minutes ago I got a reality-check/pep talk from Scott and already I'm daydreaming, straying from the path. He says it's important I stay on track and hold it together for the engagement party tonight. He says I have to look forward, not back. But in looking forward I can't have any expectations. Easier said than done. I wish there was a Present Tense Pill you could take to keep your mind from wandering hither and thither. I only have to lose concentration for a minute and I find myself in a reverie, dreaming of Christian Past . . .

Part of me is dreading seeing him. I know I shall be compelled to bring things to a climax, particularly after that phone call. No more wondering what if . . . I need to know for sure – will we ever be together again? And by forcing a response I run the risk of discovering that we will never be reunited and that the absent ache I feel is going to be with me for ever.

As much as I pretend to Izzy that I've moved on, I've never stopped wanting him, never stopped hoping he'd come back for me. I may have got myself in a right old state about other boys (mostly for something to do I now think) but Christian had the whole of my heart. And I had the whole of his. I've never felt as loved as I did with him and that's the saddest thing of all – I don't feel that lovable any more. I can't really imagine anyone being that profoundly moved by me again. But I had it once. No wonder I'm nostalgic.

'Dollar for your thoughts – as if I don't know what they are!'

I turn around and find Izzy enjoying a breakfast of Reese's Peanut Butter Cups. No pre-wedding diet for her. Or me for that matter – I wolf down three of the sickly little throat-cloggers in succession. Once sufficient saliva has returned to my mouth I sigh: 'There's something wrong when you only get to see the man of your dreams by inviting him to your engagement party.'

'Life is so warped, isn't it?' Izzy agrees, licking her fingers.

'God, I feel so, so . . .'

'Be American if you want.'

'Thank you! So *un-centered*.'

'You're bound to feel a bit "on the verge". It's a pretty mental situation.'

'Any Izzy wisdom to send me on my way?'

'Well, you know I never was sold on Christian . . . but if he rocks your world you may as well have a damn good try at winning him back.'

'Do you think marrying someone else is the best way to do that?'

Izzy shrugs. 'Let's just see how tonight goes. Maybe you won't have to.'

'Did Cindy call yet?'

'Yeah, she left a message saying her and Layla will be there early cos they know the guy that runs the bar upstairs from the restaurant. And I spoke to Zane and he's bringing Mia and Finn . . .'

'Finn?'

'Yup. And you can take that look off your face. Zane said he wouldn't be able to make it unless Finn came too. He'd already promised to do something with him tonight.'

'But I told you how rude he was to me at the dolphin pool!'

'I think you're overreacting. Besides, if he's cool about coming along . . .'

'I just think I'll feel uncomfortable having him there.'

'You said you wanted as many people to distract Nadine as possible.'

'I know, but . . .'

'You fancy him!'

'I don't!'

'Then what's the problem?'

I make a childish whining noise.

'Finn keeps the whole boy/girl seating arrangement pucker. He's coming. Deal with it.'

'Okay,' I concede, no fight in me. 'So: you, me, Reed, Scott, Cindy, Layla, Zane, Mia, Finn, Christian, Nadine and ugh! Uncle Sam.'

'Or to put it another way, three strippers, one lifeguard, one Arthurian knight, one architect, one pet correspondent, one gold-digger, one rich business-man, one accountant, one gift-shop mogul and one fish-feeder.'

'Aquarist.'

'Or for maximum mind-bending effect, think of it this way: your first love, your first Vegas crush, the man you are in denial about fancying, the man who tried to grope you at work and your gay husband-to-be.'

I look aghast.

'Table for twelve, Voodoo Cafe, 8 p.m.'

Izzy and I researched many engagement party venues on a 'the darker the better' principle. The Voodoo Cafe at the Rio hotel is on a par with the Peppermill for cave-like blackness and yet has the added attraction of disturbing witch doctor decor and strips of that eerie fluorescent light that makes your clothes look coated with dandruff. Better yet, it's position on the 51st floor affords one of the best views of the dazzling lights of Las Vegas – always an advantage to be able to yelp, 'Wow! Look at that!' when facing a lie-infested situation . . .

At precisely ten to 8, Reed leads us through the haunted house-style entrance, fumbling his way to the maître d'. I don't tell Izzy that her white G-string is glowing through her slinky black knit dress and she doesn't tell me that my freckles look like I have a horrific pigment disorder. But we both tell Scott to stop muttering, 'Heterosexual, heterosexual, heterosexual . . .' under his breath.

I've instructed him to throw 'man' and 'dude' into the conversation wherever possible and he's indulged me by removing his Superman ring and letting his eyebrows go unplucked for two days.

'Okay.' Izzy surveys the table before us. 'You need Scott to be nudgeable to your right or left, me to be kickable under the table, Nadine seated next to Uncle Sam so she'll be forced to make plenty of polite in-law-esque small talk leaving Christian free to have lots of meaningful eye contact directly opposite you.'

'And it's got to be Mia next to Christian because she's a babe but she's taken and besides she's the vocal equivalent of nails down a blackboard!' I offer.

'Good call!' says Scott. 'Who do you want the other side of Uncle Sam?'

'Layla can handle him,' suggests Izzy.

'Which leaves Cindy and Finn side by side,' concludes Scott.

'That's okay, she's used to men with bizarre fetishes,' assures Izzy.

'What's that supposed to mean?'

'Just that if he starts going on about flipper-flexibility or coral formation she'll know how to disguise her boredom . . .'

'Finn is not boring!'

'You fancy him!'

358

'I don't!'

'Fish-lover!'

'Ladies!' soothes Reed.

'Let's get some drinks,' says Scott, motioning to the waiter. 'Now, my darling wife-to-be, what nectar of the gods can we summon for you?'

'Long Island Iced Tea.'

'Is that wise?' says Izzy, no doubt flashing back through all too many of our LIIT tragedies.

'No, but I need it.'

'Go on then,' says Izzy. 'I'll join you.'

'Me too,' says Reed.

'Three Long Island Iced Teas and one Corona,' Scott instructs the waiter. 'And now I need to pee.'

'God, I'm so nervous! Do you think we look like a real couple?' I ask as I watch Scott sashay through the tables.

'It'll be fine,' says Izzy. 'What do you care what Nadine thinks anyway?'

Suddenly Reed winces. 'What is that awful noise?'

Izzy and I look up and chorus, 'Mia!'

We embrace her and Zane, who smells as deliciously arousing as ever.

'This is Reed,' introduces Izzy. 'Of course, you've already met Finn . . .'

Finn steps out from behind Zane and shakes his hand. 'Yeah, congratulations, sir!'

Reed looks awkward and mutters, 'Have you seen this great view!'

Bastard! He's used up one of our View lives and we're only minutes into the evening.

Finn turns to me. 'Congratulations to you too. Love is in the air, I guess.'

'I'm surprised you came,' I say.

'You're impossible to stay mad with! Don't ask me why – it drives me crazy!'

'Oh Christ – here it comes!' warns Izzy.

I turn around to see Nadine stomping towards me with Christian traipsing behind.

'What a curious choice of restaurant!' she simpers. 'If I'd have known I'd have brought my voodoo doll and pins.'

'And there was I thinking you never left home without them,' Izzy smiles.

Nadine blanks her, kisses the air vaguely near my cheek and then eyes Finn.

'So you're the man crazy enough to want to marry my sister!'

I let out a strangled cry but Finn just shrugs, 'I'm not Scott, if that's what you mean.'

'Oh,' says Nadine. 'It's just with your matching outfits . . .'

Finn and I take in each other's ensembles – we're both wearing midnight-blue suits, only mine is raw silk and his is velvet.

'Is it you?' She turns to Zane.

Oh good grief. 'No, Nadine . . .' I begin.

'Surely not?' She gawps at Reed.

'This one is mine,' says Izzy. 'I see the jet lag hasn't affected your tact any.'

'Well, where is he then?' says Nadine, exuding suspicion.

'Right behind you, lady!' says Scott, squeezing her ribs in a highly inappropriate way. 'So you're the sexy sister-in-law?'

Nadine recoils from his grasp and is temporarily blinded by the glare from his souped-up smile. 'You're Scott?'

'Yes, ma'am! Pleased to meet you! And I guess you're Christian?'

'Yes, hi! Congratulations on your engagement! These Miller girls are quite something.'

'Yes, I know.' Scott grins, practically winding me with his squeeze. 'We won't fight over who got the best one!'

'Oh I think I know the answer to that!' says Christian, bending to kiss me hello.

Nadine yanks him away, hissing, 'I need to sit down!'

Everyone pulls up the nearest chair, instantly throwing out my seating plan. I now have Christian on my left (as in *sitting next to me* – oh my God!), Scott to my right and Finn full frontal. Poor Zane is next to Nadine and I can already picture her sneer when she discovers what he does for a living.

'I thought your uncle was coming with you . . .' I address Christian's shirtsleeve, afraid to look him in the eye.

'Yeah, he's running late. Got to break in a new girl.'

'Oh. Right,' I mumble.

'Let's hope she knows where to find the heaviest paperweights and pointiest pens,' mutters Izzy.

'He's quite a stickler in the workplace, isn't he?' says Christian.

'He certainly likes things done his way,' I grimace.

'I can't wait to see him again – it's been years since we saw each other last.'

I pick up my killer cocktail and glug and glug.

'Do you think I should go and get Cindy and Layla?' offers Izzy. 'Everyone seems ready to order.'

'Yeah, I'll come with you, actually.'

As I get to my feet I have second thoughts about leaving Scott unattended.

'Don't worry, baby! I'll be fine!' he says, pulling me into a kiss.

I catch Finn's eye as I attempt to ruffle Scott's highly gelled hair and get a funny feeling in my stomach. I knew it would be uncomfortable having Finn here. He always makes me feel so transparent. Like frogspawn.

'You should see the way Christian's looking at you!' Izzy raves as we exit. 'All wistful and longing!'

For a moment I relish the thought, then I ask, 'Do you think Finn knows Scott is a fake? He's got this weird look on his face . . .'

'So would you if you were sitting next to Nadine. Don't sweat it, honey! Just concentrate on brushing up against Christian!'

'The old pheromone theory?'

'Works every time!'

'For you and your overproductive glands maybe!'

'Hey, if you've got it, secrete it!'

'Oh gross!' We giggle, taking the lift one floor higher to the bar.

'Jamie! Izzy! Over here!' Cindy and Layla lean back

on their bar stools in a way only professional strippers can.

'Has everyone arrived? Seth has been giving us body shots. Are we late?' asks Layla, stubbing out her Menthol cigarette.

'You're fine! Are you ready to come down?'

'Sure, here, let's just get a slug of tequila each – Seth can we get four Petron?'

'Anything for you, baby!'

'You the man!' Layla giggles and adjusts her shimmering scarlet catsuit.

Cindy looks almost demure by comparison in her sugar-pink, fringed shift dress. Demure with huge boobs, that is. As we make our way downstairs all eyes follow them. I feel androgynous verging on invisible. Izzy catches my forlorn look and gives me a boost by saying, 'Doesn't Nadine look frumpy tonight? I've never seen her so covered up!'

Izzy's got a point. Nadine has always emulated Nicole Kidman's sleek, sinewy, designer grooming but tonight she's all shapeless layers.

'I keep expecting her to pull back her drapey cardi thing and give us a puppet show!' Izzy grins.

'Who's the cutie at the table?' coos Cindy as we approach the party.

'That's Christian, Nadine's fiancé,' I force out the words.

'Yum! I love a man with a shaved head!'

'Oh! You mean Finn! He works at the aquarium at Caesar's Palace.'

'Is he with anyone?'

'No, go right ahead, Cindy. Neither of us fancy him, do we, Jamie?'

'No, Izzy, we don't.'

Uncle Sam arrives along with the main course. He smells of booze but hey, don't we all? He's as brash as ever, showing no remorse for his recent T-shirt pervings by giving me a slobbery 'congratulations' kiss. Cheek! If it wasn't for Christian I'd like to stick his over-moist tongue on to the sizzling fajita plate. The two of them indulge in lots of hearty back-slapping and 'Remember the time . . .' anecdotes and, unsurprisingly, we learn that it was good ole Uncle Sam who introduced Christian to the wonders of porn and took him to his first strip joint.

'I'll have to take you out here one night – there's some great clubs with girls that'll do anything for a buck,' he leers.

Cindy and Layla exchange a look and Nadine's face goes extremely 'po'.

'It's not really Christian's type of thing!' she sneers.

Uncle Sam laughs in her face. 'That's right, my darling! Your man is different to all the other guys in the world!'

'I'm just saying, cheap women don't do it for him.'

Layla raises an eyebrow. 'I'll have you know, some of us are very expensive.'

'Excuse me?'

'Er, Nadine . . . Layla and Cindy are strippers. As, um, in fact is Zane . . .'

Nadine turns on Zane. 'You said you made jewellery!'

'I do. But it's not all I do. Perhaps you'd like a demonstration!'

'NO!' she shrieks, glaring at me. 'Don't you know *any* normal people in this town?'

'God, I hope not!' Izzy answers for me.

'What exactly do you do to earn a living, Scott?'

'Well, I dress up in armour and pretend to be one of King Arthur's knights and knock men off horses with extremely long poles.'

'Unbelievable!' she reels. 'What a wonderful secure future you'll have together!'

I secretly admire the fact that Nadine is so comfortable with having people dislike her. I can't even dismiss her mouthiness by saying she's drunk because she's been on San Pellegrino all night. I'm just thinking that Finn has got off pretty lightly when I hear her say, 'Isn't that incredibly cruel?'

Finn goes to speak but Nadine steamrollers in again. 'Yes, well I'm sure you have plenty of excuses but at the end of the day these dolphins—'

'Nadine. Why don't you listen to what he has to say?'

'That's okay,' says Finn. 'I'm not particularly interested in winning her approval.'

Izzy giggles in delight.

'Fair enough,' I concede. 'But I would like Nadine to know that as far as dolphins are concerned, a study by DeMaster and Drevenak, published in *Marine Mammal Science* in 1988, pointed out that the survival of dolphins in aquariums "may be better than or equal to survival in the wild". And that's because they consume consistently high-quality, nutritional food,

365

receive excellent medical attention, are kept free of debilitating parasites and are spared the predators, disease and pollution of the wild.' I take a breath.

'As for the people that work in these marine environments, they couldn't be more caring and there is no way on earth they would tolerate any form of cruelty or abuse.' I switch my gaze from Finn to Nadine. 'Is your steak rare enough, Nadine? It only seems to be seeping about a gallon of blood.'

Scott lays a warm hand on the back of my neck. 'Would you look at those beautiful lights out there?' he says, pointing at the shimmering skyline. 'I kissed every bulb tonight before they switched them on, just to show you how much I love you!'

I sigh and burrow my head into his neck.

'Don't let her ruin your fun, baby,' he whispers. 'She's showing herself up, you don't need to bother.'

Amazingly conversation resumes – Layla and Zane exchange 'funniest stripping stories', Reed and Uncle Sam slur business plans and Scott tries to discover if Mia's distinctive vocal style has a psychological disturbance at its origin.

Meanwhile, Cindy listens intently to Finn's rundown of 'Do Not's' for home aquariums.

'So I shouldn't tap on the glass to say hello?' she repeats.

'No, it shocks the fish. As does switching on a bright light above the tank in a darkened room – a sudden increase in light intensity can cause fish to injure or stun themselves as they dash around the tank.'

'Poor little things!' she coos, snuggling closer. 'You know, people tell me I have the memory of a goldfish . . .'

'Jamie!' Izzy appears to be trying to get my attention.

I can't fathom the message she is trying to convey until she announces, 'Never underestimate the power of the gnomes!'

Nadine mutters, 'There's something very wrong with that girl!' but I know exactly what she's getting at – gnomes being her code word for pheromones. Time for me to get rubbing up against Christian. I shift in my seat and move my leg towards his.

'Sorry!' he says, immediately moving his thigh away from mine.

'My fault!' I insist.

Izzy rolls her eyes but surreptitiously insists I try again.

Christian rests his arm on the table. I put down my fork and slide my arm alongside his, pretending to admire the texture of the tablecloth. This time he doesn't move. I gradually relax my arm and move closer a millimetre at a time. He reaches for his wine, catches my button in his cufflink, thus causing him to jolt and spill the glass on to his chicken dinner.

'Oh my God! I'm so sorry!'

'What have you done now?' spits Nadine. 'Oh, you clumsy fool!'

'It's fine!' assures Christian.

'You can't eat that now!'

'Of course I can – it's just become coq au vin, that's all.'

'Don't be so ridiculous.'

'Nadine, it's fine. Really, Jamie, please don't worry. Now I can eat and drink at the same time – you've made my life so much easier!'

I look at Izzy biting her lip, trying not to laugh. Scott has got the sniggers too. 'How come you never cook like that for me?'

I finish my risotto quietly keeping my elbows, and pheromones, to myself.

'Dessert anyone?'

'Yes, please!' I say, reaching for a menu. Mine is the only extended arm.

'Spot the piggy!' says Nadine.

'Actually, I'll take a look!' says Finn.

'Yeah,' says Reed, 'I'll probably get a couple.'

'Layla, do you want to share one with me?' says Cindy.

'Sure. You not into dessert, Nadine?'

'I like to watch my figure!'

'I guess someone has to,' Layla smirks. My heroine.

The table is filled with banana creme pie, chocolate mousse, raspberry cheesecake, bread and butter pudding, pecan pie and tiramisu. Spoons are passed in every direction and mouthfuls exchanged, right under Nadine's nose wherever possible. Eventually she takes an extended trip to the bathroom. While she's gone Christian leans over and says, 'You've got a bit of tiramisu by your mouth. May I?'

He makes it sound so seductive, in fact it feels incredibly seductive as he strokes his finger from the corner of my mouth, lingers for a second on my bottom lip, then transfers the sherried sweetness to his own lips.

'You taste good,' he smiles. 'You always did.'

I fight to get some extra oxygen into my lungs.

'D-d-do you remember . . .?' I begin.

Nadine's skinny hand clamps down on to Christian's shoulder. 'Time for us to leave.'

I look up at her pinched face. How do these ultra demanding women pull it off? Beating perfectly nice blokes into submission so they don't have the strength to leave when someone really good comes along.

Or comes back.

Christian rifles through his wallet and pulls out a $100 bill. 'That should cover it, just let me know tomorrow if it was any more.'

'Or if there was any change,' says Nadine.

'Thanks for coming!'

Everyone bids a fond farewell to Christian. Nadine is already at the exit.

Christian turns back and bends close to my ear. 'I remember everything, Jamie.'

38

The next twenty minutes or so are a haze to me as Christian's parting words echo in my head. And my heart. I close my eyes and relive the Tiramisu dribble incident.

'Are you falling asleep, sweetie?' asks Scott.

'No, I'm fine. I'm just . . .'

'Savouring a moment?'

'Yes!'

'I have to say he was looking at you pretty intently. I got quite jealous!'

I wrap my arms around Scott's neck. 'Thanks for being so brilliant tonight. I couldn't wish for a better husband!'

'But you are, aren't you?'

I sigh deeply. Scott resumes his chatter with Izzy about the perils of peroxide and I stare out of the window at the illuminated Eiffel Tower. I know I could make him happier than Nadine. She's just a controlling bully. I would never put him down or criticise him. I'd just love him. But is that too easy? Maybe if you're spikey there is more for a man to hook on to. I don't understand love. I don't understand relationships. I don't understand what I'm supposed to be doing with my heart. Should I tell Christian how I feel or let him come to me? How do you ever judge this kind of situation? How can you distinguish between instincts and wishful thinking? It's all so confusing.

I look over at Zane and Mia. They are a couple. Indisputably. Being apart has made them appreciate each other all the more and it looks like Snugglebum City from here on in. Reed and Izzy: he wants the blonde babe, she wants the Sugar Daddy. It's a tried and tested formula and who knows, they might even live happily ever after. Layla doesn't want anyone. And is making that abundantly clear to Uncle Sam who doesn't *deserve* anyone. Cindy would rather go travelling. I think of Amanda back home, she's always been take it or leave it as far as men go. Never getting in too deep, never getting too stressed. But one day I see her pop socks being blown off by some rugby-playing lug with a heart of gold. He'll be as straightforward and easy-going as her and they'll trot through life as a team. Colin? He's had a tough time since his boyfriend of seven years dumped him but he has so much love to give I know he'll find someone. He's just the type who will. Why am I not?

So much has happened in the past few weeks to shake up my attitude to life but if you ask me whether I believe that I will find someone, I'm afraid the answer is still no. And 'afraid' would be right. I can see I'm like Finn in that respect. I think that's why it's uncomfortable for me to be around him. I look at him and I see someone who has almost given up hoping because it hurts too much. Is it that obvious with me? When I think of all the people I know, it's the ones who have blind faith in getting married that I believe will and the ones who doubt, well, I doubt them too. Is that how it works? If I doubt myself does everyone else doubt me? And when the man who was earmarked by the universe to be mine stands before me, does he doubt it too? Does he doubt so much that he walks away? Is that why Nadine wins? Because she has absolute assurance that she'll be Bride of the Year?

'You two off, then?'

I look up and see Zane and Mia getting to their feet. Mia teeters and Zane steadies her.

'I love it when she's had too much to drink, she's so cute!' he laughs.

Her silken hair slides over her face as she stumbles forward into the table, upturning two coffee cups and an ashtray. In one move Zane sweeps her up into his arms like a frail child.

'Let's get you home, baby,' he soothes. 'Finn, you coming?'

'You go ahead, I'll be fine.'

'You sure? Call me if you need anything.'

'Thanks for coming tonight!' I say, moving a chair out of Zane's path.

'So, what are you guys up to tomorrow?' he asks, showing no sign of strain from his lightweight girlfriend.

'Wedding chapels all morning with Nadine,' I groan.

'God help us,' adjoins Izzy.

'Unfortunately I'll be working,' sighs Reed.

'And I'm off the hook because I've got my class.' Scott grins, giving Reed a high five.

'Then in the afternoon my mum and two friends arrive from England,' I continue.

'Great! And the bachelorette party is the next night?'

'Yup – that's all sorted.'

'Have you got anything arranged, Scott?'

'Um . . . well . . .'

'We'll talk,' Zane grins. 'Don't worry, Jamie, I'll keep him away from the cheap women!'

'Bit late for that, isn't it?' teases Layla.

'Cheek!' I laugh, remembering just in time that she means me.

'We're going back up to Seth's bar if you want to join us,' Cindy offers.

'No thanks, I'm beat! You two go on though.'

'Finn – do you want to join us?'

'No, I couldn't drink another drop. It's a terrible thing having the DTs when you're feeding fish – it creates too much disturbance in the water.'

I laugh but Cindy just looks confused.

'I'll come,' oozes Uncle Sam.

'No,' says Layla.

'Come on . . .' Uncle Sam lunges to give her a playful squeeze.

She halts him with a hand at his throat. 'You are a repugnant, lecherous old drunk and we've had more than enough of your odorous octopus company this evening. Okay?'

She releases her grip and he falls spluttering on to a

chair, which promptly tips back. We watch with detachment as he flails around, unable to get upright. Reed goes to give him a hand but obeys the female chorus of, 'Leave him . . .'

'Are you ready to call it a night?' Scott turns to me. What a treasure. Not one blunder all night.

'I guess so,' I smile.

'Do you want a ride, Finn?'

He hesitates but Scott insists. 'I've only had one beer. It's not a problem. Let's go . . .'

We drop Reed and Izzy back at the Bellagio and then cruise down Harmon Avenue learning about live-bearing tropical fish, that is small fishes from Central America and the West Indies that produce living young rather than laying eggs. Riiiight . . .

'This is me!' says Finn. Finally a sentence without 'fish' in it.

Scott pulls up in front of the apartment. 'Do you mind if I use your bathroom? I'm desperate for a pee!'

'What is up with your bladder tonight?' I ask.

'I think it's that liquid detox thing I was on,' Scott shrugs.

Finn leads the way. I feel oddly invasive as we approach his door but curiosity has got the better of me – I always pictured Finn living in a disused swimming pool and I'm fascinated to see if he has normal things like a fridge and a toaster.

'Wow!' says Scott, first in. 'Are you expecting the Rat Pack to drop by?'

'This is fantastic!' I rave, taking in the stylish mix of

kitsch and cool. 'Look at your bar!' I rush over to inspect the chrome cocktail shaker, martini glasses, the plastic pineapple for storing ice cubes and the naughty lady swizzle sticks. 'I love this stuff!'

Scott tries out the leather pouff but realises he's inviting comment and transfers to the asymmetric sofa. 'This is a pad, man! Where d'you get all this stuff?'

'I've been collecting it for years – I'm always rummaging around junk shops and auctions and of course you can get some pretty choice items from the gift shops right here in Vegas.'

'Sam's Shopping Extravaganza?' I ask, pointing at the red dice clock on the wall.

'Could be,' Finn grins.

'What about this beauty?' I say, admiring a floral lamp with a Carmen Miranda-esque chick carved into the stand.

'That's a family heirloom,' Finn smiles.

'Vintage car, vintage clothes, vintage pad . . . What does this all mean Mr Suss-You-Out?' I ask Scott.

'You find the past more appealing than the present. You would rather live in a fantasy world of your own creation than the real world with all its faults and pain.'

Finn looks a bit taken aback.

'No offence, dude. Jamie's just the same. It's just your coping mechanism.'

'I thought at least there would be a fishing net filled with crustacea hanging from the ceiling!' I say, trying to lighten the mood.

'Follow me!' Finn smiles. 'One has to be a tiny bit predictable . . .'

He opens the bathroom door and we're bathed in blue light. Bubbling alongside the length of the bath is a tank of tropical fish.

'That's so cool!' enthuses Scott, peering at the copper and turquoise streaks flitting around in the water. 'Hey, I like this red fella! His fins look like feathers.'

'Siamese Fighter?' I suggest.

Finn nods.

'Or to give him his proper name – *Betta splendens*!'

Finn looks delighted.

'I've been doing a bit of reading . . .'

I look down and noticed that the whole side of the bath is covered in shells and driftwood and sea glass.

'All from the beach where I grew up,' he explains.

'You have a strong attachment to your childhood and this is your way of keeping the memories alive on a daily basis.'

'Scott! Give it a rest!' I sigh. 'It's beautiful.'

I bend down and trace my fingers across the fine ridges and sheeny surfaces, admiring nature's exquisite designs. Underfoot is raffia reeding. Jars of sand and fish ornaments fill the window sill.

'People are always giving me fish-themed gifts,' he explains as my eye falls on a particularly garish wooden fish doorstop.

'Guys?' says Scott, hopping from foot to foot.

'Sorry!' we giggle, leaving him to pee in private.

'Can I get you anything?'

'A glass of water would be great,' I say, following Finn into the neat little diner/kitchen unit.

'Scott seems like a nice guy.'

'Yeah, when he keeps his insights to himself.'

'You've known each other how long?'

He hands me the glass. I gulp back its contents before replying, 'Not long at all. But when you know, you know, right?'

'Yeah, it's a great feeling. Even better when they feel the same way too.'

I put my empty glass in the sink and look around the room again.

'Where do you keep your paintings?'

'In the bedroom. They're not out on show.'

'Yeah, I don't suppose landscape watercolours would go too well with shagadelic decor . . .'

'Actually, my bedroom is pretty plain. You can see,' he says shyly.

The walls, the duvet, the pillows and cushions are all a soft, soothing blue. The paintings are strewn on a big wooden table made out of an old door and other than a few candles and photographs the room is uncluttered and calm.

'Who's she?' I ask, noticing a photograph of a pretty girl wrapped in a towelling robe on a beach.

'My mum. She was in her twenties when it was taken. I love it because she just looks so happy, so full of life,' he croaks, voice breaking up.

I find myself experiencing a huge pang of loss on Finn's behalf. 'You miss her so much, don't you?'

I can see him struggling to keep his eyes from welling up. 'It was today – July 29th . . .'

Before I know it my arms are around him. For a

second his body is tense but almost instantly it begins to chug with emotion. I squeeze tighter and move my face closer to his. His warm tears mingle with my own. I run my hand over his bristley head and press my mouth above his eyebrow, feeling utterly at one with his loneliness.

'Errm . . . is everything okay?'

Finn pulls away from me, wiping his eyes. 'Sorry, man – it's just . . .'

'No, it's cool,' says Scott, remaining in the doorway. 'Anything you want to talk about . . .?'

Finn looks up at Scott and I recognise the flicker of hope I had when Scott first offered to listen to me. But he doesn't speak.

'Another time, perhaps,' Scott says softly. 'Come on, Jamie.'

'I'm staying.'

Finn looks up startled and Scott does a double take.

'That's if you want me to, Finn? I mean, I'd like to. If you want . . .'

'But . . .'

'It's okay with me,' says Scott, unsure of quite what tack to take. 'I mean, I trust you, honey and if a friend needs your help . . .'

Finn remains rooted to the spot as Scott leaves. I take a deep breath as I close the door behind him. Turning off the lights in the lounge and kitchen I make my way back to the bedroom. I walk slowly up to Finn and take his hand.

'Let's go to bed.'

39

'Where the hell have you been? We've been waiting here over an hour!' Nadine snaps the second I'm through the door.

'Yeah, Jamie,' gripes Izzy, 'your sister was good enough to fit us into her busy schedule and now we'll only have *three* hours trawling round wedding chapels . . .'

'I'm sorry, I—'

'Coming in in last night's clothes. Don't you even keep a hairbrush at Scott's place?'

I spin around and glare at her. 'I don't care what I look like and I don't care where I get married!'

Nadine gasps in horror. I have just blurted out the two most sacrilegious statements in her world.

'I'm going to have a shower. If you still want to go I'll be ready in twenty minutes.'

Izzy scurries after me, utterly fascinated.

'Don't tell me you've converted him?'

'Who?'

'Well, I don't mean the Pope, Jamie! Did you shag Scott?'

'No.'

'Oh.' She looks dismayed. 'It's just . . . you look all different . . . What happened after we left?'

I sigh heavily. 'I'll have to tell you later. Let's get this stupid ordeal over and done with first.'

'Okay. It shouldn't take that long really – I already know I want the Graceland chapel and nothing Nadine can say can put me off.'

'Lorenzo Lamas got married here!' Nadine's face shrivels in prune-like contempt.

'And Axl Rose.' Izzy grins. 'Isn't that great?'

'It's just a whitewashed hut!'

'It's an institution.'

'I've seen bigger dog kennels,' Nadine sneers, eyeing the ankle-high picket fence.

'Size isn't everything, Nadine. Besides, it's not like I'm having a lot of guests.'

Izzy looks sorry for herself for a micro-second. Obviously Dave will not be attending and her mother won't leave her claustrophobically cosy world of Battenberg, floral napkin rings and *Stars in their Eyes*, especially not to see Izzy be the centre of attention. Her father can't leave his hotel in Greece in peak season, her grandparents are too old to fly and one of her young cousins has just had his appendix removed so his mother (Izzy's favourite aunt) can't leave him. Izzy decided it was pointless to invite distant family and in the end Reed said he wouldn't ask his side of the family either, instead they would have an intimate ceremony in Vegas and then hold a big party to introduce her back home in Philadelphia.

The idea of the double wedding is also off the agenda. Izzy and I talked it through and decided that it would be better to have separate ceremonies and a joint reception. I'm ashamed to admit that the fact that it would be too intimidating for Christian to bungle two weddings with a timely declaration of love for me did play a part in the decision-making process. Anyway, the reception will be a blast. It's just as well Reed is both rich and generous because my dad is refusing to stump up a penny and Scott is essentially a student with a part-time job.

Nadine hustles us inside the chapel. With just four of us including the chap on duty the place seems crowded.

'This is ideal!' says Izzy. 'Throw in Reed and his best man and it's going to look packed to the rafters!'

The manager is a sweetie – his job is clearly a labour of love. He proudly shows us the chapel with its mother-of-pearl stained glass windows and dusty-rose carpet and blithely ignores Nadine's complaint that 'Elvis wouldn't be seen dead in here!'

'Is it okay if I supply my own Elvis – I have very specific requirements,' Izzy asks our smiling guide.

'Whatever you like, babycakes, it's your special day.'

'Special?' mutters Nadine. 'You're just part of a production line. I can't believe you're falling for the Elvis gimmick. It's just so cheesy. Next you'll be telling me your dress is a copy of Priscilla's . . .'

'No, she won't,' I smirk.

'What then?'

'You'll have to wait and see.'

'Well, I really need to get a look at it to advise you on the bouquet,' Nadine frets.

'It's not really a bouquet kind of dress . . .'

'It doesn't have to be traditional lilies, I'm having *Phaleanopsis* orchids and ostrich feathers for mine.'

'Phally-what orchids?' Izzy sniggers.

'*Phaleanopsis*,' Nadine tsks. 'They are white with a slightly yellowy centre – very oriental, very now.'

Izzy and I blink back at her. She sighs and huffs, 'The kind of thing you see as a single stem in a test-tube vase at posh restaurants.'

'Ohhh,' I say, faintly impressed. 'The thing is, a ray gun would probably be more appropriate for Izzy's outfit.'

'Oh, you two mock me but you'll be sorry. Details are so important and these things need to be planned or you'll end up with some naff ribboned thing like the ones in the display case in reception.'

'Haven't you got wedding fatigue from arranging your own?' sighs Izzy.

'Oh no, it's just got me warmed up,' Nadine answers blithely. 'In fact, the people I've been liaising with at the florist and the church say I know more than they do!'

'I don't know why you don't just give in and become a wedding co-ordinator!' suggests Izzy.

Nadine flushes pink. 'Don't be so silly! And leave my accountancy firm? It would be such a risk! I'm in line for a promotion, if I left—'

'I was only joking!' Izzy cuts in.

'Oh. Oh. Well,' she splutters. 'Yes. Haha.'

I suddenly feel uncharacteristically sorry for my sister. 'What flowers do you think would go best with a corset dress with a full skirt?'

'White or ivory?'

'White.'

'How do you feel about foliage?'

'I'd rather have flowers.'

'I mean, in with the flowers – some greenery . . .'

'Oooh, what, like, twisty twigs and dangly ivy?'

'Well, not quite, I think you need long, flowing hair if you're going to have long flowing flowers. And you don't want anything too dainty because it will just emphasise your size.'

'My size?'

'Yes, well, obviously I complement delicate petals because I have fine features and a slim frame, but you . . .'

'Perhaps I should just uproot a blossom tree and have done with it?'

'No, no. Blossom is too soft and feminine for you. I think you need something bolder, and yet classic because it is a period-influenced dress.'

'Whatever you say. Just as long as they smell nice, it's okay with me.'

Nadine scribbles busily in her wedding notebook, flipping aside swatches of duchesse satin as she writes. 'I can't believe we're trying to arrange two weddings in three days!'

'I wouldn't worry – most people in this town

probably spend about fifteen minutes organising theirs!' says Izzy.

'So I see,' says Nadine, inspecting a photo montage of previous ceremonies. 'Oh my God, this man is wearing a baseball hat on his wedding day! What is wrong with these people?'

We take the leaflets on offer and climb back into the limo Reed has laid on for our recce mission. As we cruise further Downtown, Nadine fires questions about marriage licences, videographers, confetti-throwing regulations and a million other things Izzy and I hadn't even thought of. All those years antici-pating a wedding in Vegas and all we really thought about was what we'd wear and who we'd marry. I'm oddly relieved that Nadine is here to deal with all the twiddly bits.

Next on our agenda is a spooky *Mr Benn*-esque establishment run by an eccentric ex-costume designer with a henna-red beehive and flip-flops. It is essentially a big dressing-up box with adjoining themed rooms including *Star Trek* (abundant silver foil), Bondage (wipe-clean rubber) and Viking (Izzy has Lars flashback).

'I don't think God has ever entered this house.' Nadine shivers as she tiptoes back out into the sunshine.

'Where to now?'

'The Las Vegas Wedding Gardens,' I instruct our chauffeur.

I'm rather taken with the fully astro-turfed interior,

waterfall centrepiece and mock-marble garden furniture. Until Izzy mentions *The Flintstones*.

'Next!'

Nadine concedes that the Chapel of the Bells is actually rather pretty and accidentally lets the word 'romantic' slip from her lips.

'We'll get her hooked on Vegas yet!' whispers Izzy.

At the Little White Chapel we get caught up in the outpouring from an outdoor gazebo wedding.

'Chee!' 'Darren!' the guests call to the newlyweds in unmistakably British accents. Kodak disposables jostle with hi-tech camcorders and everyone seems on an excitable high.

'That's a Neil Cunningham dress,' Nadine informs us, clearly impressed by the designer drapes of glossy cream satin. 'And look – they're throwing dried rose petals instead of confetti. Someone here has got style.'

We move closer and eavesdrop on a cluster of thirtysomething mates giggling at each other's tears.

'I didn't think I was going to cry!' sniffs one.

'Doesn't Chee look beautiful?'

'Did you see Darren's hands shaking when they lit the Unity Candle?'

'That'll be straight down the car boot sale, she won't have that naff-looking thing in the house.'

'But weren't the words lovely?'

'Ooh, yes – when she said that bit, what was it?'

'"I Chee, take you Darren to be my husband knowing in my heart that you will be my constant friend, my faithful partner in life and my own true love,"' one girl quotes word-perfect.

'Oooooh,' they wail, dabbing their eyes once again. 'Who's got the tissues?'

We watch the newlyweds and feel the love. I find myself with a lump in my throat. How are Scott and I going to pull that off?

I wander over to the drive-thru wedding tunnel and gaze up at the cherubs dancing across the ceiling. My mind drifts to Finn. I picture him feeding the fish like he does every day, but this time his tears push the water level over the top of the tank . . . I hope he's feeling okay.

'Oh my God, listen to this.' Izzy bounds over, waving a leaflet. 'They offer hot air balloon weddings here! How cool would that be?

'It's ten to one,' Nadine interrupts. 'We'll have to stop by and pick up Christian from Sam's shop on the way to the Excalibur.'

'Oh, don't worry about that. I think we've seen enough chapels for one day,' I tell her.

'Come on now – it's the last place on the list and you said Scott might be able to get a discount there,' Nadine notes.

'I wouldn't mind seeing one of the casino chapels,' Izzy admits.

'Okay, but I'm not going into the gift shop when we pick up Christian. We'll just honk and leave,' I insist.

'Deal!' says Nadine.

Our peripheral wedding experience appears to have mellowed us all. Perhaps there is magic in marriage – if only for one day.

*

'And how is Uncle Sam today?' Izzy asks as Christian dips into the limo.

'A little bruised, actually,' he replies, sliding alongside Nadine.

'Of ego or body?' Izzy enquires.

'What do you mean?' says Nadine. 'What did we miss?'

'The poor guy fell off his chair,' explains Christian. 'That stripper Layla was all over him and in the end she came on too strong and he toppled over.'

'I can't bear pushy women!' tuts Nadine.

Izzy and I look at each other with eyebrows so raised we practically have to open the sun roof to accommodate them.

'So, how come you gave up on your job so soon, you didn't even make a week, did you?' says Nadine in her native patronising tone.

'No, I . . .' I'd put Nadine in her place but I want to spare Christian. 'I . . .'

'. . . had another feature to write,' Izzy finishes for me.

'Yes, that's right,' I confirm.

There's no way Nadine will ask questions about something that could make me look good so she changes the subject, wittering on to Christian about the chapels and comparing every detail unfavourably with the wedding she has planned for the two of them. I watch him feign interest and his eyes water as he suppresses a series of yawns. I feel like I know him intimately, yet at the same time he's like a stranger to me sitting there, belonging to my sister. Could he be a

387

mere mortal after all? I've waited so long to see him again and now I'm questioning whether I still want my 'secret love'. Why is that? Izzy would probably tell me it's the coward in me. I get close to what I say I want and then I lose my nerve.

'So, it's still all on, is it? The wedding . . .' Christian looks at me with his bewitching clear green eyes. My heart melts. Of course I want him.

'Unless she gets a better offer,' says Izzy, snapping a pretzel snack and popping it in her mouth.

Nadine isn't listening. She's gazing up at the pink and blue turrets of the Excalibur.

'For fairytale weddings follow me,' enthuses Izzy, leading us through ye olde casino as Nadine sneers her way through the literature: 'Like the great Canterbury Cathedral of England, the Canterbury Wedding Chapel offers a most royal experience!'

'It'll be like Prince Edward and Sophie Rhys-Jones all over again!' Izzy winks. 'Here we are!'

Two of the chapels are way too big and conference-roomy for my taste, but I'm rather taken with the smaller one with its airbrushed clouds on powder-blue walls and white pillars tumbling with flowers.

'You can hire costumes and be married as Robin Hood and Maid Marion with a Friar Tuck vicar!' Izzy reads over Nadine's shoulder. 'Uh-oh, listen to this: "chapel doors are locked during weddings to ensure privacy!" It's like the modern day version of the father with the big shotgun.'

'Speaking of the father of the bride . . .' Nadine begins.

'He's definitely not coming. Mum thought he might crack at the last minute but . . .' I shake my head.

'That's a pity,' says Christian.

'He's only doing what he feels is right,' defends Nadine.

'How is sulking and ruining his daughter's wedding day right?' demands Izzy.

'He's not ruining my day,' I insist. 'I wouldn't want him here if he's going to be all critical and disapproving.'

'Right – Nadine's got that covered,' notes Izzy.

'Anyway, it's no big deal. Zane has already agreed to walk me down the aisle.'

'A stripper?' spits Nadine.

'A handbag!' says Izzy, mimicking her Lady Bracknell-esque disdain.

'No. I'm sorry, Jamie. No,' Nadine says firmly.

'It's not your decision, Nadine. Zane is a good friend . . .'

'. . . and think how fantastically sexy the wedding pictures will look!' Izzy giggles. 'He's wearing a G-string and a dicky bow, right?'

Nadine rolls her eyes. 'If anyone, I think it should be Christian. He's practically family. I think he would be a much more suitable choice.'

I go to say, 'I don't want him to give me away!' but realise the words hold too much meaning. Instead I simply say, 'Zane will do fine.'

'Well, we'll talk about this later but right now Christian is here so let's see you two walk down the aisle. It's important you get a feel for the distance and the pace – all eyes will be on you and you might be tempted to rush or stare at the floor because you feel self-conscious, but what you are attempting is an elegant glide. Christian has had plenty of practice with me so just relax, keep your chin up and follow his lead,' she instructs. 'Okay, go to the end and walk slowly towards me!'

Someone up in heaven is rocking with mirth, going, 'Now make them do this! That will really wreck her!'

I look at Izzy, her eyes are fixed on Christian. I know she's studying his body language for any clues that I might be missing in my internal hysteria.

He takes my hand and smoothes it on to his forearm, keeping his hand firmly in place on top of mine.

'You've never looked so beautiful,' he tells me.

'Good improv, darling! The father of the bride should always compliment his daughter just as they enter the chapel. Try to imagine you really do look beautiful, Jamie. I'm sure on the day with the veil and everything you'll look fine.'

We take a step forward.

'*She walks in beauty like the night,*' whispers Christian.

Another step.

'*Of cloudless climes and starry skies.*'

Another step.

'*And all that's best of dark and bright . . .*'

We steal a glance at each other.

'*Meet in her aspect and her eyes . . .*'

'No talking now! You are stepping towards your destiny, towards a new life. Turn and smile serenely at the congregation but don't pull faces or point. That's it, keep walking.'

I can barely hear Nadine over the deafening pounding of my heart. I am standing before an altar with Christian. I feel dizzy.

'Dearly beloved . . .' begins Izzy, adopting the vicar role and giving me the chills. 'We are gathered here in the sight of God . . .'

Nadine talks over her, busily announcing: 'Okay, once you reach this point, Christian will step aside and Scott will take his place.'

'But what if he doesn't step aside? What if Christian stands his ground?' I want to scream.

'So if Christian was the groom,' says Izzy, 'where would he be standing now?'

'Right here,' says Nadine, falling for Izzy's scam and repositioning Christian.

'How close should they be?'

'About here,' says Nadine, adjusting us like ornaments on a shelf. 'There, that's perfect! Now look into each other's eyes . . .'

'Come on, Jamie, use your imagination, pretend you love him,' Izzy taunts.

'Yes, all this will be captured on video so you want to look as dreamy as possible. That's good.'

'I now declare you man and wife!' hoots Izzy. 'Kiss! Kiss!'

'Right! I'll demonstrate this bit,' says Nadine, jostling me out of the way. 'You are standing facing each other like so . . . All the guests want to see the kiss so try to keep so that they can see both your profiles . . .

Anything with visible tongues is indescribably bad taste but a closed mouth peck lacks passion. You want something in between like this . . .'

And with that she gives Christian a three-part kiss-kiss-smooch combo.

'I videoed a selection of kisses and I feel this one works best because it sends the message that one kiss is not enough and there's a feeling of progression as the two innocent kisses give way to a more intense finale.'

'I'll keep that in mind,' says Izzy.

'Oh, I wouldn't recommend it for you and Reed,' Nadine cringes. 'Oh no, I think a simple peck would be far more palatable in your case.'

'Oh really and why is that?'

'Do you really need me to spell it out?'

'Nadine!' admonishes Christian. 'Stop it.'

'You know what, Nadine,' Izzy spits, finally losing her temper. 'I don't want your advice and I don't want you at my wedding. I love Reed and I'm going to kiss him any way I want to.'

Izzy hurtles out the door with me hot on her heels. 'Wait! Izzy!'

She comes to a sudden halt in the foyer. 'Why does Nadine say those things? She is such a bitch! How dare she?'

'Don't let her get to you,' I sigh. 'You never normally do.'

'I know, it's just . . . I mean, where does she draw the line? Why is it okay for her to be so cruel? I really wish something awful would happen to her to shake up her perfect world and her choreographed kisses . . .'

'Karma . . .'

'I am calm!'

'No, karma – it'll come back and bite her in the bum one day.'

'Do you have any idea how long karma takes?' sighs Izzy, exasperated. 'Can't you just steal her fiancé in three days' time? That would cheer me up no end!'

'I'll certainly try,' I tell her.

'I mean, I can see how it might look with me and Reed . . .' Izzy trails off. Interesting – this has never concerned her before. She looks at me shyly. 'You know, last night, I tried to come clean with him.'

'How do you mean?'

'Well, I decided I wanted to be honest about the fact that I wasn't really a lap dancer but he kept telling me that my past didn't matter and you know, in a way, I think he likes to think he's rescued me.'

'Well, let him have his fantasy then. At least you tried.'

'Yes. I just wanted you to know.'

'I know.' I smile, giving Izzy a hug. 'Shall we get some lunch?'

'Okay,' she says, brightening. 'Then you can tell me exactly what happened last night . . .'

40

'Do you want my gherkin?' I offer as I suck the last traces of tuna melt off my fingers.

'Why do you always ask that?' Izzy groans. 'Have I ever in my life accepted any of your unwanted gherkins?'

'No. I know, it just seems a waste . . .' I shrug. 'Do you think anyone *ever* eats these things?'

'Fascinating as this conversation has the potential to be, can you now tell me what happened last night? Where were you?'

I push my plate away and take a slurp of Dr Pepper. 'I was with Finn.'

'I knew it! I knew it! I told you you fancied him!' she crows.

'It wasn't like that.'

'Oh really? What was it like then?'

'It was sort of beautiful and sad and—'

'Sad? How can a shag be sad? Is he upset cos you're marrying someone else? Didn't you tell him Scott's gay?'

'There was no shagging.'

'What?' Izzy looks confused. 'Go back to the beginning. I must be missing something.'

'His mother died three years ago yesterday. That's why Zane had already promised to be with him. I wish I'd known sooner . . .'

'But what happened?' Izzy asks, getting impatient.

'I don't know, he looked so vulnerable and alone – my heart went out to him.'

'Ahhh. Sympathy shag,' she concludes.

'No. It wasn't like that at all. I just suddenly felt his pain and I knew . . . at least I *felt* that I could ease it a little. I didn't think talking would help, my instincts just seemed to tell me to hold him, so I took his hand and led him into the bedroom.'

Izzy leans in closer, agog.

'We didn't even undress, we just lay down on the bed and it was like this perfect fit – you know when you think you'll never be comfortable again unless you are lying entwined with this person? I just lay there stroking his bristley hair and holding him tight. I don't really know how to describe it but it just felt so real and, this is such a cringey word, "tender". You know, straight from the heart.'

'And you just slept?' asks Izzy, double-checking.

'Better than I have in days. You know I've had so many things on my mind lately – the wedding, Christian, my dad . . . but in that moment, lying there with him, I felt almost serene. Like he was the only thing that really mattered. I guess it must be a maternal instinct or something . . .'

'Is that what they're calling it these days? Weren't

you tempted at least to kiss him?'

'It wouldn't have been right. It wasn't about that. Scott would call it a healing. It just was what it was.'

'And how was he in the morning?'

'I left him sleeping. It was best that way. What do you say when you've shared something like that?'

'I really wouldn't know,' says Izzy, searching her mind for first-hand experience of non-shagging sleepovers and drawing a blank. 'How does it make you feel about him now?'

'I really don't know. I haven't had time to think. I left him and walked straight into Nadine's nagging and then next thing I know I'm standing in a wedding chapel gazing into Christian's eyes with you yelling, "Kiss! Kiss!"'

Izzy chuckles. 'What a trip that all was. I really think you've got Christian going now. Just how long are you going to leave it before you confront him?'

'Well, today's a write-off.' I look at my watch. 'Scott's giving me a lift to the airport in an hour and tonight will be taken up with mum and Amanda and Colin. Anyway, he knows where I am if he wants me.'

'Ooooh – look at you, Miss Laissez-faire!' Izzy teases.

'You know me – *que sera sera*!'

'Yeah, right!'

'Arrivals this way!' says Scott, leading me through an obstacle course of abandoned trolleys and pregnant suitcases. All I wanted was a lift to the airport but now he's insisting on staying to chauffeur my guests back to the hotel. I'm less worried about him meeting my mum than Colin – what if his in-built 'gaydar' starts twitching at the sight of Scott? I'm a bag of nerves but my darling fiancé seems genuinely excited and leans eagerly over the barrier.

'You don't even know what you're looking for!' I laugh.

'Well, tell me then!'

'Okay,' I say, squeezing in alongside him. 'My mum will probably be wearing some shade of purple and even if it's a jogging suit she'll be in a pair of glitzy evening shoes. She doesn't do trainers or flatties. Every pair she owns has a dagger heel or disco sparkles.'

'Go, diva!'

'Colin deludes himself that people can't tell that he's gay even though he's all flailing arms and tight trousers. He'll probably be wearing a Steps rucksack.'

'And Amanda?'

'Amanda is 4'9" with a shiny black bob, flawless white skin and red rosebud lips.'

'Sounds like the lovechild of Snow White and one of the seven dwarves!'

I giggle. 'Well, if that's the case I'd say it was Happy that got lucky because she has the most contented disposition of anyone I know. Nothing fazes her.'

'No complexes about being short?'

'Nope, you can keep your therapy! What she lacks in height she makes up for in cleavage.'

It's a fact that many a lipstick, cigarette lighter and indeed man has been lost between her cushiony breasts. If you had a rummage you'd probably find loose change and a remote control down there.

Scott pulls me into a hug. 'You must be really looking forward to seeing them!'

I am. And I can't wait for the hen night because Amanda is the cutest, giggliest, most entertaining drunk I know. You just fill her up with booze and then sit back and enjoy the show. Initially she might ask, 'Am I making a fool of myself?' but after a couple more slugs she's off to oblivion on the Vodka Express. I think the fact that she wakes up with zero recollection of what went on the night before is a kind of in-built defence system, abolishing morning-after embarrassment and/or guilt. She'll ponder the origin of her multiple bruises but refuse to take on board any revelations we might make, acting like we're winding her up when most of the time we're toning it down.

One time we were out in Torquay with Izzy for a friend's birthday bash. The birthday girl had arranged for the three of us to crash at her aunt and uncle's house so we didn't have to worry about trying to get a lift back to Exeter after the party. Mr and Mrs Stern gave us a door key before we went out so we wouldn't need to disturb them in the wee small hours. However, when we did return, desperately trying to keep quiet and not wake anyone (i.e.: lots of exaggerated shhh-ing and squealy-giggling), we couldn't get the key to unlock the front door, no matter how many times we chanted 'Open Sesame!'

It was 3 a.m. and we were knackered but there was no way we were going to ring the bell and let them see us in our lairy, 99 per cent proof state. On the other hand, the doormat didn't look big enough for three of us to kip on, so we decided to case the joint for alternative access and at the back of the house discovered a dog flap. Izzy and I looked at Amanda and then back at the flap. We reckoned she'd fit through no problem. Her main concern was her prized Karen Millen dress – she never even sat down when wearing it for fear of bending or denting one of the square sequins that covered it. So off it came. She was into reinforced underwear at the time and looked like she'd been styled by one of those shops that sells prosthetic limbs, neckbraces and surgical bandages. Not the most seductive look but well suited to the task in hand. She skilfully heaved her ample bosom through, one breast at a time, but then reached a deadlock at her hips. Izzy and I were trying to rotate her through by the ankles but we were laughing so much it made us all floppy and weak. Suddenly Amanda started kicking like crazy and the door creaked open, with her still wedged like a rolled-up newspaper halfway through a letter box. We looked up and there was Mr Stern in his paisley pyjamas. It's an image I'll never forget and one Amanda will never remember. Alcoholic amnesia can be a real plus.

'JAAAAAMIEEEEE!'

Three gleeful faces loom over me. I lunge forwards as six arms enfold me.

'I can't believe we're here!' squeaks Amanda.

'You should have seen our flight attendant – Rupert Everett with hot towels! Can you *imagine*?'

'Darling, you look so well!' coos Mum.

I step back to assess them all and see my mum is wearing the freebie Virgin Atlantic socks with her spangly stilettos. Nice touch.

'This is Scott!' I say, touching his arm in what I hope is a proprietary, girlfriendy kind of way.

'My God, your teeth are sooo white!' coos Amanda. 'Are they real?'

'She's got a weakness for complimentary in-flight booze,' apologises Colin. 'Nice to meet you, Scott!'

They shake hands looking rather too deeply into each other's eyes, if you ask me.

My mum's eyes, meanwhile, have welled up and after another exclamation of 'Oh, darling!' she gives Scott a big heartfelt, make-her-happy hug and then squeezes my hand all the way to the car.

Scott cruises down the Strip for a little introductory sightseeing before dropping us back at the Bellagio and I get nostalgic for my initial wonder at Las Vegas as I watch Colin and Amanda gawk and squawk at the fantasy hotels flashing before their eyes. My mum looks completely overawed.

'I rented *Girls' Night* a couple of nights ago but nothing really prepares you, does it?' she coos.

My heart swells with each rapturous, 'Look at that! It's so beautiful/so amazing/so BIG!' I feel like a proud parent taking the credit for spawning a genius child. 'See that volcano erupting outside the Mirage? All my own work . . .'

I answer a million questions and realise how much information I've absorbed about my home of three weeks.

'Is that the Aladdin hotel where Elvis and Priscilla got married?' asks Amanda.

'Actually, no, that was blown up in spring 1998. This new one opens in a couple of weeks.'

'But that's where he played – at the Hilton?' She points further up the road.

'That's the Flamingo Hilton. Elvis performed at the Hilton LV which is on a road that runs parallel to the Strip.'

'I can't wait to go to a buffet! Do they have frog's legs and snails at Paris?' asks Colin.

'No, it's very meat orientated, lots of Boeuf Bourguignon, that kind of thing. The baked banana dessert is fab but I think the best buffet is at the Bellagio. I thought we'd do that tonight, then just relax in the suite.'

'What's this guy Reed really like?'

'You made him sound like a bit of a Wheeble on the phone,' notes Colin.

'He's an absolute treasure, really kind,' I insist, feeling guilty. 'He's not even that bad-looking now Izzy has given him a makeover.'

'I can't believe he's letting us all stay in his suite.'

'It's fine. And it'll be all ours after the wedding because they'll be on their honeymoon in Hawaii.'

'I haven't even asked – what are you two doing for your honeymoon?' says Mum.

Scott and I steal a panicked glance at each other.

'Gosh, do you know, we haven't even thought about it yet!' I bluster.

'Well, who needs to get away when you're already in

paradise!' beams Colin. 'Do you know any good gay clubs here, Scott?'

'M-me?'

'Because you live here, darling. You must have heard of one or two,' I reassure him.

'Oh yes. Well, I'll ask the guys at work for the best place to go. I'm going there after I drop you off, which is just about now,' he says, taking a right turn. 'Ladies and gentleman, I give you the Bellagio!'

'Oh my God!' warbles Colin, gazing across the mock-Lake Como. 'I feel like Cinderella arriving at the ball!'

As they unpack I pore over my article in the bundle of *Express & Echo*'s Amanda has brought me. 'Now you're an international journalist!' she grins. 'They definitely want you to do more. And the features editor has a friend on a national magazine who is looking for writers based in America so I gave her your details. I hope that's okay?'

'Of course!' I beam.

'Can we plot Jamie's fabulous new career over dinner, I'm *starving*!' Colin pouts.

The buffet is a huge hit – I watch with amusement as Amanda, Colin and Mum create stomach-churning combinations of spinach in oyster sauce, peppered goat's cheese, seared salmon, puréed sweet potato, crab claws, carvery turkey and a cluster of desserts including the pièce de résistance – pistachio crème brûlée.

Nadine joins us a little later than arranged and

unescorted. She tells us oh-so-casually that Christian has had to go and help Uncle Sam with something in the shop and then bites off the waitress's head for bringing cloudy lemonade instead of the fizzy stuff.

'You have to ask for Sprite or 7-Up, Nadine. Lemonade here means the old-fashioned stuff,' I explain.

This sets her off on an anti-America rant which Mum thankfully curtails by dragging her off to the buffet. Naturally Nadine restricts herself to the salad bar. You'd think she'd be happy to have so much choice but no . . .

'Ten salad dressings! Ten! I ask you! What are these people trying to prove?'

It dawns on me that I have finally learned to keep my buffet-induced greed and hysteria in check. I no longer feel compelled to exploit the all-you-can-eat aspect and I'm the only one to put down my knife and fork before stomach-stretching discomfort sets in.

Could I really be getting used to Vegas?

As we stroll back through the casino I hear a bewildered old couple say to a security guard, 'We saw a sign saying "Restroom this way"' as if they've got mysteriously lost tracking a star to Bethlehem.

Before the security man answers I know where he's going to direct them to. I know where the nearest restroom is and the nearest payphone and the shortcut to the deli and the walkway to Caesar's Palace and the restaurant with the best view of the fountains and the bar where a high-class hooker can get Bailey's spilt on her dress . . . I feel a strange sense of belonging in the most transient of all towns.

'I always knew you'd end up somewhere special!' beams Amanda.

'You were always an adventurous child,' Mum acknowledges. 'And so independent. You would always march on ahead, rarely looking back. Nadine would never let go of my hand. But you – I've been waiting for you to do something like this all your life . . .'

'And all those years you never thought you were going to meet a decent man,' sighs Colin. 'Now you've met Scott and let me say, if you ever tire of him you can pass him on to me! He's divine!'

I suddenly feel fraudulent and ashamed. Is this all a big illusion? Do I even know what I'm doing? Do I even know why I'm lying to these people?

'Tomorrow can we go to the Golden Nugget?' Colin asks.

'I want to see the Freemont Street lights!' pipes Amanda.

'And the pirate ship at Treasure Island!'

'I want to see the lions at the MGM!'

'And the white tigers at the Mirage!'

Now I feel like Julie Andrews with clusters of small children to please.

'Mum?'

'Yes, darling.'

'Do you know what we're doing for the hen night?'

'Don't worry, darling. I won't be shocked by the naked men. Frances the French teacher had a stripping headmaster at her birthday party – not the real one of course, he's got a terrible body . . .'

'Mum!' I laugh. 'We're going to see Tom Jones!'

Her hands fly to her face as she does a kind of overjoyed version of Edward Munch's *The Scream*. 'Oh darling!'

We hug. Colin wraps himself around us, Amanda piles on top.

Nadine just rolls her eyes and says, 'Now if you'd said Michael Bolton . . .'

41

Like cattle being herded across a rattling iron grid, we clumsily stampede the entrance to the MGM Grand hotel. We're clinging to each other to stay upright, trying not to be swept asunder by the swarming crowds, unaware that the collective shuffling of our feet across the clash-tastic carpet is generating perilous amounts of static. Nadine gets the full brunt of the electric shock as she makes contact with the metal door handle. (There is a God.) She jumps back, zapping me and my chain gang and sparks flash as we flinch and twitch like a line of body-poppers.

We're still screaming as we skid across the marble-floored reception, conga past the slot machines and make the final sprint towards the Hollywood Theatre. Colliding at the box office we take a moment to coo at Tom's picture surrounded by glowing gold light bulbs and then enter.

As we feared the lights are already down in the auditorium and we have to burrow through the darkness to find our pink leather booth. Confused looks are exchanged as a rotund bearded man with his trousers hoisted up to his armpits paces the stage giving out about his tailor.

'That's Max Alexander,' whispers the cocktail waitress as she lays out square napkins before us. 'He opens for Tom. What can I get you girls to drink?'

'Vodka Cranberry!'

'Vodka Cranberry!'

'Vodka Cranberry!'

'Vodka Cranberry!'

'Vodka Cranberry!'

The order is repeated like a Buddhist chant around our group – Amanda, Cindy (no Layla – she had to work), Izzy, me, Mum. Of course Nadine has to be different. She orders sparkling water. At least it won't stain when I throw it in her face.

'Anyone staying here at the MGM?' asks comedian Max.

How big is this hotel? I went to the pool this morning. I took a cab. By the time I got there I needed to shave again! Have you taken the monorail from here to Bally's? How slow is that thing? My grandmother passed us with her walker. It's so slow they show *Schindler's List* on the way.' We begin to snigger.

'You know what drives me craziest here? The beds. How many layers? You've got the under sheet, the top sheet, the fleece, the bedspread, the bed cover . . . You go to bed with someone and you can't find them. It's like: "Honey, where are you?" "Meet me on level 7!"'

By now we're all laughing out loud. I can't remember the last time I saw me, my mum and

Nadine all lit up at the same thing. I feel a swell of affection. Izzy nudges me and points to Amanda – she's well and truly gone, giggling like a jiggly battery-operated toy. That in turn has tickled Cindy who, it transpires, has an absolutely filthy laugh that she really should incorporate into her act. As the waitress passes, Nadine touches her arm and whispers in her ear. Perhaps she's feeling adventurous and fancies a slice of lime. I'm surprised to see the waitress return with a full round of Vodka Cranberries, including one for Nadine herself.

'Here's to a memorable night!' she toasts.

'Here's to getting so drunk we don't remember a thing!' adjoins Izzy.

Tom bursts on to the stage with a rollicking 'Turn on your Love Light' and we go utterly berserk to 'It's Not Unusual' which he reminds us was his first hit, 'recorded in 1964'.

'I wasn't even married then,' says Mum rather too wistfully.

His powerful, dramatic vocals reverberate through my body and my earlier fretting is forgotten as I savour every lusty thrusty move. Out of the corner of my eye I notice Mum rummaging in her bag. What's that in her hand? Tell me it's not true. Tell me that lacey item is a hanky. Tell me she's reaching her arm back to stretch. I watch a pair of crimson knickers flutter through the air as if in slow motion. They miss Tom and instead encircle the microphone stand like a game of hoopla. My mum's face fills with dismay and she begins rummaging again – tell me she hasn't got a back-up pair – then I see Tom's eye take on a wicked glint. I nudge my mum. He hits the last note of 'She's a Lady' and then rumbles, 'What have we here?'

Mum looks wide-eyed with a mixture of mortification and ecstasy as he delicately displays the flimsy embroidered chiffon for the audience, little fingers cocked as if sipping tea. He pauses for a second then rubs the knickers vigorously, hungrily over his face. Nadine gives an uncharacteristic whoop. He stops abruptly, takes a final breath and says, 'I think I know this woman!'

Mum blushes *scarlet* while the rest of us just squeal. Gradually her furious facial redness reduces to a pinkish glow of joy. I've never seen her look so radiant, so alive. I feel oddly proud. She remains euphoric during 'Delilah' – leading a rhythmic sway that sends Amanda flying into the aisle – but then I see a lone tear trickle down her face during the first aching chorus of 'I'm Never Gonna Fall in Love Again'. Under the table, she squeezes my hand until it's pulsing with pain.

'Don't settle for second best, darling!' she implores, eyes searching mine in the darkness. 'Tell me Scott is The One!'

I look away. She turns my face to hers. For a moment I feel she can see the truth.

'When you were a little girl, I used to be able to tell exactly what you were thinking. I don't know what is in your heart any more,' she sighs.

I feel wretched, like I'm deceiving her *and* pushing

409

away the only person who can rescue me. But I'm too far gone now. Half of me is excited about the wedding, even if the other half is fully aware that something vital is missing. Tom starts to sing 'The Female of the Species'. It's a haunting rendition of the space song and the lyrics cut into me and twist in my stomach.

'*How can heaven hold a place for me, when a girl like you has cast a spell on me?*' he sings, sounding so plaintive and bewitched. I'm swamped with emotion and introspection – what must it be like to have a man feel like that? Izzy knows all about enslaving a man's heart but it seems I just don't have it in me to conjure up that kind of rapture. Tom does his 'dance of the seven veils' hand swirls and I'm hypnotised. The moment seems strangely poignant. The audience applauds. I turn to Mum but the rousing strains of *The Full Monty*'s 'You Can Leave Your Hat On' grab her attention and Tom unzipping his flies holds it. I exhale and then inhale the rest of my drink to drown any 'sobering' thoughts.

'*Baby, take off your dress!*' growls Tom.

'*Yes, yes, ooooh, yes!*' we sing back.

At the end of the song Izzy elbows me and I know the time has come to yell, 'GET YOUR KIT OFF!'

Tom seems taken aback. 'For our non-British guests I should explain that "Get your kit off!" means to strip, to get undressed.' he giggles. He peers in our direction.

'Where are you ladies from?'

'Devon!' we chorus, ecstatic that we've been singled out.

'How long are you here in Vegas for?'

'As long as you want us to be!' yells Izzy.

He shoots us a naughty look and segues into the appropriately inviting 'Help Yourself'.

Amanda leans across and hisses, 'Check out the trumpet player with the tufty hair!'

Izzy and I watch the indisputable cutie expertly twirl his highly polished instrument and punctuate the beats with hip thrusts. 'You should have seen him with his maracas,' she drools, nodding her head in time to his groin. Izzy and I assess the rest of the band.

'Last night of freedom shag?' she asks.

'Hmmm,' I ponder. 'I think I'd have to go for the keyboard player – he's got a touch of the Al Pacinos . . .' (He even manages to look brooding and intense when Tom sings the potentially embarrassing line, '*And Muriel plays piano* . . .' during a mesmerising 'Walking in Memphis'.)

'I'll take the sax player,' Izzy concludes. 'He'd look great perched on my bedroom window ledge!'

'Bags I the drummer! He looks a real animal!'

'Mum!' I squeal.

'Well . . .' she says, clearly tipsy. 'I need back-up in case Tom is busy tonight . . .'

We crack up. 'We should have hen nights more often!' says Izzy.

We're on our feet for the 'Kiss' finale, blowing endless kisses to Tom. And his band. And the stage crew off in the wings. And the group of Welsh lads down the front. This is fun. It gets even better when, as everyone else is ushered out of the auditorium, we are approached by a man in black.

'Is this the Ingham/Miller bachelorette party?'

We nod dumbly.

'I'm Sandy, the tour manager,' he announces. 'Would you like to follow me . . .'

My mum lunges at him, gripping his arm. 'Are we going backstage?'

'Yes, ma'am.'

'To meet Tom Jones?'

'Yes, ma'am.'

'Oh! Thank you! Thank you!' she gushes, giving him a big hug. I look adoringly at her. I feel like we've jumped back thirty years and I've been given the chance to see my mum as a teenager. I turn to Izzy.

'Reed's doing?'

'Must be,' she replies. 'I'd better give the sax player a miss, then!'

We file down an echoey corridor, Mum leading the way, quaking with anticipation. She grabs my hand. We're first to enter the plush meet-and-greet lounge with identical grins plastered across our, well, plastered faces. There are half a dozen guests in the room and one by one, Sandy hands us flutes of champagne. We try to act like this kind of thing happens all the time. Izzy and I look most convincing because quite frankly it has been happening a lot lately.

'Cheers!' we say, chinking our glasses and then decorating them, with a range of lipstick prints. I try to smudge mine off the glass but it looks worse and now I have a fuchsia thumb. I'm looking for something to wipe it on – Nadine's white trousers look ideal – when

Amanda casually asks Sandy if he knows the name of the cute trumpet player.

'That's Danny Falcone. He'll be over in dressing room B but he might swing by before he leaves.'

'Hope so,' says Amanda, switching positions with Nadine to get a better look at the door. My sister has fallen uncharacteristically quiet and is smoothing her hair into place as if she's going to be presented to the Queen. Cindy and Izzy are rather more appropriately making sure their cleavages are set at maximum impact.

And then it happens. The legendary Tom Jones enters the room. The man has a strong charismatic presence. And the bluest eyes. In both senses of the word! His twinkle is so naughty you feel like he has X-ray vision.

He moves around the room joking with old friends and welcoming new ones. Then Sandy introduces us.

'Hello, ladies, are you having a good time?'

He chugs his famously fabulous laugh as we fall over ourselves replying, 'Yeeees! Oh! Soooo good! Your voice! Take me now! Living legend! Best night of my life!', etc.

'So which of you beautiful women is about to get married?'

Izzy and I step forward. 'Sorry, Tom, I know it must be breaking your heart to hear I love another!' teases Izzy.

'I could help mend it!' offers my mum. It's a peculiar thing to see your mum flirting. Especially when she's flirting with TOM JONES.

'Thank you darlin'!' He winks at my mum. I just know she'll be digging out her pictures of him in seventies flares with Afro hair the second she gets home.

'Would it be all right if we took a photo?' I ask.

'Of course!' he grins, arms encircling us as Sandy holds up Izzy's camera. He halts before he presses the button. 'Weren't there six of you when we came in?'

We look around at each other. Amanda's missing!

'There she is, over by the door!' says Cindy. We all spot the napkin and pen situation she's got going with the cute trumpet player and cheer loudly.

There's a quick scrabble for autographs before Tom leaves and in a particularly bold move my mum steals a full-on-the-lips-kiss just before he's swept out of the room.

Izzy looks on admiringly. 'You go, girl!'

Stage II of the hen night takes place at Mandalay Bay's rumjungle – the hottest club in Las Vegas. Mum marvels at the slate-panelled walls teaming with water, Amanda strokes the fur-backed chairs and Nadine appears to be uncharacteristically taken by the fiery Cuban rhythms. We squeeze through the throbbing crowd to get to the quieter section with its S-shaped love seats, then Izzy groans: 'Oh no! Look who's here!'

I spot a rough-hewn caveman's club that turns out to be an arm. Its owner is wearing a leather waistcoat with nothing underneath and matching trousers. It can only be our favourite Scandinavian stripper. And he's coming this way.

'Uh oh, Lars Attacks . . .' cringes Izzy.

'Hey, you guys!'

'Hey, you guy!' Izzy smiles coldly.

'Aren't you going to introduce me to your friends?' He casts a lascivious eye over our party but before Izzy can dismiss him, my sister lunges forward purring, 'I'm Nadine. Shall we dance?'

I do a triple-take. Nadine who despises strippers. Nadine who expects a man to wear a tie with his pyjamas. Nadine who has only ever moved to music in her aerobics class. We all watch with amazement as she weaves her way to the dance floor, one finger hooked in Lars' belt loop.

'This I've got to see!' says Izzy, following them. 'Come on!'

We leave the others to the cocktail menu and merge deeper into the crowd. There's barely a square inch to shake, shake, shake your booty in front of the turntables, perhaps that's why Lars and Nadine have taken over a podium.

'I thought Nadine said the Lambada was just foreplay for exhibitionists!' Izzy giggles.

'It is the way she's doing it,' I say, gawping as she grabs Lars' rock-solid rump and presses her body so forcefully into him you'd think she was trying to pass through him like something out of *Ghost*. 'I don't know what's got into her!'

'But I think I know what will!' Izzy chuckles filthily.

'Noooo! She wouldn't!' I protest.

'I think she already is!'

I turn back to see her licking his neck and running

her hands over him as if she's speed-reading braille.

'I can't bear to watch!' I recoil. 'How can she do this to Christian?'

'Where's my camera?' says Izzy with an evil glint.

'Amanda's got it,' I reply, wincing as Lars slams into Nadine like a bumpercar.

'This is such prime blackmail material, we have to take advantage,' she insists.

We take one last horrified look as Nadine attempts some booty-shaking fly girl moves and then struggle back to our group. Cindy is gassing with some gal pals on a night off from Lap and Tickle (well, I say a night off – they are still being hounded and hit on by men) and Amanda is now perched on one of the bongo-drum-style bar stools with a dreamy look on her face and a Bahama Mama cocktail in her hand. She's just bought a round so we have a quick pit stop.

Every now and again, Amanda has a spasm of panic and rifles through her pockets, rummages down her cleavage and is eventually reassured that the napkin with Danny's phone number is securely stashed in her purse. 'His dad used to work with Frank Sinatra! Can you believe it! He's played with Tony Bennett and Andy Williams and Jerry Lewis and . . .'

Fascinating when you hear it for the first time but now it looks like she's going to be on rewind and repeat for the rest of the night. It suits Mum fine. She's happy to wait her turn so she can say, 'I kissed him! I kissed Tom Jones!' every five minutes or so.

'Come on,' says Izzy, wincing from her Mojita and

tucking a mint leaf behind her ear. 'Let's capture the Kodak moment!'

Back on the dance floor, some tasselled hard-body with thighs so polished bullets would bounce off has taken over the podium.

'Where are they?' I frown.

'They must be somewhere on the floor,' Izzy assumes.

We contort our way into the surging mass of sweaty bodies. No sign of them. A man grabs me by the hips and presses his scalding body into mine. He couldn't be any hotter if he were a pocket pitta just popped out of the toaster. I look around for Izzy to rescue me but she's being rotated by a Joaquin Cortés wannabe. I wriggle free and stop her spinning before she throws up.

'Where do you think they've gone?' I shout over the salsa beat.

She steadies herself and shrugs. 'No idea but knowing Lars they won't be wasting any time . . .'

'She *can't* have left with him. Not Nadine. No way. That I can't believe.'

'I tell you what *I* can't believe.'

'What's that?'

'That I'm finally going to have something in common with your witch of a sister!'

42

'Jamie!' barks an all-too-familiar voice.

I open my eyes and find myself in bed with a telephone receiver pressed against my ear.

'Nadine?'

'What the hell took you so long to pick up?'

'Gee, I don't know. Perhaps the fact that I was *sleeping*!' I groan.

'It's nearly midday,' Nadine shrieks.

'This is Vegas, Nadine. Normal rules don't apply. Where are you calling from, anyway? You were supposed to be spending the night here—'

'I am in HELL!'

'Do you want to be more specific, hell is a pretty big place—'

'I am in some godforsaken trailer park in what looks like the middle of the desert with people who have never seen a Jimmy Choo shoe in their life!'

'Any idea how you got there?'

'Listen, if you *ever* tell *anyone* that I went back with Lars . . .'

A strange wail comes down the line. If I didn't know

better I'd think Nadine was crying. 'Nadine?'

'It's nearly midday!'

'So you've said. I really don't care.'

'Christian is coming to pick me up at midday. You have to cover for me. Lars isn't sure we'll make it there in time.'

'Well, when are you leaving?'

'Just as soon as he jump-starts his pick-up truck.'

For a moment I don't say anything. I'm trying to get my head around the fact that the sister I hate is asking me to lie to the man I love. And then there's the image of Nadine in a pick-up truck to contend with . . .

'Jamie will you please *wake up*! This is life and death important.'

'What do you want me to say?'

'Oh God, that's Lars now. I have to go!'

'Do you want Christian to wait for you here or meet you back at Paris?'

'Yes! See you in half an hour!'

'Yes to what – wait for you or meet you at Paris?'

Nothing.

'Nadine?'

Perfect. I rub an encrusted eye and look over at the clock – 11.52. Eight minutes to de-thatch my hair, de-fuzz my tongue and decide on the best lie option. I smile to myself remembering the last time Amanda woke up with a raging hangover and something that resembled a naked WWF wrestler in her bed. She had no clue about how intimate they'd been but feared the worst. He seemed to have no intention of getting up but she had work to get to and after a quick shower sat in front of the mirror with her hairdryer and styling brush. The heat, noise and hair-pulling was too much for her groggy, nauseous state so she switched it off and sat with her head in her hands. He leant over the side of the bed, laid a heavy paw on her shoulder and said, 'Don't worry, you were good!'

Suddenly the doorbell rings and I'm not even upright.

'Coming!' I yell, moving too fast and getting a head rush and a stomach lurch combo. All those rum cocktails and then a full eggy breakfast at 3 a.m. . . . I'm about to pitch myself head first into the toilet bowl when the bell rings again. I take a deep 'I'm-not-going-to-be-sick' breath and head for the door. I only open it an inch deciding the less of my lying, hungover face Christian can see, the better.

He looks gorgeous, if a little bleary himself.

'Hi!'

'Hi!' I reply.

'Can I come in?'

'Er, well, Nadine's not here . . . I think she went back to your hotel.'

'I just left there, I didn't see her.'

'Oh! Right! No! I just remembered, she went to show Scott the wedding chapels, you know, get a little input from him . . .'

'I'm sure she'll be back in a minute – you know what a stickler she is for time-keeping. I'm actually a little bit early. Can I wait for her?'

The door seems to open of its own accord and in he sweeps.

'Where's everyone else?'

'Well . . . er . . .' I stumble, trying to activate my brain. 'My gang has still got jet lag so they were up and out by 8 a.m. Um, Izzy and Reed left about 10 a.m. to get his tux sorted. I tried to get up with them but I didn't feel so good so I took a couple of Advil and went back to bed . . .'

Too much information. Play it cool. I stop jabbering and attempt a cheery smile.

'How long has Nadine been gone?' he asks.

'Gosh, I don't know, I was sleeping and I've got this thumping hangover . . .'

'Good night last night?'

'Yes. Whoops!' I collide with a pillar.

'Shall we sit down?' He motions to the lounge area.

I slot myself on the two-seater, expecting him to occupy the long leather number. Instead he sits beside me. Very beside me.

Ten minutes ago I was fast asleep, most likely dreaming of being alone with him. Now here I am, dizzy and disorientated. I can't believe the face I could never get enough of looking at is inches from my own. Before I even know what I'm saying, I've asked: 'Why did you never write to me?'

He looks caught out for a minute and then sighs a heavy sigh. 'I'm sorry.'

I wait for him to elaborate, explain away the mystery I've been trying to fathom for the past ten years but he just says, 'It's amazing how one mistake can have such an impact on your whole future . . .'

He looks so sad. His hands are shaking. So are

421

mine. But there's a good chance it's just DTs. I'm desperate to reach out and touch him but I feel paralysed. I wait for him to speak. He looks up at me, I stare deeper into his green eyes. He closes them for a second and then lowers his gaze. Suddenly a smile plays upon his perfect lips. 'Cute pyjamas!'

I look down at my steamy coffee cup motif flannels and realise my buttons are all askew.

'Let me help you with that,' he says gently.

He shuffles even closer, reaches out and undoes my top button. My body surges with desire and confusion. He undoes the next one letting his hands brush against my bare skin. My heart pounds with recognition at his touch. My already spinning head is now a swirling twister. He leans closer, I can feel his breath on my collarbone. And his fingers undoing another button . . .

'Have to undo them all to get it right,' he husks.

His hand moves beneath the pyjama top and encircles my shoulder, then glides slowly down as he begins whispering my name. I feel like I might pass out. Then I feel like, very much like, yes, here it comes – I'm going to be SICK! I push him away from me, clutching my pyjama top around me as I hurtle into the bathroom. I only just make it in time. The sound effects are some of my best work ever. I sit sweating and spitting and shuddering over the bowl. Eventually he comes to the door.

'Jamie, are you okay?'

A louder voice says, 'Jamie, get your booty out here! Ricky Martin is shaking his bon-bon harder than he ever did in his life!'

422

I push my hair away from my face. What's Scott doing here?

'My God, I could just eat this man for breakfast!'

Uh-oh. I frantically splash cold water on my face, gargle and open the bathroom door. I can't quite read Christian's expression but I think I can detect disgust and suspicion.

'Scott's here,' I say.

'So I heard.'

'We've got this Ricky Martin in-joke . . .'

'Right.'

Christian follows me back to the living room.

'Will you look at his . . . Christian! Hi, dude! Er, Jamie your favourite man is on the TV . . .' He tails off taking in my dishevelled form.

'Roughest to date, baby. Are you okay?'

'Just been sick.'

'Where's Nadine?' asks Christian.

I propel myself into Scott's arms, pinching his back as I say, 'Did you have a good time looking round the chapels with her?'

'Yes,' he says nervously.

'So where is she now?' Christian enquires.

'Did she get sucked into Prada in the shopping walk downstairs?' I prompt.

'Yes,' says Scott.

There's an awkward silence, then like a late cue in an amateur dramatics production, the doorbell rings.

'Do you want me to get that?' says Christian as Scott and I remain rooted to the spot. 'It's probably Nadine.'

Yeah – in last night's disco outfit.

'NO! No. Allow me. Scott, why don't you show Christian the view from the balcony . . .' I wait until they are swallowed up by sunshine and then cautiously open the door.

Nadine is pinned to the side of the wall hissing, 'Is he here?'

'Yes! Out on the balcony. Nadine – your neck!' I gasp at the motley throbbing lovebite.

'*Don't!*' she squeals. 'Can I make it to the bedroom without him seeing me? I've got to change.'

'Did you pack a polo neck?'

She snarls and scurries to the bedroom. I head back to the balcony where Scott is giving room counts for every hotel within view. 'So pretty soon the Venetian will be the biggest hotel in the world.'

'Was it her?' asks Christian.

'Yup. She'll be out in a minute. Just getting her overnight stuff together.'

'Well, at least I won't be the one getting it in the neck for keeping her waiting this time,' he smiles.

I can't even begin to imagine what my face is doing in response.

Ten minutes of small talk later, Nadine appears with one of my scarves swathed around her neck.

'So that's what you've been up to!' says Christian reaching for her throat.

Nadine gulps, eyes wide with panic.

'I thought you said you had enough scarves?' continues Christian, inspecting the raised velvety pattern.

424

'Yes, but they have such lovely ones in the shops downstairs, don't they, Nadine?' I insist.

'Yes,' she says, looking bewildered.

'And you deserve to treat yourself after schlepping around all those chapels with Scott this morning, don't you?'

'Yes,' she bleats.

I'm better at this than I thought.

Christian shrugs. 'Right, well, we'd better be off. See you later, Scott.' He turns to me. 'About time you got out of those pyjamas, isn't it?'

I go bright red.

'She's a slob,' snorts Nadine. 'Always has been. Nothing comes between her and her pyjamas.'

'Nothing?' says Christian, raising an eyebrow.

What the hell is he playing at? This is unbearable! I liked it better when I was being sick. I want Christian and Nadine out of here now! With increasing hysteria I herd them to the door. I grapple with the door handle, somehow locking it in my panic. I feel hot tears well up but then Scott's hand closes around mine. He puts one arm around me and throws open the door with the other. I sigh with relief and then look up at the figure standing with a finger extended towards the doorbell.

It's Lars.

He's holding Nadine's handbag.

My eyes dart three feet out of their sockets.

Nadine blanches as Lars begins, 'You left this in . . .'

'. . . the bar last night! Thank God you found it, Lars! What a star you are! This is Nadine's fiancé

Christian! They're just leaving . . .' I grab the bag, foist it on Nadine, push her and Christian out the door and yank Lars inside.

I feel my legs give way and slump exhausted against the closed door.

'Is that Ricky Martin?' asks Lars, heading for the TV. 'Man, can that guy move!'

43

I leave Lars and Scott to the TV and stumble into the bathroom, turning on the shower and watching the water power forth. I'm grimy, my hair smells of last night's smoke and I've been sick. Clean would be a good thing right now. And yet I'm loath to wash away Christian's touch. I can still feel his hands on my body. What if I hadn't had to run away? Would he have carried on? Would he have kissed me? Would I have let him? Or would I have held him back and said, 'I have to know what this means!'

I hold my hand under the water and feel its warm pressure on my fingertips. What if Scott hadn't come round and what if Nadine had stayed at the trailer park? What if Christian were still here now? What if I unbuttoned him too? I'm full of swirly, sexy desire. I want to touch him again. Perhaps he's feeling the same way. Then my heart sinks. Perhaps he's venting those feelings with Nadine right now. I shudder and slide open the shower door.

When I emerge in my towel turban I find Mum flat

out on the bed.

'Hello, darling! How are you feeling?' she says, propping herself up.

'Fine now, thanks,' I smile, giving her a kiss. 'What have you been up to?'

'Everything! I'm exhausted! I don't know where Colin gets his energy. I've left him at the mall with Amanda. They're getting the pictures from last night developed! I can't wait to see the one with Tom! Can you believe I kissed him?'

She smiles dreamily.

'Anyway! I thought I'd come and see how you are and maybe have a little lie-down.'

'Recline away!' I say, plumping up the pillows. 'The jet lag gets you in the afternoon. You'll get a second wind in a while.'

'Have you heard from Nadine?'

'Yes, she's back at Paris, safe and sound,' I tell her, quickly adding: 'Cup of tea?' so that we don't get into a discussion about Nadine.

'In a minute. I've got something to tell you – I met a friend of yours at the Mirage.'

'Oh yes? Girl named Mia?' I suggest.

'No, it was a boy. Finn.'

I stop combing my hair and sit on the bed beside my mum. 'Go on.'

'I was sitting watching him in with the dolphins while Amanda and Colin were in the gift shop and he had such a natural rapport with them, such grace, I had to say something. He told me he normally works at the aquarium at Caesar's Palace but he's covering

428

for a chap called Todd for a few days. Anyway, he asked me if I was having a good time in Vegas and I explained I was here for my daughter's wedding and when I said your name . . .' she smiles.

'What did he say?'

'He said you'd been very kind to him and that you were a special person. Isn't that lovely? It's so nice to hear someone recognising your good qualities. Anyway, he asked how the wedding plans were going and I told him we had something old (your granny's silver necklace), something new (your dress) and something blue (the garter Amanda bought you), but we hadn't settled on something borrowed. So he asked me to give you this . . .'

Mum reaches into her pocket and then carefully unfolds her purple lace handkerchief. It's Finn's mermaid ring.

'I was thinking, it's bound to be too big for you. Perhaps you could wear it on Granny's chain?'

'Good idea,' I say, stroking Zane's handiwork. 'You know, the guy who is giving me away tomorrow actually made this for Finn.'

'Really?' says Mum.

'Yeah. They are great mates. You'll see them together at the wedding.'

'Well, actually, Finn asked me to tell you that he won't be able to come.'

'What?' I cry.

'He says he's sorry but he has to work.'

I look down at the ring. Surely he could swap with someone? That's if he wanted to come badly enough. I don't understand. I felt so close to him at his house. I was there for him when he needed someone, why won't he be there for me?

'Anyway, he'll be there in spirit with the ring,' says my mum, seeming to read my mind.

I slide the ring on to my finger.

'Not that one! That's your wedding finger! It's bad luck!' Mum squeals.

I switch it to my middle finger and lay down alongside my mum, rotating the ring as I stare at the ceiling.

'What did you feel like the day before your wedding?' I ask.

'I just remember my head being full of concerns like "Will everyone be able to find the church?" because it was quite tucked away with and "Will I stumble over my lines?" and "What is the weather going to do?"'

'No doubts about Dad?'

'No, we'd had a long engagement so I had plenty of time to think it all through. My biggest concern was getting a good night's sleep. I borrowed one of my grandmother's sleeping pills and practically fell asleep cleaning my teeth!'

'Did you feel groggy the next day?'

'No, not with all the adrenalin pumping away – I was on a high. There you are looking your best with all the people you love around you – it's fantastic! Your father was in his element, he looked so handsome, so happy . . .'

'Now look at him,' I wail.

'People change, darling. We all do, you're lucky if

you can grow together but that doesn't always happen. You have to accept that there will be dark times as well as magical times. The whole point is that you see it through, you don't give up believing in the other person.'

'Do you ever have any regrets?' I ask, knowing I would in her shoes.

'I don't believe in regrets, you know that. I've had thirty good years with your father and you and Nadine to show for it, how can I have any regrets?'

'What about your dreams of travelling the world?' I prompt.

'I'm here, aren't I?' she says softly.

I turn to face her, feeling so grateful that she's with me. 'Are you glad you came?'

'Do you really need to ask?' she smiles, taking my hand. 'This is like a dream come true for me.'

'Are you worried that Dad will make you pay for it when you get home?'

'Darling, I learned a long time ago that people can only hurt you if you let them. I hope he doesn't hold on to any resentment because it won't do his ulcer any good.'

I sigh. 'You are so patient with him. I don't know how you can stand it – he's so childish sometimes.'

'He's still got a lot of lessons to learn,' she says calmly.

'It just seems to me that with you, the older you get the wiser you get – you're so philosophical and cool about everything and yet you still have fun and enjoy the moment. Dad is just getting more fussy and stubborn and rigid as he gets older.'

'Then you should feel sorry for him, not get mad at him. It can't be any fun for him to be like that.'

'Then why does he do it? He's making other people miserable too,' I gripe.

'Only if they let him.'

I let out a scream of frustration. Mum laughs. 'I know it looks awful to you but I see things differently. There was a time when Ivan was the centre of my world. We did everything together. Now . . . now my centre has shifted, it's back in me. I have other interests. I have my dreams and not all of them include your father. It doesn't mean I don't love him and it doesn't mean I'm going to leave him. He's just not such an important part of my life right now. But that's not to say he won't be again. I'm not sitting around waiting for him to change but when he does, I'll be there.'

'You amaze me, Mum!' I say, sitting upright so I can get a good look at her. She seems so calm and wise. I always thought she was merely resigned to her fate but now I see she has a whole different take on things.

'And you amaze me!' she laughs. 'You tell me you've had enough of your old life and less than a month later you're swanning around a sumptuous suite in Las Vegas about to get married!'

I can't disguise the sadness that washes over my face.

'So what's the problem?' Mum asks gently. 'I get this feeling that you are still waiting for something to fall into place.'

'That's exactly what it feels like!' I say, hugging a

pillow to me. 'It's as if I've got all the elements of an amazing life in front of me and yet I've jumbled them up and put them in the wrong order and they are not quite making sense.'

'You know what you need to do?' she smiles.

'What?' I ask.

'You need to trust and let go.'

I let out a heavy sigh. If only it were that simple.

'How can I trust when nothing has ever really worked out for me in the past?' I ask her, getting up from the bed and pacing the floor. 'I mean, I want to believe in fate but that seems so passive so I try to carve my own destiny and *make* things happen, then everyone tells me I'm trying too hard . . .'

'Look how tense you are!' Mum observes. 'No wonder you can't think straight. It's like when you are trying to remember someone's name and you just can't do it and the minute you let go and start doing something else it comes to you. You've got all this interference in your brain from trying to keep everything under control but life has its natural flow. You can't change that. Everything will happen as it is supposed to happen.'

'Even if I've interfered with the natural flow and . . .' I babble.

'There's bound to be confusion when you make a dramatic change in your life. It takes time to adjust but believe me, you've got to let go. There's nothing more you can do. Give things a chance to fall into place of their own accord.'

'You'd think between your advice and Scott's

433

analysis I'd be sorted by now!' I joke.

'You're nearly there. The clarity will come and it will make all this upheaval worthwhile,' she reassures me.

'Really?' I whimper.

My mum nods. '*Being lost is worth the coming home.* Just keep that in mind and you'll be fine.'

We lie on the bed chatting until Amanda and Colin burst in, in a state of excitement.

'We've just got your wedding present!' They grin.

I feel a pang of guilt and eye their shopping bags.

'It's not in any of these! laughs Colin. Shall we tell her?'

Amanda couldn't keep it in if she tried. 'It's a night at the Venetian – honeymoon suite!'

I force a whoop.

'We just thought, you didn't have anything planned and you'll want to be together somewhere special,' explains Amanda.

'And you should see the bed!'

'Don't tell her!'

'Okay, we won't say any more but it'll be a memorable night,' Colin winks.

They stand before me with shiny eyes. I just know they are picturing wild wedding sex. I'm seeing me and Scott treating ourselves to an in-room movie.

We spend the afternoon on a hotel crawl. Colin wants to gamble in every casino and I find myself on unfamiliar turf at Harrah's, Barbary Coast and Bally's. I realise then there is no knowing all of Vegas. And that's the beauty of it. To me, at least. The beauty to Colin is that the Jeopardy fruit machines are spewing money at him wherever he goes. We hit the bar to celebrate and he orders us a glass of champagne each. Still the bill comes up cheaper than a round at our old lunchtime local.

'My kinda town,' he beams, insisting we take pictures of him showing off his buckets of shiny quarters.

'So what's the plan for tonight?'

'Well, you know Scott's mum flew in from Florida today? We're going to have an early-ish dinner, probably around 7 p.m. or something. You are more than welcome to join us.'

'No, it's best if just you and your mum go. We were thinking of going to the Hard Rock anyway,' explains Colin. 'Amanda's left a message for that cute trumpet player so he might meet us later and then Scott says there's a gay club near there called Gypsy. And it just so happened I packed my dancing shoes . . .'

'Just make sure you're home by 11 a.m. Izzy's wedding is at noon,' I remind him.

'No problemo.'

'So,' sighs Amanda. 'How does it feel to be so in love with someone that you want to spend the rest of your life with them?'

44

'What colour should I get?' Izzy rotates the nail varnish carousel with an acrylic-tipped finger.

'I think you need a pewter or some kind of metallic blue,' I advise.

'I haven't told you, have I?' she gasps.

'Told me what?'

'I'm not wearing the *Fifth Element* outfit any more.'

'Don't tell me you've gone for the Third Element – you'll get yourself arrested.'

'No,' she giggles. 'I hate to admit this but Nadine gave me an idea when she asked if I was copying Priscilla's dress. Cindy put me in touch with the seamstress at the showgirl shop and—'

'Don't tell me any more!' I insist. 'I'll wait until you put it on. Did Cindy take the other dress back?'

'No, I didn't ask her to. I'm keeping it for the wedding night.'

'You're too good to that man!' I laugh, holding my base-coated nails in front of the mini fan. 'So I guess you will need a bouquet now.'

'The naffest one I can lay my hands on, just to spite Nadine!'

'What about that calamine pink, it's got a sixties vibe.' I pointed to a vintage bottle of Mary Quant.

'Perfect. What about you?'

'I'm thinking gold to go with the embroidery on the bodice.'

'See? We can do this – these are the kind of life decisions we can cope with. I don't feel nervous yet, do you?'

'No. I think it's the fumes from the acetone.'

Izzy settles back into the manicure cubicle next to mine. I toy with the idea of asking how she's feeling about Dave but why open the wound when she hasn't mentioned him since the weeping-in-the-closet day?

'How was Scott's mum last night?' she asks.

'Oh fine. Not at all what I expected. I thought she'd be all Nancy Reagan hair with a cameo brooch pinned at the collar of her blouse – so did Scott, for that matter – but no, she turns up with frosted highlights and this low-cut, wraparound top. Scott said it was the first time he'd seen her cleavage since she was breastfeeding him.'

'She's got herself a new fella!'

'Fellas, plural. It sounds like half the widowers in her condo complex are after her.'

'So what's her secret?'

'Well, it turns out that around the time Scott moved out here – about six months ago – she got this new man-eating neighbour called Shelley and I guess she needed a sidekick to pull with because she made it her mission in life to get Miriam away from QVC and mingling with the other retirees. Now they've teamed up with this dippy woman called Sally-Sue or something and they go everywhere together and have this great social life.'

'Sounds like the Golden Girls!' Izzy chuckles.

'Exactly!' I agree. 'Only Scott reckons his mum has had enough of being Dorothy and now she's angling for the role of Blanche.'

'Proving that it's never too late to be a slapper.'

'Isn't that good to know? Anyway, she and my mum had loads to talk about seeing as they have both lived in Devon. That was quite a blessing actually – it took the focus off me and Scott and we didn't have to field any really awkward questions.'

'So how is yer man feeling about everything?'

'Fine. He said he's been a lot more relaxed around his mum since he told her he was getting married. I think it's done them a lot of good to get together again.'

'And all because of you.'

'Yeah, well, maybe it's worth it then.'

'Are you having second thoughts?'

'You know me, I'd have second thoughts if Goran Visnjic was waiting at the altar.'

After an hour in the hairdresser's being shampooed and blown dry within an inch of our lives we return to the hotel. Mum and Amanda coo over our coiffs – Izzy looks like one of David Bailey's sixties sex kittens. I, on the other hand, am pinned up at the back and raised on top for a modern-day *Breakfast at Tiffany's* vibe. At least that's how they sold it to me in the hairdresser's. Colin says I put him in mind of one of his all-time favourite *Come Dancing* contestants. I swiftly change into a white trouser suit with a pair of Izzy's new high heels to dispel that image.

Izzy keeps us all in suspense about her outfit until she hears the champagne cork pop. 'Wait for me! We have to have a toast!' she yelps from her room.

Seconds later she is standing before us sparkling in the sunlight in a white sleeveless mini-dress entirely covered with sequins and shimmering bugle beads. The skirt is short, her legs tanned and her white knee-high patent leather boots kinky. Her tiara has fluffy white showgirl plumage instead of the traditional net veil and she has attached false eyelashes to her lids. She looks OTT and utterly fab.

'I told the dressmaker I wanted Barbarella meets Priscilla!' she grins, twirling around.

'Now would that be Priscilla Presley or Priscilla, Queen of the Desert?' teases Colin.

'You look smashing, Izzy,' says Mum.

'Thank you,' she beams. 'Will you be my mum today, too?'

'Of course, sweetheart!' she says, hugging her.

'Right – a toast!' Colin grins.

We hold our glasses aloft. He clears his throat and cheers, 'Divas Las Vegas!'

'Divas Las Vegas!' we chorus, giggling.

Ten minutes later, we pile into the limo, still bubbling with bonhomie and Bollinger. Amanda can't stop giggling, Colin is puffed up with pride at being chosen to give Izzy away and Mum is loving her surrogate mum duties of hair-smoothing and hand-squeezing. Izzy, meanwhile, has fallen into a blank-faced trance. As we pull into the chapel car park she grabs my arm and cries, 'Can you go in and check he's there!'

'Of course he's there!' Colin tuts.

'Please!' she whimpers.

'All right. I'll just be a second.' I slide out of the limo and trot across to the front door. I've barely opened it an inch when a big paw yanks me in.

'Jamie! Thank God!' puffs Reed. 'Listen, can you delay her?'

'What? Why?'

'I've arranged a surprise and it'll ruin everything if she comes in before. Can you get the limo to take her round the block or something? I need her off the property.'

'Off the property? What's going on?'

'It's just she'll see . . .' he humphs.

'Okay, okay, how long do you need?'

'Just five more minutes, then everything should be in place.'

'She's not going to like this,' I mutter to myself as I scurry back outside. I tell Mum and Amanda to go and take their seats and then inform Izzy, 'The vicar's not here yet, they need you to drive around the block.'

'What? Why can't we just wait here?'

'It's just a rule they have, don't ask me. I'm going to wait here to make sure everything's sorted. Colin – say soothing things and bring her back in five minutes.'

'What if the vicar doesn't show?' Izzy panics. 'What if . . .'

I slam the door and signal to the chauffeur to get going.

At least there's not a roomful of wedding guests to appease. Just four women (Mum, Amanda, Cindy and Layla) cheerfully exchanging depilation horror stories. I step back into reception and collide with a small man shadowing Reed.

'This is Mr Sakamoto, my business partner. He's my best man,' Reed explains, eyes never leaving the door.

'Hello! I'm Jamie.' I extend a hand and Mr Sakamoto dips his head several times in quick succession.

'He doesn't speak any English but I trust him with the ring.'

'Right . . . er, Reed, is everything okay?'

'At last!' His face brightens as the door bursts open to reveal a man in a black and white stripey T-shirt and fatigues.

'*Jailhouse Rock* Elvis,' he says, nodding at Reed.

'GI Elvis,' says the man behind him in army beiges, hat in hand.

'*68 Special*.' A leather-clad stud shakes Reed's hand. 'Where do you want us?'

'Just start filling the rows from the front,' Reed instructs, ushering them into the chapel.

'*Blue Hawaii*,' says another.

'Teddy Bear.' His pal winks.

I watch in amazement as every incarnation of Elvis files into the room – I see *Fun in Acapulco*, *Kid Galahad*,

441

King Creole and the racing driver from *Viva Las Vegas* in one aisle, four outrageous jumpsuits in another – everything from fresh-faced teen to the cuddly, sideburned forty-two-year-old he became.

'One last spot there!' Reed directs the infamous gold lamé jacket to his seat.

'Do you think she'll like it?'

'More than you'll ever know!' I say, still reeling. 'I'm going to wait in the car park.'

I just have time to notice that the motel across the street has a sign saying, ELVIS SLEPT HERE on one side and HIGHLY RECOMMENDED – BY THE OWNER on the other before the limo returns.

Izzy's head is out of the window before the vehicle has even stopped. 'He's done a runner, hasn't he? Did he leave a note? Was there any clue?'

'Izzy. He's here. The vicar's here. You're here. Everything is fine,' I reassure her, helping her out of the car.

'Colin – do you think maybe she needs a slug of that whisky?'

He mouths 'She's had three' and shakes his head.

'Okay, well, deep breaths,' I say, leading her forward.

'I can't do it, Jamie!' she wails, grinding her heels into the gravel.

I turn to face her. 'Yes, you can!' I place my hands firmly on her shoulders, about to launch into a psyched-up speech when my eye goes to my wrist. A-ha!

'You can if you're wearing this.'

442

I take off my candy bracelet and take Izzy's hand.

'Oh my God!' she gasps. 'Reed ate mine, I—'

'I know,' I interrupt. 'That's why I want you to have mine.'

'I couldn't – it's twenty years old! It's practically an antique!'

I laugh and carefully roll it on to her wrist. 'To think it all began at a panto! Who'd have thought this is where we'd end up.'

'Oh Jamie!' she says, overcome with emotion. 'Everything we've been through! You've always been there for me. I don't know what I'd do without you!'

'Stop it!' I sob. 'You'll have me crying!'

'Too late!' A tear trickles down her face. 'I mean it. None of this would have happened without you,' she says, squeezing my hand. 'You're my lucky charm, you always have been.'

'Ladies!' intercedes Colin. 'We've got nuptials to attend to!'

Izzy and I compose ourselves after one more heartfelt hug and then Colin holds out his arm. Izzy takes it and I follow them through the front door, tugging at Izzy's skirt hem in a last-ditch attempt at decency. They pause outside the chapel for a second. 'Ready?' asks Colin. She nods yes, then as the door opens 14 Elvises begin harmonising, '*Ooo-ooo-ooo-ooooo. It's now or never, come hold me tight, kiss me, my darling, be mine tonight . . .*'

Izzy's gasp sucks in so much air the room becomes a vacuum. I have never seen her look so overwhelmed. Her eyes rove the aisles admiring the individual costumes and identikit quiffs. I can see it's taking all of Colin's strength to restrain her from running straight to Reed. At least I hope that's who she's trying to lunge at. Yesterday I asked her why she'd booked EP for her wedding day and she told me it was because she'd already slept with him and she didn't want the temptation of a new one distracting her during the ceremony. I'm not sure what Reed has done here but he's certainly done it in style.

I look at her husband-to-be, preened to perfection in his tux, never taking his eyes off Izzy for a second as she progresses down the aisle. I just know he's thinking, 'I'm the luckiest man alive!' and I feel a knot in my chest as she draws level with him and they look at each other with pure love.

'Do I get to keep them?' I hear her whisper as I take my position.

The ceremony is short and sweet but surprisingly meaningful. I had thought this kind of wedding wouldn't seem convincing (hence their appeal), but there is a surprisingly real sense of the solemnity of the occasion. Not that solemnity seems the right word when everyone is grinning like fools, but I actually believe Izzy when she says: 'With all my heart I take you to be my husband. I will love you through the good and the bad, through the joy and the sorrow. I will make you a part of me and in turn become a part of you . . .'

Their kiss is passionate and deep. And everyone loves it. Even the vicar has to fan himself with his prayerbook. Outside the air fills with confetti, fluttering on the gentlest of breezes. Izzy removes a cluster of paper horseshoes and hearts from her cleavage and then we pose for photographs, eagerly grabbing our favourite Elvis.

'Do you remember when Geri wore a copy of this to the Billboard Awards in Vegas?' says Amanda, hanging off the white jumpsuit with red and turquoise eagle motif.

'Will you sing "Love Me Tender"?' my mum asks another.

'Are you sure it wasn't the 69 Special?' Layla teases the black leather babe.

Colin takes his time choosing – 'It's like having The King's life flash before you!'

'I wish – God, you don't suppose they strip too, do you?'

'Izzy! You're a married woman now!' I cry.

The Elvises begin singing 'I Just Can't Help Believing' and Cindy links arms with Mr Sakamoto, instantly jettisoning him to karaoke heaven.

For a while I lose myself in the euphoria. Then Izzy dances over, arms around her tubby hubby and smiles. 'One down, one to go.'

45

Now I know where Izzy's nerves came from. I didn't think it would be this bad. I can't begin to imagine how I'd feel if I was doing this for real. I tell myself to relax and 'go with the flow', but I can't look anyone in the eye and I'm consumed with an ever more insistent desire to run away.

'Come on then, darling! Let's go and get you into your dress!'

Mum makes it sound like she's trussing me up for some kiddy party. If only. Oh to be six with bunches and an orange polka-dot dress once again.

'See you all at the Excalibur!' Mum calls to the crowd as we bundle into the cab.

'Yes, do join us at our irresistibly-discounted chapel!'

'Jamie!' tuts Mum. 'There's no need to tell everyone you got it cheap.'

On the way back to the Bellagio she chirrups excitedly about Izzy's wedding and what a special day it has already been. I stare impassively out the window at the signs for Ice Cold Beer, Grand Canyon helicopter trips and Engelbert Humperdink's three-night run at the Monte Carlo.

Zane is waiting in the lobby as arranged. He looks stunning in his tux, hair pulled back into a shiny ponytail, diamond stud winking from his ear. He gives me a big brotherly/fatherly hug, then embraces my mum. Judging by the look on her face he seems to have made as big a first impression on her as he did on me.

'You smell wonderful!' she sighs, leaning heavily on the lift buttons as we ascend to the suite.

'You wanna see his kiwi fruit,' I think to myself.

Zane settles in front of MTV and counts us down at five-minute intervals.

'Twenty minutes to lift-off. Fifteen . . . How you girls doing?' he shouts towards the bedroom where mum is zipping me into the corset, crushing my ribs with great care.

'Do you know, I would have put you in cream,' she puffs, 'but this white is really fresh and I love the gold detailing, it's so subtle. It's a shame it's got to go back tomorrow . . .'

I decided to hire rather than buy in the end. It seemed more appropriate considering my circumstances – it's not like I was going to be getting my wedding dress down from the attic for my kids to play with in years to come. I feel a pang of regret. I still can't decide whether this marriage is for better or for worse. Still, the dress is a pretty good fit. Mum takes a few steps back to get an overall view and then busily tugs here and realigns there. She steps back again for further assessment and then applies herself to fluffing

447

the petticoats and smoothing the outer skirt. This goes on for a good five minutes until I find myself laughing out loud.

'Mum! Enough!'

She looks up at my face and her look of concentration melts into sentiment.

'I wish your father could see you now! He'd be so proud!'

'We'll send him a picture.'

'Don't be angry with him,' she pleads. 'He can't help it.'

'I'm not angry. I've got the best mum in the world, I can't expect to have a great dad too. It's okay, really.'

She pulls me into what I imagine would be an intense hug were it not for the fact that I've lost all feeling in my torso area.

'Be happy, darling!'

'Jamie! Mrs Miller! It's zero hour!' calls Zane from outside the door.

'I'm ready – one more gloop of lip gloss and I'm done!'

I open the pot of iridescent apricot goo and smooth it on my lips with a trembling finger. Then I dab on a tad more golden shimmer to my collarbone and one last press of powder on my chin. My eyes well up with tears but I banish them with a deep breath and an elongated sigh.

'Okay. Let's go! We'll attach the headpiece in the car.'

One pin-skewered scalp later I feel like a bride.

'I've never seen such a long veil – you be careful you don't get it caught on anything.'

'Yes, Mum,' I smile, looping the excess yards over my arm.

'You look beautiful!' Zane sighs. 'Absolutely beautiful.'

Out of the limo, through the revolving doors and on to the escalator. As we go up, we pass another bride dressed in full Guinevere regalia. We nod as if we've pulled up to a set of lights in identical VW Beetles.

Just outside the chapel Mum gives me a last non-make-up-smudging kiss and then scoots ahead to take her seat with the rest of the congregation. As she opens the door I can sense the anticipation within. There's a low buzz of conversation and a snatch of Cindy's filthy laugh and Amanda's tinkling giggle. I smile for a moment and then remember it's me they are waiting for. My fingers go to my neck, searching out Finn's ring. I hold it tight, making a wish and then tuck it back into my bodice. Zane turns to me and says, 'Are you sure about this?'

'What?' I panic.

'I just want to hear you say that you know what you're doing, and that you mean what you are doing.'

I gulp. 'I thought you were just supposed to tell me I looked beautiful.'

'I did that in the car.'

'Can't you do it again?'

'If that's what you want.'

I look into his Bournville brown eyes. They stray

449

from mine up to the top of my head.

'Your tiara is wonky!'

'That'll do, come on, let's go,' I say, tugging him into the chapel.

The first thing I see is Scott, dressed entirely in white but for his gold cravat. We're a perfect match. I smile, reassured. He looks so handsome, so sweet. As I approach, he grins at me and everyone puts on their sunglasses. Not really. I take two more steps and draw level with Christian. He coughs as I pass him. Is that a code? Is he trying to tell me something? I try to catch his eye but Zane is blocking my view. At least he has an aisle seat – should he make a bid for me, he won't have to risk getting caught up in Nadine's never-ending layers of sage-green silk.

Mrs Mahoney aka Izzy gives me an A-okay sign and Reed, face covered in lipstick kisses, smiles soppily. There's my mum, lovely Mum, all misty-eyed, sitting next to Scott's mum who has a curious look on her face. Amanda and Colin are clinging on to each other, barely able to control their excitement. Bless. Cindy and Layla are sitting among a group of Scott's mates – I spot two knights and two off-duty drag queens. In fact, now I get a closer look at Scott's best man I recognise him as the Celine Dion impersonator we saw last week.

We reach the altar. I reluctantly let go of Zane. And push away thoughts that the last time I was standing before this altar, Izzy was the vicar and Christian the groom.

'We come together to record in the minds and

hearts of all present the ripe event of a love that has bloomed,' the vicar begins.

Not quite the wording that I was expecting.

'We gather also to mark the reality that marriage must overcome many forces that would destroy it.'

What on earth? I cast a furtive look at Scott. I left him responsible for choosing the vows.

'I charge you to see the meaning of life through the changing prism of your love; to nurture each other to fullness and wholeness; and in learning to love each other more deeply, learn to love the creation in which the mystery of your love has happened.'

Oh good grief! How's Christian going to know when to butt in with all this twaddle?

'And now, Scott, do you here today in the presence of God and all these witnesses take Jamie to be your wife . . .'

I can sense some shifting in the seats behind me but daren't look back. My heart pounds as the vicar continues, '. . . agreeing to love her and promote her joy and happiness as long as you both—'

'Stop! Please stop!'

We spin around.

Scott's mother is on her feet. She looks as surprised as us at her outburst.

The congregation murmurs in confusion. Scott and I stand paralysed.

'You're doing this for me, aren't you?' she asks tremulously.

Scott looks totally thrown.

'You don't need to. Not any more.' She pauses. 'I'm

sorry if you . . .' she trails off, taking in the astounded faces around her. 'I should have said something sooner. I just . . . I love you, son. I'm sorry I've made you hide who you are.'

'M-mum, what do you mean?' Scott falters, swallowing hard.

'I know you're . . . I know you're . . .' She looks at him plaintively. 'Do you want me to say it?'

He looks at her intently, then softly says, 'Yes. Yes, I do.'

'I know you're gay!' she blurts.

The congregation gasps as one.

Scott looks at his mother with gratitude and relief. 'Thank you,' he breaths, eyes welling up. Then he turns to me, full of concern and apology. I hear myself say, 'Go!' and watch him run to her. For a split second, I don't think of myself. I'm moved by their reunion, the intensity of the hug. And then it dawns on me: Christian didn't stand up. He didn't say, 'Don't marry him! Marry me!'

He doesn't want me.

I'm too numb to fully experience the humiliation of my current situation but there it is: the wedding is off. The fantasy dissolved. The lie exposed.

Everyone is rooted to their seats with embarrassment. The vicar goes to speak but a stronger voice overrides his.

'Okay, everyone. I think we should move through to the reception area now.' It's Nadine's voice. 'Zane – perhaps you'd like to lead the way . . .'

Mum lingers to have a few quiet words with the

vicar but the others slowly file out. Even Izzy is keeping a respectful distance from the fragile, rejected bride. Suddenly Layla breaks away from the pack and gives me a fierce hug.

'It could be worse.'

I give her a rueful look.

'You could be married!'

I force a smile. We watch the others leave. Christian turns back as he reaches the door and Layla gasps. 'That's where I've seen him before! He was at your engagement dinner, right? Some relative of that old lech?'

'Mmm, he's Sam's nephew,' I mumble, manically plucking petals from my bouquet.

Layla snorts. 'Runs in the family, then.'

'What does?' I ask absently.

'You know, octopus arms,' she says, pretending to grope me.

'What do you mean?' I say, confused.

'He was at Lap and Tickle last night, I couldn't place his face until now.'

'Christian was at Lap and Tickle?' I repeat.

'Yup.'

'I take it Uncle Sam was there too?' Horrible, corrupting . . .

'Nope, just him,' Layla insists. 'What a creep – grabbing all the girls, spilling drinks, security had to warn him twice.'

I can't believe it! She must have got him confused with another man.

'Coming out with these crazy lines . . .' Layla tuts, 'as

if spouting poetry is going to get you a free lap dance.'

Poetry? My heart chills.

'Admittedly Mariella ended up shagging him but that's only because he quoted her Leonardo DiCaprio's lines from *Romeo and Juliet*,' Layla concludes.

I feel like the room is tilting and everything is tumbling off the shelves and skidding across the floor. But I don't feel the urge to save anything. I vaguely hear Layla muttering, 'All men are bastards!' but it's drowned out by a rushing in my head like the tide pulling back from the shore. It's getting louder. I fight for air and then . . . nothing.

46

'Jamie? Jamie? Are you okay?'

'All this time I thought . . . I believed . . .' I mutter.

'I know, darling,' Mum soothes.

'I had no idea he was like that . . .' I lament.

'No, none of us did. Not even Colin.'

'For ten years . . .'

'Ten years? Oh, sweetie, you're not well, are you? You've only known Scott a few weeks.'

'Scott?' I say, bewildered.

Mum looks concerned. 'Shall we get you back to the hotel?'

'No, I want to go to the reception, for Izzy . . .'

'I have to warn you, he's in there.'

'Who?'

'Scott.'

'That's fine. I'm glad he's stuck around.'

'Well, if you're sure,' she says, sounding confused.

'Don't think badly of him, Mum. He's one of the good guys. I want him to be happy.'

'Okay.'

'Help me up?' I say, struggling to get vertical.

Half-filled with disappointment, half with shame, I follow Mum to the reception. The room is resplendent with white flowers, ice sculptures and champagne bottle pyramids. The drag queens have already shanghaied the DJ's microphone and switch from 'I Will Always Love You' to 'I Will Survive' when I enter the room.

Nadine pounces before I've even made it to the bar. That's all I need.

'I'm so glad you didn't get married,' she says, ushering me into a quiet corner.

'Yeah, you win,' I concede. 'Looks like you'll beat me down the aisle after all.'

'That's not what I meant,' she says, pulling her chair conspiratorially close to mine. 'Are you okay?'

I look up and find her usual supercilious stare has been replaced by an earnest gaze.

My eyes narrow. 'Did you go on that ride at the top of the Stratosphere?'

'What? No! Why do you ask?' she frowns.

'I don't know, you just seem different,' I muse. 'So. Was there something you wanted to say?' I'm not in the mood for playing games.

'Oh Jamie!' she sighs. 'I always thought I wanted to see you beaten, to see your spirit crushed but now . . .' She looks imploringly at me. 'I can't bear it. You've always been unstoppable. I'd hate to see that light go out of your eyes.'

I can't believe what I'm hearing.

'You've been so brave and come so far. Don't give up now,' she rallies, blinking back her tears.

All these years of whittling away at my confidence and now a pep talk? With moist eyes?

'Did you get a heart transplant?' I ask suspiciously.

'I know I've been mean. I can't help it. When I'm around you . . . I don't know, just being aware of your power to shine . . .'

'My-Power-To-Shine,' I repeat. She's got to be taking the piss.

'Yes. It makes me feel so conventional, so inadequate . . .'

'Inadequate? You? How do you think I feel? Dad is always comparing me to you and I always come up short. God, I think half of this desperation for me to get married came from being jealous over the attention you've been getting.'

Did I mean to say that out loud?

'I've always known I've had Dad's approval – that was easy,' Nadine shrugs. 'All you have to do is do what he wants, play it safe. But no matter what I do, I can never get Mum to talk about me in the same way she talks about you.'

I look at her incredulously. 'Nadine, you are way more successful than me. In everything. You always have been.'

'Yes, but you are free. Your life is so full of possibilities. Mum talks about you with such hope in her voice.'

'Hope for things that may or may not happen,' I argue. 'You know Dad just think's it's all pipe dreams with me. But you, you've already proved yourself – you've got an apartment, a car, a job with prospects, a fiancé . . .'

457

She rolls her eyes. 'He only proposed because I got pregnant.'

'WHAT?' I can't take any more revelations.

'You heard me. You don't think I'd be wearing this Mama Cass look if I didn't have something to hide . . .'

'You're pregnant?'

'Yup. And Christian's not taking impending fatherhood well. I thought I'd cured him of his philandering but this seems to have sent him back to his old ways.'

'Then you know . . .'

'What have you heard?' Nadine snaps.

'N-nothing, I just . . .'

'Did he hit on you? The bastard!'

'I didn't think he was the type to . . . to do that kind of thing.'

'We've talked about it, tried to understand why. When I first found out I was pregnant we even went to counselling . . .'

'What did they say?' I ask, astonished by her frankness.

'He's got a lot of anger. When he was a teenager he was quite the romantic, then his parents split up unexpectedly and he just shut down, stopped believing in love. He used to want to be an actor but he gave that up because it involved too much foraging around in his emotions, so he decided to study to be an architect. He had a real reputation as a "love 'em and leave 'em" ladies' man by the time I met him but he said I made him feel like that teenager again, made him feel stuff he hadn't felt in years. I think he meant it,' she says wistfully.

'Go on,' I encourage her. It's painful for me to hear but things are starting to make sense to me now.

'For a while it was great, all soppy poetry and gifts and weekends away. But then I got the feeling he didn't really like me as a person, like he was trying to shape me into something I wasn't. We were on the verge of splitting up when I found out I was pregnant. Anyway, we're not here to talk about me . . .'

'But . . . How . . .? Are you going to be okay? What do you think is going to happen?'

'Oh, we'll be okay. It's not like I've been a saint, look at Lars. I can't believe you invited him, by the way.'

'He's here?'

'Look!' Nadine points at him bearing down on Cindy.

'Oh God! Izzy must have—'

'It's no big deal.'

'He's such a hulk, isn't he?' I say, looking at his colossal thighs.

'Tell me about it!' she giggles. 'Anyway, how are you feeling?'

'All the better for talking to you – which is a novel experience.'

Nadine pulls a face. Just a normal sisterly face, not a po one for once. Then she says, 'Look, everyone here loves you. You'll get through this. And if you can get through today, you can get through anything. You know, you can be anything you want. Go anywhere you want!'

I take a deep breath. 'Okay, coach!'

'And Dad will come round in the end.'

'Actually I don't think he will,' I contest. 'I don't think he's ever going to get me. But I don't mind. I don't feel like I need his approval any more.'

'I wish I had your nerve.'

'Why, what would you do if you did?' I smile, curious.

'Give up being an accountant!'

'To do what?'

'Wedding planning,' she says with a wobbly smile. 'Every time I've brought it up to Dad he's just dismissed the idea. Says it's too much of a risk, that it's not a real career.'

'I never knew . . .'

'Well, you know how he can be. He made me feel it was such a foolish thing to want so I dropped the idea. Stopped talking about it, at least. Maybe one day . . .'

'One day soon. Do it soon, Nadine,' I urge, surprised at my eagerness for her to connect to her dream.

This is the first time in my life I've felt close to my sister. Up until now I've always considered myself to be the test case my mum and dad got wrong and then Nadine came along and did everything perfectly. But maybe she felt even more pressure than me. Maybe she felt pressure *because* of me – how could she give up being an accountant when all she hears is Dad berating me for wanting to be a journalist? How could she let him down when she's supposed to be the favourite?

'I can't believe I've said all this and I'm only on Perrier!' Nadine sighs, getting to her feet. 'Do you have any idea how hard it is for me to be surrounded by all this champagne and not be able to drip a drop?'

I look at her stomach. 'Does Mum know?'

'Not yet. I'll probably tell her tonight.'

'May as well get all the shocks over in one day,' I suggest.

'Exactly.' Nadine leads me into the crowd, making sure Amanda and Colin are being suitably supportive before she moves on.

Trying to steer clear of the landmine subject of men, Amanda chatters busily about my writing and tells me she's had a message to get a photograph of me for an end-of-summer feature the paper is planning.

'It's a spread of mock-holiday postcards from trips people have taken this year. I suggested a picture of you and . . . Oh, never mind.'

'Of me and my new husband?'

'Er . . . yes,' she blushes.

'That's okay. How about using the one of us with Tom Jones instead?'

'Oh brilliant! Yes! Loads better!'

I grin back at her.

'You're a bit cheerful, considering the circumstances,' observes Colin.

'Sorry, I don't mean to be,' I apologise. 'I think I'm having a bit of an epiphany!'

'Oh! I've always wanted to have one of those!' says Amanda jealously. 'What's it like?'

'Well, at the moment I just feel this overwhelming sense of relief, like I've been holding on to something too tight for too long and now I can let go.'

I look over at Christian and decide he and CJ may as well be two different people. I realise I have no choice now but to let CJ be just a fond teenage memory. And let Christian have a future with my sister. If that's what Nadine wants – I feel a rush of sympathy filling the place where resentment used to reside.

'Do you have a pen?' I ask the guy tending the bar. He hands me one, I grab a napkin and tell Amanda I'll be back in a second. She doesn't hear me. Danny the trumpet-player has just walked in the door.

I perch at an empty table. I need to get closure with Christian in a way we'll both understand. I know the perfect poem and start to write.

> *Since there's no help, come let us kiss and part,*
> *Nay, I have done; you get no more of me.*
> *And I am glad, yea, glad with all my heart,*
> *That thus so cleanly I myself can free.*
> *Shake hands for ever; cancel all our vows.*
> *And when we meet at any time again,*
> *Be it not seen in either of our brows*
> *That we one jot of former love retain.*

I feel strangely calm at the end of it. As I make my way towards Christian, cruise ship Jimmy gives me a squeeze and says, 'I'll do the splits if it'll make you feel any better.' I thank him but keep walking. Nadine is standing with Izzy, I expect to hear sniping as I pass but instead find them giggling and pointing at Lars, who is still working on Cindy. As I approach Christian, I ask Layla to do me a favour. She is more than happy to 'accidentally' knock a drink over his trousers.

'Shit!' he exclaims.

'Here,' I say. 'Mop yourself up with this!' and hand him the napkin.

'What's this?' he frowns, then falls silent.

I look around me. Colin is comparing thigh-grip strength with the knights, Scott is on the dance floor with his mum, my mum is getting on rather too well with the vicar, Uncle Sam (who invited *him*?) has inadvertently found himself wedged in a corner with Mr Sakamoto, Zane and Mia are feeding each other wedding cake, Amanda and Danny are sipping champagne from the same glass and EP is instructing Reed in the art of pelvic thrusts. I need a drink.

Zane approaches me with a piece of cake. 'Here, I've got something for you.'

'Thanks, but I'm not hungry.'

'Not the cake, I've got a gift for you.'

He takes a tiny box from his pocket and hands it to me. I open the lid, remove the square of foam protection and there is an exquisite mermaid charm with mother-of-pearl scales and tousled, cropped hair. It's the perfect match for Finn's ring.

'I made this a while ago,' he explains. 'I'm kinda embarrassed to admit this but I was so convinced you and Finn were made for each other. That first day I saw you – I thought you looked just like his mermaid . . .'

I look up, amazed. 'Really?'

'Yeah, I know . . . Finn's always telling me I'm a terrible match-maker. I can't help it. I just like to see people happy together.'

'Poor Finn,' I sigh. 'Next time try fixing him up with someone he actually likes.'

Zane looks confused. 'Jamie, you do know, don't you?'

'Know what?'

'How Finn feels about you? Why do you think he couldn't be here today?'

I frown. 'He had to work, I . . .'

Zane touches my chin and stares as if he's trying to read my mind. 'How do you feel about him?'

Emotions that have been squished, suppressed and ignored start to wriggle free.

Zane smiles. 'Cupid, give me back my bow and arrow!'

I don't know what to say.

'Do you want me to attach this?' he says, flipping past the dolphin and the dice charms on my bracelet. 'You know what – there are no links free.'

I look down at all the memories chained to my wrist.

'Here, you can take this one off,' I say, picking out the theatre mask that Christian gave me on our last day together.

'No sentimental value?' Zane asks.

'Not any more,' I tell him.

Zane gives me a hug and then returns to Mia who has just accidentally broken the arm off a full-sized ice replica of Izzy. I feel like an onlooker, strangely separate from everyone. Would anyone really notice if I slunk away for half an hour? There's something I need to do . . . someone I need to see.

I edge towards the door, catching Izzy's eye as I push down on the handle. She's by my side in a second.

'If they ask where you've gone . . .?'

'Just tell them . . .' I falter, unable to find the words.

Izzy gives me a knowing look. 'How about I put a little sign on your chair saying, GONE FISHING?'

Has it been obvious to everyone except me? I get a strange sensation of things falling into place and my heart awakes with a start – 'You rang?' Suddenly I'm in a tearing hurry to get to Finn. The sense of urgency gets greater with every stilettoed step I take. I dodge the dawdling families and the wolf-whistling lads and dive into a cab in front of the hotel. The driver looks bemused when I ask him to drop me at Caesar's shopping forum.

'Sick of your husband already?'

'I don't have a husband. We never got that far – he was outed by his mother during the ceremony,' I say matter-of-factly.

'Well, I suppose shopping is as good a way to get over him as any,' he replies, unfazed. 'Retail therapy they call it, don't they?'

'Actually, there's a man in the fish tank. I think he might be The One.'

The driver eyes me nervously in the rearview mirror but I carry on regardless. I like the thrill I'm getting from saying this out loud.

'Zane says we're made for each other. I'm mermaid for him and he's merman for me!' I chortle.

As soon as we reach the shops I bolt out of the car and, for the first time in my life, run up an ascending escalator. My heart beats faster as I pass Guess, Gucci, FAO Schwarz, Victoria's Secret, closer and closer. I can see the blue light from the tank reflected on the ceiling ahead, I hitch up my skirts and break into a run. I see a flipper but as I draw nearer I sense something isn't right. I squeeze closer to the glass. I don't even need to see the face – it's enough that this person's hair is swaying like seaweed in the water. I edge around the tank to find the girl with the microphone giving her aquarium talk. 'Sorry to interrupt – Finn? Is he . . .?'

She eyes my outfit. 'That's a mighty long veil you've got there!'

'I know!' I say, unravelling the various passers-by I've ensnared. 'Is Finn . . .?'

'He's at the Mirage,' she whispers. 'You're Jamie, right?'

I scurry off with the earlier rendition of 'It's Now or Never!' taunting me in my head.

The memory of Finn sleeping in my arms makes my heart ache. Of course I had wanted to kiss him that night. But I was too afraid. Now I'm afraid it'll be too late. The heat is stifling but I maintain a reasonable trot along the pavement, ignoring shouts of 'He went thatta way!'

466

The Mirage doors swing open, I hurtle through the casino and on to the Secret Garden. There's a big queue to get in but I barge to the front and puff and plea my way past the barrier. It's amazing what they'll let you get away with if you're wearing a wedding dress. The dolphin pool is in sight. I look around for someone to ask, all I can see is tourists. Oh God! Where is he? I clamber over the partition and look into the water. Is he in there? I can see a pair of dolphins swimming in perfect synchronicity but no flippers. I shuffle closer to the edge and lean over, letting go of my veil so I can get a safe grip on the edge of the pool. Suddenly I feel a strain to my head, then a tug which becomes a yank and ends with an almighty splash as I'm dragged into the water.

Floundering, I try to swim up to the surface but something is pulling me down, I force my eyes open and swish around to discover that my veil is being sucked into the water filter. I pull at my tiara but my mother has done far too good a job interlocking the pins. I'm drowning! Where's Mia and her *Baywatch* skills when you need her? I scrabble and kick at the water and then thud into a panel of reinforced glass. Am I delirious or is that Finn on the other side?

Next thing I know I'm rushing up towards the surface, gasping for air, clinging to the rubber ring around me. Finally my breathing becomes less noisy and desperate and I realise it's not a rubber ring around me but rubber arms, that is, arms in a wetsuit. Finn's arms. He hauls me up on to the side of the pool. For a while we just pant and breathe.

Finally he speaks.

'That's the first white swimsuit I've seen that didn't go transparent when wet.'

I look up at his dripping frame.

'You know the auditions for *O* are at the Bellagio . . .'

Wisecracks. I nearly drown in an attempt to tell him . . . to tell him . . . I'm too exhausted to be indignant. My humiliation is complete. I struggle to my feet, staggering under the weight of the sopping fabric hanging off me and wonder how on earth I'm going to make a dignified exit.

'Finn! What the hell is going on here?' an irate voice booms from behind us. 'We have VIP guests here!'

Finn leaps up and hurriedly apologises. 'Sir, I'm sorry, we had a little surprise planned, we just hit a technical hitch . . .'

'What kind of stunt are you trying to pull?'

'You're selling them the wedding package at the hotel, right?' Finn confirms.

'Right . . .' says the tyrant, eyeing me dubiously.

'If you give me a moment and go back to the viewing panel downstairs . . .'

He huffs, 'This better be worth it!' and exits.

Finn turns to me with a mischievous twinkle. 'I need you to play along with something.'

'If it involves going back in the water . . .'

'Believe me, you can't get any wetter than you already are.'

'Finn! For God's sake – I nearly drowned!' I protest.

'If you pull this off you might just get yourself a job here. Besides, I wouldn't let you drown.'

He gets me every time with this protective bit. I exhale noisily. 'What do you want me to do?'

As he explains his little plan I think how different I feel when I'm with Finn. How it's always unpredictable. How he fascinates me. How much I can't help but care. How I feel like he sees the real me. How I could look at his face for the rest of my life. And how, if it doesn't work out, I know I will survive. I feel like I've got my life back. I narrowly escaped by giving it away and now I'm going to make the most of every second.

'Ready?'

I nod.

Finn slides into the water and swooshes over to the viewing panel with Sprite. As soon as he's in position, I lower myself in and gently put an arm around Splash. Before I know it I'm transported through the water, arriving at Finn's side all swirling skirts and ripped tufty veil. I kiss Splash on the bottlenose as instructed, then Finn and I turn to face Sprite. He makes cute head jerks as if delivering a sermon. Finn and I let a few bubbles escape to signify 'I do's', then he takes my hand, removes a circular piece of squid from Splash's teeth and places it on my wedding finger. Splash nods his head vigorously, head-butting Finn towards me. The VIP party cheer and whistle from behind the glass. And then he kisses me. I've never been one for big wet kisses but this . . . We go spiralling up to the surface in an embrace. Then he pushes my wet hair away from my face and smiles at me. 'I can't tell you how long I've wanted to do that.'

Sigh.

As he helps me out of the pool, the sunlight converts the water racing over his body to liquid mercury. I squint at him, dazzled and then say, 'Finn – now that we're unofficially married, do you think we might go on a date?'

'What did you have in mind?' he says, raising an eyebrow.

'I don't know, something casual and low key – like a night in the honeymoon suite at the Venetian!'

Finn pulls me closer. 'Really?'

'I think you might like it . . .'

'Oh,' he says sexily, 'and why's that?'

'It's got a water bed!'

He laughs, taking me in his arms and kissing me again – sensual, penetrating kisses, hands caressing my face. My heart hurts from the pleasure of it.

'That was great!' cheers Finn's boss, startling us. 'You two should have your own show!'

Finn looks back at me and ponders, 'What would we call it?'

'Hmmm.' I think for a moment, fiddling with the zipper on his wetsuit. 'How about *Diver Las Vegas*?'

And with that, Finn takes my hand and we leap back into the pool, scattering diamond droplets of water as far as the desert.

The Paradise Room

Belinda Jones

When Amber Pepper's jeweller boyfriend Hugh asks her to join him on a business trip to the paradise islands of Tahiti she's not keen – Amber loves big jumpers and rain. She'd rather be pedalling through puddles at home in Oxford than lolling in the gel-blue waters of the South Pacific. However, the prospect of sipping Mai Tais with her long-lost friend Felicity is incentive enough to coax her on the twenty-hour flight.

Within hours of touching down on coral sands the girls venture into a seductive new world of mesmerising music, exotic black pearls and sexy strangers. And for the first time Amber falls head over flip-flops in lust, only to receive an unexpected proposal of marriage.

Will she opt for a barefoot beach wedding or cast caution – and her coconut bra – to the wind? No easy decision for a drizzle-loving gal when it's ninety degrees in the shade . . .

'As essential as your SPF 15'
New Woman

'This is definitely worth cramming in your suitcase'
Cosmopolitan

arrow books

Order further Belinda Jones titles
from your local bookshop, or have them delivered
direct to your door by Bookpost

☐	I Love Capri	0 09 941493 7	£6.99
☐	The California Club	0 09 944548 4	£5.99
☐	On the Road to Mr Right	0 09 944549 2	£6.99
☐	The Paradise Room	0 09 944552 2	£6.99

Free post and packing
Overseas customers allow £2 per paperback

Phone: 01624 677237

Post: Random House Books
c/o Bookpost, PO Box 29, Douglas, Isle of Man IM99 1BQ

Fax: 01624 670923

email: bookshop@enterprise.net

Cheques (payable to Bookpost) and credit cards accepted

Prices and availability subject to change without notice.
Allow 28 days for delivery.
When placing your order, please state if you do not wish to receive any
additional information.

www.randomhouse.co.uk/arrowbooks

arrow books